P9-DCC-908

*continued . . .*

"Fast-paced . . . deliciously steamy."—Darque Reviews

"Quirky, unusual, fun, tense, surprising, sexy, and wild!"
—Errant Dreams Reviews

## FURTHER PRAISE FOR
## CHRISTINA DODD'S NOVELS

### *Revenge at Bella Terra*

"Christina Dodd is thrilling readers. . . . Her heroes are
to die for."                           —Night Owl Reviews

### *Secrets of Bella Terra*

"Sinfully good. . . . Ms. Dodd wows me."
—Romance Junkies

"Grabbed me from the first few pages and never let
go."                           —The Romance Dish

### *Taken by the Prince*

"Delivers sensual sizzle."           —*Publishers Weekly*

"Witty, adventurous, and unexpected."—Fresh Fiction

### *In Bed with the Duke*

"A wonderful tale of love and intrigue . . . a story to be
savored."                           —TwoLips Reviews

"An adventurous romantic fairy tale."
—The Romance Dish

### *Into the Flame*

"Once again Christina Dodd weaves her spell."
—Fallen Angel Reviews

"[A] stunning tale."           —Romance Reviews Today

### Into the Shadow

"Another stellar book from a most talented author!"
—*Romantic Times*

"Sexy and . . . darkly appealing."          —*Rendezvous*

### Thigh High

"A joy to experience!"
—*Romantic Times* (4½ stars, top pick)

"[C]harming and likable characters . . . an enjoyable read."          —*Fresh Fiction*

"Christina Dodd is a master. . . . *Thigh High* is a winner."          —Romance Reviews Today

### Touch of Darkness

"A sweeping saga of good and evil."   —*Library Journal*

"Enthralling, intense."       —*The State* (Columbia, SC)

"Readers will be riveted until the final page."
—A Romance Review

### Scent of Darkness

"The first in a devilishly clever, scintillatingly sexy new paranormal series by Christina Dodd."
—*Chicago Tribune*

"[A] fast-paced . . . paranormal with a full, engaging mythology."          —*Publishers Weekly*

"A scintillating and superb novel!"
—*Romantic Times* (4½ stars, top pick)

# CHRISTINA
# DODD

## *WILDER*

### *THE CHOSEN ONES*

A SIGNET SELECT BOOK

SIGNET SELECT
Published by New American Library, a division of
Penguin Group (USA) Inc., 375 Hudson Street,
New York, New York 10014, USA
Penguin Group (Canada), 90 Eglinton Avenue East, Suite 700, Toronto,
Ontario M4P 2Y3, Canada (a division of Pearson Penguin Canada Inc.)
Penguin Books Ltd., 80 Strand, London WC2R 0RL, England
Penguin Ireland, 25 St. Stephen's Green, Dublin 2,
Ireland (a division of Penguin Books Ltd.)
Penguin Group (Australia), 250 Camberwell Road, Camberwell, Victoria 3124,
Australia (a division of Pearson Australia Group Pty. Ltd.)
Penguin Books India Pvt. Ltd., 11 Community Centre, Panchsheel Park,
New Delhi - 110 017, India
Penguin Group (NZ), 67 Apollo Drive, Rosedale, Auckland 0632,
New Zealand (a division of Pearson New Zealand Ltd.)
Penguin Books (South Africa) (Pty.) Ltd., 24 Sturdee Avenue,
Rosebank, Johannesburg 2196, South Africa

Penguin Books Ltd., Registered Offices:
80 Strand, London WC2R 0RL, England

First published by Signet, an imprint of New American Library,
a division of Penguin Group (USA) Inc.

First Printing, August 2012
10  9  8  7  6  5  4  3  2

SIGNET SELECT and logo are trademarks of Penguin Group (USA) Inc.

Printed in the United States of America

PUBLISHER'S NOTE
This is a work of fiction. Names, characters, places, and incidents either are the
product of the author's imagination or are used fictitiously, and any resemblance to actual persons, living or dead, business establishments, events, or
locales is entirely coincidental.
    The publisher does not have any control over and does not assume any re-
sponsibility for author or third-party Web sites or their content.

ALWAYS LEARNING                                                    PEARSON

Thank you to my daughters,
Shannon and Arwen,
for making me watch *Beauty and the Beast*
so many times and in so many versions
that the story is imprinted on my heart.

# ACKNOWLEDGMENTS

Leslie Gelbman, Kara Welsh, and Kerry Donovan, my appreciation for your support. Thanks to New American Library's art department led by Anthony Ramondo. To Rick Pascocello, head of marketing, and the publicity department with my special people, Craig Burke and Jodi Rosoff, thank you. My thanks to the production department and a special thank-you to the spectacular Penguin sales department: Norman Lidofsky, Don Redpath, Sharon Gamboa, Don Rieck, and Trish Weyenberg. It's been a great run—you all are the best!

Thank you to Roger Bell for critiquing *Wilder*. I hope Joyce would have approved of the story.

## THE LEGEND

Long ago, when the world was young . . . a gorgeous and vain woman abandoned her children, a boy and a girl—twins with hideous birthmarks—to the river and the forest to meet their deaths. Instead, they became the first of the Abandoned Ones, gifted with abilities that could save the world . . . or end it.

The boy was marked with a dark tattoo and given the gift of fire, and he gathered others around him with similar gifts to become the Chosen Ones—seven men and women who became a powerful force of light in a dark world.

The girl had the mark of an eye on the palm of her hand and became a seer. She turned to the devil, gathering six other gifted ones to her. They became the Others, bringing darkness and death to the world.

For centuries, every seven years, a new group of seven Chosen Ones are drafted to continue the fight against a new group of seven Others.

That battle goes on. . . .

## TODAY

Seven years ago, a new group of Chosen Ones was drafted to take up the battle against the devil and his minions, the Others. They were a disparate group: resentful, untrained, unknowledgeable, with fading gifts and nothing in common.

Until on the very day of their initiation, an explosion blew away the Chosen Ones' New York City headquarters, taking the lives of everyone who could have helped them to prepare for the fight ahead.

They quickly discovered that with few resources

and little help, they were forced to depend on one another, and together they combated the ultimate evil.

But now their seven years are almost over. Mere weeks remain. As a new building rises on the old site of the Chosen Ones' headquarters, created to house evil and tower over New York, time is running out for the Chosen Ones . . . and for the world.

# THE CAST

## THE CHOSEN ONES

❖ **Jacqueline Vargha:** Gifted with the ability to see the future and with an eye on her palm to prove it, with Caleb D'Angelo at her side, Jacqueline must take her adopted mother's place as chief seer to the Chosen Ones.

❖ **Aaron Eagle:** Raised by American Indians and marked with the wings of an angel, Aaron has a talent for melting into the shadows that surround him. But he can be truly whole only once prim and proper librarian Rosamund Hall enters his life.

❖ **John Powell:** John is famous for the strength and power he wields, and after years in exile, has returned to the Chosen Ones as their leader. At his side, his wife, Genny, has strengthened his gift of harnessing the earth's power, while finding her own ability to see the hidden talents and changes in others.

❖ **Isabelle Mason:** One of the upper-class Boston Masons, Isabelle is a physical empath with the ability to absorb the pain of others and heal them. After she accepts her fate and is married to Samuel, her gift flourishes.

❖ **Samuel Faa:** A lawyer with the ability to control minds and, after his marriage to Isabelle, a talent for mind-speaking.

❖ **Charisma Fangorn:** A young Goth, drafted for her gift of hearing the earth song in crystals and stones.

❖ **Aleksandr Wilder:** Aleksandr has no mark, no discernable gift, and is blessed with a loving family, yet he is drafted into the Chosen Ones because of his connection to the Wilder family of Washington State (the Darkness Chosen series). He is an asset to the group, until he disappears on his wedding day.

## FRIENDS AND ENEMIES OF THE CHOSEN ONES

❖ **Irving Shea:** The retired director of the Gypsy Travel Agency, and the owner of the mansion that the new Chosen Ones use as headquarters. Now one hundred years old, he has been mentor to the Chosen Ones for almost seven years.

❖ **Dina:** A mind-speaker, one of a former group of Others, and Irving's ex-lover.

❖ **Martha:** Dina's sister and the dedicated Romany servant of the Chosen Ones.

❖ **McKenna:** Scottish butler, chauffeur, and aide to Mr. Shea.

❖ **Vidar Davidov:** Owner of Davidov's Pub, located deep in the tunnels under New York City, where the Chosen often gather to regroup. Davidov sports an inexplicable knowledge about the Chosen Ones and their mission.

❖ **Osgood:** The mastermind behind the destruction of the Gypsy Travel Agency, and the director of the Others, who now wields great power over New York and across the world. The devil lives in Osgood's soul, and if the Chosen Ones cannot stop the spread of their evil, together Osgood and the devil will reign on earth for a thousand years.

# Chapter 1

———◆❈◆———

*Blythe, Washington*
*Present Day*

Konstantine Wilder sat at the head of one of the long picnic tables located among the grapevines in a valley in the Cascade Mountains, the finest land jewel in all of Washington State, smiling with benevolent goodwill at the wealth of interesting friends and beloved relatives he had amassed in these United States of America.

Some knew who he was.

Some knew what he was.

Most were neighbors.

Some had traveled far to celebrate Independence Day with the Wilder family.

Sprinkled in among the crowd were people who wandered through town during the summer season, got invited to the annual celebration, and came for the food, companionship, and vodka.

Konstantine flattered himself that they had all made a good choice. The picnic invariably boasted warm, sunny weather—Zorana might have had a hand in that, but he thought it best never to ask—boisterous laughter, interesting conversation, and easy camaraderie.

Konstantine owned more than one kind of jewel.

He gazed at the diamond in his crown, his Zorana, his wife, bustling around the tables, ensuring that everyone abandoned their cares on this American day of national celebration. He gazed at his sons and his daughters and his grandsons and his granddaughters, overflowing with welcome as they moved among the guests with platters of food; they were his rubies and emeralds and pearls.

Zorana and the family they had made loved him, supported him, fought for him and with him.

Together he and Zorana and his offspring had saved the world.

Now their home nestled into the edges of the lush green conifer forest. Their tables groaned with traditional American dishes like hot dogs, as well as more international fare, like spaghetti and fajitas, and with traditional Ukrainian dishes like patychky, cabbage rolls, and potato varenyky. His grandsons grilled meat on barbecues, and heavenly smells wafted into the clear, warm summer air. Children's voices shouted and sang as they climbed trees, swung on swings, clung to the playground merry-go-round. They fell, got up, and played again.

Life in these United States was good.

Every year on this day Konstantine affirmed that belief, loudly and with much vigor, in a speech that all respected and enjoyed, even his children and grand-children. He could always see through the eye rolling and elbow nudges to the pride that they so carefully hid.

And now . . . it was time.

Placing his big hands on the table, he slowly hefted himself to his feet. He nodded at Jasha, at Rurik, at Adrik, at Douglas. His sons rose, vodka bottles in hand. Their wives rose with them, gathered the trays of shot glasses, and, as the boys filled them, all laughed and waited for the moment when they would pass out the glasses for the toast.

In the meantime, Zorana turned to face Konstantine, and the friends who knew what to expect focused their attention on him.

He grinned. "I remember when I had to shout to make you pay attention. Now I am old, and you listen out of respect."

"You've been old for years, Konstantine." The Catholic priest had never had any respect for Konstantine's dignity.

That was all right. Father Ambrose knew Konstantine better than anyone (except Zorana), and he had always kept his mouth shut.

"I am not *really* old. Maybe ninety. Maybe a hundred." Konstantine shrugged. "Who knows? In the Ukraine, where I come from, we don't worry about formalities like birth dates."

Uncertain laughter rippled through the crowd. They didn't know whether he was serious.

He was. In his Ukrainian family, they didn't celebrate birthdays.

They celebrated transformations.

"Some of you listen with respect. Some listen because I give you vodka." He gestured to his daughter-in-law Karen, who delivered a shot to the priest.

Father Ambrose lifted his glass in salute and downed it, then took another.

Konstantine's voice swelled. "On this Independence Day for the United States of America, I thank God for the country that welcomed Zorana and me and allowed us to build our home and bear our children in peace. They are all successful. They are all married now." He patted his chest. "I take credit for that."

"Oh, Papa." Adrik, his third son, sighed.

"You wish to argue?" Konstantine demanded.

Adrik, the father to four children with his wife, Karen, shook his head. "No, Papa. I do not argue with the old wolf."

"Good. You show wisdom at last."

Laughter rippled over the crowd.

"Ah." Konstantine nodded his understanding. "When you look at Adrik, you see a successful man who pays his taxes and speaks with authority on many subjects. I see the rebellious, snot-faced boy I raised. We both survived. So I am proud." He opened his arms.

Adrik walked to his father. They hugged each other, kissed cheeks, as was traditional in their family, and both men had tears in their eyes.

They had almost lost each other, Konstantine and Adrik, and although most of these people did not realize it, their survival had been a close thing.

With a final pat, Adrik backed away. "Go on, Papa."

Once again Konstantine commanded the crowd. "The Wilder land rests cradled in the best valley in the Cascade Mountains—not that I am prejudiced—"

More laughter.

"—near our most excellent town called Blythe. You ask, Why is my land the best?" He smiled benevolently. "Because the temperatures are mild in the winter and warm in the summer. I raise grapes, and my wife, Zorana, plants a garden every year. I tell her she is too old for such labor. She tells me to shut up and plow the ground for her. Of course, I do as I am told."

"You show wisdom at last." Zorana mocked him with his own words.

By now his guests were receiving their shots of vodka and rocking with laughter.

"To demonstrate to you how fruitful our land is . . . my four sons and their wives have given Zorana and me seventeen grandchildren, and in the last year we have been blessed with not one, not two, but five great-grandchildren." Konstantine beamed and lifted five fingers. "And we have two more on the way."

A burst of applause.

"All are sons. We Wilders . . . we always have sons. Sons are good. They are hellions as they grow, but eventually they bring their beautiful wives home to us, and they make more Wilder sons who run wild." Konstantine remembered a time when his sons had been more than merely hellions—they had been shape-shifters, bound to the devil in a pact that had stretched back a thousand years. His sons, his daughters-in-law, he, and Zorana had broken that pact.

Sometimes, even now, he missed the ability to change into a wolf. But for the sake of his soul, he gladly paid the price.

Konstantine grew serious. Very serious. "Zorana and I are proud, for all our children are healthy. All are well. Except . . . in the past few years, evil has spread tentacles far and wide throughout the world, and the battle for peace has begun."

The crowd grew quiet, respectful, and some of them, who had traveled abroad, looked grim.

"At this time, we remember our oldest grandson, Aleksandr, who left us to go to college in New York City and then join the fight against evil. He has disappeared." Konstantine's voice quavered. "Almost three years he's been gone."

Zorana moved to stand beside Aleksandr's mother, Firebird, and the two women hugged while Aleksandr's father, Douglas, wrapped his arms around their shoulders. The rest of the family gathered close, too, protective of one another.

Konstantine's voice grew in strength. "As long as we hear nothing about Aleksandr's death, we have hope, and we ask that you keep hope alive as well."

Nods all around. Murmurs of reassurance.

These guests were good people. They would hope for Aleksandr's return, and they would pray.

Except . . . toward the end of the table . . . Konstantine had noticed that one man sat sour faced and shifty eyed, watching the family from beneath lowered lashes.

Konstantine didn't recognize him. He wasn't a neighbor or a friend. Yet he looked familiar, which meant . . . it was likely he was a relative. From the Ukraine. Maybe a brother, or a cousin.

He and Zorana had come to the United States and changed their last name from Varinski to Wilder because they wanted no part of the wickedness that dominated his family. And yet . . . his family had followed them here, and never, ever had it been good news when a Varinski turned up.

He sliced a glance at his youngest son. At Douglas, lost to them for so long and now returned. Douglas was in law enforcement, trusted for his consummate instincts when dealing with criminals.

Douglas had already picked up the signals from the stranger. Now, holding his bottle of vodka, Douglas moved down the table, pouring drinks and seemingly at random pacing toward the man.

"The real world, the world we know, the world of the sun, is nothing but a skin of reality barely holding in the darkness and the evil. Hell is beneath us"—Konstantine stomped his foot on the ground—"and I heard once that the devil's best trick was to convince us all that he does not exist."

Father Ambrose lifted his glass. "Hear, hear!"

Konstantine continued. "So when you pray and hope for Aleksandr, pray also for the Chosen Ones. They accepted my grandson and gave him a role to play in this fight."

Guests were hanging on his every word, clearly confused by the direction of his speech.

Meanwhile, Wilder mothers moved the younger children toward the shelter of the forest.

Zorana came to Konstantine's side to stand beside him.

His family knew trouble when they saw it.

Konstantine continued to speak, his voice commanding attention, the legend he told almost hypnotic with its dark, primitive rhythm. "Long ago, when the world was young, twins were born, marked by fate. Repulsed, their mother took them into the forest and abandoned them, and in recompense, the good God gave them special gifts. The boy could make fire, and he was rescued by a band of roving Gypsies and lovingly cared for. When the boy grew into a man, he gathered others like him, seven people with gifts who wished to use them for good, and they formed the Chosen Ones."

The Varinski now openly stared at Konstantine, his eyes black with hate.

"The girl was rescued by a witch, who abused her most horribly. When she grew into a woman, she found she could see the future. She killed the witch as a sacrifice to Satan himself, and then gathered around her seven people with gifts who wished to serve evil, and they formed the Others."

Konstantine's guests squirmed in their seats, starting to look uneasy at the turn this celebration had taken.

Konstantine's sons and grandsons followed Douglas's silent commands and moved into place around the Varinski.

"Each group of Chosen Ones serves a term of seven years, until a new group takes their place to fight the battle against the Others—and their master, the devil. These Chosen were sabotaged before they started. They came to the battle unprepared and without resources, for evil managed to breach their defenses. Their building, their researchers, their books, and their history were obliterated in one mighty explosion. And all of you must realize"—Konstantine leveled a stern look at his guests—"that the world as we know it is crumbling under the weight of corruption, blackmail, drugs, and vice."

The Varinski smiled, a wide, ugly, sneering grin.

"We have only a few weeks left before the seven years of these Chosen are up, and when that happens—" Konstantine saw the Varinski lift his hand from under the table. He saw the flash of a metal barrel. He shouted, "Get down!"

As the pistol roared, Konstantine dove sideways, sheltering Zorana with his body, taking her down to the ground.

# Chapter 2

———◆❈◆———

Konstantine held Zorana tightly in his arms, terrified that she had been shot, and crawled with her under the table.

Around him he heard guests screaming, benches being overturned.

Feet stampeded past.

"All clear!" Adrik shouted.

"It's all right, folks; we got him!" Rurik yelled.

A whistle blew, loud and long—Douglas's police whistle.

At once the crowd quieted.

"Calm down, everyone. We have everything under control. You're safe," Jasha said. "Please go ahead and return to your seats. I think we're all going to need more vodka."

Nervous laughter.

"Who is he?" someone asked.

"We're sorry. He's a cousin. Looks like he went off

his meds. It wasn't a real gun," Jasha lied with easy charm, soothing their guests. "We'll handle him. Has anyone seen my parents?"

People bent. Eyes peered beneath the table.

"They're here!" someone shouted.

Zorana shoved at Konstantine. "Get off of me, you big oaf. You're so heavy I can't breathe."

He gave a sigh of relief. If she was giving him trouble . . . she was fine. Sitting up, he looked down at her, at the smudges of dirt on her face and her angry, snapping dark eyes. "You don't usually complain when I'm on top of you."

"You usually offer me a better time than getting shot at."

"Next time someone aims a gun at you, I'll whisper love words in your ear before I save you." He offered his hand.

She took it and sat up. "Good idea. And he was aiming at *you*."

"Probably, but these young Varinskis are not necessarily well trained in the art of shooting. When you landed, did you break a hip, woman?" His question was rough; his intent was not. He had been born a Varinski. He was strong, sturdy, long-lived.

Zorana was younger than him, so much younger, but she was fragile, her bones were delicate, and as their age progressed he feared for her more each day.

She knew it, too. She mocked his concern. "I'm fine. You rolled to protect me from the impact." She looked at him out of the corners of her eyes. "Thank you, you old fool."

"You are the love of my life," he said.

"I know." She leaned her head on his chest.

Their adopted daughter, Firebird, crawled under the table with them. "Papa. Mama. You're okay?" She saw the way they held each other. "Yes. You're okay." She patted their shoulders. "You need to come out. Show everyone you're not hurt. And, Papa, you need to finish your speech."

Konstantine nodded.

Zorana rose easily. No bones cracked, although she would be incredibly unhappy about the damage done to her clothes. She bought them from Nordstrom, and she took her clothing choices, especially for their picnic, very seriously. Konstantine felt sorry for his stupid Varinski cousin; the idiot had no idea the trouble she would serve up to him.

Konstantine's knees were not as good as they once were, so he allowed Firebird and Zorana to help him to his feet.

The guests cheered.

A quick glance proved his sons had hustled the Varinski into the house, and Konstantine knew he would be bound and gagged and locked in the root cellar, with one of the boys on guard at all times.

The family would deal with him later.

"What was I saying when we were so rudely interrupted?" Konstantine boomed.

His guests laughed and clapped, reassured by his joke and his family's apparent insouciance in the face of what looked like a shocking attack. Gradually they returned to their seats and cleaned up their overturned plates, while chattering over the clink of glasses.

When most of their nervous murmurs had died down, the priest spoke in a clear voice. "If you were trying to show us a demonstration of the evil in the world today, Konstantine, you did a good job. Now, why don't you tell us the rest of the legend about the Chosen Ones?"

Konstantine slowly nodded. "As you request, Father, so I obey." And once more, he spoke. "In the modern world, the Chosen Ones disguised themselves as the Gypsy Travel Agency, a corporate identity, and that's when the current problems started. . . ."

Late that night, when the people had all gone, when the children had been put to bed, when the bonfire had burned down to red coals and blue stars peered coldly from the midnight sky, Konstantine caught Zorana's hand and raised it to his lips. "Are you ready?" he asked her.

"I can't wait," she answered.

He knew it was true. When he had met her, she was the wise woman of her tribe, the one to whom visions were given—and she had been only sixteen. Yet her elders were right: Zorana had always been wise, strong, intelligent, and courageous, and she truly anticipated this confrontation with the Varinski kept captive in their cellar.

He nodded to his sons, then warned his family, "Keep to the shadows. He may be here for reconnaissance, and he doesn't need to see exactly who watches him, and how many."

These children and grandchildren, he had trained them well. They might wish to be defiant, to challenge the Varinski themselves, but they understood strategy. They had heard the tales of the last Varinski attack; they understood what was at stake.

Only Firebird remained on the periphery of the

light. The women congregated at her back, and Zorana went to stand at her side. In this battle, Firebird had suffered the most, and like a bulwark of femininity, the Wilder women supported and protected her . . . for Aleksandr was her son, her firstborn, and every day she cried. Every day she prayed for his safe return.

In silence, Jasha and Rurik, Adrik and Douglas dragged the Varinski from the root cellar and brought him to face the family tribunal.

The Varinski was tall, but bulky, with broad shoulders and too much weight around his middle. Konstantine judged him to be about forty, at that age when men realized they were no longer the strongest, the youngest, the best. That meant he remembered the days when the Varinskis were at the top of the food chain, when a male lived for that moment he reached puberty and became a predator that would hunt and kill and earn a fortune for his cruelty.

Karen and Anne placed logs on the coals, and eager flames licked them to life.

Konstantine could have turned on the outdoor electric lights, but some scenes played better with the proper atmosphere.

Adrik and Douglas shoved the man into a sitting position on a log set close to the fire. Rurik and Jasha removed his gag and the ropes that bound him.

"You know," Konstantine said kindly, "I recognize you."

"You do not!" The Varinski half rose.

Rurik and Douglas slammed him back down.

"I do," Konstantine assured him. "You're a brother. A cousin. A Varinski."

"Yes," the Varinski muttered. "I'm—"

Konstantine held up his hand. "Don't tell me your name. It's not important. *You're* not important. If I were guessing, that's why you tried to shoot me."

The Varinski snarled.

"Fearsome." Rurik's Tasya stood in the shadows, but her tone mocked and taunted.

The Varinski snarled again, then let his defiance fade to silence.

Konstantine let that silence drag on, until the Varinski shifted uncomfortably, as if ants had invaded both the log and his hefty butt. "Compared to me and my sons, you are young. I think . . . yes, I definitely think my boys and I broke our pact with the devil before you reached puberty."

The Varinski looked aside. "Yes."

"So what you've been all your life is a pathetic loser who talked about the good old days without experiencing them," Jasha said.

The Varinski swung to face him, lips curled back, dark eyes cruel with resentment.

Jasha leaned toward him, hypnotizing him with his gaze. "I was a wolf, running free in the forest."

Rurik fed more logs onto the coals, and when the flames lit the night sky, he said, "I was a hawk, alive on the wind."

Adrik stood just out of sight of the fire's light. "I was a panther, black as the night."

Douglas watched his wife, their Firebird, slim and still, her eyes fixed on the Varinski. "I was a cougar, gleaming golden as I hunted my prey."

"Well . . . aren't you just lucky," the Varinski sneered. "You ruined it for the rest of us."

"Yes. We did," Konstantine said.

The Varinski turned on him like a snake about to strike. "The apocalypse is coming, and because of *you*, Konstantine, we Varinskis are nothing. We are no one. Of no more use to the devil than the man on the street. In this battle, we should be commanding Satan's forces, and we are mere . . . men." The Varinski choked up, showing his grief like a little girl. "I want to see with the eyes of an eagle and hunt with the cruel intent of a panther. I want to serve at the master's right hand, and foul the world with vice. Instead, I am reduced to shooting my enemies rather than ripping out their throats with my teeth."

"You cannot rip out your enemies' throats with your teeth?" Firebird said flatly. "That is a shame."

The Varinski turned from the scorn of the men to the supposed weakness of the women.

Obviously he knew nothing of the Wilder women.

In a tone of command, he said, "I know who you are, Firebird Wilder, so don't make fun of me. It is *your* son who most betrayed our loyalty to the devil. It is *your* son who tried to be something, one of the Chosen Ones. And where is he now? Vanished. Dead."

Zorana caught Firebird as she lunged at him. She held Firebird as she fought to kill him. "Listen to me, child of my heart. Listen to me." Zorana patted Firebird's hair. "He's not dead. Aleksandr is not dead. He's buried alive, but he will rise again."

Everyone froze. Everyone turned to face her.

Konstantine's heart clenched. He remembered the last time, many years ago, that a prophecy had seized her. She had been right, right about everything, and in the end all had been well. But oh, what a price they had paid in blood and tears. . . .

"Truly, Mama?" Douglas asked. "You know this?"

Zorana, too, stood frozen, her dark eyes wide and surprised. "Yes," she said slowly. "He's still alive, but smothered beneath a great weight and much guilt."

Firebird clung to Zorana. "Mama, don't lie to me. The son I cradled in my arms, the boy I saw grow into a fine man . . . is he well?"

"He is. I'm not wrong." Zorana stroked Firebird's hair again, but she gazed far beyond the circle of light. "But he is in danger. Such danger. They watch for him, wait for him. They hunger for him, need him to complete their foul scheme."

"Who are *they*?" Anne asked.

"Are they the Others?" Tasya asked.

"The Others . . . yes." Zorana's eyes half closed, and she took a long breath. "Yes, I smell the taint of the Others. I smell them and the rot that rises from the very roots of their being. . . ."

The Varinski had never seen anything like Zorana in the throes of a prophecy. He had perhaps imagined the world of the spirit, where evil and good fought for the souls of men, but he had never witnessed it.

He tried to bolt.

Konstantine caught him, threw him to the ground, planted his big foot into the middle of the Varinski's back, and said, "Adrik. Rurik. Take our guest out to an island in the Sound. Leave him there like the stray dog he is. He'll find his way back . . . but not soon." His sons did as they were told, roughly grabbing the Varinski from the dirt and pushing him out the door ahead of them.

Konstantine turned his attention back to Zorana.

"There's something else. I hear the echo of another

prophecy . . ." Zorana's voice became deep, and bleak, and as distant as the stars that twinkled in the dark skies above. . . . " 'Rising on the ashes of the Gypsy Travel Agency is a new power in a new building. Unless this hope takes wing, this power and this building will grow to reach the stars, and cast their shadow over the whole earth, and evil shall rule.' "

"What does that mean?" Douglas asked.

"It's a prophecy." Jasha remembered the first time. "We'll find out when it's time, and no sooner."

Firebird's first clean burst of hope faded. "But I don't believe it. If Aleksandr were alive, he would tell us. He would not let us suffer."

Douglas caught her in his arms and held her. She closed her eyes and dropped her head onto his chest.

"Perhaps he can't," Douglas said.

"And you, my daughter, you underestimate the power of guilt." Konstantine had killed in his day. He had been the embodiment of evil. He had repented . . . yet he still carried a burden on his soul. "Our Aleksandr was raised to be a man of honor. *You* raised him to be a man of honor. If the Others captured him, tortured him, and he gave in . . . he would never forgive himself. If he is alive . . . someday we will know it." He gazed at Zorana, watching the power of the prophecy leave her, seeing once more the burden of worry oppress her.

Yet the foresight compelled Zorana to say one more thing. "Yes, we will someday know what tore his soul from his body and left him the empty, seeking shell that I sense. But not this day. Not today."

# Chapter 3

*Deep Beneath the City of New York*
*Present Day*

Charisma Fangorn was so busy shaking the heavy plastic grip on her flashlight, trying to eke another minute's worth of illumination out of the wavering bulb, she never noticed the abrupt drop-off—until she stepped out into nothingness.

Her flashlight went flying, a brief glow of light that twirled away from the hot, close air of the tunnel and into the void. Then the glass shattered, plunging Charisma into bleak darkness. She landed on her feet, on the sharp stone edge of . . . somewhere. Her foot slipped off. She fell again. Landed on her hands and knees, irretrievably off balance. On a stair. Stone stairs. She tumbled, curled into the fetal position, protecting her head with her arms, hitting each step, bruising each rib, her hips, her knees, her elbows. She hit bottom face-first, felt her chin split and her eye blacken, and something snapped in her shoulder.

Pain crashed through her, overwhelming her.

She tried to scream. Tried to move. Got her breath. Screamed, except . . . it sounded like a whimper.

*Oh, God. Oh, please. Please, God . . .*

*No, don't pray. They'll notice you.* Down here the mouth of hell lurked too close and yawned too wide.

She rested there, gasping, getting control, subduing the agony, praying—not praying—*wanting* to be well and whole. And knowing that, even if she escaped alive, she would never be whole again.

Without moving, she tried to look behind her.

Where was behind? The dark was . . . blacker than anything she had ever seen.

Except for the eyes, glowing eyes, dozens of eyes, that followed her, moving, shifting, circling.

She needed to get up. Get moving. Find her way out. Now.

But . . . agony. Pain everywhere. *Agony* . . . her collarbone was broken.

She breathed again, in through her nose, out through her mouth, as her yoga teacher had taught her, controlling her mind, soothing her nerves. . . .

Every time she broke a bone in her battles alongside the Chosen Ones, the pain blistered her. Usually, though, she got hurt during a fight, and adrenaline kept her going. This time . . . she had nothing except a warm, flat stone surface under her body, a darkness so thick it smothered her, and fear. So much fear.

She tried to remain still, to allow the agony to subside. But it didn't, and she could no longer stay still.

She groaned.

How could she have been so unwary? She knew the treacherous passages down here. In the last three days—or was it five days?—she'd been all over, looking for the way out. But she was as lost as she had been the first day in these underground tunnels.

There was no way out.

Just as there was no end to the pain. Or the fear.

So dark.

So hungry. So thirsty.

That was why she'd fallen. She'd been down here for days. Three days. No, more, because she'd been without food for at least four days, had drained the last of her water more than forty hours ago.

Five days. Probably. Maybe. Her phone was dead—not that it did her any good, so far underground.

The stones in her bracelet hummed softly, warning her.

She wanted to snap at them. Which made no sense. They were stones. Although they spoke to her, they did not live.

They warned her that danger lurked, but what good did that do? She knew she was in trouble. She was dying of hunger and thirst, her body was broken and bleeding, she was half-insane with the need to sleep, and she kept thinking she would gladly die of any of those causes . . . because when she looked behind her, or in front of her, she saw those eyes, glowing eyes, in the dark.

She had to find the wall, to get her back against it, to prepare her weapons for a fight to the death. The wall . . . was not too far. A few feet, perhaps. She could move a few feet.

Cradling her useless arm, she sat up.

Her head swam. Her face was swelling. The darkness had already blinded her. She hoped . . . she hoped *her* eyes didn't swell shut before she had taken out some of *those* eyes.

With her free hand, she reached, groped, found a wall. A stone wall. Yes! Triumph!

"Yes, Samuel, it's a crappy triumph, but I take what I can, you asshole. All right?" She didn't think she'd actually said the words out loud. She thought that, with her swollen lips and dry mouth, she only mumbled.

But for a moment, the gibbering quieted, and she felt the intense stares as she inched her way to the wall and propped herself up. There. Now all she had to do was stand up. Easy. Nothing to it. Soon.

New York City was one of the world's great cities. It bustled. It roared. It created fashion. It made money. It sold knockoffs.

It covered one of hell's doors to the world.

Like their kin, the rats, the demons would wait until she was unconscious, near death, and then they would take her, bite by bite, tearing her flesh, consuming her while she still lived. . . .

The demons had appeared in the world about four years ago.

Charisma had seen them first. She had been patrolling, and she got the itchy feeling of being watched. She saw glowing lights out of the corners of her eyes, swung and faced them. The lights blinked out. She told herself she was imagining things.

In her business, it was easy to imagine things.

In her business, sometimes she would rather go crazy than have to face the truth.

She hadn't said anything to the other Chosen. After all, she'd never really *seen* anything. But finally the Chosen Ones' seer, Jacqueline Vargha, had pronounced, "Hell is bubbling like a cauldron, and creatures are escaping, with scaly skin and teeth and claws and ravenous appetite and little glowing eyes. . . ."

Then every one of the Chosen Ones admitted to glimpsing at least one flash of a demon in the dark. Even Samuel said he'd seen something peering at him from beneath a grate in the street. Of course, being Samuel, he jabbed it with the sharp cane he now carried. The thing had screamed and slithered away.

Being Samuel, and a mind controller, he also said the things had no minds of their own. They were simply eternally hungry creatures that hunted and ate and hated everything that lived in the world.

Most of the time, Charisma could barely tolerate Samuel. He was a boor, and only his wife, Isabelle, could keep him in check.

But now Charisma wished Samuel and his stupid cane were here, because the eyes had moved closer, and for the first time she could hear the demons' low gibbering.

They were excited. They smelled blood. They were salivating over the idea of fresh meat.

Charisma shuddered. She always carried a gun, a small pistol. It was loaded. Full of bullets. She needed to get it in her hand and take aim, and shoot them one by one. . . .

No, wait. She'd lost her pistol somewhere. Where had she lost it?

*Oh.* She remembered. She'd fallen down before, on the very first day, before she'd been lost . . . or before she had admitted to herself she was lost. She'd heard something, something that sounded like a child wailing. She'd been running, trying to catch up. She'd turned a corner, saw a demon, squat and scaly, loping along ahead of her, its head thrown back, its lipless mouth open and imitating a human baby's cry. Furious, exhausted, ready to kill, she had pulled her handgun, tripped on a loose stone, landed on her hands and knees.

The pistol fell, skidded toward one of the cracks that yawned so unexpectedly in the ground. She'd flung herself after it. Missed.

The demon cackled and kept running.

The pistol fell off into the void. Charisma waited, listening for it to land, thinking that perhaps she could go and get it. At last, long moments later, she heard a faint, far-distant thump.

She didn't want to go down that far.

Here in the tunnels she was too close to hell.

She hadn't come down here to look for hell. She'd come down because . . .

Because she'd witnessed a kidnapping. A human child snatched from its parents and carried below the city. She had fought the demons, rescued the baby, returned it to its parents, and realized that somewhere during the battle, she'd lost her crystal bracelet.

But she couldn't give up that bracelet. She'd made it for herself, back when the earth's stones had first started to speak to her, drilling the stones and threading them on a sturdy chain. She never took them off. This bracelet contained the first crystals that had spoken to her, and she had worn it always. . . .

She was Charisma Fangorn, one of the Chosen Ones, and her gift was that she could hear the earth song.

For almost all of her life, Charisma had been aware of the earth, speaking through the stones at her wrist, crooning like a mother to her beloved child.

As a child, Charisma had reveled in those loving tones, and, believing everyone heard the same song, she had spoken to her mother about the pleasure she felt in hearing it.

Two things.

One—that mother wasn't her biological mother, and she was an altogether pretty poor excuse for a human being.

Two—that woman whom Charisma thought of as her mother started farming her out as a healer at markets and street fairs across the western United States. Charisma hated it, hated the nomad lifestyle, where she . . .

Not important now.

Eventually, there on the site of the demon battle, she had found her bracelet, and now the stones urged her, *Wake up. Wake up!* That more than anything proved her situation was desperate, for her gift was fading as hope failed in the world, and the voices of her stones had almost vanished.

Charisma's eyes popped open.

The darkness pressed in on her.

The glowing eyes were closer. A lot closer.

Charisma pulled her shoulder in. In a slow, desperately painful movement she pressed her back against the wall and staggered to her feet.

The glowing eyes surrounded her, but they hung back.

Yes. She tried to smile. They were afraid. Because . . . she was one of the Chosen Ones. She would make them suffer. She would die fighting.

A few levels up, the walls were slimy and cold. Down here, the heat from hell's fires radiated up Charisma's back and fought off the chill of death.

Charisma bent, inch by painful inch, down to her boot and pulled her knife. She grasped the handle in her sweaty palm. She wished she could say the blade felt familiar, but no. She lost her knives in fights every day, every week, until Irving bought them by the case and kept them in the hall closet for the Chosen so they would never be without.

God bless Irving. Almost a hundred years old . . . she had never thought he would outlive her.

No, Charisma would fight to her last breath. . . .

She breathed in and out, the sound rasping in her ears.

The gibbering got louder, more excited.

She lifted the knife. Narrowed her eyes. Braced herself.

And staggered when something heavy, cold and slick and silent, fell on her from above.

She screamed, the pain in her injured shoulder agonizing, then screamed again as that *thing* sank its teeth into the muscle above her collarbone. She stabbed, impaling it, and heard it squeal and struggle. She lost her grip on her knife. She grabbed, dug her fingers into some body part. A nose. An eye. She didn't care; she knew only that she suddenly had a handle with which to throw it, and she did, flung it as hard as she could, the way a person threw a cockroach or slug or spider or snake.

A thump. A squawk. Four pairs of eyes went out. She'd knocked them over like bowling pins, and that made her happy. But when she lost the knife, she'd lost her last weapon.

The chattering grew guttural, angry, intent. The eyes slid closer. Closer. Glowed hotter, red and blue.

Her shoulder throbbed. The bite spread cold down her arm and up her neck. Venom. She'd been poisoned. The world wavered. She was going to die. . . .

She heard an unexpected rush of movement from the side.

Driven by instinct, she crouched and turned to fight.

Loud and deep and animal, something roared and threw an object that clattered and rolled toward the demons.

And right before her eyes, a bomb exploded.

The demons screamed.

Light flashed scalding white, showing her the silhouette of a creature that stood between her and the demons. Tall, hairy, misshapen, a creature from a child's nightmares, with long arms outstretched—toward her.

She tried to cover her light-blinded eyes. The ragged edges of her collarbone scraped together.

The demons scattered.

The beast roared again, closer this time; then like a vengeful god it grabbed her, lifted her, flung her over a broad shoulder, and bounded like a lion up the stairs.

Her arm hung uselessly down the beast's back.

The pain was excruciating.

She welcomed unconsciousness.

She was going to die.

# *Chapter 4*

———◆———

Charisma drifted toward consciousness.

The first thing she heard was the sound of water rippling over stones, like a delicate brook down a mountain slope. She heard birds tweeting, too, and realized she was warm and comfortable, snuggled into her bed listening to her sound machine.

She usually set the machine to play the ocean shore, not the babbling brook, but this was nice. Relaxing. Soothing. Although some memory niggled at the corner of her mind. . . .

Then she moved.

*Wrong!*

Every joint ached and burned.

Instinctively, she reached for the bracelet on her wrist.

It was there, her crystals strung on a wire and held close against her skin. The stones whispered a faint reassurance, so faint she could scarcely hear it, but even so . . . she knew she was safe.

She opened her eyes to darkness. Total darkness. Her night-light had burned out.

She moved again. And groaned. What had she done to herself this time? She couldn't quite remember. . . .

Then, in a rush, she did.

Lost. Hurt. Attacked. Saved by . . . *something*.

Where was she?

It wasn't just dark.

She couldn't see.

*She couldn't see!*

She sat straight up, groped for her eyes. She was blindfolded!

From the side, she heard someone move. Her wrists were caught and held. "Don't." A man's voice, deep, rough, and scratchy. "Your eyes were injured in the blast."

Blind. She was blind. *And imprisoned.*

Panicked, she struggled.

"Don't," he said again. "You'll hurt yourself. The doctor said to leave the bandages on as long as possible."

"The doctor?" Her mouth was dry. Her voice was shrill. "What doctor? Who are you?"

"Dr. King. He saved your life."

This guy didn't tell her who *he* was. Like she wouldn't notice *that*. "I'm not stupid, you know. I remember what happened. I fell down the stairs. I broke my collarbone." Although it felt better. For a new break, surprisingly better. "So *what* are you claiming could have killed me?"

The voice didn't answer.

She started to struggle again.

He shook her wrists. "Do you remember the bite?"

She froze.

The demon. The bite.

"Yes." On her shoulder. The cold had radiated down her arms, her legs.

"Some of the demons are venomous. That one was, and the venom worked on you. By the time I got you here, you were delirious, with a high fever. I sent my people to find Dr. King, but he's busy. He came as soon as he could—"

"You have a specialist who makes house calls?" She poured scorn into every syllable.

"He knows I can't come to him. And he works down here a lot."

"So I'm still below the city?"

"About three levels under Central Park."

"Why so far down? Why Central Park?"

"I'm safe here. And I like Central Park." The man sounded almost whimsical. As if he didn't get much company and was enjoying her visit.

"Safe from what? Who are you?"

He sighed. He loosened his grip. "If I let you go, will you listen to the story before you tear off the bandage?"

"Yes." Because his hands like manacles around her wrists made her panic even more.

Cautiously he released her.

She could feel him hovering, waiting to make a grab if she made the wrong move.

"Water," he said, and put a bottle in her hands.

She should sniff the contents. She should make sure this wasn't drugged. But she was so thirsty, she couldn't wait. Lifting the bottle, she drank, and drank, and when he pried the bottle away, she fought him.

He won, of course, for she was abominably weak. "Stop! You've been on an IV. Your stomach's not ready to be inundated!"

She lowered her hands to her sides, gripped the blanket that covered her legs, and realized—"I need to go to the bathroom." She wished she didn't. She couldn't imagine where she was, what kind of primitive facilities there were, whether he was a leering pervert who would watch her . . . or whether he was a demon who faked being human to trick her into revealing secrets of the Chosen Ones.

Why else would he blindfold her except to conceal his disgusting, eerie, reptilian face?

She heard a rustle of material. His voice came from close beside her, at almost the same level as her head. "I'm going to help you get up." He put his hands under her arms and lifted her to her feet.

And she realized she'd been resting on the ground.

As if he knew what she was thinking, he said, "You were delirious, dying. You kept flinging yourself off the bed onto the floor and burrowing into the dirt."

Her mind seized on the oddest detail. "Your floor is dirt?"

"You're in a cave, okay?" He guided her with his hand under her arm. "Finally I realized you were special. Different. You get your strength from the earth, and you needed the earth to heal."

Kudos to this guy for figuring it out.

The voice continued. "So we put you on the ground and covered you with blankets, and you got better. It was a close thing."

"I feel a little achy now. That's all." She rotated her shoulder. "Even my collarbone is better."

"That's because you've been unconscious for eleven days."

"What?" She jerked her head toward him as if she could see him.

"Eleven days," he repeated. Taking her wrist in his grip, he placed her hand on a doorframe. "Here's the bathroom. I took out the lightbulb. You'll have to grope around, but it's small, with a sink and commode. There's a lock on the door. You'll be okay."

"Why would you take out the lightbulb?"

"I don't know. Maybe because you seem to be the kind of person who doubts me when I say your eyes are injured and would hit the switch to prove me wrong."

"Sarcasm." She rather appreciated that. Made him seem more human.

Not that she'd ever had a conversation with a demon, but she didn't think they had the wit or intelligence for sarcasm.

As promised, the room was blessedly tiny, the door had a lock, and she didn't need her sight to do what she needed to do. She washed her hands at the sink—by the shape and heft of the fixtures, she would guess they dated from early twentieth century—and stood there, trying to understand her situation, to figure out what to do next.

She was dressed in a long, voluminous, sturdy cotton nightgown that smelled like dirt and age, and covered her from her neck to her toes.

Was that creature telling the truth? About anything?

One thing he'd said that she knew was true: She was underground. She could tell by the sense of still earth around her, from the way sound hung in the air, then slowly faded. For her, the earth was the womb from which she was birthed—and the tomb where she would die.

But . . . had the demon's venom truly been so strong it almost killed her? Had she been down here eleven days? Add the days she'd been lost in the tunnels, and she knew the other Chosen were frantic, uncertain whether to say a prayer for her soul or continue their hunt for her. And they didn't have any moments to spare on hunting for her—the Chosen Ones were the last line of defense against hell's increasingly strong assault on the world. And they were almost out of time.

Only weeks remained before darkness covered the earth and hell reigned for a thousand years.

Her heart pounded. She desperately needed to go back up into the city as soon as possible, yet . . . yet she could feel a weariness tugging at her senses, a faint chill and numbness remained in her fingertips, and if her sight was truly affected, how could she escape?

In an abrupt fury, she reached up and tore off the blindfold.

*Oh. Oh!* She blinked. She could see light around the door. A dim light, but still—a light.

After a moment of staring, fireworks began exploding along her optical nerve and she had to turn her head away.

So she wasn't blind. But she did have visual problems, and when she remembered the demons and the utter darkness, and then that radiant explosion . . . how could she be surprised?

A light tap on the door, and the creature called, "Charisma, are you all right?"

She tied the blindfold on again, unlocked the door, and yanked it open. "I'm fine."

"I see." He readjusted her blindfold, his hands careful not to touch her skin. "Are you satisfied now? You took it off. Dr. King will not be pleased."

"I had to know."

"And?"

"I could see."

He took a long breath, which she could read as either disappointment or relief. Then, taking her arm, he walked her across the room . . . she guessed. "We honestly didn't know, so that's a good sign."

"You say I've been here for eleven days, and since my collarbone is feeling pretty good, I tend to believe you."

"Why, thank you."

More sarcasm. She would have to be careful. She might begin to like him.

"Here's a chair." He put her hand on it. "If you can, we'd like you to try some broth. Can you do that?"

She smiled toothily. "I can always eat." Although she wasn't particularly hungry, and that was a bad sign. Usually when she woke after an injury, she was ravenous. So when the scent of chicken broth wafted past, she seated herself, found the mug he placed in front of her, and drank little sips. It was salty and rich, not tainted with the bitter taste of drugs or poison, and, possibly even more miraculous . . . not from a can. "My compliments to the chef," she said.

The scrape of a chair, and his voice was close and to her right. "I keep the Belows safe, and in return they bring me food."

She remembered taking food from Irving's kitchen at the Chosen Ones' headquarters and passing it out to the street people, and remembered, too, that some of them carefully stowed it away. *For the Guardian*, they whispered.

That made her frown. "You've got a racket going."

"I suppose you could say that. But I actually do keep them safe." His voice grew sober. "I never ask for anything in return. They bring the food because I need it, and because they want to pay me as best they can. They have their pride, you know."

"Okay." That made sense.

And she was finished with the broth. She groped, found a table before her, put down the mug. He helped her to her feet, and she followed where he led. "In all this time, why haven't my eyes healed?"

"That particular demon's venom is primarily a neurotoxin, although Dr. King thinks he delivered a load of harmful bacteria, too. The neurotoxin attacked your nervous system—you suffered vertigo, convulsions, pain, and you were panicked because you couldn't see. Dr. King thinks the shock of the flash to your eyes, combined with the venom, injured your optic nerve, and if we let it rest . . . Here's your bed."

Her legs wobbled as he lowered her to sit on her pallet.

The broth should have revived her, and maybe it did. But she was still weak, her head swimming.

Beside her, the creature steadied her with a touch and waited, maybe in concern . . . or maybe because he anticipated the pleasure of tearing out her throat.

She wasn't afraid. She had always known she would die down here, and for right now . . . she had to know whether this man, this thing, would murder her. . . .

So she attacked.

# Chapter 5

—◆—

Charisma lunged toward the voice, shoved at the creature.

He toppled with a hard thump.

She landed on top of him. Kneed him in the groin.

He gasped in pain.

She lunged for his throat.

But he was very tall.

And she was blind.

She missed his throat, caught a handful of the cloth at his chest, gripped it, and clambered up him, planting her feet and knees hard into his belly and his chest. She lunged for his face.

He caught her wrist.

She still had one free hand, and she knew how to kill. She was ready to take him out, but . . . he was warm.

She hadn't expected that. She had really thought he was a demon, cold-blooded, pretending to care about her, presenting an illusion of humanity to lure her into some foolish revelation about her friends and her mission.

Instead he was a . . . well, she still didn't know what he was. But sitting on top of him, she remembered how he had come to her rescue, and her fight instinct cooled. He breathed in and out, his massive chest rising and falling. His heart hammered beneath the knee she had planted on his breastbone. Beneath the loose clothing he wore, his body parts appeared to be in approximately the right places, so he was . . . a mammal?

Probably some form of humanoid, a species that was perhaps not an enemy, and she was trained not to kill on anything less than a certainty, or in self-defense.

He, inconveniently, didn't try to beat her unconscious or slice her to pieces. Instead he remained motionless, and after a moment of indecision, she swept her hand across his chest.

It was heavy with ribs and muscles, and abruptly tapered to a thin waist and hips. His cotton tunic left his huge upper arms and shoulders free to move. And they really were huge, abnormally so. The arm felt human, with muscles and an elbow and more muscles and a wrist . . . but coarse hair about an inch long covered the skin. His coat felt like that stray German shepherd that appeared whenever she bought a meatball sandwich at Luigi's Roach Coach.

This guy was not formed right. "Lift a lot of weights?" she asked.

"Yes. And I indulge in an unwise use of Rogaine, too."

She half laughed, because it was the polite thing to do when someone joked in the face of . . . of being so very, very different. Her heartbeat began to calm.

Maybe everything about him was the truth. Maybe he was merely one of the unfortunates who lived beneath the city because above, they would be the objects of horror and mockery.

Beneath the rough weave of the tunic, she felt the heat of his skin, and over that, more of that coarse, long, thick hair. A ruff of hair—of fur—circled his throat.

He didn't wear a collar. He didn't smell like a dog. He didn't smell like flea shampoo. He smelled like a man who used Dove, probably in its liquid form, and rinsed in rainwater.

She hesitated, her fingertips hovering over the top of his jaw.

"Go ahead," he said, his voice rougher than before. "It's a little late for you to worry about intruding on my personal space."

She nodded. "Truth."

With the flat of her hand, she stroked his cheek, then his temple. The hair here grew back toward his ears, like a man's beard, but smooth. And softer than the hair on his arms.

Up the center of his face, from the point of his chin to his forehead, his features were shaped like a man's— and covered with fine, short hair like the coat on a dog's face. Except for his lips. They were smooth, soft, sculpted in the same shape as human lips.

He was definitely the guy who had saved her ass. She remembered the outline she'd seen when that light blasted her eyesight away. "Why didn't the light hurt your eyes?"

"Since I set off the bomb, I knew enough to close them."

"Makes sense. Are you a werewolf?" She was joking. Since Aleksandr, one of her fellow Chosen Ones, had disappeared, the Wilder family had visited the Chosen Ones more than once: Aleksandr's parents, Firebird and Douglas, along with his grandparents, Konstantine and Zorana.

Konstantine had raised a family of shape-shifters, and had a great deal of knowledge of the creatures that populated the night. He had snorted when Charisma asked about werewolves and vampires and ghosts.

She believed him, too.

But this creature beneath her gave a sigh. "Maybe."

She gave a quavering laugh and slid her hands into his long hair. The ends swept his shoulders, and the strands felt clean and glossy to the touch. But when she allowed her fingers to delve into his hair and touch his scalp, she gasped, and he flinched away.

The skin there covered . . . something. Something weird. Harder than bone. With a seam.

"Who are you?" she breathed. "What happened to you?"

He took her hands and held them, not to imprison her as he had before, but as if he wanted comfort for himself. "They call me *Guardian*."

Her heart picked up the beat again. "What do you mean, they call you *Guardian*? Who calls you that? Is it your name?"

"The Belows call me that. The people who live down here. So I guess it's my name." He shrugged, a massive roll of his shoulders that for her seemed like a roller coaster. "Say, could you do me a favor?"

"Maybe."

"Could you get your knees out of my stomach?"

"Sure." Hastily she slid off him and settled on the ground, sitting on her heels. "Could you do me a favor?"

"Maybe."

"Tell me how you got the name."

He took a breath, and another, then said, "When I first got down here, I was, um, sick. Out of my mind. Wounded. Terrified, like an abused wolf cub. Moises found me and he coaxed me into this cave with a trail of bread crumbs."

"Literally?"

"Pretty much. I was starving. Moises told Amber about me. Taurean overheard."

"These are all Belows?"

"Sometimes they go above. But yes. They are my . . . staff, I guess you'd say. My friends. I trust them."

"It's good to have friends." Charisma missed her friends. Missed them terribly.

"Taurean announced to the Belows that a guardian had arrived." Reflectively, he said, "I vaguely remember the clamor that resulted."

"So *Guardian* is like a title."

"Yes. And a legend."

"A legend." She clutched his hands tightly.

He gave her a light squeeze back. "Does that mean something to you?"

It did mean something. *She* was a legend, or part of one, and in these uncertain days, she knew never to discount a good legend. "I'm Charisma Fangorn."

"I know. In your delirium, you told me."

What else had she told him? Uneasily, she said, "Tell me all about *your* legend."

"The Belows believe that in times of trouble, someone comes to them—apparently, it's always serendipity—

and he protects them from the dangers down here. In normal times, it's all about the Aboves who are creepy enough to come down and scrounge for slaves, or the serial killers who prey on the disadvantaged, or the rich boys who come down to get their fill of rape and pillage. These days, of course, it's all of those, plus the demons."

As he spoke, Charisma slid her crystal bracelet up and down her arm, trying to coax the stones into speaking to her. Who was he? What was he? Was he really a legend, and did he have a part to play in the fate of the Chosen Ones?

The stones were silent, their magic exhausted . . . or perhaps it was that her magic had abandoned her. "So you fulfill the duties as Guardian? And you took that as your name?"

"I don't remember my real name. I had some kind of surgery on my brain." His voice grew strained and scratchy. "I'm not right in the head."

"Oh. That explains your, um, skull." He was crazy. That was what he was saying. He was crazy.

Not that she hadn't met a lot of crazy people, and conducted business with them, too. About half the street people and ninety percent of the people who lived in the tunnels should be on meds and weren't, and Charisma thanked them when they brought her reports of weird creatures and demon attacks that no one else believed.

Although . . . although perfectly respectable people were starting to report such oddities, and they hated when the police doubted *their* sanity.

The trouble was, of course, that Osgood owned the city, and the police department, and Osgood did not want those reports circulated. He wanted the populace quiet and docile . . . until the seven years were up. Until it was too late.

So respectable citizens kept quiet when they saw scary things, and Charisma listened to the street people and never feared them.

But then, she'd never been blindfolded and trapped underground by one before.

But he seemed to get it. "I'm not violent or anything. As far as I remember. I can't recall much before I was down here."

"You have amnesia."

"That's what Dr. King tells me. He says my mind will release the past when it has healed from its trauma."

"Amnesia isn't so bad." Really. She hoped.

"I suppose not, although I do hope I don't remember *I'm* a serial killer."

"Oh, me too." Except . . . "Why did they operate on your brain? Whoever they are?"

"They told me they would make me what I was meant to be." His voice changed, grew deeper, with a growl that sounded ugly and hostile.

And it seemed death hovered close in the heated air.

Yet Charisma had never learned to shut her mouth. "What were you meant to be?"

He yanked his hands away from her grip. He sat up, towering over her. "A monster. A beast. A fiend. A twisted horror worthy of nothing but disgust and terror."

Never had she felt so inadequate. He had saved her from certain death, and now his pain was palpable, yet she had no way to help him. "You're not so bad."

"You haven't seen me!" His voice stripped away any illusion she harbored that he wasn't dangerous.

He sounded . . . angry, a creature on the razor's edge of violence.

"No. I haven't seen you." She edged back, wondering whether to rip off her blindfold and *run*.

But slowly he brought his rasping breath under control. "I saved you, Charisma Fangorn. I nursed you. I'm invested in you. I won't hurt you now."

"Reassuring." Not really. Sounded stalkerish. Perhaps it would be better if she attacked again, knocked him out, and made her escape. If only . . . if only she hadn't wasted her strength on her first ineffective attack. If only she weren't so exhausted . . .

"You're drooping." Taking her arms, he pressed them to her sides, lifted her to her feet, picked her up, and placed her on her bed on the floor. "Go to sleep."

Alarmed or not, she was almost asleep now.

"When you wake up again," he said, "you can take a shower."

"A shower." The faintest spark made her straighten.

"You've been burrowing into the ground for eleven days."

"I'm dirty." She touched one hand to her chest and felt the crust of filth there. "A shower . . ."

But when she thought about the effort to wash herself, she realized he was right. She was finished. She was . . . exhausted.

She slithered backward onto the pillow.

He caught her by the shoulders and eased her flat onto her back.

And she was asleep.

# Chapter 6

———⬧———

Guardian stared at Charisma where she lay lax with fatigue in a thin cotton nightgown, resting in a hollow in the earth. In the days since the attack, she'd lost weight, leaving her painfully thin. Her tan had faded and she'd grown pale. Her black hair had grown out to show strawberry blond roots, and in her delirium, she'd dug herself into the hard-packed ground, pushing dirt under her nails and into the creases of her knuckles.

Yet . . . yet he liked to look at her. He liked to think about who and what she was. He had grown fond of her.

Eleven days ago, Taurean had come running to him with a report that one of the Aboves had lost her way in the tunnels. She'd been down a long time, watched by a hunting pack of demons who waited for her strength to fail before they tore her apart.

Although Guardian feared a trap, Taurean's urgency had sent him out after her.

Taurean had led the way, loping along while informing Guardian that this was one of the *good* Aboves. Charisma Fangorn had been kind to Taurean. She even listened when Taurean told her about the terrors that stalked the night . . . terrors no one perceived but Taurean. Charisma didn't call Taurean crazy; she said Taurean was gifted, and she thanked her with offerings of food and blankets.

Taurean had told him that Charisma saw what nobody else above wanted to see, and she fought for the lost children, and poor families, and for people like Taurean.

Guardian hadn't necessarily believed everything Taurean said. Taurean was . . . special. Different. But he patted Taurean on the shoulder and promised to save her friend.

Guardian had reached Charisma barely in time . . . and still he had been too late.

Dr. King spoke from the door behind him. "She came to consciousness?"

Guardian swiveled to face his friend. "She did."

"She was aware? Coherent?" As always, Dr. King was impeccably dressed in a suit, white shirt, and tie. His wingtips shone with polish, and his Breguet pocket watch was a work of art.

"She ate," Guardian told him. "She drank. She went to the bathroom. She abused me verbally. She tried to kill me. Considering what she's been through, she is doing well."

Dr. King laughed, a deep, contagious laugh that made Guardian smile despite himself. "That is better than I ever dared to hope." He walked forward, his bag on one shoulder, his other arm swinging awkwardly.

He knelt on the floor beside Charisma and studied her relaxed face, then placed a hand on her forehead and nodded. "Almost no fever. Good." Holding her wrist in his hand, he took her pulse. "She's a lucky girl. If it hadn't been for you, we would have lost her."

Dr. King was like everyone else who worked below ground—he didn't fit in among the Aboves.

He worked with the poor and disabled. He was African-American. He was a dwarf, the smallest man on earth.

He probably could have gotten along with the Aboves, but he didn't fit their profile for a dwarf. He had trouble sidling up to an examining room table, not just because of his height, but because of the constant ridicule by his peers.

Worse, his IQ was off the charts. Guardian could only imagine what it had taken Dr. King to get through medical school, working the long hours and battling his colleagues' overweening egos. But he kept his diplomas framed on the wall in his underground office to reassure those who doubted his medical qualifications.

Dr. King opened his bag, donned sterile latex gloves, turned back the collar on Charisma's nightgown, and examined the demon's bite.

After the attack, it was an hour before Guardian got her back to safety, another hour before Dr. King arrived, and in that time, the poison had invaded her system and the wound had turned septic. Dark red streaks ran under her skin, down her arm, and up her neck. Froth bubbled at the edges of the open wound, and a sickly sweet stench rose from it.

Guardian and Dr. King had worked through the

night, opening the wound to cut away the dead tissue, disinfecting and cleaning, applying heat and cold. . . .

The bite was closed now, resulting in a hard blue mark that looked as if she'd been branded by evil. And perhaps she had.

"That's probably as good as it's going to get," Dr. King said, and closed her nightgown tightly at her throat.

Guardian squatted beside her and stroked her hair back from her forehead. "She freaked out about having her eyes covered."

"Of course she did. Wouldn't you?" Dr. King pulled off his gloves and put them in the trash.

"Yes. But I think I convinced her of the danger of taking off the blindfold." Guardian looked around his lair. The massive stone cave extended three football fields in length and rose six stories. Golden stalagmite pillars lifted their arms to support the weight of the earth above. Elaborate primeval buildings, like multistory palaces, now in ruin, had been shaped out of the walls, complete with windows and turrets and stairways. A small, pure shallow brook gushed from a hidden grotto in the far wall, cascaded over a waterfall and through a riverbed, and disappeared through a hole in the opposite wall. Here and there, high in the ceiling, sunshine beamed down through hidden skylights. . . .

For all the time that Guardian had lived down here, he had never seen a hint of who had constructed this immense underground chamber, or when, or how the ancient builders directed the sunshine from the city so far above down to this place. But he couldn't argue with their success—where the sunshine touched the ground, crimson flowers bloomed.

He liked this place, halfway between the corruption of the city above and the fires of hell below. As best as he could tell, this was where he belonged. Among the Belows, this place was a legend . . . and so, now, was he. They had seen something in his deformity and his madness. They had brought him here to heal. They called him *Guardian*, and depended on him to protect them from the demons below and the cruelty above.

He did his best.

He could spend the rest of his life here. If things continued as they were, he would. If he never remembered who he was and what he was, he would be here forever.

Forever.

Forever.

The word echoed in his brain, bouncing back and forth against the metal plate that formed the back of his skull.

Dr. King patted Guardian's knee. "How about you? Still having nightmares?"

Guardian fought back his terror. Opening his eyes, he saw Dr. King watching him with that world-weary concern he so often showed. "I don't sleep much," Guardian said.

"Not sleeping will make you crazy faster than anything."

"I'll take my chances. The real demons scare me less than . . ."

"Than the phantoms in your mind. I know. I've heard you scream in your sleep. Raises the hair on the back of my neck." Dr. King rubbed his bald head. "Not easy to do."

"Ruffles my fur, too," Guardian joked, "and that's a lot of fur to ruffle."

Dr. King didn't laugh. "You are so—and I use this word rarely—normal."

Guardian rudely snorted.

"No, it's true." Dr. King shook his finger at Guardian. "You have a sense of humor. You seldom get angry. Nor do you pity yourself much. You react like a man who is used to being treated kindly. Fairly. There was no abuse in your childhood, not from your parents or from your schoolmates. You weren't born this way."

Guardian lifted his hands and showed them to the doctor. "Are these the hands of a man?"

Rough blond fur covered the backs of his hands. His pale palms were bare, but on his right hand the skin looked artificial. On this hand, he had no fingerprints, and that added a dimension of science fiction to his deformity. He flexed his fingers; they worked well, although the two in the middle were stiff in the joints.

Bitterly he said, "I don't even need to look in the mirror to see what I am."

# Chapter 7

———✦———

"**Y**ou take your appearance too seriously. It doesn't define who you are." Dr. King patted Guardian's knee again. "Leave the easy judgments to everyone else, concentrate on the work you have to do, and be thankful that somehow you were given the weapons to do it."

"Right." *No point in complaining to* me, Dr. King meant. Dr. King faced his own, more serious challenges. "How much longer will she have to wear the bandage?" Guardian asked.

"A week. A month. I wish I knew for sure." Dr. King donned another pair of gloves, eased the blindfold away from her left eye, then her right, lifted the lid and checked the pupils, and shook his head. "The bomb flash burned her retina, but the poison is what did the damage, and I don't know how that poison works."

"Demon poison? No, I don't suppose you do. I don't suppose anyone does." Tests needed to be run, but what hospital would run tests on a poison they didn't believe existed?

"That she's recovered at all is because you recognized the one thing that would heal her."

"Her connection to the earth. I don't know what gave me the clue. . . ." Guardian realized Dr. King was looking at him carefully, considering him again, judging him again. He snapped, "I don't!"

"You don't remember any more than you did?"

Guardian shook his head. "I don't even know whether recognizing her gift is something I knew before, or if it was simply good observation skills. Down here, I have had to develop *those*."

Wearily, Dr. King loosened his tie. "I think when you remember, what you remember will be extraordinary."

"Then why, whenever I try to remember, do I feel sick with anticipation and dread?" Thinking about the past made Guardian want to run away, farther than he had ever run before, away from everyone and everything . . . but how could he run away from himself?

"An extraordinary life doesn't necessarily mean an easy life. Sometimes the events that shape us are extraordinarily difficult." Dr. King stripped off the gloves again and trashed them. "With you looking like you do, I think that's a safe assumption."

"How do you know I wasn't born this way?"

"It would have been in the papers."

"The ones at the check stands!"

"At the very least. No, someone fooled around with your brain. Hurt you terribly. Made you look like a monster."

With what he considered formidable restraint, Guardian said, "I don't believe a man can *think* himself hairy."

Dr. King waved him to silence. "The human brain is God's most powerful creation. Nothing man has done has ever come close to the glories of a man's mind. Or a woman's. We haven't begun to tap the potential hidden within, and most researchers are afraid to try, for whom do we experiment on? Only the most morally decrepit would dream of using a human guinea pig. Unfortunately, I have more than once met the morally decrepit, and it seems to me their numbers are growing exponentially."

Guardian's mind roamed the miles of dark corridors beneath the city where horror lurked. "Are we calling the demons morally decrepit now?"

"No." Dr. King might be small, but he stated his opinions definitively. "The demons are exactly what they seem—beings forever damned to hell until there's nothing left of humanity inside them, until they're just distilled drops of pure malevolence. No, I'm talking about the people in this city who deliberately market drugs to children, who terrorize already miserable prostitutes, who spread disease and pain and filth, and take pleasure in holding power over others. . . ." His small fists clenched. "I'm talking about Osgood and his minions, and all those who take their example from him."

Yes. Yes. Osgood hadn't brought evil to New York, but he had tightened its grip on the city. He had made evil impossible to escape. Guardian felt sorry for Dr. King, on the front line of the battle. "You see too many of the wounded."

Dr. King shrugged. "Who else will treat them? God gave me hands, however small, to help, and I will. But you, my friend, show the classic signs of amnesia. That

mind of yours is not damaged; it's as sharp as a tack."
Dr. King waved a hand at the books that lined the
shelves in the library alcove. "You remember the real
world." He chuckled. "You remember the kind of magazines at the grocery store checkouts."

"*That* I wish I could forget."

"You don't remember your past because you don't
want to remember. I think someday you'll see something or do something that peels back the first layer, and
then it'll be like peeling the dead skin off a burn—each
layer will be agony, but it must be done before you can
heal."

"Once again, Doctor, you've given me something to
look forward to." Guardian hadn't realized he was
watching Charisma, but when she shivered in her
sleep, he pulled the covers up to her neck.

Her sweetly round face with its flashing dimples im-
plied an artless disposition and a character that had
never viewed the ugly part of life. A rose tattoo climbed
her spine and blossomed behind her left ear, and,
asleep like this, she looked young. So young.

But only a fool would ignore the calluses on her
hands formed from hours of self-defense classes, the
scars that slashed the creamy skin, the well-toned muscles, and the stubborn tilt of her chin. She trusted no
one, certainly not *him*.

He told himself Charisma had earned his fierce dedication; he had met no other seasoned warrior who
would face the dread forces of hell, could fight and defeat them, and then fight another battle against pain
and poison to live and fight again.

Yet his primal need to protect and defend her was
more than admiration. When he looked at her, he didn't

feel like a monster. For the first time in a long time, he felt like a man, a young man who dreamed of one woman who saw past his beastly form and loved him.

"How pathetic is that?" he murmured, then glanced up and away, hoping he'd revealed nothing of his longing to the good doctor.

If he had, Dr. King gave no indication. "Guardian, when I think of what you have done to survive, and the monsters you've faced down here, I know you'll come through just fine." In a voice grave and sad, he said, "Which is more than I can say about this poor soul. I've never seen anyone survive the demon's venom. I suspect . . . Well. We'll see."

Guardian, too, had seen the results of the demon's bite. But during the days and nights he'd cared for Charisma, her fierce battle against death had given him hope. "All she needs is a miracle to remain alive."

"Exactly right. And we can all use one of those, I suppose." King picked up his bag. "I'll check in tomorrow. When she wakes again, you know the drill. Give her fluids; feed her; try to keep her as quiet as possible. She can bathe if she feels up to it. Don't let her take that bandage off."

"I'll do my best. It should all be doable, as long as she doesn't kill me." Guardian watched Dr. King walk toward the door.

Dr. King said, "Call if you need me, but I think the worst of the crisis is over."

"What will happen to her now?" Guardian waited, hung on a hook of hope and fear.

"I can't say for sure, but she's a fighter."

"She'll get better; then she'll leave and return to her life above."

"Yes." The doctor viewed Guardian with something that looked like pity.

So maybe Guardian hadn't been as discreet about his emotions as he had hoped.

Dr. King continued. "I know it's hard, but try not to take it to heart."

It was far too late for that.

# Chapter 8

—◆—

Guardian escorted Dr. King through the narrow, winding tunnels, up two stories to the broader corridors that crisscrossed a mere fifteen feet beneath the city.

"You don't have to walk with me." With one hand, Dr. King balanced his bag on his shoulder. He wore a band around his head with a flashlight that lit his way, and that left his other hand free . . . to carry his small, custom-made pistol.

"Not usually." Guardian turned his head as they passed a crossroads, and saw a glint of pale, glowing eyes that blinked out as soon as he spotted them. "But with caring for Charisma, I haven't been patrolling the tunnels, and it doesn't take long for the creatures from below and above to grow bold."

As they spoke, a skinny, dirty, snarling man rushed at Dr. King, his fists raised.

Guardian strong-armed him, slammed him against the wall, and snarled back.

Dr. King watched calmly as the mugger ran away. "Not just hell's spawn, I see."

They stopped by the fold-down ladder that led up into Central Park at the back of the Metropolitan Museum of Art. Guardian looked the fifteen feet up toward the hatch. He could see light around the edges, and for a moment dreamed of fresh air and sunlight on his face.

But this was closer than he ever before dared come to ground level.

The monsters in his nightmares were monsters in truth.

Stretching tall, Guardian brought the ladder down to rest on the ground.

Although perhaps . . . perhaps whoever was after him had forgotten.

He took the first few steps up.

"Don't!" Dr. King said.

"It's been more than a year since I've attempted to surface."

"Things haven't improved. They're getting worse. Whoever is after you has more resources than ever before. Don't try to go up!" Dr. King caught at his leg.

Guardian looked down at him. "All I'll do is open the hatch for you. Then I'll stand aside. I promise." He climbed again.

Even here, he could feel fresh air washing over his face. He clicked the latch and swung back the hatch. For one blessed moment, he saw a glimpse of the real world, where, as the sun set, the shadows lengthened and a breeze ruffled his fur.

Then Dr. King clambered past him, moving fast and chattering nervously. "Go back. Go back! Don't worry about me; I'll get home. It's not quite dark yet, and I have friends on the streets, too."

"I know you do. And my people have instructions to look out for you."

Dr. King stood on the ground and looked down at Guardian. "You'll go back right away to check on Charisma? Because she should be watched."

"Right away."

"You'll be able to find your way back to the Guardian cave?"

"I can follow a scent clearly in the dark, and my night vision is superior. The benefits of looking like a dog, I suppose." Guardian was only half joking.

"Not a dog. A wolf, wild and lethal." Dr. King glanced around nervously. "Go on now. Quickly. You've exposed yourself, and that's dangerous to us all." Taking the hatch out of Guardian's hand, Dr. King slammed it almost on Guardian's head.

The tension and hopelessness were getting to Dr. King.

Guardian waited one more moment at the top of the steps, toying with the idea of opening the hatch and springing into the real world. But he had read about Central Park and the Metropolitan Museum of Art. He had seen movies about it, and perhaps in his past he had walked its paths. He knew people were always there, and he didn't dare show himself.

His dream of the real world should remain just that—a dream. It must.

He climbed down, lifted the ladder, then ran back and down two levels to his cave.

He entered and, with a glance, confirmed that Charisma still slept, that her blindfold was in place. "I'm back," he said softly, and knelt beside her. "Don't worry; you're safe."

Without warning, she sat straight up. In a clear, strong voice, she said, "Of course. Why didn't I think of it before?" As if she could see him, she turned her head toward him. "I need you to get Isabelle."

Stunned by her sudden shift from sleep to consciousness, he asked, "Who's Isabelle?"

"She's our healer. When she puts her hands on me, I'll be well. I'll be able to see. I'll be able to fight. Get Isabelle," she said. Then, more faintly, "Please. I need Isabelle. I don't have much time."

Had she subconsciously heard the doubt and worry in Dr. King's voice? Or was her body speaking to her?

She groped for his hand. "You'll do it?"

Guardian stood. "Yes."

"I knew you would." She lay down, turned on her side, pulled the covers over her shoulders, tucked her hand under her cheek, and once again she was asleep.

But finding this Isabelle was more easily said than done. Who was she? Where was she?

He again ran toward the exit from the cave.

The narrow, dark tunnels twisted and turned beneath the city. He was on the hunt; he needed to consult with one of his people, someone who roamed the streets and knew New York intimately. Taurean or Amber or Moises were the most reliable, but right now, he would talk to any one of his troops. All of them were more street-savvy than he was . . . he, who didn't dare put his head up to look at the stars.

He found Taurean first, huddled at the bottom of the same ladder where Dr. King had gone up, staring wide-eyed up the steps.

Taurean was tall, over six feet, square-jawed, with a dark stubble on her upper lip and long, dark black hair that hung down her back in a profusion of curls. She shambled rather than walked, cowered rather than confronted, and when Guardian asked how old she was, she told him she was seventy. She was so swift and strong, he could hardly believe that, but at the same time . . . maybe it was true. On her good days, she was his best right hand. On her bad days . . . she feared the New York streets. She feared the people above, and when she grew terrified, she could throw a punch that would knock a man out.

Guardian did everything he could to keep her out of trouble.

"Taurean, can you help me?" he said.

"Yes?" She seemed unsure, listening to something he could not hear. Then she nodded. "Yes. I'm good today."

"Do you remember Charisma? You helped me save her."

"That was a long time ago."

"Eleven days . . ." *No, don't go there.* "Charisma said she needs Isabelle. Do you know where to find Isabelle?"

"Isabelle . . . Mason. Yes. She's at Irving's house: Upper East Side, neo–French Classic style, nineteenth century, dozens of bedrooms. Entry: marble floors, gilded ceilings, matching Chippendale tables, Chagall hanging on wall. Library: tall, wide fireplace with leather chairs and sofa, two pool tables and a gaming table, mustard-colored walls, mahogany shelves filled with leather-bound books and antiques, Aubusson rugs, floor-to-ceiling shelves." Taurean recited so matter-of-factly, Guardian never doubted a word. "Irving's bedroom and private library: two joined rooms with books, relics, his bed with gargoyles carved in the wood, a library table, chairs and ottomans, shelves of books, skulls, teeth, artifacts, and scrolls—"

" 'Kay!" Guardian held up a restraining hand. "Okay. Isabelle is at Irving's house. Can you fetch her?"

Taurean thought for a moment. "I know where to go." Head cocked, she listened again. "But it's a mansion."

"Is that a problem?"

"I don't like mansions. Beautiful mansions. Glorious, old, revered, with cruel people who lie in wait . . ." A tear slipped down her face.

"You can't go by yourself. So come on, then." He took the first steps up toward the street. "I'll help you find Isabelle."

Taurean didn't budge. "No, Warrior. Don't do that. You know *they'll* come."

"I don't want you to be afraid." He offered her his hand.

"I'm not afraid as long as *they* don't come. They're bad people. They hurt you." Taurean put her hand on Guardian's arm, but that hand trembled.

"You said Irving's mansion is on the Upper East Side. It can't be far."

"A few blocks."

Guardian wanted to help Charisma, to get her what she needed to heal. He was selfish, too; at the idea of seeing the night sky and the stars, feeling the wind on his face, a spark of excitement rose in him. "We'll run."

"Promise me"—Taurean grabbed his ear as firmly as a mother disciplining her child—"promise me if *they* come, you'll save yourself."

He stared at her. "No. I won't leave you to them."

She pinched his ear hard. "Yes. I can make myself invisible, a pitiful street dweller. But the Belows can't live without you. Promise me you'll save yourself."

"Okay. Okay! I promise. But you're afraid, and I haven't been up for so long. Maybe they think I'm dead." Surely they had given up. "I'd like to see this Isabelle, too. Only from a distance, of course. No reason to scare the woman with a face like mine." He led Taurean up the ladder. "Charisma seemed so sure Isabelle would rush to her side, and she said she was a healer. So, a doctor, I guess. If Charisma hadn't gone back to sleep, I would have had her write a note, because what kind of doctor would follow either one of us under the city?" He threw back the hatch. He stepped out into the enclosed garbage area for the museum, and reflected briefly that his first breath of fresh air smelled of rotting leftovers from the cafeteria. He reached down for Taurean's hand—and something scraped against the building, and an alien odor touched his senses.

Men. Humans. Police. Nearby.

And *them*.

"Run!" he shouted at Taurean.

With a gasp, she vanished down the rungs.

Floodlights flashed on, illuminating him, baring his hideous form to the whole world.

A man's shocked voice said, "Holy shit, what is that?"

In one bound, Guardian jumped halfway back down the ladder. In another, he reached bottom.

Taurean was nowhere in sight.

So Guardian kept his promise. He ran.

Behind him, he heard shouts. The creak of wood as men poured down the ladder. Pounding feet.

Spotlights blasted through the stark night of the tunnels.

Gunshots roared and echoed along the stone walls.

He dropped flat to the ground.

A man's voice yelled, "Aim carefully. I want him alive!"

Terror froze Guardian in place.

He knew that voice. He knew that man.

He feared that man.

Someone screamed at him. *Run!*

Or maybe it was his own mind he heard.

He didn't care if he was shot. He had to *run*! Rising onto all fours, he used his hands and feet to gain a speed these humans could never emulate.

Behind him, a flash of light. A blast and an unearthly high whistle. Screams of surprise.

His underground friends did not allow trespassers— and they would protect Guardian, their Warrior, who protected them.

Another explosion; the reverberation rolled down the tunnel, shaking the ground, overtaking him, passing him.

Smoke tickled his nose.

He took the first passage to the left. He rushed along another corridor, down another stairway, plunging deeper into the secret places beneath the city, where night clung eternally to the walls and only a creature like him, deformed, mutilated, outcast, could find his way back.

He ran until his heart wanted to burst and his lungs burned, until he smelled no other creature, heard no sound other than his own breathing. Until he was alone, as he would always be.

But somewhere in the passages above, a man—and a woman—hunted him. He remembered them.

Lifting his head to a sky he would never again see, he howled out his fear and rage.

And the demons cowered.

# Chapter 9

Taurean waited until the number six subway rumbled past, then crawled out of the underground onto the tracks. She walked a hundred feet to the 103rd Street station, climbed up on the platform, and headed for the exit, talking to herself all the way.

No one said anything to her about how she'd arrived and the way she departed. She was homeless and crazy. So she might as well be a ghost.

She headed south on Third Avenue, toward the Upper East Side. Outside, the city was as quiet as it would ever be; the sun wouldn't be up for another hour, but already it turned the sky a light tan. As she trekked along toward Irving's house, she said, "See that color? That means there's an air stagnation warning. Again. I remember when the wind off the sea used to blow the smog away occasionally. Now it seems every day it gets thicker and harder to breathe. Glad I don't have asthma."

Outside a corner bakery, a short, chubby guy who was sweeping the front walk glanced at her and backed up toward his door.

She told him, "Of course, I also remember a time when I was an art historian, when I was welcome at homes like Irving Shea's, when I appraised the objects of the wealthy with a cool eye."

"Yeah, I remember that, too," he said.

She nodded regally and walked on. "I remember a time when the world was full of beauty and I never imagined that cruelty prowled the mansions." She stopped, and leaned a hand against a lamppost. "Or that madness lurked in my own mind."

A lot of things had happened since then: years in an institution, years on the street.

She straightened. "But I recall the way to Irving Shea's mansion, and I will get there, give my message, and get back before Guardian worries too much about me. Because he proved one thing tonight—even one level down is too close. Those people who hunt him are always watching, waiting like spiders in their webs, and if it hadn't been for me, they would have caught him." Recalling the gunshots, she frowned. "I hope they didn't wound him. We can't survive without him down there. Oh, look! Here we are!"

She stared up at the grand steps that led from the street to the mansion's massive front entry. The lights on either side of the door were not authentic. "But they were last time I was here. Probably they were broken in one of the recent riots, and replaced." Windows on the second level were lit, and in the entry, too. She put one foot on the broad concrete step—and stopped. "I can't climb those stairs. I don't belong. Not anymore."

Day's light grew, but slowly, blocked by the murky air. "No one will see me," she assured herself, and slipped around the corner, close to the building, and crept toward the back, toward the servants' entrance. Lights shone from the ground-level windows in the basement. "That used to be the kitchen." She saw it in her mind, and recited, "Kitchen is as big as a lobby. Open pantry shelves. Cupboards to the twelve-foot ceilings, gas stovetop with six burners and a grill, two ovens—no, three. And a huge fridge. Ugly table, though." Getting on her belly, she low-crawled under the wrought-iron fence that protected the property and peered in the windows. Yes, it was the kitchen . . . and people were in there. Three people.

At once she tried to crawl back, terrified that they would find her, hurt her.

Then she remembered . . . she had a message. For Irving. So she ducked out of sight and scratched on the window. She waited a moment, then poked her head back around and checked.

The people inside the kitchen stared at her: an older man in a black suit and tie, a small, gray-haired woman in a black dress and wearing a scowl, and an old, old man seated in a wheelchair, eating from a bowl at the kitchen table.

New kitchen table. "Granite tabletop with oak frame," she said. No one moved, so she scratched again, and waved frantically. "I have to talk to Irving," she shouted, and pointed into the house and then at herself, over and over, until the man in the suit moved toward the back door.

On her hands and knees, she rounded the corner of the house.

He opened the door.

Light from inside streamed out and illuminated the concrete stairs that led down to the kitchen.

He stepped out and said, "Miss, can I help you?"

"I have a message for Irving," Taurean shouted again.

"Come in, then."

He was a very odd man, formal in the way he dressed and the unique lift of his speech, but at the same time he seemed unfazed by her—and that didn't happen often.

She crawled to the stairway.

"Can I help you rise?" he asked.

"I have to keep my head low. They're after me, you know."

He nodded as if he knew who *they* were.

That did not happen often, either.

She sat on her butt and eased herself down one step at a time.

He stepped aside as she got to the bottom, and with one final glance at his calm face, she scurried into the kitchen.

"Would you like me to leave the door open," he asked, "in case you wish to leave suddenly?"

"No. They're out there. Shut them out."

He did as she instructed.

The big room was warm and bright.

The woman watched her suspiciously.

The old man observed her with bright, birdlike curiosity.

"I have to give a message to Irving," Taurean shouted.

"I'm Irving," the old man in the wheelchair said.

She frowned. "No, you're not. Irving Shea: tall, dark

skinned, dark haired, dark eyes, first African-American CEO in charge of a major corporation in New York, drinks tawny port and coffee."

"I am Irving. I'm simply much, much older now. See?" He pointed to his face. "Dark skinned. *White* haired. I have arthritis." He showed her his twisted fingers. "And hearing aids, so you don't have to shout."

She walked toward him, head bent, staring hard. "You are Irving Shea. You're like a fine house with good architecture that's too old to salvage."

Irving chuckled. "Exactly. And I think if I remember correctly, you are . . . Jessica? Jessica Bellwether?"

Taurean jerked back. "No, I'm Taurean. Jessica's dead. I haven't been Jessica for a long, long time."

"I see." Irving tapped his spoon on the table. "I'm eating my breakfast. Would you like to join me?"

She thought about it.

"When a warrior eats at my table," Irving said solemnly, "I honor her presence whether she be friend or foe."

She relaxed. She understood that kind of reassurance. "All right."

The woman in black spoke, harsh and abrupt. "You're dirty. You need to wash before you sit down at the table."

Taurean glanced down at her hands and clothes in bewilderment. They were black. She rubbed at the stains on her hands. "How did I get dirty?"

"From crawling under the fence and living like a—" the woman snapped.

"Martha, that's enough." Irving cut her off. "Taurean, there's a powder room in the corridor outside the kitchen. McKenna can show you the way."

The man, McKenna, stepped toward her.

She shrank back. He was male. She was in a mansion. He wanted to take her off alone.

He stopped. "You smell a little like gunpowder. Were you setting off fireworks?"

Taurean's mind cleared. She remembered. The tunnel. Guardian. The police. The people with the nets. "Yes. We scared the monsters away."

"Good for you." McKenna waited.

Taurean thought he was the kind of man who waited without chafing at the delay. He was also short and rather hobbitlike in appearance, with wild eyebrows and a kind smile with white teeth.

She was over six feet, scrawny, and she knew how to punch.

McKenna was no danger to her.

She went with him to the powder room.

He showed her the soap and towels and left her alone. She locked the door and took a sponge bath. After all, she might be insane, but she recognized French milled lavender soap when she used it.

It took her a long time, and when she was done, she quietly opened the door and crept along the corridor toward the light. The people were still in there, three of them, and she heard Irving say, "She testified at the trial, but the Beckers got the best lawyers and the boys walked free. She disappeared after that and I heard rumors that she—"

McKenna looked up, caught sight of her, cleared his throat.

Irving stopped talking.

"Taurean, the gunpowder is all gone," McKenna said. "For Mr. Irving, Martha prepared oatmeal. Would you like that, or would you prefer bacon and eggs?"

"Do you have watermelon?" Taurean asked.

"For breakfast?" Martha said. "I mean, no, we don't have watermelon."

"Then I'll take soup." They'd set a place mat and silverware across from Irving, and Taurean seated herself there.

"Last night, I made a cream of tomato basil soup, and have some leftovers. Would you care for that, or does something else appeal?" Martha seemed a lot nicer now. Probably because Taurean was clean.

"I'd like that." Taurean put her napkin in her lap, and for the first time in a long time, she felt like . . . like Jessica again. Civilized, clearheaded, knowledgeable.

Martha set a large bowl of soup before her, and put another, smaller bowl of croutons beside it. "They're baked with Parmesan cheese," she informed Taurean. "Good for floating on top."

Taurean dipped her spoon in, tasted the soup, and after one taste, ate eagerly until the spoon rattled on the bottom.

Martha whisked the bowl away, refilled it, and this time sprinkled the croutons on the top without asking.

Irving waited until Taurean had had two spoonfuls before he said, "You wanted to see me?"

"What? Oh, yes." Taurean put down the spoon. "Charisma said she wants Isabelle to come to her."

*"What!?"* The incredulous outburst struck her from all sides.

She covered her face in fear.

"It's all right," Irving said in a soothing tone. "We shouldn't have shouted. We appreciate your bringing the message. But understand, my dear, we thought Charisma was dead."

Taurean peered from between her fingers. "Almost," she whispered. "That thing bit her. She almost died, but *he* wouldn't give up. He put her in a cradle in the earth, and she lived."

No one seemed to understand that, but it didn't matter. All three smiled, and Martha clasped her hands at her chest, "Praise God. The Chosen will be so pleased."

"No." Swiftly, Irving turned on her. "Do not tell them!"

"But, Mr. Shea," Martha said, "they'll be so relieved!"

"Do not try to contact them," he said sternly.

"Yes, Mr. Shea." But she bit her lip and looked rebellious.

"Where is she?" McKenna asked.

"In the earth," Taurean said again. She'd already told them that.

"Who is *he*?" Martha asked. "The man who wouldn't give up?"

"He is our Guardian."

Martha frowned as if Taurean were mocking her.

Irving looked worried. "If Charisma is alive, why does she need Isabelle?"

"She said to bring Isabelle." It was the only answer Taurean had.

"Bring her where?" McKenna asked.

"Into the earth," Taurean answered.

"Into the tunnels?" McKenna clarified.

"Yes. Into the tunnels." Taurean enunciated each word, wondering why they didn't understand. "She was lost. He found her. He saved her. But she wants Isabelle."

"Eat your soup." Irving raised a shaking hand to his

chin and stroked it. "You see, Taurean, the trouble is—Isabelle can't come right now. The Chosen Ones, including Isabelle, are in Switzerland at a bank in a vault deep underground, trying to open a safety-deposit box consigned to the Gypsy Travel Agency."

Taurean picked up her spoon. Her fingers were trembling, she noticed. "Why are they doing that?"

Irving said, "Because if they aren't successful, in less than a month, the devil will sign the papers that give him a thousand-year lease on the whole world."

# Chapter 10

The five Chosen Ones and their mates huddled close in the confines of the Swiss bank's underground steel-lined vault.

Samuel reflected that there wasn't enough room to do anything *except* huddle close. The room was long and narrow, cool, and austere, containing only a marble countertop and a safe.

The bank president, Adelbrecht Wagner, used a handprint reader, a series of voice commands, and a key to open that safe. "There you have it," he said, as if everything should be easy. Removing a long gray metal box, he placed it on the marble counter. "I will leave you alone now to discover the contents of your safety-deposit box. I hope you have better luck this time than those other times when Samuel visited."

"Ha, ha." Samuel laughed feebly and without humor. He'd been here half a dozen times trying to fig-ure out how to do nothing more complicated than remove the safety-deposit box from the room. Last time, whatever was inside had zapped him so hard he'd been unconscious for a half hour.

"I will lock you in. This is our highest-security area, and no one is allowed to wander unsupervised." Wagner was six-foot-six, fair and blond, with long arms, long legs, and big fists. He was not a man who encouraged challenge.

Yet John Powell, the leader of the Chosen Ones, six-foot-five and a man who wielded power with supernatural ease, stood toe-to-toe with him. "Why lock us in? I thought there were guards at the door."

Samuel wanted to snort. This whole stupid idea of all of them coming together to free the contents of the safety-deposit box was John's, and now . . . he had the guts to challenge the restrictions of this top-security Swiss bank?

*Good luck.*

"Yes, of course. Well-trained armed guards. Should any unauthorized person wander through this level, they aim to kill." Wagner stared unblinkingly at John.

"Good to know." John stepped back. "I feel safe."

"Exactly our intention. Now I will lock you in." Wagner gestured at the button on the wall. "When you're ready to leave, ring that and I will come to release you."

Samuel offered his hand.

Looking a little puzzled, Wagner took it and shook.

"Thank you, Wagner. It's always a pleasure to see you again." Samuel used the moment of contact to make sure that Wagner's mind was still firmly under his control.

It was. Wagner had no ulterior motive except to protect the clients of his bank.

Yet as he shut the door behind him, as the thick steel closed so quietly and the turn of the key in the lock was so final, the Chosen Ones looked uncomfortable ... except Aaron Eagle, who, as the world's most proficient thief, had spent more time in closed bank vaults than the rest of them.

Aaron strolled to the box and fiddled with the latch, then shook his head and backed away.

Isabelle restlessly rotated her shoulders. "Sammy, couldn't you have controlled Wagner's mind and made him leave the door unlocked?"

Isabelle Mason was Samuel's wife, the love of his life, with a high-class Boston accent, delicate bones, and exotically slanted blue eyes. She never raised her voice; she never broke a sweat—and oh, God, how could he forget? She was the healer for the Chosen Ones.

That meant she absorbed injury in order to heal them, and in doing that ... she absorbed their pain.

He couldn't stand to see her hurting. That was why he tried to keep her away from trouble.

Not that she ever listened to him.

But he did everything he could to make her happy, so now he said, "I could try. But when it comes to mind control, it's best to keep it simple, to never go against ingrained behavior—and Wagner's compulsion to protect the stolen billions in cash and jewels is ingrained in him. I convinced Wagner that we all have the right to be in here. For now, that's enough."

"You're right." Isabelle smiled at Samuel, her lips trembling. "Ever since you and I were trapped together, I get a little uneasy underground."

He caught her hand and placed a warm, intimate

kiss in her palm. In a deep voice that both reminded and enticed, he said, "Some good things occurred while we were trapped together, too."

Her smile strengthened. "I know."

"Nothing like those good things are going to happen now with the rest of us here," Aaron said. "Right, Samuel? *Right?*"

Samuel grinned at his friend. "Right."

John Powell, who harnessed the power of the universe and, as needed, kept the Chosen Ones focused on their goals, took a long, patient breath. "Guys, stop joking around. Let's see if this works."

They stood in a circle—actually the shape of the vault created more of an oval—and one by one they prepared for the ritual they could only pray would release the contents of the safety-deposit box.

First their seer, Jacqueline Vargha, joined hands with her husband and their director of security, Caleb D'Angelo. Then Jacqueline joined hands with Aaron, who joined hands with his wife, the antiquities expert and librarian Rosamund Hall. Then Rosamund joined hands with John, and he took the hand of his wife, Genny.

In their infancy, Jacqueline, Aaron, and John had been given supernatural gifts, and although Caleb, Rosamund, and Genny were not gifted, each Chosen had found the perfect mate. And since John and Genny had first met, Genny had developed the disconcerting ability to see talent in other people.

Now Samuel and Isabelle were left, still separate from the others.

Isabelle took Caleb's hand and placed her other palm against the side of the box.

Samuel leaned his cane against the wall. He took Genny's hand and placed his other hand on the other side of the box.

And they waited.

"Nothing's happening, John," Samuel said.

"I know nothing's happening," John said irritably. "Samuel and Isabelle, try joining your hands."

Samuel put his hand over hers, gently turned her hand up, and intertwined their fingers. And although he was tired of standing, grumpy at being here, and worried to death, still the touch of Isabelle's skin against his brought all his love for her rushing back to him.

He glanced up with a smile, expecting to meet her gaze.

But she was staring at the box with a startled expression.

"For the hundredth time, John, *why* does Isabelle have to be here?" Samuel picked up his cane and leaned on it.

John Powell fixed his icy blue eyes on Samuel, and he looked like a linebacker scoping the new tackling dummy. "For the hundredth time, Samuel, Isabelle has to be here because we've all, one at a time, tried to unlock the safety-deposit box and failed, so we needed to try opening that box together."

"I've never tried by myself," Isabelle said.

Of course. She would say that.

"I feel responsible." Jacqueline sagged against Caleb. "I'm sorry, everyone. I saw everyone here, and when John suggested that if we did our thing where we held hands and got that jolt of approval that we get when we're all together, maybe the magic that guards the box would dissipate and hand over its contents . . . well, that seemed sort of a good idea."

"It was worth a try." Rosamund gave her a hug.

Genny joined in the hug.

Samuel waited for Isabelle to rush over and do the female thing and hug and pat and reassure.

Isabelle still stood there. "I could try," she said dreamily.

Samuel was pretty freaking pleased with his level tone when he said, "Isabelle, you're our healer. How does having *you* try to free the safety-deposit box make any sense at all?" Samuel turned back to John. "And maybe having all of us here might be the key, except all of us are not here. We're missing Aleksandr and we're missing—"

A stifled sob interrupted him.

"Crap." He glanced around. The embracing women had gone from sad to desolate. They'd lost Charisma less than two weeks ago, and even *he* knew he'd been insensitive.

"If Charisma were here, it might work." Jacqueline's voice rasped with the effort to hold back her tears.

"We can't give up on her." Genny held Jacqueline's arm. "I know that your visions will help us find her."

Samuel felt bad. It was all so bleak. Charisma was like a kid sister, annoying, smart-assed, tattooed, rebellious, strong, careless. . . . He had never gotten along with her. Yet she had been a part of his life for almost seven years. She had mocked him. She had exulted when he'd at last won Isabelle. She had protected his back in every battle.

But how to say what was in his heart without embarrassing himself by . . . by sobbing? "Look," he said, and he used his hearty voice. "I'm sorry. I miss Charisma, too. You know I do. No one except Isabelle has ever managed to give me as much hell as Charisma. That woman was born to be the boss."

Still crying, Rosamund took off her glasses and wiped the lenses.

Jacqueline stood with her hand over her wet eyes.

Genny buried her head in John's dark shirt.

And Isabelle stood with her back to him and her head bowed.

The guys were glaring at him.

"I'm sorry." Samuel really was. "I'm sorry I said anything." He wished he'd kept his mouth shut. But he couldn't keep quiet now. "I'm just so tired of visiting this bank every damned year trying to open the damned safety-deposit box when we don't even know for sure what's in it."

Just like that, Rosamund stopped sobbing and exclaimed, "I know!"

# Chapter 11

———◆◆◆———

**"I** know you know," Samuel said hastily, trying to head Rosamund off before she got rolling about Lucifer and the feather and the prophecy and all that other stuff she loved so much because she was an antiquities librarian and such cool stuff was her specialty.

Not that he didn't agree it was cool.

It was just that he'd heard it. So. Many. Times. Before.

But there was no stopping Rosamund. "It makes sense, Samuel."

*Agree with her. Just agree with her.* "I know. You're right. Really. I know."

"God's beloved angel Lucifer tried to lead an insurrection against God, and God expelled him from heaven." Beneath her glasses, Rosamund's violet eyes shone with conviction. "As Lucifer fell to earth in flames, his angel wings incinerated—"

"Except for two feathers, one from each wing." He flapped his hands like tiny wings. "Yes. Yes. I know."

Rosamund was exactly like the stereotypical librarian: She never wore makeup, her curly hair rioted wildly around her head, and she loved telling the details of her research.

Every single damned detail.

She continued. "Lucifer descended into hell, where he rules today, but as the devil he continually walks the earth trying to corrupt the souls of men. Occasionally he takes possession of a body, and occasionally he is invited into the soul of a wicked person. Right now, that's Osgood."

Rosamund's husband, Aaron Eagle, leaned against the wall and smirked at Samuel.

"Osgood had one of the feathers buried in the foundation of his building to conceal it, so no one could use it for good, and as a charm to ensure the building would stand forever. But Charisma said"—Rosamund's voice quavered for a minute—"Charisma said nothing could contain the feather, and it was working its way from the concrete foundation into the earth under the building. So if *this* safety-deposit box contains the second feather, and we think it does, we have them both."

"Except that we don't have the first feather," Samuel pointed out in a level tone.

"We just have to *find* it," Rosamund said.

"Yes, but, Rosamund, even if your theory is correct, we don't know whether having the contents of the box is going to help us." Caleb had heard all this before, too. The smug bastard was goading her.

"It will!" Rosamund said. "Jacqueline's prophecy says—"

"I've heard the prophecy," Samuel said.

Nothing could deter Rosamund. "It says, 'Some

must find that which is lost forever. For rising on the ashes of the Gypsy Travel Agency is a new power in a new building. Unless this hope takes wing, this power and this building will grow to reach the stars, and cast its shadow over the whole earth, and evil shall rule.' "

"The key word here is *wing*." Jacqueline loved her prophecy, sought new meanings in it every day.

As far as Samuel was concerned, prophecies were tricky things, and he saw no use in looking too hard at them. "I got it!" he said.

John checked his watch. "Look, Samuel. We don't have forever to fool around in here before the president of the bank shows up with the Swiss police and slaps us all in prison for trying to retrieve something we don't have permission to retrieve."

The injustice of that statement made Samuel want to pound his chest and roar. "I know that. I'm the mind controller who's holding the guy in check!"

John continued. "Even if Rosamund is wrong about what's in there, and I don't think she is, it's still something that could help our cause. The Chosen who put it here had to be safeguarding something important. I don't know how it will help us. I don't know why. But we've got to try something, because right now, we're getting our asses kicked and *we've got no time left*."

"Believe me, I know we're getting our asses kicked." Samuel pointed to his hip. "My hip is still broken from having that cooking show bitch who just happened to be an Other throw an industrial-size smoothie maker at me with her damn mind. . . . It's not funny!"

Everyone tried to wipe the smiles off their faces.

"We know it's not funny," John said. "You were hurt, and that's not funny at all. But, man, when I realized you were mind-controlling the wrong person and that sweet little cooking show diva suckered you. . . ."

Aaron gave a crack of laughter.

"Really," John repeated. "It wasn't funny at all."

Samuel glared. He knew they all thought he should let Isabelle cure him.

But he was tough enough that a cracked hip wasn't going to do more than slow him down, and he couldn't stand to know that she was taking his pain as her own. . . .

Come to think of it, where was Isabelle? Usually when he got into a fight with the other Chosen, she stepped in to mediate.

He glanced around.

She was still standing with her back to him, facing the safety-deposit box, and her head was cocked.

"Isabelle, what are you doing?" He started to reach for her.

Jacqueline caught his wrist in her hand, her grip strong. "Leave her alone."

"Why?"

"She's listening."

"To what?"

"I don't know. I can't quite hear it. But she can."

Immediately the silence in the small vault grew intense, profound, and held the faint, bitter hint of desperation.

The Chosen were here because they needed what was in that safety-deposit box. They needed something that could give them an advantage in the fight to defeat Osgood. All the chatter, the explanations, the teasing masked the frantic worry of eight people who stood, backs against the wall, mourning their losses while trying to find the proper weapon to battle the forces of evil before those forces controlled the world.

Now, at last, someone had made a breakthrough. *Isabelle* had made a breakthrough. And even Samuel knew that if Isabelle had to suffer to find that weapon, she would choose to make the sacrifice—and he would have to let her. His heart squeezed with fear and love.

This time, would he lose her forever?

Reaching out, she stroked the gray metal safety-deposit box. "So much pain is contained within. So much loneliness. So many years of being imprisoned."

The Chosen exchanged glances.

"Is it a person?" John asked quietly. "Like a genie?"

"It is a piece of a puzzle that waits to be moved into position." With a sure hand, Isabelle flipped back the latch of the safety-deposit box.

"Wait a minute." Genny's voice, too, was quiet. "Could we have done that at any time?"

Aaron was their expert thief. "First thing any self-respecting burglar tries is to see whether the door is left open. I tried it. It was locked."

Isabelle smoothed her palms across the metal again, then flicked her wrists as if clearing away the dust of years. Or perhaps she had just wiped away the magic, because at once she lifted the long, narrow lid and looked inside.

Samuel stepped forward, at her right shoulder, prepared to protect her.

Everyone else crowded close, unafraid, curious.

The reality of the box's contents made Samuel sigh with disappointment. "Just once," he said to no one in particular, "couldn't we find some ancient artifact encrusted with jewels? Do we always have to end up with dry bones and sandstone tablets and"—he gestured—"this?"

A ripple of assenting laughter went through the Chosen.

A three-foot-long, twelve-inch-wide, black iron sword case rested inside the box. Patches of rust discolored the hinges, and the massive utilitarian lock looked like something out of the Old West.

"We're going to need WD-40 to crack that baby open." Caleb reached out to touch one of the corners.

The sword case shimmered as if gathering energy. A spark arced.

Caleb slammed against the far wall as if a giant hand had shoved him.

"Caleb!" Jacqueline ran to his side.

He sat up, shaking his head as if his brains were scrambled. When he recovered enough to see everyone staring anxiously, he said, "Apparently it's going to take more than WD-40." With Jacqueline's help, he staggered to his feet and in an apologetic tone said, "I'm fine. Really. That's what I get for grabbing at a magic object. I do know better."

John studied the sword case. "The thing is, an angel's wing feather would fit in there. I mean, theoretically—I've never actually seen an angel's wing feather. But—"

Samuel interrupted. "But have we got the safety-deposit box open? Only to be unable to take the contents?"

"Another test?" Genny asked.

"Another puzzle to solve?" Aaron asked.

"Why does every damned thing have to be so hard?" Rosamund asked.

Everyone stopped and stared at her.

"What? I'm not allowed to get discouraged?" she snapped. "Isn't the next question always, 'Rosamund, what should we do now?'"

"You know a lot of stuff, Rosamund, and you usually *know* what we should do now," Aaron pointed out.

"Probably there's something in a book in Irving's library about a rusty sword case that gives off sparks—but I'm *here*." Rosamund ruffled her long, carroty curls. "Underground. The guards took away our phone and tablets. How do you expect me to do research?"

"Cranky," Samuel muttered, but he really wasn't paying attention to anyone except Isabelle.

Isabelle studied the case as if it were a foreign friend whose English she didn't quite understand. Cautiously she stretched out her hand over the box, then withdrew it. Stretched out her hand again.

No one else was watching her; they were squabbling about what to do next.

So only Samuel saw her lean forward, pick up the rusty iron sword case, and turn to face the room. "Okay." She started toward the door. "Let's go."

The squabbling stopped. Everyone stared at Isabelle, sensitive, noncombative Isabelle, holding the magical case that shimmered . . . and seemed to embrace her.

Samuel knew exactly how the case felt. He liked to embrace her, too.

Jacqueline clapped her hands and laughed.

Aaron said, "The box wanted a woman's touch."

"Maybe the box needed to be healed of a long-ago hurt?" Genny suggested.

"It's what's in the box that was hurt." Isabelle's eyes half closed. "All these years it has barely survived in loneliness and pain. Now it has hope, so it chose to come to me."

Everyone started toward the door.

John stopped them with a gesture. "The Others are watching, and now that we've freed the box, they'll try to take it. So remember the plan. Each couple is going to get back to the States by a different path. Be cautious. Be observant. Especially you, Samuel and Isabelle—you've got a precious cargo there. No cell communication, no Internet, no way for the Others to track us. *They are watching.*"

"We remember, but we need to go now." Isabelle seemed itchy, worried, as if the feather were urging her on. "Let's *go*."

Samuel looked at his friends, his comrades, the Chosen Ones. "You heard what the lady said. Let's go."

# Chapter 12

———◆◇◆———

**G**uardian was tired. He was dirty. And even after days of fighting demons, his rage still simmered.

Stripping off his battle gear, he dropped it in the basket outside the cave.

He never took that stuff inside. He believed the cave would be the last citadel to fall to the demons. He would never stain his peaceful home with the residue of war.

Then he trudged in.

Two days ago—or three, he wasn't sure—Charisma had asked for Isabelle. She had claimed Isabelle would heal her, and he'd experienced the kick of hope that Charisma could be healed. He'd left her sleeping and he'd been foolishly optimistic, imagining he could fetch her friend to heal her.

What an idiot he'd been.

*They* were after him . . . whoever *they* were. He didn't remember their names, but he knew they would always be after him. And he would be forced to remain belowground forever.

The upwelling of fear, frustration, and rage had sent him rampaging through the tunnels, seeking the bands of demons and destroying them. Now he was back, filthy, hungry, and exhausted. And a failure—Taurean had found him and reported that Isabelle was in Europe with no date set for her return.

Guardian so badly wanted to be able to talk to the people at the Upper East Side mansion, tell them how to find him when Isabelle returned, so he could help hasten Charisma's recovery.

But when he questioned Taurean, she looked confused and upset, afraid she hadn't done enough during her visit and afraid to go back. So for now, he would do nothing until he had talked to Charisma.

One glance at her cot on the ground proved she wasn't sleeping now. In fact, no sign of her remained except a faint, womanly scent that teased his nose with false promise.

Regret pierced him. And concern.

While he was gone, had she slipped beyond all help? Had she succumbed to the demon's venom?

No. His people would have found him, told him.

No, it had to be the other choice. She had recovered enough to leave.

He had hoped for this. Yes, he had. He didn't need a woman here, distracting him from his fight, teasing him, touching him, reminding him of what he could never have.

And yet . . . on his arrival, Charisma was the first thing he had looked for.

He hurried deeper into the cave, searching for someone who knew where she had gone, and when, and why. "Amber!" he shouted. "Where is she?"

Amber popped up her head from the hollow in the rock where she preferred to meditate. She spread her hands and frowned as if she didn't understand.

He indicated Charisma's empty bed. And knew a chill of fear, for Amber covered her mouth in horror.

Charisma hadn't left on purpose.

Somehow, she was gone against her will.

Instincts screaming, he put his nose to the ground and went on the hunt.

Charisma knew where she was; she was lying on her back in a hollow in the earth in Guardian's cave. She knew why she was there; she was recovering from a demon's bite. The packed ground was hard and cool against her back. . . .

But something unfamiliar was poking her shoulder blade. She groped for it.

It was a button.

A button. On the ground.

The ground felt velvety, smooth. Not like dirt at all. And it had a button. It had . . . a lot of buttons. It felt like . . . upholstery, fancy rolled upholstery like on the antique chairs at Irving's mansion.

She didn't want to look.

But no. It was okay. The demon's venom had hurt her vision, so she wore a blindfold. She couldn't see anyway.

So she opened her eyes.

She *could* see: shiny metal and wood. Red velvet upholstery.

A coffin, her coffin, held her close.

She took one long breath to scream—and the heavy lid slammed down on her, hard and fast, muffling her, imprisoning her forever.

In the dark and the forever, she panicked.

She couldn't get her breath. She couldn't breathe.

She wanted out. *Get me out!*

Abruptly, she stood alone at the base of a tall, sheer rock mountain. A small, dark cave beckoned.

She knew she had no choice. She had to go in. On the other side of the mountain was everything she wanted. Her friends. Her life, free from cruelty, evil, and anguish. She could linger here, but nothing would change. She had to go in.

She had to look for her destiny.

She also knew . . . knew she might never find it. Many paths led into the darkness. Only one was the right path. She might be—probably would be—lost in the dark for all eternity.

Charisma woke in truth.

She pulled air into her lungs in a mighty gasp.

She was standing up. In the dark. In utter and complete silence.

No birds chirping. No brook babbling. Still underground . . .

She reached out her hands, hoping to encounter . . . something. A wall. A piece of furniture.

Nothing.

But she wasn't blind. No. She wasn't. She was wearing a blindfold, and all she had to do was take it off and she would see . . . something. Everything. And that stuff about her eyes being burned was just so much bull fed to her by someone who was now playing games with her. Or who existed only in her nightmares.

Where was Guardian? *Had* she dreamed him? She wanted Guardian.

It struck her how much she hoped he wasn't a figment of her imagination. Like the coffin, like the cave, was Guardian a part of her subconscious's ravings? Was this a trick? Was this all madness . . . ?

She realized she was standing rigid, with her hands straight at her sides as if she were afraid to take off the blindfold.

But she was Charisma Fangorn. She was afraid of a lot of things—in her business, only the foolish didn't fear the dark—but she was not afraid to take off that blindfold.

No, removing the blindfold wasn't what she feared. It was seeing what lay beyond.

Lifting her hands took effort, but she touched the knot at the back of her head, untied it—wouldn't it have just been easier to push it off her face?—and unwrapped the blindfold. And stared at . . . nothing. *More* nothing. Total darkness.

She saw nothing. She heard nothing. She felt no draft of air, sensed no other being. She was alone except for . . . except for the earth.

Panic built in her mind.

She was far below ground. She could feel it. She could smell the deep, rich, life-affirming, death-dealing earth. She could feel the first faint spark of excitement from the stones at her wrist.

But how did she get here?

She knew the answer. Pretending she didn't would not help her.

In her sleep, she had heard the call of the earth and followed it. Sleepwalking.

How many times had this happened in the safety of the mansion? Usually she awoke before she wandered very far and took herself back to bed. Once or twice she'd come to consciousness to see Martha or McKenna talking to her gently.

This time . . . this time Charisma had escaped from the Guardian cave.

Or maybe *that* had been the illusion.

She groped the spot on her shoulder where the demon had bitten her.

The bite wasn't an illusion, and she was thin and weak, so Guardian was *not* a figment of her imagination. *Please. Be real.*

But how could he, or anyone, find her and return her to the surface? She was lost again below the city, marooned in the deepest dark where no light could ever penetrate, where even the demons did not come.

She could go forward. She could answer the call of the earth.

But . . . she was so afraid.

The earth beckoned her to its heart, wanting her to come, to face what she must become. She knew that transformation must involve pain and anguish, a release of self, and ultimately . . . death.

The coffin and the cave were real. She knew it in her heart. Death stalked her, and challenges waited in the utter dark of that endless, twisting cave. Her destiny was calling to her, even though she tried to ignore its grave demand.

"Charisma . . ." Her name echoed softly, eerily.

She held her breath.

Had the earth developed a real voice to call her?

"Charisma, don't move." Soft and low. "You're on a bridge."

No, that couldn't be the earth. It didn't sound like its call.

"There are chasms on either side of you," the voice said.

*Oh, great.*

"Did you hear me?" The voice was deep, but distorted, as if it came across a great distance.

"Yes, I hear you," she said.

"Speak softly." The voice sounded nearer. "The rock here is rotten and pockmarked. A loud voice or sudden noise could start an avalanche."

Nearer. And clearer.

It was *his* voice. Somehow Guardian had found her.

"We want to be very quiet," he said faintly, "very cautious not to dislodge a stone."

She nodded. She was not about to say another word.

She could see a dim red light now, moving slowly toward her from far away, casting its feeble illumination on a narrow path cut into a sheer cliff.

Of course. The way to the heart of the earth would always be challenging.

Who made up these stupid rules?

Now he started across the bridge toward her—the really narrow stone bridge that groaned under his weight. She felt the rock shift under her feet, and moaned softly in terror.

He moved even more slowly.

She couldn't see him, only the hand holding the flashlight with the red filter.

Red for improved night vision, of course, and possibly to be healthier on her eyes. But better safe than sorry.

The bridge groaned again, as if protesting his weight.

The light stopped.

In that low, soft voice he said, "This won't support me. You'll have to come here."

"Okay." In an abstract corner of her mind, she noted that she sounded a little squeaky.

"Are you afraid of heights?"

"No." Still squeaky.

"That's good." He spoke so soothingly, she knew he was worried.

But she *wasn't* afraid of heights. Not normal heights. But heights above a bottomless chasm in a midnight dark cave in the middle of the earth—well, that was a different story.

He shone his flashlight slowly across the bridge, giving her a sense of where she must step.

The way was narrow, the darkness beyond bleak, and every step was littered with pebbles and slippery, broken stones. She edged forward, each movement an agony of fear . . . and all the way, she fought the demand of the earth to come the other way, into the harsh unknown.

Guardian spoke softly, constantly encouraging her, and she concentrated on him, used him to block out the increasingly strident call of the earth.

At last she took the step that took her off the bridge and onto solid ground.

As she did, the stone cracked.

Her foot slipped.

Guardian grabbed her, saved her from the chasm.

The bridge broke.

In a mighty roar, boulders poured into the gap.

He pulled her into his arms, and she clung to him, burying her face in his fur. He backed away from the cataclysm, keeping her close, protecting her as the stone continued to crumble beneath their feet.

At last the tumult died.

They halted, panting.

She thought she felt his hand touch her hair. "Very bravely done," he said. "But I think we must not linger. I've never been here before, but nothing about this place is safe."

"No kidding." Her voice had returned to normal, if normal meant it wobbled only a little.

He placed her in front of him and guided her with his light. "How are your eyes?"

"No problems so far."

"Good." He sounded so pleased. So relieved. "You've had time to heal. If . . . if they continue to be well, I could show you my cave. It is more hospitable than this place."

"I would like that. Let's get out of here." She was feeling more like herself every moment.

Maybe because he kept his arms around her and walked close behind her, and this felt like . . . protection.

# *Chapter 13*

———◆———

**G**uardian and Charisma climbed out of the depths, and as they did, he marveled that she had come so far on her own, through a night so dark even he had been blind much of the time. Something had taken her into the hidden parts of the earth, something that frightened and appalled her. Yet for all that he'd known this woman for such a little time, he knew she would stand up against any fear, and face it straight on.

He could learn a few things from her . . . perhaps if he did, the fact that she was soon going to see him in all his beastly glory wouldn't worry him.

Yes, he could face down a hundred demons without a quiver—but one small woman made him tremble.

He sighed.

"What?" she asked. "Did I take you away from something important?"

"Not at all. Nothing is as important as the safety of

my guest." He debated telling her the truth. "We're getting close to the Guardian cave."

"Yes."

"There's light there."

"Yes?"

"I wonder what you'll think when you see me."

"Do I seem the delicate type?" She turned so quickly, he almost lost his grasp on the flashlight. "Go ahead. Show me."

He realized his jaw was unattractively ajar. He shut it. "I'm not ready," he said, and sighed. He sounded like a virgin.

"What have you got to do?" she asked. "Shave first?"

"You have a smart mouth." He'd had to face this particular fear before. He'd had to brace himself for other people's horrified reactions.

But Charisma *mattered*.

"Yes, I do have a smart mouth. Also, I'm insensitive to others' feelings." She paused. "What are you going to do about it?"

He found himself grinning. "I'm going to scare you with . . . *the monster*!" Like a Boy Scout trying to frighten the other campers, he raised the flashlight under his chin.

Her loud, terrified gasp startled him. He hadn't expected her to actually . . .

*Shit*. Now she was stifling laughter.

She wasn't afraid. She'd been pulling his paw. "Fine." Disgusted, he brought the flashlight out a little farther so she could actually see him.

Silence.

How odd to stand here in the dark, the only puddle of light the one he directed at himself, at his misshapen body wrapped in a cotton tunic, and wait for judgment from a woman he barely knew, but cared about too much.

Finally, she said, "You're very tall. I envy you that. I'm on the petite side."

"You're short," he said without thinking.

"I see I'm not the only one who's insensitive."

Apparently she wasn't as impressed with his looks as he expected. Or maybe she was just being tactful—although that seemed out of character. "So what do you think?"

"Of you? I think there are monsters, Guardian. I've seen them. I've met them. But you're not one of them." She took his hand, the one with the flashlight, and shone it in front of them again. "Come on. I want out of here before I . . ."

"Before you go back to wherever you were going?"

"I wouldn't know how," she admitted. "Not while I'm awake, anyway."

They started walking again.

"That must have been quite a dream, to take you so far in the dark," he said.

"I don't remember." Her voice sounded obstinate.

Whatever she had dreamed, she wouldn't share it with him.

He understood. Most of his dreams weren't fit to share, either. Most of his dreams would scare a demon into church.

The trail became a tunnel. The tunnel began to lighten.

They approached the large, arched entrance of the Guardian cave. Here light seeped in from above. He looked down at her, saw how thin she was, remembered her illness and Dr. King's worries. "How are your eyes?" Guardian asked. "Should you put on the blindfold again?"

"Not yet." He heard the note of panic in her voice. "Let me see where I am. Let me see that this is not a fevered figment of my imagination."

"It's pretty fevered," he said. "Trust me. When I first saw the cave . . . to start with, I was crazy, so maybe it doesn't matter what I thought then. But I still think the cave is . . ." Words failed him. He stopped her with a hand on her arm. "We can check it out, but only if you'll promise me that if your eyes hurt, you'll let me know."

"I'm stubborn, but not stupidly stubborn. I'm not going to risk my eyesight for a tour."

"Then come on." He stopped her just outside the entrance. "I envy you this first glimpse. It's . . . bizarre. Odd. Fabulous. Glorious. A place beyond reason."

"Okay!" She smiled. Dimples quivered. Her green eyes lit up with curiosity and greed. "You've sold me. Let's see it."

He guided her into the cave. His people were out searching for Charisma, and Guardian and Charisma were alone.

Inevitably, she looked up. "Wow. Just . . . wow." She pointed up at the ruins high in the wall. "What's that?"

"No one knows for sure."

She faced him, planted her hands on her hips, and glared.

"Okay! This is pure speculation. It's my theory based on nothing but gut feelings and the legends surrounding this cave. I think that long ago, a race of guardians came into the cave and made it their base. Here they lived, built homes and workplaces, and ventured out to

fight the hell spawn that wander the underground."
There. He felt foolish.

She nodded thoughtfully, and looked up again.
"Sounds reasonable to me. Someone created this place,
and those ruins are spectacular. How do you get up to
them?"

"You don't." He was firm. "There's no way up."

"Really?" She considered him suspiciously. "You've
never gone up there?"

He grimaced and confessed, "Once. On a high ladder and with some climbing. That convinced me I
never want to go back."

"Ghosts?"

"I felt like I was being watched every moment."

She shivered. "Cool."

"I think whatever spells they cast, whatever protec-
tions they created are still in place. That's why the
Guardian cave is safe."

"Cool," she repeated.

Light shone down from the ceiling through skylights.

"How do you get electricity down here?" she asked.

"No electricity. The Belows tried to run a cable for
me. Like rats, the demons chewed it through."

She paced into the cave, ten steps, twenty, craning
her neck, trying to see everything at once. "What gen-
erates the lights?"

"In the daytime, it's sun." He glanced up. "Not
much more daylight now. At night, the stones themselves are phosphorescent."

"*Really?* No electricity? No television, no Internet?
Wow." She clasped her hands. "That sounds kind of
peaceful."

Guardian grinned at her enthusiasm. "No Internet,

but Dr. King carries a MacBook back and forth for me. He charges it on the surface, brings it down, and I use it."

She paused, thought hard. "Dr. King. I remember that name. You said Dr. King saved my life."

"He did. He's a great guy." For a lot of reasons.

"But he's the one who didn't want me to take off the blindfold."

"For your own good." Guardian carefully, tentatively asked, "After so much exertion, how do you feel?"

"Good." She put her palm to her chest and took a breath as if testing her lungs. "Yes. I'm good. Better."

Relief melted into Guardian's bones. "Good. I want you to . . . heal."

"Me, too, honey." She sounded precisely like a tough girl.

He supposed, with the tattoos and the leather, she fit the definition of a tough girl. But he'd seen her helpless and near death, and as far as he was concerned, she was delicate and far too mortal.

She wandered over to his desk and touched the computer. "So you watch movies and stuff?"

"I do. But more important, and I don't like to brag"—he had his tongue firmly in his cheek—"I'm actually quite a brilliant programmer."

She faced him. "If you can make coffee and know how to run a vacuum, you're the perfect man."

He knew that in this light, she could really see him now. But she didn't flinch. In fact, she seemed only slightly impressed.

Her indifference made him stand a little taller. "I can clean the demons out of a tunnel."

"Close enough." She turned back to the cave.

Here and there furniture stood against the wall: a

cupboard, groupings of chairs, and occasionally a folding screen placed to give privacy. Steep, narrow steps had been cut twenty feet up into the stone walls, leading to the alcoves carved into the rock. Up there, on one side, was Guardian's library, with a long bookcase cluttered with a million books collected by other Guardians of other times, and a battered, broken recliner Taurean had procured for him from an estate sale. Free, of course. On the other side was his bedroom.

Like the world's most improbable tour guide, Guardian said, "The place is a legend underground, always a sanctuary for the Warrior who defends the innocent, somewhere the demons cannot come."

"That is a good spell. I wonder how they did it." She ran forward a few steps toward a bird pecking into the dirt on the floor.

It fluttered and flew.

She laughed. "I wasn't sure the birds were real."

"They were here when I got here. I think they get trapped belowground, and somehow the lucky ones find their way here."

As day faded to night, a faint glow began to emanate from stones placed into the walls and ceiling, like streetlights created to keep the night away.

"Amazing." She waved an all-encompassing hand. "Why? How?"

"Maybe it's magic. Maybe it's the ghosts. Maybe it's the memories of the ancient people who channeled the water and built the buildings." Guardian looked at the library, willing an answer, and knowing it was not there. "I've looked and have found nothing—no paintings of Stone Age animals on the walls, no scrolls filled with ancient hieroglyphics. But it can't be a mistake that it was built so close to the mouth of hell."

"It's definitely a sacred cave of some kind."

"That being the case, we have the knowledge that someone before us fought to hold back the forces of evil. And that is a very great thing to remember. The battle has been fought before, and won." Guardian allowed the peace of the cave to sink into his bones. In a low voice, he said, "We have to have faith we can win again."

"That's the problem," she admitted. "I've lost faith. All I can see is a long fight against a rising tide of malevolence, and beyond that the coffin and the dark cave with too many paths . . . and only one is right."

"Dr. King says . . . if you don't know the right path— help comes to those who ask."

"Do you believe that?" She faced him. "Do you really believe that?"

"I try." He looked at her; she was grubby, defiant, with a frown of worry that wrinkled her brow.

She didn't run from him, screaming. She didn't seem impressed by his fur or his paws or his misshapen body.

In his eyes, she was beautiful, and even more so because she gave him hope. "I didn't used to believe in anything, except living one day at a time, struggling, fighting, sleeping, eating, getting up to do it again. But lately I've started to think . . . there might be more."

She observed him, intent and quiet. "I pray you're right."

"I do, too." He listened to a commotion outside the cave. "Charisma, you should rest."

"What? Why?"

"Because I have a battle to fight." He turned as Moises burst into the room, Taurean on his heels.

"A group of the Belows," Moises said in a gasp. "Attacked. Come! Now!"

No. Guardian wanted to stay with Charisma.

Charisma put her hands on his chest and shoved at him. "Go on. You were bragging about what a great warrior you were. Prove it."

She made him smile. "Taurean will feed you," he said.

"Good. I'm hungry." She shoved at him again. "You take care."

He headed out. At the door, he turned and found her observing him. "Put your blindfold back on. Rest!"

"When you come back, you'll find me exactly where you want me," she promised.

He pointed a stern finger at her, as if demanding she keep her promise.

Then he ran out, changed back into his fighting garb, and went to do his duty . . . as Guardian.

# Chapter 14

———❖———

Charisma woke slowly to the sound of rushing water and the twittering of birds.

But this time she didn't automatically think she was back in her room in Irving's mansion. Nor did she assume she was in the Guardian's cave. Her dreams were vivid, even more than the real world, and she didn't know what to believe.

Cautiously, she groped her face.

Yes, she wore a blindfold, and that was the reason she couldn't see.

She sat up slowly, leaned forward, and rubbed her feet. They were sore, as if she'd wandered far underground.

She didn't want to remember answering the call of the earth.

Even worse would be if she discovered that she'd hallucinated the whole episode. That would definitely head her right toward the loony bin. But also . . . she

liked Guardian. He had faced death to rescue her. Plus
he had a sense of humor. And a guy who looked the
way Guardian looked . . . well, he could either laugh,
or he could rampage around like Frankenstein's monster and kill a bunch of people.

Then she'd have to take him out.

She didn't want to do that.

He wasn't that bad-looking, really. It was all a matter
of perspective.

Should she take off the blindfold?

Yes, with Guardian she had seen the cave. But afterward her head had hurt and her eyes had throbbed,
and she knew she had done too much.

Charisma flexed her shoulders. She felt pretty good
now, with a lot of stiff muscles, but . . . she took a long
breath, trying to gauge the change in the air.

Someone was watching her. She called, "Hello?"

Footsteps approached.

"Be calm. You're safe." The voice was male, deep,
warm, reassuring, with a tinge of a Western accent.

Something was off about the footsteps, about his
voice, and about him, but she couldn't figure out what.
First she had to ask, "Where am I?"

"Can you guess?"

"Yes. I'm in the cave." She felt relief, as if the weight
of the earth's call was not so burdensome, and a
warmth enveloped her. "But I don't know you."

"I'm Dr. King."

Again she got that sense of wrongness. His voice was
at the wrong height. "Guardian speaks well of you."

"I have my moments." Dr. King's voice was self-
deprecating, amused. "I'm here to help you."

"Nice, but . . ." But if Isabelle were here, she

wouldn't need a doctor. Why wasn't Isabelle here? "Listen. I have a vague memory . . . didn't I ask for my friend?"

"Yes! Good recall." Dr. King sounded pleased. "But your friend Isabelle is out of the country with the rest of your friends."

Charisma groaned. "That's timing. Are they okay?"

"I believe Mr. Irving Shea reported they were on a mission."

"Do you know where?"

"Switzerland."

"Good." That meant they were making another run at opening the safety-deposit box, and Charisma knew as well as any of them how important that could prove in their battle against evil. "Just hearing that makes me feel better."

"Excellent." Dr. King's voice shifted away. "Meet Amber."

The faintest rustle of material brought Charisma's head around to the side. A whiff of patchouli teased her nose.

"Amber is one of Guardian's people . . . you'll feel comfortable with her."

What did that mean? Did he realize she wasn't comfortable with him? "Nothing against Amber, but where's Taurean?" Charisma had liked Taurean. The older woman was tall and peculiar, and gloriously free with her delusions.

"Taurean is not always available when we need her," Dr. King said.

"I suppose not." But how disappointing.

Dr. King continued. "Amber will guide you through your ablutions and get you something to eat—"

At the mention of food, Charisma's stomach growled.

"—and then, if you don't mind, I'd like to examine your eyes for distance and acuity."

Should she tell him she'd already had the blindfold off? That she'd seen Guardian and viewed the cave?

Naw. Doctors got weird about their patients testing their limits before they were told they could.

So Charisma allowed Amber to lead her from the bed to the bathroom to the table, where the smell of something more than chicken broth made Charisma's stomach growl.

She really did feel better.

She ate a bowl of beef pho.

She ate pesto pasta salad.

She ate Popeye's chicken and biscuits.

By the time she pushed back from the table, she was smug, full, and happy—and curious. "Where is Guardian?" she asked.

"He had demons to chase," Dr. King said.

"Good man." Although she wished Guardian were here right now.

She heard the sound of a chair being pushed close, then the tap of shoes on wood.

Suddenly Dr. King spoke close to her face. "It's twilight in the world above."

She had slept the clock around . . . again? That demon poison had seriously whacked her.

"Let's take off that blindfold. I don't think there'll be any shock to your eyes, but please keep them closed until I tell you and then open them slowly. If you're in pain or if you see fireworks, close them. You're the one who knows best what you can bear."

The blindfold fell away.

Charisma opened her eyes slowly.

The first thing she saw was a bald, African-American dwarf dressed in a suit and tie, standing on the chair in front of her. "Dr. King?" she asked.

"That's right."

Now she understood why she had thought there was something off-kilter about him. He was not at all what she expected. "I thought you'd . . . have a full head of hair."

He grinned and relaxed. "I'm gay, too."

"Of course you are. But I can't *see* that."

"What *can* you see?"

Slowly she turned her head. "Amber is very pretty." She sounded surprised, she realized. She was surprised; she had been expecting a small, cheerful Buddhist statue of a woman. But Amber was petite and curvaceous, with curly blond hair that hung in wisps around her Marilyn Monroe face.

Amber placed her palms together and bowed.

Charisma bowed back.

They smiled in perfect accord.

"Shall we replace the blindfold?" Dr. King asked. "Or, if you like, you can simply close your eyes and Amber will guide you to the shower."

"That's right." Charisma clasped her hands in delight. "Guardian promised me a shower."

"In the stream."

She shut her eyes and stood. "Lead me to it."

# *Chapter 15*

———◆———

As Guardian approached the cave and removed his fighting gear, he remembered the last thing Charisma had said to him.

*When you come back, you'll find me exactly where you want me.*

He wanted so badly for it to be true. If she was still here . . .

She wouldn't leave without saying good-bye, though. He was pretty confident of that. For all that she was a smart-ass, she was polite and—he hated to make her sound mundane—she was nice.

*When you come back, you'll find me exactly where you want me.*

He entered the cave with his hopes high.

As it was every night, the cave was dark enough to allow for sleep, yet the glow from the stones acted like a night-light. On the other side of the folding screen, he could hear splashing in the stream, and he caught the scent of soap, and Amber, and Charisma.

His heart lifted. He came around the corner toward the bathing pool—and there Charisma stood, in the waterfall, her eyes closed, head back, back arched, arms outstretched, wearing nothing but a smile.

His mind went blank. He froze. For a really long time, he stared, numb, mesmerized, stammering in his mind. He stared so hard and so long without blinking that his eyeballs ached.

Other parts ached, too.

Silly. This was silly. He was being ridiculous. During Charisma's illness, he'd cared for her, sponged her down when she was burning with fever, dealt with every body function. He had seen her naked and at her worst. Of course he had. And this was exactly like that.

Except it wasn't.

She was glorious. Breasts and hips thrust forward. Water foaming around her calves. Still too thin, but taut with muscle.

The woman he'd cared for had been on the verge of death.

This woman was embracing her return to life.

Could she return him to a real life, too?

Turning, she groped for the soap on the stone shelf. Her buttocks. Her spine. Magnificent.

She created a lather. She washed her face, her neck. Turning again, she washed her arms, her breasts, her belly.

She had been dirty. She was washing. Nothing extraordinary about that.

But he couldn't tear his gaze away from her hands

as she . . . caressed herself. She traced the shape of her body, the length of her thighs, exploring the changes that had occurred. She turned and, in profile, put her foot on a rock and bent to wash first one foot, then the other. Her fingers, her palms never stopped moving. The white lather slid across her soft skin, over old scars and new, taking with it the sweat and anguish of her recovery and leaving her, if the expression on her face was anything to go by, delighted.

And a delighted Charisma was like a child, uninhibited and joyful. She splashed. She sang and danced. She laughed aloud for no reason.

At last she put the soap back, picked up the shampoo, and washed her hair. Then once again she leaned back into the waterfall, arched her back, and opened herself to the experience.

He had never seen anything so beautiful.

He thought he was going to expire from lust.

He should go away. Leave her to her privacy.

He should.

But it was too late.

She was climbing out, moving slowly, eyes closed and hands outstretched. She found the towel folded neatly on a rock. She dried her hair, her face, her body. . . .

Her voice made him jump. "Have you seen enough, Guardian?"

She hadn't looked. He had not once seen the flash of her eyes.

Yet she stood smiling, eyes closed, head cocked, waiting for his reply.

How had she known?

He cleared his throat. "You're happy."

"I feel better. Lots better. Dr. King had me take off the blindfold. He thinks my vision will continue to improve. And I just got to take the best shower I've ever had in my whole life, because I've never been that dirty before in my whole life. Of course I'm happy. Aren't you?"

*Happy* was not exactly the word for what he felt. "I'm happy for you." He cleared his throat. "How did you know I was watching?"

"I sensed someone watching me. I sensed you. And I've learned to listen to my instincts. They've kept me alive." She waved a hand back at the waterfall. "This reminds me of a place in Tahiti. My mother decided we should move there, and I spent a glorious year swimming, fishing, running naked."

He would have liked to have been there.

"I used so much sunscreen. . . ."

Guardian believed that, because every inch of her was pale, covered with light freckles.

She said, "You've been demon hunting."

That pulled him back from the brink of some awful revelation: a confession of desire, or maybe just a request to kiss every one of those freckles, followed by an unmanly whimper. "Yes." He clipped the word.

"Then I imagine you're ready for your shower. I'm out. So, your turn!" She stretched out a hand.

Amber arrived—where had she been hiding?—to take it and guide Charisma toward the cupboard and the clothes stacked there.

"Whether you like it or not, I've got to get dressed!" Charisma called.

He wanted to say no. Command her to remain naked. He wanted to look at her, to torment himself with what he could not have.

He looked down at himself.

He was filthy. Covered with blood. Hairy.

He was a monster.

A very tired monster. Getting down on all fours, he dashed into the bathing pool and allowed the cool water to wash away his desires, and bring some sense into the aching hollow left behind.

# *Chapter 16*

———◆⬦◆———

Guardian climbed out of the pool and shook like a dog. Straightening, he reached for the towel Amber had left for him—and met Charisma's inquisitive gaze.

"Are you supposed to have your eyes open?" He was proud; he sounded so calm, so reasonable. Not at all disconcerted to be seen naked by the woman who made his libido—and other things—stir.

"Probably not," she said, "but Dr. King said to close them if I saw fireworks. Not from seeing you. But at the back of my eyes. So far, no problems."

"Good news." Guardian maintained eye contact. Better than checking her out and . . . stirring.

Strange. It had been fine when he'd been peeking at her. But to know that she'd been watching him, seeing the whole him for the first time . . . he didn't like that.

Truthfully, he would never want this woman to look at him. Not if she viewed him as an oddity. As a curiosity. Something inhuman, without rights, that belonged in a zoo.

She stood, hands on hips, blindfold tied around her neck, dressed in black pajama pants with vivid pink and green and yellow stripes, and a perfectly normal cap-sleeved, lime green T-shirt . . . except for the nipples that poked at the material, calling for his attention. Not that her nipples weren't normal, but he wasn't used to seeing them outlined so clearly when . . .

*Focus on her eyes.*

*Focus. On. Her. Eyes.*

"Except for the hair and the shape of your body, you're very human," she said. "Are you sure you're not a werewolf?"

"I don't change with the moon. I don't change at all." He gestured at himself, realized he'd just directed her gaze downward, and hastily wrapped the towel around his waist. "This is me, all the time."

"So you don't like looking like this?"

"Who would?"

"Did you think I would run away screaming?"

"No. You're kind."

Throwing back her head, she laughed—and she most certainly was laughing at him. "*Kind* is not usually the word applied to me, not even by my friends. No, *you're* kind. You do the right thing. I've met enough men who were cowards, or cheats, or liars, to be able to look beyond your appearance." She was still smiling, and smiling invitingly, when she said, "I find you attractive."

His face grew hot. How could he flush underneath this growth of hair? "You're grateful to me."

"Most definitely. But you're not the first person to

save my life. My friends do it all the time, but I've never wanted to see any of *them* naked."

"You . . . you . . ." She actually wanted to see him naked?

But why? Why would any woman want to see him naked?

Yet if Charisma said she wanted to see him, did he dare accuse her of vulgar curiosity? Or of mocking him? "You did see me naked, or at least stripped down to my fur."

"I suppose you could get lasered."

"What?"

"You know, go into the city, go to one of those laser hair-removal places, get the full treatment." She was laughing again, teasing him.

But less than forty-eight hours ago he had tried to go into the city, as she so casually put it, and he had been forced to run for his life. The lights, the horrified voice saying, *Holy shit, what is that?* And that other voice, the one that spoke in his nightmares, saying, *Aim carefully. I want him alive!*

If he ever was in doubt that he was a *thing*, a disgusting, mutilated creature of the night, those voices had thoroughly reminded him of the truth. He was a monster to be taunted and caged.

"Guardian?"

Charisma's voice woke him from his bitter reflections.

She took a step toward him, extended her hand. "I wasn't serious about the laser hair removal. I was trying to defuse the tension. If I offended you, I'm sorry. Really."

"No. It's fine." Amber had left a clean black tunic for

him with a wide embroidered band at the neck and long, full sleeves. He pulled it over his head—at least it covered up some of his fur—and came out to see Charisma observing him.

"That is so romantic," she said. "You dress like a sheik."

He stumbled into an explanation. "Pants don't work for me. I don't have a tail, thank God, but I have narrow wolf-hips, too. Dr. King lets us use his credit card, and Amber orders these djellabas for me online."

"You may see me as tough and mean and completely unfeminine, but trust me on this: Looking like a sheik is romantic." Her smile faded, and she looked wistful. "I'm a woman, and I know romantic when I see it."

"I do not think of you as unfeminine." He couldn't believe she even suggested such a thing. "Quite the opposite."

"I don't think of you as a freak, either, but you don't believe *me.*"

*That's different.* But he wasn't dumb enough to say that. She'd tie him in knots trying to explain how it was different.

"I used to be a girly-girl. I wore tight skirts"—with her hand, she measured a hem halfway up her thighs— "tight sweaters, and this diamond-studded leather collar. I wore all this great makeup, really dramatic stuff. And my shoes. I had the best shoes."

In his mind's eye, he could clearly see her as she had been, wicked, smart, and sarcastic.

"Actually, I still have the shoes, but I can't chase demons in four-inch heels." She sighed deeply. "I miss those early days, when I was young and innocent and didn't realize how bad it was going to get."

He didn't tell her how much worse it had become in the two weeks she'd been out of action. Although she looked as if she were just about to ask. . . . Hastily, he asked, "Why did your mother take you to Tahiti?"

"Oh." Charisma's shoe glow faded. "My mother."

He had diverted her, but not happily.

She looked around, saw the motley assortment of chairs and stools Amber had grouped together around a glass-topped coffee table, and wandered over to sit down. Picking up a few of the magazines, she flipped through them and tossed them aside. "These are so old, you could set yourself up as a doctor's office."

He followed. And stood. And waited.

Charisma fidgeted, and finally said, "All right! If you're going to interrogate me . . . my mother calls herself a free spirit."

He folded his arms. "What does that mean?"

"It means her whims drive her. She does whatever she wants without regard to how it affects anyone else."

"Specifically you?"

"Oh, yeah." She stretched out her legs, propped her feet up on the table. "You'd think I'd be over that by now, wouldn't you?"

"She's your mother." He wanted to sit in the chair next to her, to take her hand and pat it, and tell her everything would be all right.

"That's the problem. I'm still attached to her. You know?"

But patting Charisma's hand wasn't all he wanted to do. He wanted to hold her, to kiss her lips, her neck, to lift her shirt and lower her pants. He wanted to do the friendly stuff, and the more-than-friendly stuff, and a whole lot of things he had no business imagining.

"When Mom was seventeen, she got married to a very nice man. A rancher. In Idaho." Charisma tweaked the hem on her pajama pants. "She got bored. She ran away and joined a commune somewhere."

He pulled up a stool, not too close, and straddled it. "Communes were still around?"

"Might have been a cult." Charisma's grimace grew more pronounced. "Mom was never very clear about what or where, and she can't tell the same story the same way twice."

In lieu of tasting Charisma's nipples, he should express some comforting sentiment. So he said, "*You* certainly always tell the truth!"

Somehow, that didn't come out as the compliment he had intended.

But Charisma didn't seem offended. "Truthful to a fault, I've been told. Which possibly isn't always the most diplomatic way to be. My friends usually forgive me. In time." She looked wistful, as if she missed her friends. "Anyway, when I was an infant, my parents abandoned me in this commune, so Mom picked me up like a stray dog and brought me home to her husband. I thought he was my daddy until the day she decided she was bored—"

"Again?"

"Nothing held Mom's attention for long. Anyway, she decided we should move on. I cried about leaving him. She told me he wasn't my real daddy and she wasn't my real mommy, but she'd saved me, so I had to go with her."

"How old were you?"

"Six."

"Six?" Guardian was appalled. "She blurted out that you were adopted when you were six?"

"With my mom, it was best to get used to the occasional surprise or two. But I admit, that was the first, and the most"—Charisma groped for the word—"shocking."

"I can imagine."

"Hey." Charisma leaned forward and touched his hand. "No need to feel sorry for me. The fire that melts the candle also tempers the steel. I am tempered steel."

"Yes. You really are." He freely offered his admiration. "You're the first person Dr. King and I know of who survived the demon venom. How are your eyes?"

Charisma looked startled. Lightly she touched her lids. "I guess they're fine. I haven't even thought about them."

"Good. But a little while longer and we should cover them."

"Yes, I suppose." She untied her blindfold from around her neck and looked at it with disfavor.

"And you should rest."

"Yes."

"After you tell me the rest of the story about your mom."

# Chapter 17

As Charisma twisted the blindfold, she intently watched the motion of her hands. "Listening to my story is sort of like watching a train wreck, isn't it? You can't tear yourself away."

"It's more like standing on the tracks, waiting for the train to hit. I know it's going to get worse, but I can't imagine how."

Charisma acknowledged his quip with a brief smile. "I don't want you to get the wrong impression. Mom wasn't the wicked stepmother. She wasn't really a mother at all—I remember feeling responsible for her from the time she left Daddy."

Charisma had never had a real childhood, and somehow Guardian found that to be a tragedy equal to any fairy tale.

"Mom and I lived all up and down the West Coast. She made beads or flutes or clothes and sold them at the weekend markets. One awful year she decided I had a talent for singing and dancing, so we followed the kiddie pageants. She really got into that for a while, but she got bored. Like always. Thank God"—Charisma rolled her eyes—"that pageant thing was excruciating."

He pictured the ultimate stage mother shoving a young Charisma into the limelight. "Were you afraid to get up onstage?"

"No, I'm not shy." She airily waved away his concern. "But talk about cutthroat! Those moms and those kids would kill for the Miss Congeniality title, much less to be Little Miss No-name City."

He couldn't help it. Although he wasn't amused, he laughed. "What next?"

"We lived in ghettos, in condemned housing, in caves when necessary. Not nice caves like this, either." Charisma kicked at the hard-packed dirt floor. "We're talking bear droppings on the floor."

Fascinated, he scooted his stool closer. "That could have ended badly."

"Yeah. Even in those days, it occurred to me I could *be* bear droppings." Charisma spoke matter-of-factly, without self-pity. Her childhood had been difficult. She accepted that. "When I was ten, I lucked out. Mom took a job on a cruise ship, and smuggled me on board. When we got to Tahiti, we abandoned the cruise and stayed."

He didn't remember a single thing about his childhood, and Charisma had all this angst. . . . He was in awe.

"Tahiti was the best thing that ever happened to me. Mom worked at a resort. In between swimming and climbing trees and exploring the island, I went to school and found out it wasn't stultifying and didn't stunt my imagination, like she told me it would. It was wonderful. I loved school—loved reading, math, history." She tied the blindfold around her neck like a bandanna. "Then I went through puberty and I discovered I could hear the earth sing."

*Um . . . huh?* "The earth sing? Like . . . singing rocks?" Was she pulling his leg?

"Yep." A glance proved she was quite serious.

He tried to figure out what exactly he should say to this woman who seemed so normal, yet claimed to hear voices from the earth. He finally settled on, "Singing stones. That's interesting."

"What? Why that tone of voice?"

"I've just never heard of anyone who has heard the earth sing." He thought he did a wonderful job making his voice neutral.

Not good enough, apparently, because her voice rose. "So you don't believe me?"

"You have to admit, it's different."

"So is being a hairy half man, half beast, but I haven't accused you of being a Hollywood makeup artist." She grabbed a tuft of hair on his chin and yanked hard enough to bring tears to his eyes.

He had to retreat, to pull his foot out of his mouth and save this blossoming relationship. Without pausing a beat, he said, "So what do singing stones sound like?"

Leaning her head back, she laughed with hearty enjoyment.

He liked that about her. She didn't cover her mouth like some women. She didn't disguise her merriment.

It pealed forth to brighten the heart . . . and it did brighten his.

"Occasionally I get uneasy. I wonder if you work for the demons, and if all this"—she waved a hand toward the ceiling far over their heads—"is an elaborate ruse to trap me into betraying my friends and all that we fight for. Then you show me that sly sense of humor, and I believe in you again."

He looked around at the massive cave. "This would be a *very* elaborate ruse. Are you worth so much trouble?"

She answered easily, "I don't know my place in the bigger scheme of things, but I do know I'm here on this earth for a reason, and I never make the mistake of thinking that what I do is trivial. I trust in myself. I am important."

Somewhere, deep in his soul, her words and her confidence resonated. It was as if at some time in his life he, too, had been precious, loved, important.

He closed his eyes.

Faces crowded into his mind: men and women, boys and girls, smiling at him. Voices rang in his ears: scolding him, praising him, teaching him, laughing with him. A vision filled his brain: of a bonfire that lit the night, mountains that protected a narrow, fertile valley, and stars that studded a sky so vivid he could have reached out and cupped each twinkling light in his palm. In this fantasy, love held him close, protecting him from harm.

But it wasn't a fantasy. He knew these people, those voices, this place. Revelation was so close. . . .

He stopped breathing as he hovered on the precipice of a memory.

Then, before he could grasp it, a woman laughed mockingly, and her voice, husky and low, jeered at him. *You are nothing. Nobody. A fool. In your heart you knew the truth, but you delivered yourself into my hands . . . and now you pay the price.*

*You should have listened to your grandfather.*

*You should never have trusted me.*

He groaned, deeply, mournfully.

Charisma watched in horror as his lips peeled back from his teeth. His eyes opened wide, and deep within a dull red glowed. He rose slowly, stretching himself to his full height, and in a guttural voice he roared, "No!"

Madness possessed him. Or fury. Or pain. Something far beyond her experience transformed Guardian from half man to all beast.

She leaped out of her chair, ready to defend herself.

He didn't seem to know she was there.

Picking up his stool, he flung it against the stone wall.

Charisma lifted her arm to guard her face.

Too late. The polished wood shattered and, like hail, splinters pelted her skin.

No time to worry about that. She couldn't take her gaze away from Guardian.

She had never seen evidence that he was, as he claimed, insane.

Now . . . now she believed it.

His neck thrust forward. His shoulders hunched. His head swung back and forth, looking for something else to attack.

His eyes fixed on her, gleaming, violent, ferocious.

She shoved her chair toward him, like bait to distract a predator, and backed up, putting distance between them, never looking away.

Lifting the heavy straight-backed chair over his head, he slammed it into the coffee table. The thick glass top exploded, a million shards blowing across the cave on the winds of rage.

Blood started from tiny cuts on his face and arms, and his bellow sounded like anguish.

He was a savage. A lunatic. In the grip of emotions she didn't understand.

She crouched into a defensive posture.

He noted that. Gave a derisive laugh. He gripped the edges of his tunic. . . .

And she saw his hands change.

He changed.

His fingers grew longer; the joints enlarged; the nails sharpened into claws that could slash her skin to ribbons.

With a mighty heave of his shoulders, he tore the cotton from top to bottom. He shrugged out of it, dropped onto all fours, hands and feet on the ground. With another feral roar, he raced from the cave.

Charisma straightened, adrenaline rushing through her veins. Her head swam, and a cold sweat covered her forehead.

The silence in the cave was deafening.

Her wobbly legs demanded she find somewhere to sit—now. She groped her way to a chair, sank down, and panted as if she'd run miles. Closing her eyes, she listened to the rushing of blood in her head and prayed for her heart to calm.

And jumped when a woman said harshly, "I've never seen him like that. What did you say to him?"

Charisma's eyes flew open.

Amber. It was Amber.

"I didn't say anything. I don't know." Charisma tried to remember. "Something about . . . being relieved that this wasn't all a ruse. Something about . . . me being valuable."

"You made him change!" Amber pointed a finger at her. She accused Charisma in her posture and voice . . . did Buddhists make accusations?

"I didn't mean to." Charisma remembered her question: *Are you sure you're not a werewolf?*

He had denied it. He had said the moon didn't influence his form.

But he did *change*. "I said that I never make the mistake of thinking that what I do is trivial. I told him I was important. That couldn't be it. Why would that set him off?"

Amber folded her arms forbiddingly across her chest. "Dr. King says he has memories at war in his head."

"But he didn't hurt me."

"He has never hurt any of us. He only hurts the demons . . . and the bad people." Amber stared out the door where Guardian had disappeared. "I hope he doesn't get killed this time."

"Me, too." Something about this woman drove Charisma to confession. "I like him. You know?"

Amber smiled and bowed her head, her serenity returned. "I am happy to hear that. I would hate to think he frightened you enough to make you run away."

Closing her eyes again, Charisma thought about leaving while Guardian was gone, making for Irving's house and safety. But she wasn't well enough to fight yet. Obviously. So what good would she be to the Chosen Ones? And although Guardian had terrified her with the threat of violence and insanity, he had also reassured and comforted her.

Even in his frenzy, he hadn't threatened her.

"He's a puzzle I need to work out." He was, despite his beastliness, very much a man, and in his torment he thrilled and attracted her. But she didn't need to explain *that* to Amber. "I feel that if I could help him unravel the truth of his past, he would be free from so much anguish. And I feel I owe him that much."

"That is a worthy goal indeed. It does you honor." Amber bowed again. "Now, let me help you to bed. Moises and I will clean up the mess."

"Who's Moises?" Charisma let Amber help her to her feet.

"He's . . . there." Amber waved a vague hand toward the darkest part of the cave.

Charisma glanced, but saw nothing but shadow.

"Moises is one of us. He chooses to serve Guardian, as we all do. Like you, we are soldiers in the battle against evil." Slowly they made their way back toward the pallet dug into the earth, Amber supporting Charisma all the way. "You've overreached your strength," she scolded.

"Yes." Talking with Amber had clarified Charisma's thinking.

So Guardian provided her with a few challenges. He was hairy, had an unpredictable temper, and made unscheduled changes in body type.

But he had saved her life, and she would help him. Somehow they would figure out what had happened to him. Somehow they would discover what horrors lurked at the back of his mind, and somehow they would return his memories . . . whether he liked them or not.

As they neared the pallet, Charisma viewed it disfavorably. Yes, she had needed to be close to the earth to heal, but she was better now. And she was clean. And the pallet was not. The sheets and blankets were as filthy as before.

Apparently, Guardian's staff didn't quite comprehend all the niceties of caring for guests.

"Is there a real bed?" Charisma asked. "With a mattress?"

"Only Guardian has a bed here." Amber pointed up a steep stairway, where a dim alcove had been carved into the rock.

"That'll work." Charisma's eyes were aching. She needed to sleep. "Could you help me to it?"

Amber so obviously worshiped Guardian that Charisma expected her to object. Instead, she inclined her head and did as Charisma asked.

# Chapter 18

———⬥———

Charisma woke, nerves tingling, aware she was not alone.

Daylight seeped into the cave.

Her vision was better. She knew because her eyes didn't ache and she could clearly see that Guardian stood over her.

But although her heart quickened, she refused to show fear, or even to feel it.

Because she remembered her resolve to help him retrieve his memories, but also . . . right now, he looked normal. He looked like the civilized yet powerful creature who had rescued her from a demon attack and tended to her injuries. Normal. For him.

Except for a slash that started at his throat and disappeared under the neckline of his white djellaba, and a patch of missing fur on his cheek. But his eyes were blue, with no infernal red glow, and a quick glance at his hands proved that they looked like a man's hands—

but still hairy. "Heck," she said sleepily, "hairy's not a big deal. I've seen grown men who have as much hair on their backs as you've got on your whole body."

He half grinned, but exhaustion drew his face in austere lines. "You're in my bed," he said in a neutral tone.

She looked around the rocky alcove, at the massive antique bed, the curtains that protected it. "I didn't feel like sleeping on the ground anymore, and this is the only bed here. Big, too. And comfortable."

"They brought the mattress down for me."

"Who?"

"The Belows." He looked faintly damp, and smelled of soap. He had showered again. "You're better?"

"I would be if someone didn't keep interrupting my sleep." She turned over with her back to him. "Come to bed. It's big enough for the two of us. I hope you don't snore." She waited to see what he would do.

A few moments later, the covers shifted. The mattress compressed. He pulled the bed curtains shut. And he was next to her, their world reduced to the size of a mattress.

What was he thinking? What was he doing? Was he perturbed with her? Was he uncomfortable? Did he think she was coming on to him?

Because she wasn't. No, no, no.

When she chose to sleep in his bed, her decision had been all about comfort and recuperation, and not about intimacy. If there'd been another good mattress available, she would have selected it. She might think Guardian attractive in an odd, primal way, but she planned to help the man, not dance the horizontal mambo with him. . . .

Possibly she was still scarred by her experience with the last guy. That jerk. Probably she had started to get over it, because ever since she'd been down here with Guardian, she hadn't thought of the creep at all. Not once.

Part of the problem here was that sleeping with a man *was* intimate, whether or not that was what she intended.

His voice made her jump. "You've got my pillow."

"Oh!" She pretended to be surprised.

Like she didn't already know she had his pillow.

The whole bed was this giant phallic symbol, with tall, smooth, polished posts on each corner and heavy purple velvet bed curtains enclosing the California king mattress. The sheets were silky-smooth, latte colored, and she'd guess about a thousand thread count, and a dozen pillows were tossed against the tall mahogany headboard. More to the point, the whole contraption carried a faint hint of Guardian's scent.

How did a man manage to smell like long, lazy days on a sandy white beach? Like blue skies and carefree memories? Like callused hands smoothing lotion over her skin?

Charisma was a smart girl. She *knew* the scent was pure testosterone. But knowing the facts didn't make any difference, because she had sought out his pillow, buried her face in it, taken long, deep breaths, and fallen asleep holding it crushed in her arms.

Then she dreamed of him. And her. And them.

Now he insinuated that he wanted his pillow back.

He didn't know about her dreams.

She should be grateful.

She flipped over to face him.

He rested on his back, close to the edge of the mattress, staring straight at the ceiling.

*Wow.* He looked uncomfortable. "Here." She thrust the pillow at him. "I didn't realize it was yours."

"Thank you." He took it without looking at her. "I'm sorry I frightened you," he said.

"When? Oh, you mean earlier, when you got upset?" She was faking her way through all kinds of stuff today. "I wasn't frightened."

He turned his head to look at her.

"I was *terrified*." She used a joking tone, but she wanted to see what he had to say. "When you throw a tantrum, you get right with it."

He looked back at the ceiling. "That was a little more rage than I've experienced before."

"Why is that?"

He stuck the pillow under his neck and sort of mashed it around. "I heard a woman's voice in my head, mocking me for being a fool."

"Who?" Charisma sat up. "What woman?"

"I don't recall who she is. I only know I felt such an upwelling of hatred. . . ."

Charisma slithered back down onto her non-Guardian-scented pillow. "Bummer."

"Not that that should have made me become more of a monster. I usually have better control. I simply think that the memory of her cruelty, combined with what I felt when I saw you . . . and you were still here, and, well, beautiful . . . That woman's voice stripped me of something I don't ever recall experiencing down here." He moved restlessly beneath those really great sheets.

"What's that?"

"For the first time in my memory, I experienced a moment of . . . hope."

She liked that. Very much. Because he made her spirits lift, too. Was this hope? It had been so long, she wasn't sure. But it felt like it.

*Play it lightly, Charisma. He's a little stressed.* "Yeah, seeing me naked will do that."

Startled, he looked back at her and grinned. "Absolutely true."

"Good answer." She tucked her hand under her cheek and scrutinized him. "That's quite a couple of wounds you've collected. I suppose the cut is more dangerous, but that one on your face looks like it really hurts."

Lightly he touched the raw spot on his cheek. "I raced out of here without putting on my superhero tough-guy uniform, and it's never a good idea for me to fight demons unless I'm wearing it."

"Okay." Now he was playing it lightly. "I'll bite." She snapped her teeth. "What's your superhero tough-guy uniform?"

"It's sort of like a skin-diving suit, durable and slick. It fits me tightly, and it stops most of the trouble with the demons. They like to rip off my fur."

"Ouch."

His blue eyes grew gray-blue and stormy. "This time I hardly noticed."

His ears grew a little more pointed.

She told herself it made him look elfish, like an unshaven Orlando Bloom. "What a good way to work out a shit-ton of rage. You got your exercise and killed a bunch of demons. Has one ever bitten you?" She waited anxiously for the answer; although she felt so much better, sometimes a wave of fatigue and depression passed over her. . . .

"They don't bite me."

"What? Really? Why not?"

"Because I would taste nasty."

"Which means you would be tasty to me." *Probably not the smartest thing to say, Charisma.* Hastily, she added, "About those wounds—you don't want an infection. Those demons are filthy. Did you put antibiotic ointment on your cuts?"

"Yes, Mom." He studied her, and something about the way she lay, totally at ease with him, seemed to ease his tension. "I always enjoy watching the demons when I sing to them."

"Why? What happens?"

"They don't like it."

"Do you have a good voice?"

"Nothing operatic, but pleasant, yes."

"That's fine for you. When I sing to the demons, they applaud."

Guardian gave a crack of laughter. "Not true."

"I'd prove it by singing a few bars, but you look so tired, I don't know if you're up to fleeing."

"But the earth sings to you."

"The earth doesn't require that I sing back." Whimsically, she added, "In fact, I'm sure the earth prefers I don't."

The smile that played around his mouth made his blue eyes crinkle and his face look so . . . human. He said, "You never told me—what does the earth sound like when it sings?"

# *Chapter 19*

---

When Charisma remembered the days and months and years of hearing the earth crooning to her, when she remembered those times that she believed the support would always be there for her, her eyes half closed, and she caressed the quiet stones at her wrist. "Like a welcome home. Or a promise made with love." Her eyes snapped open, and she glared. "Or the rumble of oncoming trouble."

"When you first heard the earth sing, was it home and love, or was it trouble?" Guardian's voice was a low, tired growl.

"Home and love. I thought everyone heard the earth, and I went prancing off to tell my mother about my wonderful new gift." Charisma tried hard not to judge the foolish child she had been. "I was always trying to please my mom, one way or another. The stones warned me not to share our secret, but I didn't understand. Yet."

"Your mother saw in you the potential to make money?"

"You've never met her, and you've got her figured out," Charisma marveled. But she wasn't really surprised. His tribulations had made him sensitive in ways most men—most *people*—were not. "Yes, she saw far more potential in my weird ability than when I was little Miss No-name City. All of a sudden we were outta Tahiti and back in the States, hitting every weekend market in a tent covered with astrological symbols, with me as the prime attraction."

"As a fortune-teller?"

"Good guess." Charisma tried to smile, but her lips were too stiff. "She tried the fortune-telling thing first. But she lied all the time. To everyone. To me. So I balked at telling lies, and she had to change the act. She had me make charms for people. Bracelets made of crystal to protect them from harm, or to help them find love, or to give them health."

"Wasn't that like telling lies?"

"No. They worked." Charisma found satisfaction in telling him that.

Interesting. She wanted to impress him.

She continued. "People would come into our tent. They would tell me their stories—how their husband cheated on them, their children neglected them, they had cancer, they were infertile, they were dying. While I listened, I'd string the stones, and when they left they carried the strength of the earth around their necks or on their wrists."

He sat up on his elbow. "You cured the dying?"

"No. No. I never cured anything, but I helped them find peace in their fate, and a respite from pain. That was a very great thing, wasn't it?" Still unsure, all these years later, she appealed to him.

"That is a very great thing." Gently he reached out and smoothed her lower lip with his thumb. "But you spent your adolescence listening to unhappiness."

"Until then, I never knew there was that much misery in the world." For all that it had been years and years since that horrible time, Charisma discovered she couldn't bear sympathy. Not from him. Not now. She turned her head away from his touch. "I went to child protection and told them I hadn't attended school. My mother told them she'd been homeschooling me. She had no proof, of course, no test scores, no paperwork, and when examined, I was remarkably ignorant."

He closed his hand, pulled it back to his side. "You faked it."

"No, really! A year in school in Tahiti didn't exactly prepare me to do more than read a lot." She smiled at the memory of herself, always sitting with her head in a book. "Not that that wasn't educational. But my reading taught me a lot about how this parent/child thing was supposed to work, at least in the real world, and I knew I wanted more than being a freak my whole life." Bitterly she added, "Especially a freak that Mom dressed up like a ten-year-old, because a kid magic healer sold better to the tourists than a teenage magic healer."

He didn't answer right away. He seemed to be thinking of a way through this potential minefield. At last, he said, "I take it you won the battle to grow up."

"I had to win sooner or later, didn't I?"

"No. Some children never do get away from the desire to please an abusive parent."

Charisma had never actually put it into words. She tried out the thought: Her mother had been abusive. She'd been raised by an abusive parent. It was almost a relief to acknowledge that simple fact. "But I mostly turned out all right."

This time he didn't hesitate. "Yes, you did. You're dynamic, interesting, intelligent, funny."

"Right. I am." She nodded. "Thanks, Guardian."

"I didn't do anything." His voice was husky with exhaustion. He rolled onto his back.

"You did. You really did." Imitating his earlier caress, she slid her thumb across his lower lip.

He closed his eyes as if her touch pained him. "So you went to school . . . ?"

"I got caught up in school, went to college, got a degree, got drafted by the Chosen Ones—"

His eyes popped open. They really were very blue. "Down here, I've heard rumors about the Chosen Ones. You're one of them?"

"I am. And proud of it."

"Pardon my ignorance," he said in a humble voice, which she didn't believe for a minute. "But what exactly is a Chosen One?"

"It's almost like a fairy tale. But not a Disney fairy story. One by the Grimm Brothers. And it really is grim." In a soft, slow, easy tone, she slid into the story. "Long ago, when the world was young, a young woman lived in a poor village on the edge of a vast, dark forest. The face she saw in the reflecting pool was glorious in its splendor, and all the men of the village competed for her favors, desiring her as their wife. Their good opinion of her was matched only by her good opinion of herself, and she declared she would take only a man whose magnificence matched her own. So she took the eldest son of the local lord, a lazy lad as famed for his dark, wavy hair and deep-set blue eyes as for his vanity. . . ."

His breath grew heavy, deep, regular.

He was asleep.

Gradually she let the story trail off. Silently she studied his face.

In sleep, without the animation of humanity and emotion, his features looked oddly more menacing, as if the beast in him lived vividly in his subconscious. Lightly she stroked the thin, short, pale fur that covered his face; it was smooth and soft to the touch.

After a moment, she pulled her hand back.

She had no right to touch him. It was a violation of his personal space. But she'd dreamed of this: exploring him, discovering the planes and textures of a body so different from any she'd ever seen. In her dream, he had allowed her to do as she wished, then insisted on returning the favor. In her dream, he had been wonderful, gentle, and so slow.

Damn dream.

Damn chastity.

Damn his testosterone, clinging to her skin from his sheets and his pillow. . . .

The hair on his face expanded at his hairline to become a luxurious mane, like a lion's, and with one finger she stroked a single strand. It, too, was silky, inviting her to slide her hand along its length. . . .

She didn't dare touch his scalp. He had something under his skin there, something mechanical. Something horrific. *That* she remembered from her first, brusque exploration of him, and for the first time she felt well enough to do more than simply wonder what had happened to him. She thought about it, and thought hard.

Had someone viewed him as an opportunity to make a name in the scientific world, captured him, and operated on his brain?

Or was the reality even worse than that?

After getting to know Guardian, she felt guilty for ever doubting him, fond of him for his understanding and humor, and, face it, she was hot for his body.

What a mess she had landed herself in now. She should go back to Irving's mansion, get back to work fighting Osgood and his minions, do what she was supposed to be doing as one of the Chosen Ones.

But with the rest of the Chosen Ones out of town, she had no backup. She was still weak and way out of shape. She had sworn she was going to help Guardian discover himself once more.

That was a noble goal, too. Wasn't it?

Yes. It was.

Although she'd known him only a little while, she saw in him a deep, pure character that needed only one thing—someone to believe in him.

Sitting up, she leaned over him and inhaled his scent. And closed her eyes.

Sunshine. A warm, sandy beach. His hands on her skin . . .

She pulled back and opened her eyes, and grounded herself in the here and now. She wasn't on a beach. She was in this cave with the sound of water babbling across the stones, in this bed with an absolutely fabulous broad-shouldered creature whom she'd viewed naked. . . . He looked human where it counted . . . maybe a little better endowed than most men, but—

*No.* She scooted back toward her own side of the bed.

She did not have to give in to this lusty desire to roll on the bed with him. Giving in to that urge had always proved to be a disaster. And face it, no matter how tempting Guardian might be, with the world on the brink of being sucked into a living version of hell, she didn't have time for a full-blown, sweaty, moaning, good-time affair.

So. She would be good. Logical. Restrained.

Right after she gave him a single, logical, restrained kiss. Just one kiss.

Little by little, she eased back toward him, knowing this was a weak yielding on her part. An invasion of his privacy. Stupid beyond belief.

But he was so deeply asleep, and she so wanted to taste him, just once. This way she could do it without explanations or complications. . . .

Very gently, she placed her palms on either side of his head, compressing the pillow as she leaned in to hover over him, her mouth over his mouth, almost touching. . . .

She waited for—wanted—a moment of sanity to save her. But he seduced her with his scent, with the warmth of his breath, with his aura of danger. Slowly, she eased her lips onto his. . . .

And screamed when his eyes flew open, and he flipped her on her back, stared into her eyes, and snarled like a beast who had snared his prey . . . at last.

# *Chapter 20*

———◆———

Guardian held Charisma trapped beneath his body, keeping her in place with his hands, his weight, his aggression. His furious gaze held hers, and in a guttural voice, he said, "Slumming?"

"What? No!" She was so embarrassed. He'd caught her kissing his unconscious body, like some pathetic spinster out for a clandestine thrill. "Listen, Guardian—"

But he didn't listen. Instead, he crouched over her, keeping her imprisoned with his knees beside her hips. He gripped her upper arms, holding them close to her sides. And he *kissed* her, a full-octane, open-lipped kiss that gave no quarter, but ravished her mouth.

She struggled, trying to free her hands, to touch him, tame him, appease him, but he refused to cede an inch. Instead, his tongue sought hers. His breath filled her mouth. And she was reduced to clutching the tunic material at his waist.

When they were both breathless, he lifted his head

and stared into her eyes, and pressed his erection against her belly.

Large. Hot. Determined. His motion was not a promise, but a threat.

"Guardian. Don't." She didn't really mean *don't*. She simply meant, *You don't understand*, and, *Not while you're angry*.

But he didn't want to hear it. He took her lower lip between his white teeth and nibbled until desire overwhelmed wisdom and she opened her mouth to him.

He kissed her again, using his tongue to stimulate her, to imitate intercourse. In and out. In and out. A crude technique. And effective, because he swept her along, filling her senses, making her clench her legs together tightly, trying to ease her desire with pressure and movement. She whimpered, begging, needy, desperate to be one with him.

When she had touched him, kissed him, lusted after him, she hadn't meant to start *this*. Nothing in her dream was like *this*. *This* was not a warm beach filled with leisurely lovemaking. This was a race: panting, heart racing, muscles straining. This was a blistering competition for dominance—and she had lost before she started.

He let go of her arms.

Finally she could touch him.

But he hadn't released her hands to allow her freedom. No, he did so for his own pleasure, so he could push her shirt up. He spanned her rib cage with his fingers, plumped her breasts, ran his thumbs over and around her nipples . . . and all the while he still kissed her, as if kissing her fulfilled his every desire, as if kissing her heated him, made him hard, and harder.

Still he caged her with his body, holding her in place, immobile, while he did as he wished with her. She wanted to entice him with rhythm and movement, and all she could do was grip the fur at the nape of his neck, open her arms, and offer herself.

At last he lifted his head from her mouth.

She opened her eyes to see his face, so close to hers. His eyes, angry and oddly vulnerable. His lips, soft and smooth, wet with kissing.

He looked down at her chest, and he growled, low and deep. Bending, he feasted on her breasts. He sought her nipples with his wet, open mouth, tasted them as if her flesh gave him pleasure, and then firmly, thoroughly suckled on her, pulling against each breast with a pressure that made her cry out with lust and frustration.

He flamed with passion. He burned her with the heat of his demands. He ruthlessly compelled her sexual pleasure, and when she surrendered, he demanded more. He left her no choice. He wanted everything, every piece of Charisma that she was, every piece that she would become.

With every movement, every aggressive sexual demand, he dared her to try to escape. He wanted her to fight him, to challenge him.

She should be afraid of his strength, she knew. She was a fighter, but she had no chance against him, his power, his anger. She was a fool to trust him . . . yet she kissed his chin, stroked his back, his buttocks, his thighs.

She trusted him, God help her, when all evidence proved his ferocity.

But she knew his ferocity would take a different path tonight . . . and she wanted to walk that path.

He lifted her butt, pushed her pajama pants down, and settled her beneath him again.

It was a cruel parody of intercourse, with him on top, yet still clad in his djellaba. His knees pressed against her hips and kept her legs clamped together, yet his cock pressed lower, nudging at her slit.

He slid his finger between her tightly closed legs and found that she was damp, swollen, in such need. He moved his finger lightly against her clitoris, barely brushing the tip, a tease that made her claw at him first in frustration, then, as she climaxed, in satisfaction. "Good," she whispered. "So good." She had neglected her sexual needs for so long—with her history, it seemed a smart thing to do—but now she begged him, "Please, Guardian. Come inside me."

"No."

"Please." She tried to spread her legs, to pull him into her. She slid her hands down to his hips and tugged at his tunic, trying to rid him of that single layer of cotton. As if that were all that separated them.

He held himself absolutely still, not breathing, not yielding.

She undulated beneath him.

He held steadfast.

But she was Charisma Fangorn. She knew how to free herself if necessary—and now it was necessary. Twisting onto her side, she extricated herself from the cage of his legs, got onto her stomach, and lifted herself to her knees.

A mistake, perhaps. She had turned her back to him. She had lifted her bare bottom into the air.

She was vulnerable. She was sexually available.

She almost heard the crack as his control shattered, like thick river ice breaking in the spring thaw.

He seized her hips in his hands, slid one arm under her belly to hold her in place. "You don't understand what you've done," he said in that dark, menacing voice that sounded more beast than man.

She braced herself, expecting assault, but his fingers lightly brushed her exposed bottom, her thighs, moved more intimately to circle the entrance to her body.

He was teasing her.

For a man wild with desire, he showed a magnificent ability to take his time.

She pushed herself onto his finger.

He allowed that.

Generous of him.

He used first one finger; then, with more difficulty, he used two and slid deep, testing her depths, her heat, her passion. He filled her, used his other fingers to open her to his view. "Look how swollen you are. You need me . . . to taste you."

"Oh, God." At the mere idea, she almost came again.

"To use my tongue on you." His voice grew ever smokier. The atmosphere in the confines of the bed grew more heated, more intimate. "To teach you what happens when you provoke a man who's more than half animal."

"All men are more than half animal." She was pleased at the response, pleased she could even speak.

He allowed her barely a moment of pride before he struck, replacing his hand with his lips, bringing all the skill and dedication he had used in kissing her mouth . . . to kiss her there. He sucked on her, thrust his tongue inside her, used his fingers to counterattack.

And she never had a doubt he was attacking. She had won; he had never meant to go so far.

But he would not go down in defeat. He would employ her tactics. He would use her body against her. . . .

In a moment of clarity, she saw them as they were: in a massive, legendary cave, on a giant bed, a petite woman on her hands and knees, a gigantic beast of a man behind her, both absorbed in the passionate battle between them. Both would lose. Both would win.

Who would claim victory?

# *Chapter 21*

———❖———

Charisma bent to the mattress, pressed her face against it, breathed in the fragrance of Guardian, of sex, of struggle, of war on the battlefield of this bed, *his* bed. The aromas heightened her senses, made her ever more susceptible as, behind her, Guardian used his tongue, his teeth, his lips to sample her, savor her. He gave her his fingers, whispered his enjoyment of her short, sharp cries, the demands of her body, the taste of her climax.

By the time he rose onto his knees, pushed his legs between hers, and spread her wide, she was crying in completion and demand. She half turned as he pulled his tunic off, and saw him bare, a creature of manlike proportions. But his face looked very human now; he was a man intent on possessing a woman, and he wore that particular determination easily, as if he could not be dissuaded.

*Thank God.*

Still half turned, Charisma pushed herself up until

the backs of her thighs were against the fronts of his. She slid her arm around his neck and pulled his head down to hers. Passionately, she kissed him, giving him what he had given her—fever, delight, delirium.

When she pulled away, he skimmed his palm across her shoulder and curled his hand around her throat.

She stared into his eyes.

He stared back, his mouth taut, his nostrils flared, his expression implacable.

A lesser woman might think he hated her; she recognized a desire so plain and stark, it could be satisfied with nothing less than a mating.

"I haven't got a condom," he said. "Will you get pregnant?"

"No. And I haven't had sex since—" No, she wouldn't think of that. "I haven't had sex for a long time, so I won't give you a disease. You?"

His bitter laughter mocked . . . himself. "You're safe from disease, Charisma Fangorn. But you're not safe from me. I'm going to fill you. I'm going find out what you feel like inside. Velvety sandpaper? Hot enough to burn me to a cinder? I'm going to revel in your body, make you come so hard and so often you'll be sorry you started this."

"I thought you were asleep. I didn't mean to start it. But since I have"—taking his erection in her hand, she stroked it, smoothing the silken length from the base to the tip—"I promise I won't be sorry. Not if you follow through on everything you've promised." And she smiled, a slow, sexual curl of the lips that made him yank her against him, her back to his front, while he stroked her breasts and belly. And lower.

Shamelessly, she leaned her head against his chest,

put her hands behind her so her breasts thrust out and into his palms, and reached up to caress his face.

His erection pressed into her back and hardened yet more.

"Now. Lean down," he said.

No, not said—commanded.

Charisma obeyed.

Why wouldn't she? She was getting what she wanted, and maybe . . . maybe more.

Maybe, with the length and breadth of him, and his heat, and his magnificent primal fire, he would brand himself on her, this man she would never, ever forget.

She got on her hands and knees . . . but that wasn't enough for him. He pressed his broad hand into her shoulder blades, moving her head down to rest once more on the mattress, and brought her bottom close enough to rest against his groin. She spread her legs wider, rubbed herself against him, seeking satisfaction, trying to hurry him . . . because she needed this. Now.

But he took his time, arranged her legs to his satisfaction, then used his fingers to open her. . . .

He pressed inside, so big and hot she wanted nothing more than to welcome him, all of him, into her body. Inch by inch he stretched her, torched her with each new advance. He made her whimper. He made her struggle, try to take control.

He laughed at that, a brief snort of derision. Wrapping his arm around her hips, he lifted her to him, a position that left her helpless, clawing at the sheets as he surged inside. All the way inside—he pressed deeply, his hips against her bottom, and held her there as if savoring the penetration. Or perhaps his suspension of movement was a clever strategy to force her to realize exactly what she had started.

A very clever strategy, for as she hung there, dependent on his strength, on his tenderness, she knew a moment of primitive feminine fear. He could hurt her—or he could take her to ecstasy.

Her inner muscles convulsed on him; she didn't know whether this was pain or passion, whether the spasms that racked her were nothing more than a continual orgasm . . . or an introduction into a new world, painted with brand-new colors, where she breathed sensuality and wore desire like a garment.

Perhaps he'd been waiting for that internal caress along the length of his cock. Or perhaps his own needs drove him to start the long strokes, in and out, moving her on him, a slow, precise movement that stretched her patience as she waited, nerves screaming, for his next motion. In and out. In and out.

Grabbing the pillows, she buried her head to muffle her moans.

And, of course, she managed to grab *his* pillow, permeated with his scent, and those male pheromones went to her head like a drug, so that she climaxed in one long, continuous ache of pleasure, with higher and higher peaks.

In her mind's eye, she pictured his face. And he was beautiful to her. Her lover.

Each time he thrust his erection inside, he made every inch matter. Each time he withdrew, his penis tugged at her flesh. His speed increased, matching her needs, directing her desires.

She wanted to move, but instead he used his strength

to move her, goading her from one shuddering climax to another.

Faster. Harder. Faster. Faster.

In all the universe, there was only his touch: his arm around her hips, his hand stroking her spine from buttocks to shoulders, over and over, as if driving pleasure along her nerves, through her veins, and into her mind, there to change her forever.

Faster. Harder. Faster.

And then—a breathless moment of waiting, a suspension of movement. With a deep roar, he pulled her tightly against him, his balls against her clit. His cock pulsed inside her as he came, filling her even more. She climaxed with him, writhing with bliss, squeezing the pillows in her fists. For a long moment, it seemed as if time stopped. . . .

And then it was over.

He lowered her to her knees.

She collapsed onto her stomach and concentrated on pulling the pieces of herself back together. Not an easy thing, for she would never fit together in the same way. He had exhausted her in every way; she could feel the weeks of illness and inactivity in the trembling of her muscles and the weariness that dragged her down. Yet she luxuriated in a surfeit of pleasure so elemental she had been only half-alive without it. "That was great," she breathed.

He didn't answer.

"Spectacular."

He didn't answer.

Had she screamed so loud she'd hurt his hearing? Had she killed him with an overdose of addictive, mind-blowing sex?

Was he ready for another round?

She lifted her head out of the pillows.

While she'd been concentrating on getting her breath back, Guardian had managed to pull on his djellaba. Now he reclined on his back on his side of the bed, his eyes fixed on the ceiling, his hands tucked under his neck.

He looked . . . calm. Offhand. As if world-changing whoopee happened every day.

"Guardian?" She touched him lightly on the arm. "Are you not talking to me?"

"Of course I am," he said. "Could you return my pillow?"

She sat up and back on her heels. *"What?"*

"Could I have my pillow back? It's my favorite."

"I heard you the first time. But you . . . Why would you . . . We just . . ."

He turned his head and looked at her.

That was not the face of the man she'd pictured in her mind.

The face he showed her now was set as a stone-carved statue, indifferent and implacable. Except for his eyes. His blue eyes were as cold as chips off an iceberg.

She couldn't believe it. She was sitting here, her pajamas pulled down to her ankles, her sleep tee rumpled, still wet and aching between the legs . . . and he was asking about his *pillow*? This wasn't happening. "Oh, come on." She tried a half laugh, tried to make it a joke, when she was irked. And hurt. "I knew you were mad when we started. I know it was intrusive to kiss you while you were asleep, but it's really not that big a deal. It's not like I fondled you, or sneaked a peek at your man goodies."

"Why would you have to sneak a peek? You got a

good look at my man goodies earlier today, when I showered."

*Pause. Think hard. Try to understand what's going on here.* "I'm sorry. I didn't realize that offended you, too." But she couldn't stand to apologize. Not in this case. "I mean, fair's fair. You got an eyeful of me, too." She had to say it, because she wasn't going to sit here and take all the blame for . . . whatever it was he was blaming her for.

"I wasn't offended. I was just wondering whether that's what made you think you could score some beast points while you were slumming in the cave." His voice was cool, reasoned.

"Listen to me. You are not a beast. And I am *not* slumming." She was the *opposite* of cool and reasoned.

He continued as if she hadn't spoken. "I'm told women have this fantasy about beasts, about size and duration and hot, animal sex. I hope I managed to fulfill all your expectations."

"It's not like that." Her voice rose. "I didn't want you because you're a novelty. I want you because you're Guardian. You saved me from certain death. You're smart and funny. Women have fantasies about men like you, too, you know!"

"You didn't like it when I touched you." He enunciated, as if he couldn't say it clearly enough.

"What? That's not true. We just performed the best horizontal mambo *ever*." She waved at the sheets.

"I didn't give you a lot of choices."

"I wasn't exactly objecting!"

"There are ways to make a woman give it up."

"Got a lot of experience with making women give it

up?" *No! Stupid thing to say. Mean thing to say.* She was sorry.

"I read a lot." The line was funny. His delivery was not. Hostility had begun to seep through.

She had to figure out how to defuse this situation, how to get back to at least the relationship they'd enjoyed before. . . .

Before.

*This conclusively proves something, Charisma. You're bad at sex. Buy some new rechargeable batteries and give up on the real thing.* So she pulled up her pajama pants and straightened her shirt, and said, "Look, Guardian, I'm sorry I caught you off guard and kissed you while you were sleeping. I guess it was like taking advantage of you, but I wanted to see whether your . . . lips . . . were as soft as . . ." She faltered under his glare.

"When we were talking. Remember when we were talking? You were telling me about your mother, and I ran my thumb along your lower lip." He repeated the motion roughly, contemptuously. "Did you think I didn't notice that you turned your head away?"

She was floored. Such a small mistake on her part. Such a massive misunderstanding. It made her feel a little faint.

No, it wasn't the misunderstanding that made her droop onto the pillows. Fireworks flashed at the backs of her eyes. She had trouble catching her breath. In a colossal piece of bad timing, the venom had chosen this moment to overwhelm her. "But I didn't turn my head away because I don't like you to touch me. I did it because—"

"I know why you did it. I'm good enough to fuck.

But don't put my filthy paws on you without permission."

"No!" She closed her eyes, rubbed her head, opened her eyes again.

"I'm nothing but a novelty, a plaything to use while you're out of the sight of real life, and to abandon when you go back to the surface to be with *real* people. Yes, I may be a pathetic creature, a man who's forced to live alone and finds his usual satisfaction with Rosie Palm and her five sisters"—lifting his open hand, he closed it into a fist—"but I have my pride, and I have no intention of providing you with a diversion while you recover. So from now on, you keep your hands and your lips and your body to yourself. You sleep on your side of the bed and I'll sleep on mine. Now, if you'll excuse me"—he pulled his pillow out from underneath her head—"I need to sleep. Tomorrow I plan to give Osgood and his minions a surprise, and clean up the area under his building." Turning his back to her, Guardian plumped his pillow and . . . well, he didn't relax. The air around him shimmered with heat.

What happened to her intention to help him find himself? She had only made him feel worse.

Her hand hovered over his shoulder, then fell away. She was faint, exhausted, and he wasn't going to listen to her tonight. Better save her breath for tomorrow.

Tomorrow he would listen to her.

Or else.

# Chapter 22

Guardian watched the procession of demons crawl out of the hole that led down to the deepest depths of hell, up the steep, winding stone stairway, and into the foundations of Osgood's building. How long ago had Osgood—or rather, the devil that possessed Osgood—conceived the plan to blast the Gypsy Travel Agency to smithereens? How long ago had he plotted to build on the ruins? Because that stairway looked as if it had been constructed millennia ago. That kind of forethought—no, foresight—made Guardian's battle against the demons seem even more futile.

But he couldn't sit by and watch them swarm through the New York City tunnels. He had to fight. He had to do what he could to stem the tide.

And really, what else would he do with his time? It wasn't like he could stop by a bar at night and lift a few beers with the rest of the guys.

Of course, if he'd kept his big fat mouth shut, he could be boinking Charisma. . . .

*No. Don't think of that.* He wouldn't think about her two-toned hair or her pink, puckered nipples or the way she whimpered, deep in her throat, when he used his tongue on her, pulling her honey out of her body for his own delectation. He wouldn't think of holding her body against his, plunging into her heated depths, finding a satisfaction and release that broke open his defensive shell and left him vulnerable. And for shit's sake, he wouldn't imagine what it would be like if she wrapped those full, soft lips around his dick and—

*Son of a bitch.* He needed to concentrate on what he was doing.

Quietly, he moved into position and aimed his ammunition—a massive spotlight—at the stairs. In one swift move, he flipped it on.

Blinding white light blasted the scurrying little bastards. The ones who caught the full force of the beam staggered, lost their footing, fell screaming into the depths. The others scrambled around, blinded and confused, gibbering frantically.

Guardian always liked this part. He should go back to the cave and create a video game called Killing Demons for Fun, with different levels involving lights, singing, and extra points for head chopping.

When he had knocked the greatest possible number of demons off the stairs, he waved the spotlight randomly around, picking the stragglers off with a blast of light that made them moan, run, and sometimes, shrivel into little burned black husks.

But fighting them involved more than just eradicating them. He had to lure them in so he could get his hands on them.

He didn't bother to shoot them anymore.

Now he used a hatchet to slash off their heads. He didn't know whether that killed them, since he didn't know whether they were alive, but it seemed the only way to actually eliminate them.

During this part, he had to be careful. If they overwhelmed him, they would drag him down, tie him up, and leave him.

He didn't know why they didn't kill him. It couldn't be for anything good.

Sooner or later Taurean would find him, but it was always an unpleasant few days, and after spending so much time caring for Charisma, he didn't have any more days to squander.

So now he pretended to be completely occupied with his light, pretended not to hear the patter of padded feet behind him.

The nasty little cockroaches fell for this trick every time.

They got close, beautifully close.

Then, turning suddenly, he blasted them with the light.

Screaming. Shriveling. A full-fledged retreat.

Yay for him.

Eventually, of course, the overwhelming odds got him.

The demons sprang at him from all sides at the same time. They leaped from the walls. They fell from the ceiling. They were endless, nasty, disgusting things, neither human nor devil, just drops of distilled malice with feet and hands, and two eyes, usually. And teeth. Way too many teeth.

His lungs burned. His heart pumped with adrenaline. He fought them, as he always did, his skills honed by too many battles like this one.

One dropped from the ceiling, grabbed the hair that had escaped Guardian's superhero suit, and swung like a monkey. It opened its wide mouth. Fangs gleamed.

A blast of foul breath made Guardian stagger. *This is it. He's going to bite off my face.*

The demon met his eyes. Froze. Shuddered. Dropped to the ground.

Guardian didn't understand. What was it with the demons not wanting—or daring—to bite him?

Slamming his foot into the middle of its back, Guardian leaned down and cut off its head.

The demons gibbered in horror and attacked again.

So now he fought. And he sang.

He liked Broadway show tunes. When he was feeling ironic, he sang songs from Disney's *Beauty and the Beast* or *Phantom of the Opera*. But he favored *The Sound of Music*. The theme song and "Do-Re-Mi" made the demons cry in pain, and "How Do You Solve a Problem Like Maria" made them cower and cover their ears.

But he saved the best for last, when he knew he was tiring, to drive them away so he could escape. When he had worked out enough frustration and anger, he pulled in a long breath.

The demons froze. They knew what was coming.

He lifted his voice, sang the first few words: "Climb every mountain. . . ."

They retreated.

"Ford every stream," he sang louder, more powerfully. "Follow every rainbow, till you find your dream. . . ."

The demons whined. They sniveled.

Like a magic act, they disappeared back to the depths from whence they came.

Hands hanging at his sides, Guardian stood alone in the dark.

His spotlight was gone. Some of the braver demons had smashed it. Happened every time.

He winced as he cataloged his cuts and bruises. Turning, he trudged back toward the Guardian cave.

The Guardian cave . . . and Charisma.

Inevitably, his mind returned to the question that gnawed at him.

When he rejected Charisma, what *had* he been thinking?

Or rather—when had he started thinking like a girl?

Yeah, he got his feelings hurt when he touched her and she turned her head away. So what? When had his feelings become so delicate?

More to the point, when had his pride become more important than getting in Charisma's pants?

She was valiant, strong, stunning, funny, sexy, and he had wanted her from the first time he picked her up, carried her to the cave, and watched her fight to recover from the demon bite.

Sure, maybe the reason she was willing to hump his brains out was because she had some perverted male beast fantasy. At least she was freaking horny, so hot her skin sizzled against his. Last night had been the best sex he ever remembered.

Okay, it was the only sex he ever remembered. But he was pretty sure it wasn't the first time he'd had sex; it had been like riding a bike. He had the balance; he had the moves . . . he knew how to pop a wheelie.

He grinned. When he was a kid, he had flipped a lot of wheelies on his grandparents' gravel drive, but in those innocent days, he had never imagined . . .

He froze. He stared into the eternal night of the underground.

But . . .

He saw his bike, the best blue mountain bike ever made. He saw the nubby tread on the front tire, saw it start spinning as he pushed off. He leaned over the handlebars. Heard the spit of gravel behind him. Felt the wind in his hair as he picked up speed. Saw the flash of green and brown as the forest whipped by on either side. He broke out into the valley. The grapevines. The garden. The milling crowd of people.

Independence Day. Fourth of July. The annual picnic.

Right in front of the house—right in front of it—he shifted back on the seat, pulled on the handlebars. The front tire lifted smoothly, and he rode past his parents, his grandparents, the whole crowd, thirty feet down the road and into the grapevines. Then he smoothly lowered the tire and lay low, because when his mother and grandmother got ahold of him, they were going to shriek.

But while they were scolding, he knew his father and grandfather and uncles would be giving him the secret thumbs-up. And his cousins would never top this. When he thought about how—

He heard the sound of soft feet pattering behind him.

The stench of rotting garbage wafted to his nose.

He was cloaked in darkness, below New York. And something hit him from behind. It knocked him onto his knees.

Bruises on bruises, and all for one lousy leftover demon.

Getting painfully to his feet, Guardian plucked the little rodent off his neck, dangled it in the air, and then dropped it down a shaft that went to China.

It shrieked all the way down.

Then he sought in his mind for that moment on his bike on the road on Independence Day in front of his family. . . .

His family . . .

Somewhere he had a family. A human family. Family who cared enough to grab a boy and lecture him on the dangers of popping wheelies. He saw his mother and grandmother shaking their fingers at him, while in the background Grandpa gave him a thumbs-up.

The vision had vanished. But the faces remained.

He remembered no facts, only a moment in time.

But it told him so much—and *he had remembered.*

He remembered his family, and he wanted to remember more. To explore his mind, to find the ragged remnants of sanity and recollection and weave them together into a whole life. His whole life.

But right now, no matter how much he struggled, he was here. Underground. In the dark and the still heat, and his mind would not cooperate.

So he would move on to his next priority. He had to go square things with Charisma.

If he handled this right, he could be popping wheelies with her all night long.

# *Chapter 23*

———✦———

Guardian stood by the table in the middle of the cave and stared, and listened.

The stone walls stretched four stories into the air. The rock ceiling was lost in the dark, but closer to the ground, the stone lights glowed with soft phosphorescence. No movement, no human voice disturbed the quiet. Even the stream seemed to babble more quietly.

Was Charisma gone?

Probably. He had been a real piece of shit last night. A big, dumb, male POS.

It didn't seem fair. Say one or two stupid things about not wanting to have sex with a woman who was just using his body for thrills, and she took him seriously.

Now he was never going to get laid again . . . and it was more than that. He'd grown accustomed to her face. He liked coming in and knowing he was going to get to talk to someone who didn't believe he was a mythical Guardian. Or maybe she did believe it, but she was some kind of Chosen Ones legend, too, so it was like Mr. Incredible and Elastigirl at home after fighting all the battles.

If she were still here, this evening he might have suggested they cuddle in his extended-length, extrawide recliner and watch *The Incredibles.* They'd share a little popcorn, a few kisses, and all the while they'd be thinking about the moment when they went upstairs and . . . and . . .

A meal had been set out for him: a chipped white bowl with blue stripes, a bent spoon, a glass of milk, a black-spotted banana that looked as if it had come out of a Dumpster, and a piece of bread sitting on a paper towel spread with a thick, dark spread that he hoped was peanut butter.

He sat down.

The banana smelled; it was incredibly overripe. And he kept catching a funky, yeasty scent, too. Probably the bread was moldy.

Apparently Amber had wandered off, possibly to take Charisma back up to the surface, and Moises had taken over his care. Guardian knew from hard experience that Moises was never too fussy about using the right utensil for the meal, or about the meal itself.

But fighting made Guardian ravenous, and if Osgood won his battle, the food down here would get worse. A lot worse.

Above the bowl sat a book, a large, thick, leatherbound tome. Its pages were yellowed and it smelled like dust, and the title, in gold on the cover, proclaimed, *When the World Was Young: A History of the Chosen Ones.* Pulling it toward him, he opened it.

From behind him, Charisma said, "You asked about the Chosen Ones."

He jumped. He hadn't heard her walking up behind him—and no one sneaked up on him.

Except Charisma. When she wanted, she could move as silently as a ghost.

"I found that on your bookshelves. *When the World Was Young* is our textbook." Walking around the table, she sat opposite him. Looking worn and serious, she said, "I thought you didn't believe me about the Chosen Ones, so this might convince you."

"I believe you!" He tried to inject sincerity into every word. "Why wouldn't I?"

She looked directly at him, and her eyes burned like liquid emeralds. "You don't believe that I don't care about your appearance. Surely you're inclined to doubt me about the Chosen Ones. It *is* a ridiculous story."

He needed to remember what he wanted. He wanted to keep her here, to enjoy her body and let her enjoy his, and never mind all his tender, hurt feelings. "I've been thinking. It doesn't matter whether we tell the truth to each other. It doesn't matter whether we believe each other. We can enjoy each other's bodies—"

"Without trust." Swiftly, unexpectedly, she slapped one hand flat on the table, leaned toward him, and smacked him hard across the side of his head. "That's for what you said last night." She did it again. "And that's for what you said just now."

He rubbed his ringing ear.

Apparently Charisma did not like being called a . . . a liar.

"That's just my opinion," he said.

Her eyes narrowed dangerously. "Opinions are like assholes. Everybody's got one."

She just called him an asshole.

He started to feel like he needed backup in this battle of wits. He wished he could confer with the men in his family. He didn't remember them, exactly. He didn't remember their names, or what their voices sounded like. He didn't even know whether they were still alive.

But he knew they lived in his memory. He had seen them. And that was something.

Charisma settled back in her chair, and she didn't look as if smacking him had improved her temper. "You are going to listen to me. *You* misunderstood *me*. *You* did *me* an injustice. So you might as well stop acting like you've got a stick up your butt."

He straightened, all ruffled dignity and indignation.

"That stick looks like it got jabbed up a little higher," she said.

She didn't give a crap about his dignity.

He needed to remember that he didn't give a crap about his dignity, either. He needed to remember he was here for the sex.

Picking up the toast, he took a bite.

That spread on top was *not* peanut butter. That was the yeasty smell. It also tasted salty and vile. He should have remembered—Moises was Australian.

It was Vegemite.

If Guardian had been alone, he would have spit it out. But the dignity he didn't care about made him chew slowly, painfully, and swallow.

He couldn't swallow enough. The taste was still in his mouth.

Charisma continued. "Last night, when you touched

me and I turned my head away, I did it not because you repulse me, but because I was talking about my mother. Maybe I'm a little oversensitive, but I don't like being pitied, and you were feeling sorry for me right then."

"No, I—"

She gave him a *don't bullshit me* look.

He shut up. And took a drink of milk.

It was curdled.

"It's not all about you," Charisma said. "It's not always about the way you look. I mean, talk about oversensitive. Last night I think I successfully proved your touch does not repulse me."

He grunted a nonword, and swallowed at least seven times. If there was anything that could make the Vegemite taste good, relatively speaking, it was spoiled milk.

"I'm not saying you don't have challenges when it comes to your appearance, but everything in the world does not boil down to whether or not you've got a few extra hairs."

He fake-smiled.

"So we can pretend last night didn't happen, if that's what you want." In a very sensible voice, she said, "It would be the smart thing to do."

He forgot the disgusting tastes in his mouth.

Pretending last night didn't happen was *not* what he wanted. "I can't forget!"

"We're fighting a war with Osgood and his demons, a war we're losing. A war that takes every second of our time." She looked down at her hands, flat on the table, and asked softly, "Do we really want to take time away from our battles to fall in love?"

*Yes!* "I hardly think last night was love."

She looked up at him, challenging him. "If you're practicing slap-downs, that one gives you first prize."

Had he ever in his life been so bewildered?

Maybe. In that other life with those other people.

But mostly he thought he didn't understand women, and he most definitely didn't understand Charisma. "I wasn't trying to slap you down. I was stating an obvious fact."

"That I'm vulnerable where you are not? That I've invested more thought and emotions into our relationship than you have?"

"No." He'd spent the day trying to convince himself he was happy to have meaningless sex with her. Did that make him thoughtless and emotionless?

Maybe. Possibly.

Probably.

"I actually thought I could fall in love with you." Her voice broke.

That was pushing it a little too far, and suddenly he forgot today's resolve and found himself stumbling into all of last night's bitter emotions. "In love with me? Really?" His voice rose. "If things were different, if we weren't fighting a war, if I could walk the streets of New York City without being chased and trapped like an animal, would *you* walk with me? Could you bear to see people point and stare? Yes, all cats look gray in the dark, and down here it gets really dark. But I don't want an underground lover who'll leave me as soon as the sun shines. I want one who's with me forever." When he finished, he glared indignantly, then realized— he had blown it again.

He wasn't a good liar, and he was never again going to get a chance to be her lover.

# Chapter 24

————❧————

Charisma sat back in her seat and considered Guardian, and tried to understand him.

An impossible task. He was *such* a guy.

He apparently wanted to have sex with her.

*Duh.*

He also wanted her to like the way he looked.

She did.

But he didn't believe her when she said she did, and he expected her not to mind that he called her a hypocrite, something she had never been called in her whole life. Quite the opposite. Isabelle and Genny were always on her to soften the way she expressed her opinions.

Perhaps she had misunderstood him as badly as he'd misunderstood her. Perhaps he was racing neck and neck with her, caught by surprise by the empathy and affection between them.

Who was going to be the mature one and take the

chance that this relationship could build into something . . . magnificent?

But they didn't have a lot of time. The world as they knew it would end in a few weeks. So if they didn't talk now, they would never talk.

But the whole idea of putting herself out like this made her sick to her stomach. She *hated* being the mature one.

She took a breath.

She folded her hands on the table.

She looked at him, or at least past his left ear. "My last boyfriend was one of the handsomest men I've ever met. Tall. Dark hair. Blue eyes. Irish and charming as hell. Ronnie seemed like my perfect mate. He liked the music I like. He liked to eat adventurously. He worked at a soup kitchen feeding the poor. He even liked to go shoe shopping. Perfect. He was perfect. Gorgeous. Perfect."

Guardian apparently wasn't completely dim-witted. "What was wrong with him?"

"Did I mention the guy was great in bed? Great in bed. Perfect. He could get me in the sack just as quickly as you did." With a liberal touch of enmity, she added, "And I didn't even have to beg him."

Guardian winced.

"Apparently I'm easy."

Guardian winced again.

*Good.* He deserved a little discomfort. "Ronnie was so perfect, it was almost like he had inside information about my likes and dislikes."

"Who would have told him—"

"But I didn't figure out someone had sold me down the river. No, I was in love. I mean totally, completely, shit-faced in love." Even now, twenty months later,

Charisma burned with humiliation. "If Samuel, who treats me like the village idiot, had met him, he would have used his mind control on the guy and Ronnie would have blurted out the truth. So Ronnie stayed away from my pals. Which should have tipped me off." She repeated, "Shit-faced in love."

"What was the truth?"

"He was one of the Others." When Guardian looked confused, she pushed *When the World Was Young* toward him and tapped the cover. "The Others are the bad guys, people with paranormal gifts who oppose the Chosen Ones. Ronnie's gift *was* seduction. He was like a snake, a smooth-skinned, sleek, and beautiful boa constrictor who hypnotized me so well I never even saw the coils as they slipped around my throat."

"The Others have someone on their team to seduce women?" Picking up the black-speckled banana, Guardian peeled it. "You know, my high school guidance counselor never suggested that as a job possibility." When he heard what he had said, he looked surprised, as if the words had popped out without his volition.

"Did your high school guidance counselor suggest *Guardian* as a job possibility?"

"Probably not. I don't remember. I don't remember my guidance counselor or high school, but that sounded so natural." He used the spoon to scoop out most of the brown spots, and frowned. "I wonder which high school I went to. Hairy High?"

She hadn't thought she could laugh right now. But she did, a little too long and with a slight edge of hysteria.

He reached across and patted her hand. "Want some banana?" He offered her the poor, battered fruit.

"Thanks. One was enough." She put her hand on her

stomach. "And that Vegemite is awful. I can't believe you ate it. I spit mine out."

He glared as if he had a bad taste in his mouth, which made her laugh again. Then, on a caught breath, she said, "The Others recruited Ronnie to seduce me—and kill me."

"Kill you?" Guardian put down his banana and pushed it aside. "I would have thought he wanted to pry information out of you. Or money. Or something."

Her throat closed. So she shook her head.

This was harder than she expected.

"Then why seduce you first? Why not hire an assassin?" Guardian sounded indignant. "What's wrong with the world? Doesn't anybody do anything the easy way anymore?"

She almost laughed again. Then she almost cried.

He pulled the paper towel out from underneath his bread and handed it to her. "Here. Although I hope you appreciate the sacrifice, because if I ate the paper towel, it would taste better than the Vegemite."

She nodded and blew her nose. "I haven't ever cried over Ronnie. I have ranted, raved, sworn, glared, sunk into a depression about the fact that I'm the only one of the Chosen Ones who has never found true love. But I never cried. And here I am, all emotional."

"Realizing that you're of no value to a person who is dear to you is a hard thing."

"It's worse than that." Embarrassing and painful. "I really loved him. I really thought that he was the one who could restore my powers."

"I . . . What?"

Now she was on familiar ground. She loved studying *When the World Was Young*. She loved being part of a legend and watching it evolve. She loved explaining how the rules worked. "First, there're supposed to be seven Chosen. Always. Since the world was young. So I'm part of the current batch, and we were chosen—picked—but with reservations. Our powers were much diminished from previous generations." She looked down at her bracelet, at the stones that were so stubbornly silent, and rolled them around her wrist. "It wasn't our fault. The system is flawed. The Chosen Ones spend seven years kicking bad-guy booty, for which we get paid nothing; nor do we bring in money. It's all gratis, as it should be."

With fine irony, he said, "Yes, I've noticed myself that superhero work doesn't pay as well as it used to."

"So, more than a century ago, the Gypsy Travel Agency was formed to raise money to support the Chosen Ones as they performed their duties. The trouble is, the Gypsy Travel Agency was run as a corporation, and as we all know, corporations are corrupt."

He put on a surprised face. "I'm stunned."

"They can get away with funny financing if they're not connected to an ancient struggle between good and evil. And they did. But eternal laws are not meant to be broken. When they are, someone has to pay. Since the Chosen Ones are on the side of honor and integrity, and we were supported by corruption, as punishment, we were losing our powers."

"As usual, the people on the front line paid for the screwups at the top."

"Yes. And it sucks. It really does. But there was a way to fix the inequity." She leaned forward, eyes gleaming. "We Chosen found that whenever one of us bonded with our one true love, we would get our powers restored."

His gaze fell to her fingers as they tweaked her silent stones. Yeah, between her nervous habit and the story of Ronnie, Guardian was smart enough to figure out that she hadn't managed to find the guy.

She put her hands in her lap. "True love worked really well for the first five. Jacqueline found Caleb, Aaron found Rosamund, John found Genny, and Samuel and Isabelle found each other." She smiled at the memory of that tumultuous courtship. "It's like connecting with their mate plugs them into a power source, and they're all *amazing*. They really are superheroes."

"But?"

"But we lost Aleksandr Wilder."

"Aleksandr Wilder?" Guardian said the name slowly, as if he were testing it out. "Is he dead?"

"No. Or at least, he was alive last time we saw him." Without realizing what she was doing, she rubbed her closed fist over her chest, over her heart. "We lost him, not to death or terror, but to a woman."

Guardian stared at her, his blue eyes wide and unblinking.

She smiled, soft and sad. "I've never forgotten my last glimpse of Aleksandr, young, smart, laughing, in love. . . ."

"Aleksandr Wilder," Guardian repeated again, his gaze out of focus, his fists clenched on the table. Then he snapped to the present and stood. "I've got to wash my hands. They smell like rotting banana."

Charisma gaped, surprised by his abrupt change.

Either he was bored by her reminiscing, or he was jealous of Aleksandr, or . . . his hands smelled like rotting banana and he wanted to wash them.

Because without another word, he turned his back and walked away.

# Chapter 25

———— ❈ ————

Charisma found Guardian washing in the waterfall. Showering, actually. He turned his head to look at her—obviously he would not allow her to sneak up on him again—and then returned to soaping himself thoroughly.

She approved. Not only had he smelled like blood and demon guts and sweat and fighting, but now she got to see him naked.

Charisma was not one to deny herself the creature comforts. So to speak.

She dragged a chair—a new chair that replaced one of the ones Guardian had smashed—close to the stream. "Getting those hands clean?" she asked.

"Peeking?" he retorted.

*Don't be snotty with me, mister.* "I don't have to peek. I've seen it, and I've felt it. This is more like after-season reruns."

The trouble with her snark, of course, was that

she saw him grin before he disappeared under the water.

He thought she was amusing. Was there any greater flattery? The man was too charming for his own good.

When he came out, he had a bottle of shampoo and he proceeded to use it vigorously ... all ... over ... his ... body.

Charming. And a tease.

"About Aleksandr Wilder ... it sounds as if you were a little in love with him, too." He sounded stuffed up, as if he had water up his nose.

*Good.* He *was* jealous. "No. Aleksandr and I were good friends. Of all the Chosen, we're the ones who are about the same age. Plus we had a lot of interests in common. In college, I majored in earth sciences. He majored in engineering and mathematics. He tutored calculus in the summer."

"You were geeks."

"A very rude, blunt person might say that," she said primly; then she grinned. "Thank God for Aleksandr, because he's done some ... I mean, he did some fabulous computer stuff for the Chosen Ones. Hacked information for us, built software, did research. Brilliant guy."

"What was his gift?"

"He didn't have one." She laughed at the expression on Guardian's face. "Remember I said the Chosen Ones' gifts were fading? The board of directors had trouble finding seven Chosen Ones to fill the quota, so they drafted Aleksandr."

"If he didn't have a gift, what was the point?"

"It was his background. He's a Wilder, a family famous among the folks who fight this battle."

"What did they do?" Again that stuffy, stifled voice.

"Old Konstantine Wilder is from the Ukraine, from the oldest and most famous crime family ever. The way he tells it, a thousand years ago, the original Konstantine Varinski made a deal with the devil. In return for giving him and all his descendants the ability to transform into beasts of prey, he promised that they would serve the devil in all his guises. To seal the deal, he killed his own mother—"

"Nice guy."

"—and sacrificed his soul and the souls of his descendants. The current Konstantine and his wife, Zorana, immigrated to the US, changed their name to Wilder, had four kids, and twenty-five years ago they broke the devil's pact."

"Not an easy deal, I don't imagine." Guardian stepped out and grabbed a towel off the rock shelf, and he seemed not at all concerned about covering up.

In fact, Charisma would have said he was flaunting himself.

She gave him full flaunting points.

Guardian said, "If Aleksandr Wilder had no gift, I still don't see why he was drafted as one of the Chosen Ones."

It took Charisma a moment to gather her thoughts, ignore the beast that stood naked before her, and get back to the conversation. "When he was only three, Aleksandr performed a very important task in the breaking of the pact. He went through fire while sheltered in his mother's arms. He was a whiz kid without ever having done anything that he could remember."

"So he can walk through fire? I'd say that's a pretty cool gift."

"Well, no, not exactly. His mother is the fire walker, and it could be that her gift protected him."

"Did he ever try to work the fire thing?" Guardian tossed the towel over his head and started drying from the top down.

"When he was a kid, he was showing off for his cousins and picked up a burning brand. That didn't go well. On his right hand, his fingers were fused. But the gifts of the Chosen Ones were fading, and he had connections, so he got picked for the team."

"He skipped out when the going got tough." Guardian's tone was critical.

"No. Well, sort of." Her voice softened with affection. "He was so much in love. I only saw the girl the one time. Beautiful. Blond hair. He met her on the steps of the courthouse . . . and they disappeared."

"Never to return?"

She soberly shook her head. "Ever since, I have searched for them both, but not even my stones have given me an inkling of where they are or whether they're alive."

Guardian pulled on one of his djellabas.

"None of Aleksandr's replacements lasted. Ella Owoso. Stewart Mickelson. Carl Badden. Lily Carter. Good people, all of them, gifted in magical ways. But unseasoned, unprepared for the fight. We trained them, but nothing we could do could prepare them enough. The battle just keeps getting more savage, and none of them lasted more than a year. Carl made it only two weeks." Charisma couldn't even mourn them; she had known each so briefly, she couldn't truly recall their faces. "After losing so many, we gave up. We couldn't bear the heartache of losing those good people. The thing we're all afraid is that . . . we need seven Chosen Ones. We *require* seven Chosen Ones to defeat Osgood. Since we've had such bad luck with replacements, we suspect that Aleksandr Wilder is *the* seventh Chosen One. The right one. The only one who can do whatever needs to be done with whatever powers he has or doesn't have."

Guardian put his hands on his hips and stood over her. "So what about this Ronnie?" he asked quietly.

"I'm the weak link of the Chosen Ones. I haven't found my true love; I don't have enhanced powers; I'm pretty much just a street fighter who survives on my wits and my knowledge of where evil's going to pop up next. So unfortunately, I was primed for seduction. I met Ronnie, who was rescuing a nun from a gang of murderous thugs—"

Guardian snorted.

"Exactly. I fell for a cliché. And I didn't question his motives or his background or his knowledge of my likes and dislikes, because I really, really wanted to find my true love, get enhanced powers, and stop being a drag on the Chosen Ones."

"I can't believe you were ever a drag on anyone."

*Oh, God.* How pathetic was she? Guardian was being *kind.* "I do my best, but compared to the others . . ."

She was so glad Samuel couldn't see her now. He would rub his eyes and pretend to cry like a little girl, and Isabelle would have to tell him to stop.

Or worse, he would be embarrassed for her and avert his gaze.

"This Ronnie tried to kill you?"

"He tried."

"What happened?"

She looked up into Guardian's eyes. "I killed him."

# Chapter 26

————◆————

*Aleksandr Wilder.*

*Jacqueline and Caleb. Aaron and Rosamund. John and Genny. Samuel and Isabelle.*

*Konstantine Wilder.*

*Aleksandr Wilder.*

The names buzzed in Guardian's brain, stinging him, demanding that he recognize them. And he wanted to; he really did.

But how could he concentrate on the elusive shadows of his past when right now Charisma was here, and she was breaking his heart with her tale?

Ronnie deserved to die. But Charisma should never have had to do it. This affair should never have happened. If Guardian had been there . . .

But how could he have been? It was about twenty months ago when Guardian had first made his appearance in the tunnels. About twenty months ago that any of his memories began. Half-crazed as he was, he would have been no good to her then. But still, the conviction pounded at his mind.

If he had been there, Ronnie would have never happened.

But while Guardian was not there for her then, he was now.

He heard the tremor in her voice when she said, "When the affair was finished, as I stared at his body lying dead on the floor, the thing I hated most was that I had to tell the Chosen Ones. I mean, I had to. I was pretty battered; plus I was covered in blood; plus I was . . . bitter. I was in such bad shape, not even Samuel gave me a bad time." Her beautiful, plush, rounded lips quirked and quivered. "Although for once I had given him good reason."

"I don't like this Samuel who always gives you a bad time."

She dismissed Guardian's hostility with a wave of the hand. "He's like a brother to me. We butt heads. We make up. We fight. We make up."

"I don't know why this man would fight with you."

"I don't know why *you* would fight with me, but you did."

The two of them stared at each other, neither lowering their eyes.

She was probably right, and he wasn't going to win this one, so he inclined his head. "So we are back to the question, Why seduction and not murder?"

"Exactly. Why go to the trouble to seduce me first? Samuel shows a remarkable affinity for knowing how Osgood's mind works—"

"You trust Samuel?"

"With my life. But you have to realize—he's a lawyer." She grinned, a lopsided grin that made fun of Samuel, lawyers, and herself. "Samuel has seen evil. He understands evil. He knows the way evil thinks. He says Osgood has almost unlimited power, and that's boring."

"So Osgood uses the Chosen Ones for entertainment."

"Yes. And he couldn't lose with me. If I was killed, the Chosen Ones were down to five, the struggle would be more hopeless, and . . . my friends would know I had deceived them. That I had a secret affair when I should have known better. I would have besmirched the memory of Charisma Fangorn by my own stupidity and shame. If I wasn't killed . . . I had wasted time and energy proving to myself that true love was a chimera." She took a painful breath. "And, of course, I had to tell the Chosen Ones about the whole foolish affair."

"Have they reproached you?"

"Worse. They were kind." Crimson burned along the top of her cheekbones.

"*Did* this Ronnie convince you that true love was a chimera?" Guardian waited a little too anxiously for her reply.

She chuckled a little. "No. That's not possible. When I am with the Chosen Ones, I see true love at work every day. In my friends. I see the miracles their love creates, and I believe. In the end, he was an illusion, a hope unfulfilled—and a failure."

But she hadn't started this conversation to tell Guardian about a murderous affair, only to dismiss the results so cavalierly. Something was off, and it niggled at him. Something she'd said earlier . . . "Who sold Ronnie the information to use against you? Who told him your likes and dislikes? Who betrayed you to him?"

She looked down and away. "You already know the answer."

Guardian knelt before her. He took her hands. "Your *mother* did this to you?"

"I told you. I was only ever an opportunity to her." Charisma set her chin. "Ronnie offered her money."

"And she took it." He chafed Charisma's cold fingers. "What did you *do* to her?"

"Nothing. I found her in a hotel in Times Square, where she was thoroughly enjoying her ill-gotten gains. I showed her the bruises on my throat where he had tried to strangle me, the stab wounds I received during the fight. I thought if she actually saw the damage she'd helped inflict on me, she would finally get it." Charisma looked at him and rolled her eyes, as if amused at her own eternal optimism. "Mom pointed out that I wasn't supporting her anymore, and as far as she was concerned, I should have been. Because she saved me from the trash bin. So in her opinion, selling me out was acceptable behavior. And payback for turning her in to social services, for my going to school, going to college, and leaving her behind."

"Isn't that what children are supposed to do?"

"One would think. Ronnie hurt me. He did. In all ways. But I cherished this secret hope—I didn't even realize I held it—that at the proper moment, my mother would step up to the plate for me. Love me, support me, care for me, fight for me. Instead, she sold me. It took her a lot of years, but she killed my faith in love. Or at least, my faith that I was lovable. Once I lost that . . . the earth doesn't sing to me anymore." Charisma smiled, tried to joke. "It barely hums."

"That breaks your heart."

"Since the day I went through puberty, the earth was always there, helping me, warning me of danger. To have lost that support—it's like losing my mother all over again. Worse. She never . . ." Charisma shook her head. "You know."

"If you're trying to convince me there are worse things than fur on my back, you've done it." He was quite serious.

"That's progress, I guess. And I do have a point for telling you this whole pathetic story, and it has to do with you and me. You don't believe me when I say I don't care what you look like." She looked into his eyes and said, "I don't care what you look like."

"You care what *I* am like."

"Give the man a gold star."

He deserved a gold star. She deserved a gold star. They both deserved a lovely meal with delicate china, glowing candlelight, fine food, and excellent wines. But in lieu of that . . . "I've got beef jerky and some crackers stashed in Tupperware under the bed."

Her eyes got wide and round. "I'm starving."

"Me, too." Still holding her hands, he stood. He pulled her into his arms. He held her. Just held her. "It's not that you're not lovable. It's that there's something seriously wrong with your mother. I'm about halfway in love with you myself right now."

She stood stiffly for a moment, then hugged him and buried her head in his chest. He had to bend to hear her say, "Tell me sweet lies and feed me beef jerky, and I'm happy."

"They're not lies." He tilted her face up to his. "Shall I prove it to you?"

She nibbled on her lower lip to subdue her smile. "How ever will you do that?"

# *Chapter 27*

———◆———

L inda Gómez had always considered herself lucky. She was very pretty, which made men admire her, and she was very smart, which meant that if she wanted something from a man, all she had to do was smile at him, flatter him, behave as if he were handsome and young and clever. It worked every time, and she'd built a good life for herself with the proceeds.

Her first two husbands had paid for her education as an investment banker, and she'd received enough in the divorces to keep herself in the style she preferred.

The third husband had been a mistake; when he disappeared, he cleaned out her bank account and broke her heart. But like a miracle, this job had come along. . . .

She'd worked for Osgood for three years now, and all she could say was, he was amazing. The man understood money and power and how to accumulate both. It was a pleasure to watch him operate, and the first time she realized he would do anything to get his way, she had felt a kinship—and at the same time a little shiver of fear, because . . . he really would do anything to get his way.

He made her uneasy, with his pale skin and slight body, and those unreadable hazel eyes that seemed to change color: brown to green to the most frightening blue glow, although she told herself the blue glow was an illusion of the light. She was determined to believe that.

She thought sometimes that he would want to sleep with her, and she thought she would do it. But when he put his hands on her shoulders, or touched her hand to emphasize his point, she froze in fear.

His flesh felt old, soft, flaccid, cool . . . terrifying, as if only the thickness of his skin protected the world from the accretion of cruelty and evil.

Osgood knew he frightened her. He knew she recoiled when near him. And he didn't seem to care, except . . . she thought he smiled inside, and bided his time.

Now she sat in the sunshine, outside on a park bench, and ate her lunch with Burke Brennan, one of the researchers in the ancient sciences division. He was droning on, as he usually did, about his latest discovery and how cool it was that he worked for Osgood, the only wealthy person in the world who understood the necessity of preserving the world's treasures before they were lost forever—

"Yes," she blurted, "but don't you ever wonder if we're stuck?" As soon as the words were out, she wanted to clap her hands over her mouth.

She hadn't even realized she'd been thinking that, and now she'd said it. Out here. In the open. Where anyone could hear. She looked around fearfully to see whether anyone had heard her, and then up at Osgood's office building, looming against the horizon.

"What?" Burke looked confused and annoyed that she'd interrupted him.

No one had heard her except Burke. And he was a good guy, a lowly guy, not at all in the confidence of the upper levels of the organization.

Good thing. Not that Osgood would care what she said, but . . . he was a man who valued loyalty, and took any attempt to defect to a different organization coldly.

"Linda? What are you talking about?"

She ate a couple of bites of her Asian chicken salad and tried to figure out the best way to explain so Burke, not the most sensitive of guys, would understand. "I mean, it seems as if I never leave Osgood's shadow." She shouldn't be saying this. She really shouldn't be saying this. She knew better. But once she got started, it was as if the dam had broken and the words had to tumble out. "I live in an apartment Osgood owns."

"Me, too, but it's so close, and he gives me such a good deal, it's no hardship."

"Exactly. To live anywhere else would be foolish. I eat in his restaurants."

"The food is good, the service is excellent, and the prices are reasonable."

"Yes. I buy my groceries at his grocery store."

"Is Buster's owned by Osgood? I didn't know that. Great store, though."

"Great store." She supposed she was being foolish.

Clearly Burke thought she was foolish.

She played with her fork. "And Osgood bought all the land around his building, and tore down a bunch of historical sites to make this park." She gestured around at the trees and the lawn, the picnic benches and the fire pits.

"It's for us. For his workers." Burke seemed to think she didn't realize what a great guy Osgood was. "So we would have someplace to come to relax. All of us work hard for Osgood, and it's good of him to care."

"Yes." She stared at what was now the tallest building in New York City, and she wanted to vomit. Osgood Headquarters was plain stark stone, almost obscenely, sickly white, without windows on the bottom floors, and only a few on the floors above. From this distance, when she stared at it, it looked like a prison tower that captured workers and held them within. While the other tall buildings in New York were frequently covered in clouds, the prison never was. It rose into a patch of clear blue sky . . . but above it, the sky was deeper, darker blue, as if the building stole pieces of heaven to create a more impressive backdrop for its pale stone.

In appearance, it seemed to be an insolent gesture to the cold, far heavens.

As Linda watched, she noted masses of small, hunched, bug-eyed creatures that clung to the side of the building and stared out at the city. They circled the building at about the fortieth floor, and she laughed when she saw them. "I didn't know we had gargoyles on the building."

"What?" Burke followed her pointing finger. "Oh, yeah. Not the cute Disney ones, either, but real gargoyles, all bug eyes and lolling tongues. Grotesque. I'll bet they're patterned after Notre Dame or Saint-Étienne de Meaux."

"Those are cathedrals, right?" Linda used to be a practicing Catholic. "I should go to France and tour the cathedrals."

"Good idea. I was going to say that maybe you should take a vacation."

She could light candles and say a prayer for her own soul.

"I was going to suggest that you take a few mental health days, visit one of Osgood's resorts. . . ."

She whipped her head around and glared.

He was an idiot, incapable of foresight or imagination.

"I seem to remember that churches offer sanctuary from evil." She wanted someplace safe to flee. Not that she needed to flee. Not that Osgood would pursue her if she did. She simply had this feeling that someone was watching her all the time.

"Yes, for all the good that ever did the poor pilgrims."

"What?"

"Churches might offer sanctuary from evil in its spiritual form, but they're no match for real people with evil intentions. Do you know how many people were slaughtered in churches by the Vikings? They weren't Christians; they didn't know the rules, or care either." Burke was just getting warmed up. "Then we have Henry the Second's knights, who pursued Thomas Becket into Canterbury Cathedral to kill him most gruesomely. They cut off the top of his head and scattered his brains all over the floor."

Linda stared at the ground chicken on her lettuce leaves and felt light-headed.

"And let's not forget what happened to the nuns

who were raped and slaughtered in . . ." Burke's voice trailed off. "Wow, look at that. That is a really cool animation."

"What?" She glanced at Osgood Headquarters, then at Burke. Then she whipped her head around to stare hard at the building.

The gargoyles were climbing the sheer stone face of the rock, straight up toward the top. They scuttled like cockroaches, their long arms reaching ahead, their hands attaching to the stone as if they had suction cups for fingers.

"It's like the Haunted Mansion," Burke said, "all scary-cool illusion. I am *im*pressed."

The gargoyle who lingered behind turned to look over its shoulder, and Linda saw a swift, avid, bright blue gleam in its eyes. For one moment, those eyes fixed on Linda in malicious humor—and hunger. Then the creature looked toward the top of the building and climbed, ascending rapidly up the vertical wall, all the way up until the tiny figure vanished onto the roof and out of sight.

Numb with shock and horror, Linda dropped her fork.

It clattered onto the bench, then onto the concrete.

"Are you okay?" Burke looked at her in concern.

He was so stupid. Ridiculously, absurdly stupid, blindly determined to see what he wanted to see.

"An animation? Are you *crazy*?"

"Of course. What else would it be? I mean, gargoyles aren't *real*."

She stood. "I've got to get out. I've got to get out."

"Of where? You're not in anything."

She looked at the simpleminded fool. She couldn't

stand him. She couldn't stand this place. She couldn't go back to her office. She couldn't look at Osgood and pretend she didn't know who and what he was.

Turning her back to the building, she started to walk to the edge of the park.

"Where are you going?" Burke called.

To her apartment. To pack up her things.

The creepy sensation of being watched made her shiver. She glanced behind her, up toward the top of the building.

Again she thought she saw the blue gleam.

She broke into a run.

No, not her apartment. She could never go back there again. She had a credit card. And she could stop and get money. She could get away. Get out of New York. Out from under Osgood's influence.

She only hoped, for the sake of her eternal soul, that it wasn't too late.

# Chapter 28

❖

At the top of his building, Osgood greeted his favorite little demons. "You grow strong," he said. "The daylight doesn't hurt you."

"By your grace, master, we eat well." Ipos scurried toward Osgood, but stopped just out of reach.

Foolish Ipos feared Osgood would hurt him . . . as if Osgood needed to touch him to hurt him. "Have you frightened them, the homeless, the crazed, the people who roam the night?" As always, Osgood kept his voice soft and bland. "Are they whispering of the creatures who attack and leave nothing but a few bones?"

"They are frightened, master. They speak of the bones." Ipos's tongue lolled out of his mouth as he remembered the taste of soft flesh.

How easily the fool fell into Osgood's trap. Osgood lifted his hand, and with malevolent intent he squeezed his age-spotted hand into a fist.

Ipos gagged. He clawed at his throat. His tongue

stuck out straight as an arrow. His scarred, hideous, scaly face turned purple.

"Bones. You leave only bones." Osgood looked around at the crowd of demons. "And what did I tell you?" He pointed at Nergal.

Nergal clasped his long-fingered hands before his chest in supplication. "That we should leave blood and flesh that has been rent and torn."

"What else?" Osgood pointed at Raum.

"That we should leave faces, so all could see the terror and know fear."

"And do you do these things?" Osgood asked.

Ipos's huge frog eyes bulged as he died.

The other demons chattered, scattered across the roof, and cowered.

"Do you?" Osgood asked. He kept his voice quiet, but all of them recognized the danger that stalked them. With a gesture, he could clear the roof. With another gesture, he could bring up their replacements from hell.

Nergal prostrated himself on the ground. "We do now. We will do as you tell us in every matter."

"Very good." Osgood compelled each demon to meet his gaze.

Each shivered and moaned.

"Then you all may live," he told them.

"Thank you, master." The chorus of squeaky little voices grated on his nerves.

Yet he quite enjoyed unlimited power.

*With my permission.* The voice spoke in Osgood's head. It was that other being entwined with his soul, the Evil One, the Dark Prince, the devil himself. Osgood had proved himself worthy of their union; now they were one.

But Lucifer liked Osgood to know who allowed him to hold the power.

Osgood could scarcely forget.

He dropped Ipos's already decaying body. "Nergal, you're the leader of my guard."

"Thank you, master." Nergal crawled over and tried to kiss Osgood's brown leather oxfords.

"Get rid of that thing," Osgood ordered.

Nergal looked at Ipos, then up at Osgood. "I do not eat in front of the master."

With ill-concealed irritation, Osgood said, "Drop him off the edge."

"Yes. I knew that." Nergal hoisted Ipos onto his broad shoulders, took him to the balustrade, and hoisted him over.

The other demons ran, chattering, to watch.

Osgood knew what they saw: the falling body turning to sparks and flames, and disintegrating into oblivion.

No matter. He could always make more demons. Lost souls he owned in plenty.

He called his demons back. "How are my dear little Chosen Ones doing?"

"The Chosen Ones have run away. Five of them. Left the country." Nergal snorted moistly. "As if they will escape us."

Osgood wasn't so stupid as to imagine the Chosen Ones had fled.

They were up to something.

"Where have they gone?" he asked.

"They went to the airport. Pardon, master. I can't read. I couldn't go in. . . ." Whining. Nergal was whining.

"What did they say to one another?"

"They watch for us. We can't get into Irving's mansion. It's protected." More whining.

Osgood had never liked Nergal. "I like to be kept abreast of their movements. It entertains me. Perhaps you can recruit a human to do your bidding."

"Recruit?" Nergal nervously rubbed his spatulate fingers together.

With formidable patience, Osgood said, "Explain to the human that if the human does what you tell it to do, you won't eat it . . . yet."

Nergal's eyes lit up. "But I like to eat humans."

Osgood leaned down.

Nergal scrambled back.

"I chose you to be the head of my troops for a reason," Osgood said. "Because you're smarter than the others."

"I am. I am."

"Don't make me throw you off the building, too."

"No, master, no. We'll recruit a human. We will."

Raum tugged at Nergal's long earlobe. "Can't we use the human we already have?"

Nergal snapped at Raum, his sharp teeth removing the end of Raum's finger.

Raum attacked, and the two demons rolled across the roof, kicking and squealing, until Osgood picked them both up by the napes of their necks.

At once, they went limp.

He shook them. "You already have a human who spies for you?"

"Yes, master," Raum said.

With a flick of his wrist, Osgood flung Nergal over the edge of the building. "Very good, Raum. You are leader now."

A sly gleam lit Raum's eye. "Thank you, master. You have made a good choice."

Osgood thought perhaps he had. He dropped Raum back on the concrete floor. Pulling out his handkerchief, he wiped his fingers. "What about dear Charisma? Did she suffer before she died?" He felt a special grudge toward Charisma. She had managed to be so cheerful in the face of every adversity.

"She's still alive," Raum answered boldly, as if he were not afraid.

"Still alive." Osgood stroked his chin. "How is that possible? Must be the Chosen's natural immunity. How did dear Charisma escape you?"

Raum scuffled his feet. "I'm sorry, master. Must be the Chosen's natural immunity."

*Ah.* A demon who tried to be clever. "What"— Osgood smiled with cruel intensity—"does *natural immunity* mean?"

Raum made a humming noise as he tried to guess. "That she can fly?"

Osgood prepared to destroy him in some new and marvelous way.

"It doesn't matter, master." Raum spoke with absolute certainty. "All that has done is give dear Charisma another few days or weeks before death inevitably takes her away."

Osgood experienced a surge of affection for the little demon. He had such an optimistic outlook. "True. Let's drag out her torment a little longer."

He turned toward the door that led to the elevator going directly to his office.

Raum continued to speak so soothingly, for a very long moment Osgood didn't realize what he meant.

"Even though she is in her last days, she does not battle us. She lives with the Guardian. She loves the Guardian. And—"

Osgood swiveled on his heel. *"What?"*

"Dear Charisma lives with the Guardian in the Guardian cave. Just the two of them. Together. Our human recruit has seen to it that they spend time in . . . romance." Raum thumped his fists together. "He does not come out to do battle all the time. She stays within the cave. They . . . romance." He thumped his fists again.

"You stupid fool. Separate them. *Separate them!*" Osgood's voice rose to a shriek.

Two of the demons jumped off the roof.

Osgood surveyed the remaining crew. He wanted to kill them. Rend them limb from limb.

Only one prophecy stood in the way of his ultimate reign over the earth and all its minions, a horrible foretelling only he knew.

Three years ago, he had craftily obstructed its fulfillment, and again twenty months ago. Now his own creatures told him they had facilitated bringing that prophecy to reality.

Raum backed up toward the concrete balustrade. "Yes, master. The human recruit suggested this method to keep the Chosen One and Guardian out of the way as you complete the conquest of the world. The human recruit is stupid and lowly."

Osgood paced slowly toward him.

Raum spit on the ground beside him to demonstrate his contempt for the stupid human. "We, the demons, will attack the Guardian cave—"

In protest, the remaining demons hummed and squawked, then fell silent under Osgood's glare. He said, "You cannot attack the Guardian cave until the conquest is complete. It is . . . protected." And nothing he could do would change that until the Chosen Ones had lost the final battle.

In the tone of a creature eager to please and be spared the wrath of his master, Raum said, "Then I will instruct the human recruit to separate the Guardian and the Chosen One by whatever means possible. It will be done as you wish, master."

"See that it is." Osgood looked out over New York City. His city. His.

His far-reaching gaze lit on Linda. Linda Gómez. She was running away from his building, glancing over her shoulder as if she were in a panic. "What is wrong with my employee?" he asked.

Raum seemed to anticipate Osgood's question. "She saw us climbing the building."

"Did she?" Osgood was angry. He was displeased. He was . . . worried. "My children! You have done so much work today. Are you not hungry?"

Raum moaned softly and rubbed his strong, pudgy hands together. "Always hungry. Always hungry."

"You can have her. Take her. Eat her." Osgood looked around at the creatures that hopped and clapped at his feet. "And what instructions did I give you?"

The demons looked confused.

But Raum was crafty. Fire and pain honed his mind with malice. "Leave blood and flesh that has been rent and torn. Leave her face, so all can see the terror and know fear. We will do as you instruct, master. We will leave parts."

"Very good," Osgood said. "Make her suffer."

# *Chapter 29*

---

Charisma stopped halfway up the stairs, leaned her hand against the rock wall of the cavern, and took a breather.

This was *so annoying*. She was going up to take a nap, and on the way to the bedroom, she had to take a break.

She felt better. She was working on getting her stamina back: She ran laps around the gigantic cave, did push-ups, lifted weights. And yet, when the fatigue hit her, it was sudden. Her energy simply vanished, and she had to rest.

Worse, when the fatigue dragged at her, when her resistance was down, she couldn't fight the summons from the earth. It called her persistently, demanding she come down into the depths. . . .

She inhaled deeply.

She was not a seer, yet she knew that when she obeyed, when she followed the call and descended into the depths of the earth . . . there she would confront her innermost fears. Everything she was would be burned away, leaving nothing of the Charisma she was.

She shivered.

She was afraid.

Shaking her head to free herself from the faint, far call, she started back up the stairs.

She concentrated on the moment: on lifting her left foot, placing it on one of the high stone steps, then her right foot, placing it on the next step.

She was one of the Chosen. She was used to being healthy. Even when she was injured, she recovered quickly. Her drive was a point of pride to her . . . and yet here she was, seeing the world through a gray fog of weariness. The only cure was rest.

Or Guardian.

Even the thought of him lifted her spirits.

Possibly her affair with Guardian had contributed to her delayed recovery.

Every day he went out and fought demons. Every night he came home to her arms. In his big bed, they didn't spend a lot of time sleeping.

Before, when he had lived alone, he had indulged a virgin's curiosity about women and sex, and done extensive research on women's bodies and what pleased them. Prepping for the pop quiz, he told her, in the hopes that she would arrive to save him from his loneliness.

If today was to be the marathon of breathtaking sex the previous nights had been, she needed to rest.

At the top of the stairs, she walked the short corridor, turned the corner into the bedroom.

In the past three days she had been reveling in sensuality, in the constant knowledge that he worshiped her. And not just her body. They also talked.

Not as much as they had the first few days before they had sex, but—

*What was that?* Could it be . . . ?

On the bed. Shoes. Red patent. Black soles. Pointed toes. Stiletto heels.

She stopped breathing. She stared. She circled them. She looked at the box. She looked at the cloth shoe bags. She looked at the brand.

Lanvin. Designer. *Stunning*.

Her fatigue vanished. Awe and pleasure took its place.

With great deliberation, she reached out and smoothed her finger reverently across one shiny surface. "Ahhh." So rich it felt almost alive.

She slid her hand under one of the soles. She lifted it to her face, sniffed the luxurious leather, rubbed her cheek on the heel, and turned it from one side to the other and gazed some more. "Magnificent," she murmured. "Size six." Exactly her size.

Taking the other one, she seated herself on the old-fashioned armless rocking chair. She removed her sensible brown flats. After a moment's thought, she shimmied out of her jeans.

These shoes deserved a long, bare leg.

They deserved a great short skirt, too, but she didn't have one, so her T-shirt tail would have to do.

She balanced the shoe on the floor and slowly eased her foot inside. And moaned with pleasure. It was a sudden reminder of simple joys, before life had gotten so complicated, so dangerous.

The leather inside was opulent. It fit perfectly.

She donned the other one.

She stood.

She had never worn more flawlessly engineered, extravagant, and *uncomfortable* shoes in her life.

Guardian eased into the room. He leaned against the wall in one corner, grinning as he watched her turn her foot from side to side as she admired the red, the black, the toe, the high heel, the way her foot looked encased in such luxuriantly sexy, shiny shoes. "Do you like them?"

"Oh, Guardian!" She put her hand over her heart. "This is the best gift I've ever received. Thank you!"

"I'm glad." He pushed off from the wall and strolled toward her.

"How did you get them?"

He rumbled with amusement. "There was this thief."

Her mouth quirked in answering amusement. "Was there?"

"Who was apparently smart enough, or lucky enough, to steal ten pairs of designer shoes, various colors and sizes, and dumb enough to think the tunnels would be a good place to sell them. I went to him to explain that we didn't want the underground swarming with cops, and for some reason, he took one look at me and ran away."

She chortled. "He just doesn't know you like I do."

"I would hope not." His blue eyes twinkled. "I don't know where they came from, but these were your size, so—the spoils of war."

"What did you do with the rest of them?"

"Amber took them. She sold them." He stepped closer. "Are they comfortable?"

She faced him. "Not at all. They're pretty. That's enough."

They locked gazes.

"Would they be more comfortable if they were waving in the air?" he asked.

"Perhaps you should help me find out." Hooking her thumbs into the elastic at the top of her panties, she slid them off her bottom and let them drop around her ankles. Stepping out of them, she walked toward him.

The heels rang assertively on the stone. She pulled off her shirt as she moved, and dropped it on the floor.

He picked her up by the thighs, wrapped her legs around his waist, and turned to the bed. "Is that better?" he whispered.

"Much better." His erection pressed between her legs.

"I meant . . . is that better for your feet?"

"So did I." As her back hit the mattress, she smiled into his face.

For the moment, the beast had cured her fatigue.

Charisma woke to the increasingly insistent summons from the earth.

*Come down, Charisma. Come down and meet your fate.*

"No," she moaned. "Can't you leave me alone?" She rubbed the stones at her wrists, trying desperately to get them to speak; then, in a surge of determination, she batted away the earth's call and concentrated on the here. The now. The crumpled pillow where Guardian had laid his head. His scent mixing with the scent of great sex. The aroma of food wafting up from below . . . she was starving.

Making love with Guardian had a tendency to make her hungry.

She loved the way he talked to her, all warm and sexy, confessing that her beauty made him weak and drove him to his knees, when she knew she wasn't an extraordinary beauty, and even on his knees his strength far surpassed hers. She loved his fascination with her breasts, her throat, her spine. She loved that he found erogenous zones in places she had never imagined: the palms of her hands, the backs of her knees, her toes. He seduced her with every kiss. He begged to go down on her, to bury his face between her legs, taste her, suck on her. The man showed an enthusiasm for lovemaking that inspired her to try to match him for inventiveness.

Best of all, he wanted to try out everything now! At once! ASAP!

Of course, he had a point.

They did not know whether they had tomorrow.

On that cheerful thought, she sat up. And saw, draped carefully across the high back of the old-fashioned rocking chair, a button-down blouse. And not just any blouse . . . its severe lines contrasted with the red satin material. That blouse was a businessman's wet dream . . . especially when worn with the red lace bra placed beside it. On the chair's seat was a black pencil skirt. A short black pencil skirt. With red lace panties to match the bra. And placed on the floor in front of the chair were her red-and-black Lanvin heels.

"Oh, Guardian," she breathed, "you are a naughty, naughty beast." Sliding off the mattress, she approached the chair and ran her fingers along the red satin. It was cool to the touch, and slick, and it shimmered as it moved. Picking it up, she held it to her shoulders. It would fit perfectly. Every piece would fit perfectly. Guardian's surprise was thoughtful in every way. . . .

And she knew exactly how to surprise him in return.

Before the night was over, she would make her beast howl for mercy.

# Chapter 30

———◆❖◆———

The table was perfect. White linen tablecloth, sterling silver platters that glittered with the flames of tall white candles, and bold black-and-gold china plates. The wineglasses sparkled, the silverware gleamed with the elegance of lovingly used antiques, and on Charisma's plate, Guardian placed a single yellow rose.

At the aggressive click of stiletto heels, Guardian turned. And stared. And lusted. And sweated. And *stared*.

When he had come to Amber with the stolen shoes and the proposal that she sell them so he could give Charisma a gift, he had been very specific about the clothes he wanted her to acquire. Amber had not spoken a word to him, but he was still pretty sure she hadn't approved.

As far as he could tell, Amber didn't approve of any lascivious activities, and for sure she didn't indulge in them.

Nevertheless, she had followed his instructions to the letter, and now . . . this was his reward.

Charisma. Long bare legs. Shimmering red blouse. The shoes. Most of all, the light that shone from her like a beacon of happiness . . . he'd done exactly the right thing.

Going to the bottom of the stairs, he waited until she was close before offering his hand.

She stopped on the last step, and smiled as she entwined her fingers with his. She kissed his hairy hand. She slid her other hand into his hair. She pressed her body against his. "You are the most magnificent man I've ever had the good luck to meet."

"Why, yes. Yes, I am."

She kissed him on the lips once, hard.

His free hand touched her thighs, slid up toward her bottom.

And she stepped away. "No, you don't. I saw the lit candles and smelled the food. What do we have?" She stepped down onto the packed dirt floor. She walked toward the candlelit table.

He watched her bottom sway, her calves stretch and contract, her hips thrust forward suggestively. And he recognized that those heels were the best feat of engineering ever created by mankind. He started to speak. Realized he had no voice. He cleared his throat and started again. "For your pleasure, I sent out for dinner from Lizzie's. It's a small, quiet restaurant on the Upper East Side."

"I know it." Her voice, too, was breathy. "It's fabulous."

He followed her, irresistibly drawn by this need to be with her. "They're always nice to my people. They agreed to prepare our order without asking too many questions, they created a menu that could be eaten at any time, and they even sent down the table setting."

She picked up the rose. She caressed the petals with one fingertip, then breathed in its scent. "Magnificent!"

One by one he removed the covers from the silver platters. "Iced shellfish platter with oysters, clams, and shrimp. Caprese salad drizzled with aged balsamic vinegar. Roasted asparagus served with homemade mayonnaise. Crab-stuffed avocado with grapefruit vinaigrette. Cold sliced filet mignon on beefsteak tomatoes with Roquefort cheese. And for dessert, bread pudding with golden raisins and bourbon sauce."

She wet her lips. "My favorites!"

"Really?" Guardian pulled out the chair and held it.

"My dear man, Lizzie's couldn't have created a menu more likely to satisfy almost my every desire." With a voluptuous slither, she slid into her seat.

She watched as he walked around to his place at the table. He wore a long black tunic trimmed with black embroidery; the candlelight and the dark color gave him an austere aspect, more beastlike and less human.

She liked it. As he seated himself, she leaned toward him. "I *have* got a beast fetish. I saw the Disney movie about a dozen times. I even saw *La Belle et la Bête*. But the rest of this is your fault."

"*My* fault?"

"What did you think was going to happen when you . . . you snacked on me like I was a Hostess Twinkie?" She leaned her elbow on the table and widened her eyes at him. "Did you think I was going to *not* like it? Maybe your experience is from reading how-to books, but as a researcher, you get an A in Holy Shit That Feels Good."

"So I am your fantasy." He pulled the iced champagne out of the silver bucket, popped the cork, and poured two stems full of bubbling pink liquid.

"Yes. Perhaps on some subconscious level, I always knew what fate had in store for me." Lifting her glass, she inclined it toward him.

He reached across and clinked his glass against hers. "Are you happy?"

As she watched him slide a crab-stuffed avocado onto her plate, she said, "In all my years I have never been so happy. And I remember all of mine. All twenty-eight of them."

"It doesn't sound nearly as impressive when I say you've made me happier than I've been in the twenty months that I remember, hm?"

"I'll accept that compliment in the spirit in which it was offered." She tasted the avocado and crab, and moaned with pleasure. "That is absolutely delicious."

He slid a selection of shellfish onto her plate.

What a perfect time to destroy his concentration!

"By the way," she said casually, "the panties were very pretty, but lace is itchy."

"I'm sorry; are you uncomfortable?" He offered the asparagus.

"Not at all. I simply am not wearing them." She observed with satisfaction as Guardian froze, became a tall beast statue with glittering eyes and a spoonful of homemade mayonnaise. "In fact, I'm not wearing any. I thought, better that you be uncomfortable than me."

He jerked back into motion. He placed the asparagus on her plate. "You're trying to kill me."

"There are worse ways to die." She took a deep breath that riveted his gaze to her cleavage. "Sit down and eat. If you can sit."

After that, as she tasted the fabulous series of courses, she guided the conversation into safe channels. Restaurants she'd enjoyed. Irving's kitchen, where the Chosen Ones congregated. The close friendships she'd formed with the women of the Chosen Ones. Davidov and the miraculous beer he brewed.

And all the time she spoke, he ate, he replied, he smiled, he frowned, he gave every appearance of paying attention . . . but occasionally, while he was serving another course or pouring another glass of wine, his gaze dropped and, as if he could see all of her, his eyes burned a virtual hole through the table.

Superman would have been proud.

Every time he did, she crossed and uncrossed her legs. She couldn't help it. Even his arousal thrilled her.

He talked, too, and his story of seeing a demon jump into an endless chute straight down to hell when he sang, "Raindrops on roses and whiskers on kittens," made her laugh so hard she was weeping.

When she lifted her head from her napkin, she asked, "Where did you learn all the lyrics?"

He gestured toward the laptop on his desk. "When I first came down here and Dr. King was trying to rehabilitate me, he brought me movies."

"Cheerful movies," she guessed.

"Yes." Guardian tapped his spoon against the table and confessed, "But I already knew all the lyrics."

"Isn't that *interesting*?" She took her last bite of steak and pushed her plate aside. "Where do you suppose you learned them? Glee club at Monster High?"

He grinned to acknowledge her teasing, but sounded thoughtful when he said, "I think it was someone's favorite movie. My mother's or my sister's or . . . my grandfather's. Or something."

"You remember that?"

"No. Not quite. But it's so close. . . ." He clenched his fist.

She gazed at his hand, at the straining fingers that looked as if he could crush the silver spoon he held. "In some ways, you remind me of Aleksandr Wilder."

He looked up so quickly she flinched. "What? Why?"

"He wasn't like the rest of the Chosen Ones. We all are adopted, and we all have parental problems, some bigger, some smaller." She grimaced to acknowledge her own.

Wordlessly, Guardian offered her bread pudding.

"Yes, please. A little. I'm so wonderfully full." She watched him spoon it into a bowl and drizzle it with bourbon sauce, as she tried to explain what she meant. "Aleksandr isn't an orphan. He came from a happy family. His parents lived on the coast overlooking the Pacific Ocean. His grandparents lived in the Washington mountains in this gorgeous valley—he used to show us photos—and they'd host these family gatherings. Aleksandr would talk about the Fourth of July." She gestured widely. "The whole town would come out, and they'd eat and drink and dance. At night they'd have a bonfire, and when everyone left, the family would stay up all night, talking."

"You suspect I'm Aleksandr Wilder?" Guardian's deep rumble of a voice seemed stifled.

"Oh, no. I didn't say that. I don't mean that. I wish I did. It would solve so many problems." That sounded cold, and she hurried to clarify. "I can't see anything of him in you. When he disappeared he was almost twenty-five, and really, he was just becoming a man. The rest of us had grown up when we were very young. He had such a sheltered, happy upbringing. So it's what I think your background must have been that reminds me of him. You've dealt with challenges that would fell a lesser man, and you do it with such grace and ease."

She found it hard at times to decipher Guardian's facial expressions. The hair covered a multitude of quirks easily read on a less beastly man. Yet the more she knew him, the more she prided herself on being able to read his thoughts through the emotions that shifted behind his blue eyes.

Right now was not one of those times. If he'd been practicing enigmatic, he had perfected the look.

He said, "You said the Wilders could transform themselves."

"At their own will, into actual animals like hawks and panthers, and with the aid of a deal with the devil." She was so sorry she'd started the conversation. It had been thoughtless of her to even hint that she knew the secrets of this lonely man. "I know you can't remember what happened to you, but if you made a deal with the devil and transformed yourself into this and can't figure out how to get back, you got screwed."

"Isn't that likely to happen with the devil?" Guardian smiled faintly.

"Of course, but the Wilders' deal was based on a promise to *serve* the devil. If that's part of your promise, and you spend your time killing demons, then the devil got screwed, too."

"Too true."

"Don't you think you have a family of beings just like you somewhere? Yetis in the Himalayas or something?" She leaned across the table and put her hand over his. "That you got captured by a mad scientist who was experimenting on you? That plate in your head means someone was doing something awful."

"You've thought about this."

"I'm used to being busy," she said apologetically. "I'm used to a daily adrenaline rush. Here, it's peaceful. I like that. For the first time in years, I've been able to read, to listen to my body as I work out, to nap. But I can only read so many books, run so many laps, take so many naps. I have time on my hands, and so I think"—she grinned at him—"deep thoughts."

"About me."

"About you. And you and me. And how happy you have made me. If I could, I would save this day encased in amber and wear it as a memory I could revisit when we . . ." She faltered.

He looked across the table at her. "When we have to part?"

"Yes."

"Today is not that day, Charisma."

She looked at him, bathed in candlelight, his strength of character clear in his expression. She watched the way he moved, with the balanced grace of a large man in a small environment. She noticed the little things she liked so much: his blue eyes, his warm smile, the way *he* watched *her* as if she was precious as a diamond with the warmth and sparkle of a whole mine full of rubies.

To her, he was the handsomest man in the world.

She blotted her lips with her napkin, folded it, and put it neatly beside her plate. She pushed back her chair, and the scraping sound echoed softly through the cavern. "No. That's not today. In fact, that exquisite meal has fulfilled every desire, every appetite I have . . . except one." She walked toward the stairs, then half-way turned and looked over her shoulder.

He was fixated on her butt.

As he should be.

She reinforced her physical invitation with a verbal one. "Come and help me fulfill *all* my desires."

# Chapter 31

———◆———

Guardian followed Charisma, but slowly, waiting for that moment when she climbed the stairs, watching as she lifted each stiletto-clad foot, observing as each time her skirt hitched up a little.

He didn't need to see what was or wasn't beneath her skirt. Knowing she was bare, that no barrier existed between her pussy and his touch, fired his imagination. All the way through dinner, he had been plagued with fantasies that kept him hard and frustrated him at the same time.

He knew she had given him a lot to think about; the information about Aleksandr Wilder felt real, important, worth investigating.

But nothing was as important as taking her into his arms and—

High on the stairway, with one foot resting on one step and the other on the step below, she turned and asked, "Aren't you coming?"

"Not yet," he muttered. "But it's a close thing." He ran up the stairs after her.

When he got to the bedroom alcove, she stood behind the old-fashioned brocade-upholstered rocking chair. She was smiling. "Here," she said. "Sit."

He frowned. This was not what he had planned.

But she beckoned and pointed, and he obeyed.

For him, with his long legs and broad shoulders, the chair was uncomfortable. The seat was low to the ground, and narrow. The back was high, tall enough to support his head. There were no arms, no place to put his hands.

But when Charisma came around to face him, and bent and kissed him, and slipped her tongue into his mouth, then leisurely sucked on his tongue . . . he suddenly had a place for his hands. He cupped her breasts and pressed them through the slippery red satin, feeling the lace that supported them, the hardening nipples that invited his mouth. Putting his fingers to the top button of her blouse, he opened it to her waist, and pulled away to enjoy the view.

Her breasts were small, firm, the skin pale through the red lace, and those nipples . . . what a beautiful pink, like two small rosebuds. "Come here," he whispered.

"Why, Mr. Guardian, whatever do you have in mind?"

He pulled on her waist.

She put her hand on his chest to stop him. "I have an idea." She sank onto her knees in front of him. "Let's do something new, shall we?" Putting her hands on his tunic, she pushed it up over his knees, over his thighs, and slowly, slowly pulled it along his erection. Each movement of the silky material caressed and tormented, and when she bared him to the open air, she smiled and cooed, "Look at that. You're asking for a kiss."

He wanted to moan at the thought.

She placed her hands on his thighs, leaned forward, and took him into her mouth.

And he lost his breath. He lost his mind. He couldn't move, caught in the exquisite agony of her full lips massaging the length of his cock, her wet tongue working the head, her breath, warm and moist, adding an erotic balance to the torment.

He wanted to come there, now, in her mouth.

And he wanted to hold off, to get inside her, to fill her and love her and hear her scream her satisfaction.

So he gripped the seat with his hands, his fingers digging into the wood and upholstery. He leaned hard against the back of the chair, making the effort a counterpoint to his need.

When she sucked on him, he groaned low and deep in his chest. He heard himself; he sounded like an animal in agony.

And he was. In such agony.

He didn't know how he could get any harder . . . and yet he did.

He didn't know how he could contain himself . . . and yet he did.

Finally she lifted her mouth. She looked deep into his eyes and licked her lips slowly, deliberately. She rose. "You are so stubborn, Mr. Guardian; you should have a reward."

She might be giving him trouble verbally.

But he didn't care.

Because she put one hand on his shoulder to steady herself, and lifted one foot up and over his leg to rest on the floor beside the rocking chair.

He saw everything in a flash: a fluff of blond hair, the attractive, plump flesh, and the portal to heaven.

As she set her foot down beside the chair, her heel echoed off the stone floor. Lifting her other foot, she performed the same ritual, and again he caught a glimpse of . . . everything. When she set her second heel down on the other side of the chair, when he heard that snap, the hem of her tight skirt rested at the top of her thighs.

She was completely open to him. Completely. Open. To. Him.

Yet he was at her mercy.

The little witch knew exactly what she was doing, too. Her eyes lit with mischief and desire, and she scraped her short nails across the cloth on his chest. "Your heart is thundering, Mr. Guardian. Is there anything I can do to help?" Leaning forward, she put her left breast near his mouth. "Maybe you'd like a taste?"

He pulled her toward him. He took her breast into his mouth, sucked on the nipple through the lace, and listened as she moaned and rubbed herself against him. He did the same with the other nipple, and chuckled when she undulated against him, pressing her body against his in irrepressible need.

Yes, she wanted him as badly as he wanted her.

She caught his hands when they wandered down to touch her, to arouse her. "No!" she said. "Let me." She leaned back and sank down, her firm thighs flexing as she lowered herself. Gripping his cock, she held him firmly in place and smoothly slid down onto him until she was seated on his lap with him all the way inside of her.

With her hands on the tall, narrow back of the rocking chair, she pressed forward, then back, then forward. The motion of the chair thrust him first deeper, then forced him to withdraw, little increments that taunted and enticed. She moved them slowly at first, forcing him to enjoy the subtleties of the motion. Then faster, increasing the pressure, her pussy so warm and tight and silky he wanted the moment to go on forever.

He gripped her thighs, stroked them, marveled at their strength and her passionate determination.

Far below, he could hear the ripple of the stream as it flowed eternally across the rocks. The stones in the cave glowed softly, giving up their light.

Close at hand, the rocker scraped across the floor. The world narrowed to the two of them, here and now.

Her chest began to heave as she gasped. Her damp breasts in the red lace bra swelled. She blushed with arousal. Inside, where she wrapped his cock in heat and glory, her muscles rippled and convulsed.

And the way she squirmed—she was rubbing herself against him, using him to give herself pleasure.

With that, he could help.

He could most definitely help.

Gliding his hand close between their bodies, he opened her, and used his thumbs to stroke her clit.

She moaned, and began the sweetest begging babble. "Oh. Oh, Guardian. Yes. Please. More. Like that."

She began to lift herself, at first a bare inch, then, as their urgency increased, in fantastic, long sliding motions that made him clench his teeth and fight off his orgasm. He moved his hands to her bottom to hold her, help her, and the flex of her muscles against his palms was a rhythmic sexual accompaniment to a moment he would never forget.

The rocking grew more vigorous.

The pleasure intensified.

Charisma's face glowed. Her eyes closed. Her lips opened as she panted, and clearly she was waiting . . . waiting. . . .

Guardian's balls drew up tight against his body. He was waiting . . . waiting. . . .

Charisma threw her head back. She cried out. She strained. Her nails dug into his shoulders, and her pussy clutched his cock.

He came, pumping into her, filling her, each thrust a blessed relief, a joy, an enchantment that lit his dark world.

This woman—funny, innovative, horny, intelligent, *his*—made him know, for the first time that he could remember, that love took physical form. That love could possess his mind. That love was real.

They finished.

The rocking slowed.

Charisma collapsed into his arms.

They subsided slowly, reluctantly yielding to the return of life beyond this blissful madness.

He closed his eyes, breathing in her scent, knowing that no perfume could ever set his senses on fire like the fragrance of Charisma's skin against him.

Wrapping her arms around his neck, she looked up and said, "I love you."

He started to speak, to protest.

She put her finger on his lips. "I know. It's stupid. There isn't time. There isn't hope in the world. But you make me imagine a better world, and you make me a better me. You are my hero, Guardian. Promise that no matter what happens, you will never forget me. Promise you'll love me as I love you."

He agreed. He hoped. He loved.

Which was why it was such a surprise when, later that night, the nightmare ripped him from his happiness, and he woke screaming.

# Chapter 32

————◆≫≪◆————

**P**etrified by the shriek of anguish, Charisma sat up in bed.

It was daytime. Sun streamed through the skylights of the cave. And all too easily she could see the terrifying sight of Guardian beside her, rigid on his back, his eyes transfixed, staring at nothing, while a long, terrible scream came from deep in his chest.

She had seen Guardian roaring out his rage. She had held him in the ecstasy of orgasm. She had never imagined he could scream like that, as if the tortures that endured in his nightmares lived in him during the day.

Charisma had always heard one should never wake a person in the throes of a nightmare.

She didn't care.

"Guardian!" she shouted, and put her hand on his chest.

His hand whipped up and grabbed her wrist. He squeezed; then, at her pained cry, he came to consciousness. His horror pulsed from him, and he threw her hand away. He leaped from the bed. Leaning a hand against the bedpost, he stood, head down, gasping and shaking.

"What was it? Guardian, what happened?" She glanced at her wrist.

She bruised easily.

He looked up at her, then away, as if he didn't want her to glimpse his terror. "A nightmare. Usually I don't remember what it is. This time . . . I do."

As if he were a scared, dangerous animal, she crept toward him and tentatively offered her hand. "Can you share it with me?"

He stared at her hand, but he didn't take it. "I can. But I wish . . . I wish I still didn't know." Slowly, stiffly, he reclined on the bed.

He didn't reach for her, but he didn't reject her when she rested her head on his chest, wrapped her arms around him, and whispered, "Tell me."

When he started, his voice was hoarse, but gradually it smoothed, as if the memory drew him in. "I saw bright lights. Brilliant. Round. Boring into my eyes. They strapped me down. They always did. Everyone in scrubs. Surgical masks . . . all I could see was their eyes."

"An operating room?" she whispered.

Guardian seemed not to hear.

"A couple of them were crying. Not most. Most of them . . . liked their jobs. The doctor . . . liked his job." Guardian's nails scraped on the sheets. "He loved what he was doing. He believed in what he was doing. Smug bastard. He told me he intended to place a homing device in my brain. He said if I did what he wanted, I could have anesthesia."

"My God." She brought herself tight against him, tried to give him strength.

"I refused. So many operations. No anesthesia. Never. Not once. Sometimes I passed out; sometimes I didn't." He lifted his right hand and examined his palm, opened and closed his fingers, then dropped it to his side. "I could endure this. I always had before. He believed he could force me to betray everything that I am. But I was . . . taught better than that."

Charisma stroked her hand over the thick fur on his chest and wished she could do something to make this giant, strong, invincible warrior stop trembling. And wished she could stop trembling, too. Wished she could scrub the images from her mind—of Guardian, abused and terrified, determined to be strong, to do the right thing. "He cut your skull open while you were . . . awake?"

"Of course," Guardian said, as if it were a foolish question.

And she supposed it was.

He continued. "While they used the electric clippers to shave my head, he held the bone saw beside my ear. The saw was high-pitched. Loud. Then he took it away. Again, he promised anesthesia if I would do as he commanded."

"They were going to place something in your brain no matter what decision you made?"

For the first time, Guardian looked down at her and stroked her cheek, giving her comfort when he was the one who needed it. "With *him*, it was never a good choice. Only a less painful choice. He showed me the metal plate he would install, with a trapdoor that would let him in and out of my head whenever he wished. He described the way it would feel as he ripped through my skull. The slow cut, the fiery agony."

"What did he want you to do?"

Guardian put his finger over her lips. "Let me . . . finish."

She nodded.

"He used his scalpel. Peeled back my scalp. The cauterizing iron sent the smell of burning flesh up my nose."

A wave of nausea passed over Charisma, but she fought it back. After all, she was not the one suffering.

"He used the bone saw." Guardian's expression was pure desolation. "I didn't pass out. I wanted to. I tried to. All I could do was scream. Nothing . . . could ever . . . compare to the pain . . . and the terror."

Tears welled in her eyes.

"When I stopped screaming, he showed me the homing device he would implant."

She hid her head in Guardian's chest, not wanting to hear any more.

"He burrowed it into my brain." Guardian stroked her hair, giving comfort, getting comfort. "They screwed the metal plate onto my skull. They shut the trapdoor. They sewed the incision shut. And that was when I faced the fact . . . that he was never going to stop. He had to win. He would seek to inflict his will on me forever. He would keep me and torture me until I died, or he died, or I yielded. But I also realized . . . I could escape. Only one way. But I had to escape."

"You had to do what you could," she whispered.

"Yes. But I had to do it before they put me back in my cell. So I bided my time. Pretended to be weak while I prepared myself to transform. In the recovery room, I begged one of the nurses who had cried for me to loosen my bonds." He shook in a palsy. "And as I lay there on the bed, quietly, I changed. Mutated."

She lifted her head and stared in shock. "Changed?"

"The nurse screamed and screamed, but it was too late. When I had become *this*"—he gestured at himself—"I was strong. I was invincible. I tore the place apart. I demolished the operating room. I rampaged through the facility, ripping out their electricity, their lines of communication. I found and destroyed every phone." In a low voice, he said, "I killed the cruel ones. All of them."

"The doctor?"

Guardian's face contorted. "He disappeared."

"He had prepared a way to escape? Just in case?"

Guardian nodded sharply. "He had told me who he was. Smith Bernhard. I refused to call him *Doctor*. Bernhard thought himself a genius. And perhaps he was. He despised the rest of the world as weak. For the sake of his experiments, he believed he had the right to kill and mutilate anyone and anything."

"Without guilt?" Stupid question. *Obviously*.

Guardian's low growl was truly that of a beast primed to attack. "He considered it a duty to his genius."

She stroked him, smoothing her hands through his hair, along his cheeks, down his throat.

Gradually his snarl faded to nothing, and he was her man once more. "When I couldn't find any trace of Bernhard, I didn't waste time. I had to get out. I knew he would be back for me. I knew I couldn't lose him for long. So I ran out into a snowstorm."

"Where were you being kept?"

"Somewhere over the Canadian border. Far north. So much snow, so deep. But I took a jeep. I drove south. When the gas was gone, I ran."

"You had just had surgery."

"When I changed, I was healed." Bitterly he said, "It's the side benefit for surrendering my will to his."

"You did what you had to. You seized an opportunity. You know it's true!"

"I do. But I did it to save myself."

She sat up and stared down at him. "And I'm glad!"

She half expected him to smile at her indignation.

Instead, he soberly examined her. "I know you are."

"Not just because you saved my life, either!"

"I know." Finally, he nodded. "I know."

She didn't know how else to convince him he'd done the right thing. What to say? How to explain how much he meant to her? To all the people he protected?

She'd said it all last night.

Anyway, he didn't seem interested. "Along the way, I stole a truck. I stole a car. I scavenged off the land. I came to New York City. I hid, and I forgot . . . it all."

"You may have forgotten then, but now . . . you remember so much."

"I remember . . . him." His eyes narrowed. "And her."

Charisma's breath hung in her throat. "Her?"

"A woman as bright as the sun, as sultry as the night."

"Who is she?"

He shook his head. "I don't know. Only that she's there in my mind, with Bernhard."

The tightness in Charisma's chest lifted a little. "So she's a villain?"

"She betrayed me."

Charisma didn't want to know. But she had to ask. "*Are* you Aleksandr Wilder?"

"I don't know. The barriers to my memories are breaking down, but . . . not all the way. Not completely."

She leaned against his chest. She searched his face and tried to see any resemblance to the Aleksandr Wilder she knew.

She could not. The boy Aleksandr had been had nothing in common with Guardian. Yet . . . the story he told . . . of refusing to change, of becoming a monster to escape. Who else could he be?

There were so many difficult questions to pose now. So many quandaries to face.

She was almost relieved when footsteps sounded loud on the floor downstairs, and a man's voice called, "Guardian! Charisma! They called me. They said Guardian had another nightmare."

# *Chapter 33*

———— ❖ ————

Charisma hadn't seen Dr. King for four days, but here he was in the Guardian cave, waiting for them as they descended. Dr. King stood on a chair by the table still littered with the remains of last night's dinner. "I'm sorry I haven't been down," he said. "Up above, things are disintegrating. Gangs are roving the streets, raping and killing. They fear nothing except—"

"The demons?" Guardian asked.

"Exactly. Respectable people scarcely dare leave their homes. I'm working day and night." Dr. King looked worried and harried, as if the weight of the world rested on his shoulders.

Ill at ease, Charisma stared down at the packed dirt floor.

While she had been down here with Guardian, talking and eating and making love, the city had been under attack. Civilization had been collapsing.

But she had an excuse. She had been ill. Really ill. Truly . . . fatigued.

Yet Amber watched her critically.

Taurean fidgeted by the entrance, studiously avoiding Charisma's gaze.

Was Charisma guilty of shirking her duty? Should she be ashamed?

"But enough excuses." Dr. King dismissed his own problems with a sweep of the hand. "When Moises heard you scream, he came for me. What happened?"

Guardian paced along the river, then back, as if his great strides would shake off the memories. "Another nightmare."

"What did you dream?" Dr. King asked.

Would he answer? Would he tell Dr. King?

Everything was changing, and Charisma felt the pressure of fate pushing her, and Guardian, to a new moment.

Most of all, she felt . . . *heard* the thrumming of the earth grow louder, demanding she come below, into its heart.

"I dreamed the truth." Guardian stopped and faced them. "I dreamed about the doctor who did *this* to me."

"The surgery on your head?" Dr. King scrutinized Guardian, his dark gaze weighing and curious.

"The doctor who made me take this form." Guardian swept his hand from his head to his toes.

As if the news rendered him weak, Dr. King sank onto the chair. "Do you know his name?"

Guardian turned away, as if the name were too bitter to speak.

"Smith Bernhard," Charisma told Dr. King quietly.

"My God. Bernhard is insane." Dr. King's revulsion matched hers.

"You know him?" Charisma had never imagined such a link between Guardian and Dr. King.

"Smith was one of the doctors who worked in the hospital during my residency," Dr. King said. "He wanted to . . . He tried to persuade me that I would do better to donate my body to science than get a degree in medicine."

Charisma didn't think she could be more horrified. Yet now . . . she was.

"We knew, all of us who worked with him, that he was up to something dreadful. One of the watchmen caught him experimenting on one of the coma patients. The administration hesitated to turn him in to the police." Dr. King's mouth twisted. "It would have reflected badly on the hospital's reputation. By the time the police went to arrest him, he had disappeared. I hoped never to hear his name again."

A movement caught her eye. She looked quickly and saw a man peering at her from behind a stone. He was handsome; his fresh complexion marked him as a young man. Yet he stared at her with eyes too anxious and a palpable apprehension, and when she stared back and smiled kindly, he slunk back behind his stone.

Moises. She thought he must be Moises.

"Tell me about the dream," Dr. King said to Guardian, and listened without interrupting as Guardian told the tale.

After the first few words, Taurean stumbled closer, wringing her hands, and then stopped, transfixed by the story.

Amber sank to her knees, shaking and crying.

Charisma felt ill as she heard it all again.

Dr. King, too, looked sick, and when Guardian fell

silent, Dr. King said, "Most physicians live to relieve suffering, but this . . . I have to apologize for my profession."

"You have nothing to apologize for." Guardian stepped forward. "You saved me, Doctor. If not for you, I would still be cringing in the dark."

"I don't believe that." Dr. King shook his head. "You've got a strength of character that puts me in awe."

"And yet I became what Bernhard demanded I become." Guardian lifted his hands and looked at them, turning them back and forth as if he couldn't believe what he saw.

"You did what you had to do to get away," Dr. King said.

"See?" Charisma said softly. "I told you."

Guardian held her gaze with his. "I can't go back to my human form."

"We don't know that," Dr. King said in a suitably pontifical doctor voice.

"*I* know." Guardian lowered his hands and looked into Charisma's eyes. "I need the pain and despair to tap into that wild part of me—and not even to be human again would I suffer so much."

"No. Of course not." Again, Dr. King stood on the chair. He leaned his hands on the table. "What else have you remembered?"

"I see faces in my head. I hear names and think I should know them." With a cool gaze, Guardian looked far across the cave toward the high cluster of homes built into the wall. "But nothing more beyond those moments in the operating room."

"I think that's quite enough for one day," Dr. King said. "You'll find, now that the memories have started to return, that you'll get them back in fits and bursts."

"Great. I can't wait to remember more of the same," Guardian said sarcastically.

Charisma grinned. He sounded almost normal.

Dr. King turned to her. "While I'm here, I'd like to examine you."

Instantly she said, "I'm fine."

"Nevertheless, you're my patient, and you went through a terrible ordeal yourself." Dr. King reached into his bag and pulled out his stethoscope. "I won't take a minute."

As the doctor listened to Charisma's heart, took her blood pressure, and looked into her eyes, Amber began to clear the table: carefully placing the burned-down candlesticks in boxes, throwing away the leftover shell-fish, and boxing up the other remains to be given, Charisma knew, to the poor. As she answered Dr. King's questions about any aches and pains, Moises scuttled up and grabbed the boxes, and put them in the basket that went back and forth to the surface.

Within minutes the table was back to normal, battered and plain, as if the most romantic evening of Charisma's life had never occurred.

When Charisma left the cave, she knew she would leave no sign of her passage except a hollow indentation in the earth.

Had she been nothing but the briefest interlude in Guardian's life? Was she to be wiped away as if she had never lived and almost died, fought and learned to love here in this cave?

Dr. King smugly said, "I have never seen anyone recover from the demon's venom. Charisma, you are truly a miracle."

"You're a great doctor," she said.

"Thank you. I pronounce you totally cured." Dr. King beamed for another minute. Then his face fell, and he sighed. "But as much as I would like to stay down here, I have a patient load that would drop a lesser man." He hopped off the chair and picked up his bag. "Still, everything today is a good thing. No man would want to remember what you have remembered, Guardian, but it's a huge step on the path to recovery. And, Charisma, I am releasing you from my care." With a satisfied good-bye, he left the cave.

Charisma sneaked a glance at Guardian.

He stood grim faced and silent.

He was probably absorbed in the new memories that crowded his mind. But did he realize what the doctor's words meant to her? To them?

Taurean sidled up to Charisma and tugged at her sleeve. "I have a message from Irving."

Charisma didn't want to hear it. She didn't want the claims of her real life to intrude yet more. "Yes?"

"He said to tell you that the Chosen Ones are expected to return soon. Isabelle is coming home. You should come back to prepare."

Charisma's dismay compounded.

She wanted to see her friends.

But she wasn't ready to leave.

She needed to confirm that Guardian was indeed Aleksandr Wilder, because the Chosen Ones needed Aleksandr.

But how could she do that if he couldn't quite remember?

Did she dare tell the Chosen Ones what had transpired, knowing the anguish Guardian would feel when they stared? Kindly, of course. But they would stare. . . .

Yet did she dare not tell the Chosen Ones?

What if she was wrong?

Amber stepped forward, her smile tight and superior. "Guardian cannot take you to the surface. But if you will prepare, I'll make sure you get home safely."

Charisma looked helplessly at him.

"I *can't* take you to the surface. The homing device . . ." His voice was stiff, his face emotionless, as if he were already separating himself from even the thought of her.

"I understand." She straightened her shoulders. "Thank you for allowing me to recover down here with you. But it's time for me to again become Charisma Fangorn, Chosen One. I have a job to do, and not much time left to do it. I have to go back."

"Yes. You have to go back." Guardian's blue eyes flashed with, she thought, an echo of her anguish. "I'll take you as far as I can."

In a burst of inspiration, she said, "Take me as far as Davidov's Pub. It's underground. Nothing can harm you there."

# Chapter 34

The tunnels smelled of sweat and fear. Dirt shifted down, as if New York's chaos weighed too heavily on the ground. A bird fluttered and swooped, desperate and trapped forever underground. The Belows huddled in small groups for safety, muttering fearfully, and watched Guardian and Charisma pass.

With each step, Guardian suffered a disorienting sense of déjà vu.

He had walked this tunnel before.

He had suffered the agonies of love before.

He had felt lost and uncertain before.

But he had never held Charisma's hand as he walked before, had never looked at her sweetly rounded, pixie-ish face, had never experienced this roiling sense of despair and finality.

Could he bear to let Charisma go?

Would they ever see each other again?

How would he survive the loss?

She squeezed his hand in excitement. "That's the brew pub," she told him, and hurried her pace toward the short, wide steel door at the end of the long corridor.

Guardian had seen the door before, but never ventured close. Now he read the nameplate: DAVIDOV'S.

Charisma stepped up confidently and knocked.

As if their arrival had been anticipated, the door swung open at once.

Guardian's jaw dropped. He'd been expecting a rotund German brewmaster in a dirty white apron.

Instead, he got Vidar Davidov: thirty years old, six and a half feet tall, two hundred and fifty pounds of pure muscle. Davidov's casual, well-worn blue jeans and collared, short-sleeved navy blue shirt made Guardian think of a successful investment banker on the golf course. But his blue eyes and shoulder-length wavy blond hair probably made Charisma imagine a Viking warrior on the prow of a ship, holding a long sword and preparing to raid the villages.

"Charisma! We were worried." The buff, handsome, confident bastard opened his arms wide.

Charisma walked into his embrace.

Davidov held her and rocked her, then lifted her chin and examined her face. "You look tired, little one."

"I need a good night's sleep and I'll be fine," she said.

"Hm. Yes. Come." He wrapped his arm around Charisma's shoulders and led her in. "It's not safe out there."

"Not even outside your pub?" Charisma asked in dismay.

"Inside no one can harm you," he assured her, then flicked a glance at Guardian, a glance that felt as if it left Guardian naked and defenseless. "You, too, Guardian. Don't linger on the doorstep. Come inside. Shut the door. Here you can relax at last."

The guy knew his name. Okay, that wasn't too weird—Davidov owned an underground bar; Guardian had been around for twenty months; it shouldn't be too much of a mystery.

But Guardian didn't like this Davidov, didn't like the casual way he led Charisma to a barstool, didn't like his self-assurance and his overweening masculinity. He made Guardian feel, not ugly and deformed, but young and foolish.

Either way, Guardian didn't like it.

On the other hand, the inside of the pub gave him the impression he'd come home. Somehow, in this place belowground, Davidov had managed to make the single big room look like a forest, with oak-paneled walls and branches artfully arranged on the tall, fifteen-foot ceiling. Deep cushioned seats and padded leather benches surrounded the well-worn wooden tables.

Guardian took a long breath. The air smelled like woodlands in spring.

The pub would easily hold fifty.

They were the only ones inside.

And Davidov had known they were coming.

Weird.

"Come and sit at the bar," Davidov said. "You can tell me what you've been up to."

Charisma followed without hesitation.

Guardian stood in the middle of the room and tried to figure out how Davidov had created lighting that gave the impression of a sunshine-dappled day in a medieval forest.

"Come, Guardian." Davidov's authoritative voice was impatient. "We haven't a lot of time left."

"Are we in a hurry?" Guardian strolled to the bar, a slab of granite set on a dark wood base, and pulled back one of the padded leather swivel stools. Even for him, the seating was comfortable.

"There're not many days left before Osgood extinguishes hope and civilization on earth. I would think the Chosen Ones wish to use their time wisely."

"Don't pay any attention to him," Charisma said to Guardian. "He's always rude to the guys."

"Is it so surprising that I like women?" Davidov's smile caressed her face. "They're rational beings."

"Men are not?" Guardian snapped.

"Not where women are concerned," Davidov answered.

Guardian could hardly argue about that. But, for the way Davidov was staring at Charisma, Guardian wanted to punch out his headlights.

Just when Guardian was ready to launch himself over the bar, Davidov announced, "Charisma, for you, a nice, clean pilsner, with lots of strength-producing carbonation."

"I knew beer gave me gas. I didn't know I got strength, too." She grinned at Guardian and touched his leg. "Doing okay?"

He nodded, because he couldn't bluntly announce that losing her would never be okay.

They had to do this.

And he needed to stop being such a whiner.

"Gas is good. Healthy." Davidov smiled as he poured a sparkling glass mug full from one of the kegs set into the wall. He set the foaming golden beer in front of her. "You'll like this one."

"I know I will." She took a sip. "And I do."

"For you," Davidov said to Guardian, "at first, something mild. Soothing." He poured from a different keg into a larger, heavy pewter tankard. "This is an ancient brew from Scandinavia, given to the warriors when they came home from their voyages. It's always been one of my favorites."

As Davidov placed it in front of Guardian, Charisma leaned up and over and stared into the contents. "It looks blue."

"As blue as the place where the sky meets the sea," Davidov agreed.

Guardian took a cautious sip. "Good. It tastes like . . . a summer sunset, or a breeze off the sea." He glanced at Charisma. "Not that I remember either one of those things."

She spoke in a rush, as if by impulse. "You *could* see those things. You could come to the surface with me."

The knot in Guardian's chest, the one that had begun to loosen, tightened once more. "They'll come for me. Bernhard and the woman."

"I'm one of the Chosen Ones. We're good at what we do. You can stay at Irving's house. We can protect you."

Davidov wiped the taps with a towel, and listened.

Patiently, Guardian said, "Even if I wanted to be seen by your friends or anyone else in the city—and I do not—do the Chosen Ones really have the resources to protect me? As Davidov pointed out, you're overextended and running out of time." He pushed his tankard aside, did the same with her mug, faced her, and took her hands. "And if I leave, who's going to protect the Belows?"

She shook her head and looked down. "I don't know. But you and I . . ." She shook her head again.

He shouldn't say it. He shouldn't even suggest it. Yet he blurted, "You could stay down here. With me."

"I can't."

"You mean you won't."

Her hands convulsed in his, and she sounded wretched and upset. "If I stayed, one day I would give in."

"To what?" What was she talking about?

Charisma withdrew her hands from Guardian's grasp. "To the summons of the earth."

Behind the bar, Davidov made a sound, like a wince made audible.

She turned to him. *"What?"*

"Ask me a question," he said.

"I don't know who imposed the rule," Charisma explained to Guardian, "or why, but Davidov can give answers only if someone asks the right question."

In his turn, Guardian examined Davidov.

So this alluring creature wasn't human, or if he was, he was bound by some magic.

That explained a lot.

"Ask," Davidov told Charisma.

Charisma slid her mug close and took a long drink.

For strength, Guardian supposed.

Carefully she placed the mug on the bar. Spun it a few times while watching intently. And finally she said, "What does the earth want from me?"

"I don't know," Davidov replied.

"Helpful," Guardian said.

"Unlike you youngsters, I reply only if I *know* the answer," Davidov said with withering scorn.

Charisma placed a restraining grip on Guardian's arm. "Vidar, what will happen if I ignore the call?"

"The earth cradles us, and to you she has given great gifts." Davidov's voice grew deep and lyrical. "A mere week ago you burrowed into her and she saved your life. What do you think will happen if you ignore the call? She is the goddess earth. She is powerful."

"I know. I know I should obey. I know I'm needed." Charisma whispered, "But I'm afraid."

Her hand on Guardian's arm trembled. "Afraid of what?" he asked.

Her eyes lost their focus, and she seemed almost to be talking to herself. "It's so deep. The passages are dark and dangerous, and at the end . . . what is within is beautiful and terrible."

"It's perilous," Davidov concurred. "Most who attempt to reach the gate never arrive. And if you do face the challenges and get inside, you'll come back changed."

Charisma's trembling increased. "The earth wants a sacrifice. I don't want to be that sacrifice."

# Chapter 35

---◈---

Guardian turned from Charisma to Davidov, listening, trying to understand. "The earth is calling you to a specific place?"

Charisma took a shaky breath. "It's not so much a place as a goal. Or a destination. Sort of the holy grail of caves."

Guardian tried to understand. "It's a cave?"

"I don't know. But, yes, I think so. A sacred cave. Or rather—*the* sacred cave." She faced Davidov again. "Right?"

He shrugged and wiped the bar.

"Vidar, will the summons ever stop?" she asked.

"The stones at your wrist are dying. So yes, when the earth is tired of treating you as a favored daughter, when you have killed your gift with neglect, the summons will stop."

She groaned and covered her eyes.

Davidov pushed her mug toward her. "Finish. Taurean is waiting outside the door to take you to Irving's. It's time to go."

How did Davidov know that? Why had Taurean come? Why not Amber?

Why did Charisma have to leave at all?

Davidov answered as if he heard Guardian's rebellious questions tumbling through his mind. "Taurean knows the way to Irving's better than the others, and even the gangs hesitate to mess with a six-foot-tall madwoman. Charisma will be safe with her."

"I can take care of myself." But when Charisma lifted the mug to her mouth, her hand was shaking.

Guardian couldn't stand it.

The minutes were ticking away. Their time together was fading. Charisma wore despair like a too-heavy cloak.

Somebody had to be strong—did he really have to be the one?

Yes. At this moment, he was the one. In a steady voice, he said, "I trust Taurean with my life. And, more important, Charisma's life."

She closed her eyes, then opened them. "Listen. I can't go yet. We have to find out whether you're Aleksandr Wilder. It's important. I told you why."

"I can't force my memory," he told her.

"He had blue eyes," she said.

"So do I." Guardian widened his eyes at her. "So I must be him."

"You're so sarcastic. He wasn't sarcastic. He had humor, but it was . . . gentler." She searched his face again. "The middle fingers on his right hand were fused."

He opened his hand like a starfish and showed her all five fingers.

"But you said there were operations." Taking his hand, with her touch she explored the pale, lined skin on his palm, and slid her fingers through the fur on the back. And held his hand.

"Underneath my fur there are scars. Lots of them. Some from fighting. Some of them . . . I don't remember getting. My hand . . . yes. Maybe Bernhard fixed it." He shrugged. "I don't know."

"Aleksandr was shorter than you," she said.

"Maybe I grew."

"He was even-tempered."

"I'm not."

"He drank Coke."

"I love Coke. Even warm and shaken up, which is the way they usually arrive in the Guardian cave." He tried to make her laugh. "My delivery system is flawed, but it's the only one I've got."

She smiled absently, intent on one thing. "He was good with computers."

"I'm good with computers."

"A lot of guys are." She took a drink of her beer and contemplated him.

He took a drink of his and contemplated back. "I thought you were trying to convince me that I'm Aleksandr?"

"Not trying. I would like you to be. I would *love* you to be. We need our seventh Chosen."

Davidov made a humming sound.

She turned on him. "I know. You told us. We need seven. Always seven. And we believe you. We seven were totally unprepared when we started, but the enemy was less powerful then. Now, every time we bring in someone gifted and unseasoned, the enemy kills him. Or her. They've lasted only months. Then weeks. We can't keep doing that to people. It's virtual murder." She turned back to Guardian. "I told you: We think Aleksandr Wilder is *the* one. The one fate has decreed as our seventh. If I bring the Chosen Ones down to meet you, we have a way of knowing when we have the right person. See, when we join hands, this kind of electrical shock goes through us—"

"All right," Guardian said.

"Really?" Her eyes brightened. "I can bring them to see you?"

"Yes." He half laughed, although he was not amused. "I'll hate it. I don't want to face them, to observe as those humans react to the sight of me. But I'll do it."

"We remember Aleksandr," she said. "We loved Aleksandr."

"And the shock of expecting to see something of Aleksandr in this carcass will be horrifying to them." When she would have objected, he held up a hand. "But I'll do it. Send word to Davidov. He'll send word to me. We'll set up a meeting. Maybe, in the meantime, I'll remember more." He stood and offered his hand. "Now, Charisma . . . you really have to go."

She slid off the stool, breathing heavily. "I don't want to leave you."

"A wolf and a bird might fall in love, but where would they make their home?" Davidov asked.

For that bit of philosophical wisdom, Guardian wanted to smack him.

But then, right now, frustration made him want to put his fist through the wall.

Sliding her arms around him, Charisma hugged him.

He hugged her back, holding her too tightly, never wanting this moment to end.

Davidov rattled the mugs as he cleared them away, like a bartender announcing last call.

The man was a pain in the ass.

Charisma stood on tiptoe and kissed Guardian's lips. Gently, she disengaged herself from his embrace. She went to the door, opened it, turned, and looked at him in desperate longing. "I will always love you." She walked out into the dark tunnel.

He heard Taurean speak to her.

The door shut firmly behind her.

Guardian stood frozen in place, his hands heavy at his sides.

He had never been so alone.

Davidov got out a new pewter tankard. "You two remind me of Romeo and Juliet."

"The play?"

"No, the actual kids." Davidov chose a different keg, one at the far end of the bar.

"Sure." Guardian lifted one foot, then the other, and moved himself back to his seat. "I need to get drunk."

The liquid that streamed from Davidov's tap was dark amber, unfiltered, almost without foam. When the tankard was full to the brim, Davidov placed it on the bar. "This will get you more than drunk. Trust me. I always serve my patrons exactly the right brew at exactly the right time." With a flick of the wrist, he shot it down the bar to Guardian.

Guardian caught the mug, pulled the brew toward him, and took a sip. Hearty. Toasty. Almost beefy. "This is fabulous." He didn't know why, but he was surprised. "What is it?"

"It's an ale originally brewed in the Ukraine as far back as the Middle Ages."

Guardian tipped the tankard back and drained half in a single long swallow. "In the Ukraine?"

"The Wilders are from the Ukraine."

Guardian put the tankard on the bar. "Yeah. Why that brew for me?"

"Quaff up."

"Quaff up?" Guardian guffawed, and drank once more.

"Charisma forgot to tell you one thing about Aleksandr Wilder." Standing in the shadows at the end of the bar, Davidov looked almost sinister.

"What is that?" The percentage of alcohol in this ale must be over the moon, because Guardian felt the kick already.

"One of the reasons Aleksandr was picked to join the Chosen Ones was because the Chosen Ones frequently sport a mark or a tattoo somewhere on their bodies that gives hints at their gifts."

"She told me something about that. The marks expand when they fall in love." The room spun once, and tilted.

"Aleksandr Wilder had no gift." Davidov wandered closer. He still looked sinister. "But he had a mark."

That helped Guardian focus. "What mark? Where?"

"On his chest. It starts on his left shoulder."

Guardian slid his hand under his tunic and groped his own shoulder.

"It extends across his chest."

Guardian dug under the fur on his body, followed the raised pattern across his chest.

Davidov's voice was soothing, but his words burst like fireworks in Guardian's mind. "The colors are the same as the ones sported by the Wilder family. But according to Aleksandr's grandfather, the grand old man, Konstantine Wilder, the pattern has never been seen before."

Guardian put his chin down on his chest, parted the hair, and looked.

A beautiful decoration of reds, blacks, and blues was hidden beneath the fur. "Shit," Guardian said in a daze. "It's true. I'm Aleksandr Wilder."

The room listed like the *Titanic* when it struck the iceberg.

In slow motion, Guardian looked up at Davidov. "What did you put in this ale?"

"Vitamins. Minerals. A hallucinogenic." Davidov observed Guardian's eyeballs roll back in his head, his knees collapse. Watched him crumple to the floor. "We can't wait for you to remember in your own time," he said to Aleksandr's unconscious body. "So that brew will open the floodgates."

Turning, Davidov went into the back room, collected a pillow and blanket out of the closet, went back. He lifted Guardian's big, hairy head and slipped the pillow under it, threw the blanket over the long body.

Going to his computer, he reflected on how incredibly handy these gadgets were, and wondered why it had taken people so long to figure them out.

Flipping through his contacts, he found the one he wanted and made the call.

It took five rings, but at last a face filled his screen.

Konstantine Wilder. The old man looked older, but still hearty, annoyed at being interrupted from whatever he'd been doing, and then . . . astonished. "Vidar Davidov? Is that you?"

"It is indeed. Greetings, Konstantine."

"You don't look any different than you did the last time I saw you . . . *sixty years ago*." At the last three words, Konstantine's genial voice boomed out.

"I don't change. That doesn't matter. I have news. Important news." Davidov pushed the subject of his eternal youth aside. "Konstantine, I've found your grandson. I have Aleksandr Wilder."

# Chapter 36

———— ✦ ————

"**I**n the nineteenth century, mansions abounded on the Lower East Side of New York City, packed onto the city lots with very little green space. But no luxury was spared when designing the impressive exteriors and opulent interiors, and many of those homes remain today. Of course, a lot of the mansions have been turned into museums and high-end restaurants." Taurean led Charisma south on Third Avenue, sounding like the city's most informative tour guide.

It was late afternoon, yet the sun was dim in the sky. The smell of smoke wafted through the smoggy air. Toward the East River, a fire lit the sky. Sirens shrieked. People hurried along the streets, glancing behind them, too aware, too frightened.

The city was dying.

Charisma felt like dying, too. At least that would relieve the pain of leaving Guardian behind. It was worse than anything she'd ever felt.

Yes, she would be glad to see her friends. She missed the Chosen Ones. They were warriors, comrades who had together faced battle time and again. They had one another's backs, always, and that built a closeness that went beyond friendship.

She was bringing them great news. Because of her adventures in the tunnels below New York, she had possibly found their long-lost comrade. They would be so excited. They'd go to Davidov's. They'd set eyes on Guardian. . . .

And he was right.

No matter how much she told them about what had happened to him, no matter how much she prepared them for his appearance, they'd be shocked and incredulous. They'd watch him surreptitiously. They'd avoid his gaze.

Because it was one thing to have seen the inhuman creatures crawling out of the gutters, to know that monsters existed. It was another to see a friend who had been so altered as to be unrecognizable. Men who returned from war, scarred and mutilated, had suffered such travails: society's embarrassment and the discomfort of their friends.

Cheerfully oblivious to Charisma's turmoil, Taurean continued with her travelogue. "Also, as you can see, with the current warfare on the streets, the entire area is in danger of imploding. Rival gangs are confiscating homes and using them as bases, destroying the priceless antiques and works of art within. Frequently the mansions are private homes that are occupied when they move in. Needless to say, the families are tossed out or murdered. The police are helpless—or, in the case of those whom Osgood owns, they look the other way. Demons are appearing, mostly at night, and catching lone people on the streets and devouring them. They always leave faces. . . ."

"Just because you're paranoid doesn't mean they're not after you," Charisma muttered.

Taurean proved she had good hearing. "They are after *you*. All of you. If the Chosen Ones don't save the world, you're all going to die a horrible and painful death. And that will be better than living in the world left behind."

"You're cheerful," Charisma said.

Taurean pondered that. "I'm crazy. I see things as they are, not as I want them to be."

"That's important for me to remember."

"That I'm crazy?"

"No. That I should see things as they are, too." Because no matter how awkward the meeting between Guardian and the Chosen Ones would be, something wonderful could come out of it. They would join hands. And if that searing approval zipped through them, if confirmation occurred that Guardian was indeed Aleksandr Wilder, and if in addition he was indeed Charisma's true mate . . . the fire would strengthen them for this last, great battle.

It was their only chance.

But no matter how Charisma twisted and turned things in her mind, even when she visualized victory for the Chosen Ones, she couldn't imagine a life afterward for her and Guardian.

He was a beast, hairy and abnormal.

She didn't care; she loved him.

But even at the best of times, in the real world he would be treated with horror. At the best he would be an object of scorn, a headline on the scandal sheets beside the checkout counter in every grocery store. At worst, he would be a thing to be imprisoned, observed, dissected.

No matter how much she loved him, she couldn't live forever belowground. Sooner or later she'd go mad from the darkness and the stifling air, from longing for a life in the sunshine.

Guardian couldn't live above.

As Davidov said, a wolf might love a bird, but where would they make their home?

"I don't even know why I'm worried about the future," Charisma told Taurean. "From the way things look up here, the Chosen Ones don't stand a chance of surviving."

"The monsters have always been out there. Human monsters. But now even the monsters are afraid." Taurean pointed at one of the mansions. "Like in there."

"The Becker mansion?"

"I worked in there. The monsters hurt me. Human monsters. I hope the demons eat them. All of them. I don't want the demons to leave even their bones."

Charisma had never imagined the shy, gentle, awkward Taurean could be so rancorous. But Charisma said, "I've met Mr. Ambrose Becker. He's a vicious, disgusting pig."

"So is his brother. And his cousin. I want their names, their bodies, their memories wiped from the face of the earth." Taurean's tone went from ominous to bright. "Here we are! Irving's mansion!"

"Yes. And my home for almost seven years." Charisma sagged with relief to be here. "The place looks the same." Unlike the rest of the mansions defaced with graffiti and with boarded-up windows.

"Tall, grand, a home built for display," Taurean said. "It's the last fort that will fall."

"There's some comfort in that." Charisma started up the front steps.

"No!" Taurean sprang after her and stopped her with a hand on her arm. "We go around by the kitchen."

"Why?"

"That's where the food is."

"Of course." Because someone who lived on the streets and in the tunnels knew her priorities.

At the corner, Taurean cautiously peered around, then sidled down the wall toward the kitchen.

Charisma followed, not sidling but staying close to the mansion.

The city had a claustrophobic feel to it, as if no one here should show themselves as a target, as if everyone here were trapped and no amount of struggle could free them.

Dropping to the ground, Taurean struggled in a low crawl to the basement kitchen window. She plastered herself against the glass and knocked hard. "It's Taurean!" she shouted. "Remember me?" She must have gotten a positive response, because she pointed to Charisma, then at the door, and crawled in that direction.

Charisma walked around, and when McKenna opened the door, she cried, "McKenna!"

When she had first come to live at the mansion, she and the stuffy butler had often butted heads.

In the intervening years, either she had grown more straitlaced or he had loosened up, because she tried to rush forward, into the familiar safety of the house McKenna ruled with an iron hand so she could hug him, kiss his shaven cheeks.

Taurean strong-armed her back. "No! It's a dangerous passage. We have to stay low." Seating herself on
the stairs, she inched her way down on her bottom.
Turning back to Charisma, she said, "Come on. Don't
be afraid. You'll be okay."

Sometimes Taurean seemed so normal that Charisma couldn't help but wonder whether she was mess-
ing with her now.

Then she remembered Taurean's revealing words
about the Beckers, and she sat on the stairs and bumped
her way down.

At the bottom, McKenna helped Taurean to her feet,
and then Charisma to hers, and when Charisma flung
her arms around his neck, he beamed. "I am so glad to
see you, Miss Charisma. So glad. The Chosen will be
thrilled."

"They really are all back?" At the thought of seeing
her friends, a little of the burden Charisma carried
lifted from her heart.

"Just back." McKenna's voice, with his hint of a
Scottish burr, was as comforting as hot chocolate on a
cold day. "What good timing you have!"

"I came as soon as I got the message you sent."

"Message?" McKenna frowned. "What message?"

"The one about returning to see Isabelle."

"I didn't send a message."

"Somebody did. Taurean told me. Taurean,
who . . . ?" Charisma turned to face Taurean.

But Taurean was gone, fleeing without a word.

# Chapter 37

———— ❖ ————

"That's weird." Charisma stared at the place where Taurean had stood. "I wonder who told her to fetch me?"

"I don't know." McKenna shut the door. "But in the case of Taurean, she's been watching the house. I tried to get her inside to have a meal, but she would have none of that. So I left food out for her. Somebody ate it."

"It was probably her. She was very intent on reaching the kitchen." No wonder. The kitchen was cool and quiet, redolent with the aromas of bacon, rosemary, and garlic, and in here, with the hum of the refrigerator and sound of water boiling on the stove, Charisma was free of the earth's call.

Almost.

"My point exactly. She may have seen everyone arrive." McKenna lifted the lid of a pan to stir the contents.

Charisma peered inside. Stew. She loved McKenna's

stew. "She said the Chosen Ones were *expected*, not that they were all here."

McKenna lifted a hand. "I do not understand the efficiency of the underground network, but we can't argue with its success."

"I suppose." But Charisma felt still uneasy, as if she'd somehow missed something she should at once see.

"Come, Miss Charisma; the Chosen are all up in Mr. Shea's room. They will be so glad to see you."

He walked her up the stairs to the grand entry hall, then up the long, curving stairway that led to the second floor. As they entered the imposing upstairs corridor, lined with dark oil paintings in gilded frames, she could hear her friends' voices as they babbled and laughed.

Charisma smiled at the racket. "Sounds like they're celebrating."

"They are." McKenna wore smugness very well.

"Did they get it? Did they get the feather?" A spark of hope lit in her soul.

"They did. Or at least a case that looks as if it could contain the feather."

Charisma's smile faded. "Why not open the case and find out?"

McKenna hesitated, grimaced. "It's not that easy."

She already knew the answer, but she asked anyway. "It's bewitched?"

"Yes."

"They're in Irving's room because he's the man who owns all the best research books on how to open the box?"

"Yes."

Charisma seethed with frustration. "Why does everything have to be so difficult?"

McKenna chuckled. "You sound exactly like Mr. Samuel."

"With my luck, we're probably long-lost siblings." Dreadful thought.

"You do not look at all alike, but at the base your personalities are so similar, I have wondered about some hidden bloodline myself."

"Don't flatter Samuel so," she snapped.

"Exactly right." McKenna bowed and gestured toward Irving's room. "Would you like me to announce you?"

"No. Please. Let me announce myself."

They exchanged smiles.

She slipped into the room.

Irving's private library was unlike any Charisma had ever seen. Bookshelves lined the giant room. Books of every kind lined the bookshelves. Ancient books. New books. Loose manuscripts. Egyptian scrolls made of papyrus and filled with hieroglyphics. Stone tablets. And scattered here and there, two dozen e-book readers of every variety. If the books weren't enough to keep the casual peruser busy, mixed in among the books were relics and oddities: African witch doctor masks, shrunken heads, glass jars with questionable contents that looked very much like petrified male body parts, dried flowers, glass beads, wigs made of human pubic hair. . . . Charisma had never cataloged the contents. Usually after a few minutes she was so grossed out she preferred to ignore the whole disgusting display.

Through the double connecting doors, Charisma could see Irving's bed. She didn't know how he slept with those gargoyles staring at him from the posts.

But it warmed her to see her friends all gathered together.

In the center of the room, Irving sat at the end of the long library table, in his wheelchair, a dark metal box stretched before him.

By the bar, Martha stood with a tray, collecting dirty glasses and putting out clean ones.

Across the table from Irving, Rosamund sat in a leather desk chair, a tall stack of books at her elbow, a book open before her, looking at another book that Genny held in front of her nose. John stood behind Rosamund, pointing at the open page. Aaron stood off to the side, arms crossed.

They were all frowning intently.

In the far corner, Jacqueline stood twirling the illuminated globe of the world, an orb so large it required its own maple stand. As it circled, she ran her fingers along the smooth surface as if seeking a moment of revelation.

Caleb stood beside her, his hand outstretched, ready to catch her if a prophecy struck.

Isabelle sat beside Irving, stroking the long, slender metal box with a loving hand and talking animatedly to Irving.

Samuel stood beside her right shoulder, and, like Aurora in the fairy tale who touched the spindle on an enchanted spinning wheel, he deliberately reached out with one finger and touched a corner of the box.

A spark arced.

Samuel was slammed back against the bookcase.

A mason jar fell on his head and broke, sending glass and human teeth in an explosion across the room.

Conversation died.

Everyone stared at Samuel in disgust.

"Why do you keep doing that, man?" John snapped.

"I keep thinking the charge will run out." Samuel touched his face. "Geez, I'm bleeding!"

"Serves you right. Magic taps into the energy of the universe." John sounded as if he'd completely lost patience. "Unless the eternal generator dies, which would make our current crisis look like a cakewalk, this box will not open without the right spell."

"All right, fine. It was a stupid idea." Samuel used his handkerchief to blot his head. "This time I really knocked my hip out of joint. Somebody help me up." He held up his hand.

Charisma judged that her moment had come. "Samuel, I hope none of those teeth were enchanted. You could end up at the dentist getting a tooth extracted from your brain."

A moment of silence, of wide-eyed stares.

A gratifying shriek of joy.

Jacqueline and Genny, Rosamund and Isabelle rushed toward her. They surrounded her, hugged her, and exclaimed over her.

When the female joy had subsided to a manageable level, the guys moved in.

They hugged. They thumped on the back and said hearty, encouraging stuff.

When they were finished, she went to Irving and knelt beside his wheelchair. "How are you, dear friend?" she asked.

"I'm not senile. I'm not sick. I'm not in pain unless I try to walk. So I'm good." He patted her cheek.

"Let's keep it that way."

"I'm scarily close to a hundred years old, darling."

He patted her cheek again. "I can't keep that way much longer."

"We're almost to the end of the seven years. Don't you want to see us finally triumph over the forces of evil?"

"Wherever I am, I'll know. And I know you'll succeed." He looked around at the gathered friends and comrades. "I have every faith in you."

"Good to hear." John ran his hand through his hair, and a little of the weariness lifted from his face. "Faith is exactly what we need right now."

Charisma stood and walked to Samuel, who still sat on the floor against the bookshelves, looking disgusted. She offered her hand. "Imagine my enjoyment to see you knocked on your ass."

"By something supernatural. Not by you." Samuel grasped her hand and let her pull him up. Sweeping his arm around her, he pulled her close. Gruffly he said, "Good to see you, peewee."

"Good to see you." She turned to the Chosen Ones. "You wouldn't believe where I've been."

# *Chapter 38*

———◆❖◆———

**H**ours later, Charisma sagged in exhaustion.

She had told the Chosen Ones how she was lured underground, how she got lost, how she had almost become a demon snack.

She had told them about the demon bite, and about Guardian and how he had saved her.

She told them about her eleven days of oblivion and her slow recovery.

She *did* not tell them about the intimacies she had shared with Guardian.

This wasn't like the last time she had kept an affair from them.

With Ronnie, she had been seduced.

This time she had been the seducer.

This time she knew she had found her one true love. And this time she understood all too well that they could never be together.

God help her to find the strength to endure the upcoming challenges without Guardian's tenderness and care.

Finally, she had explained to the Chosen Ones the possibility that Guardian might be Aleksandr Wilder.

They had been horrified at the details of his imprisonment. They had dismissed her worries that they would be shocked at his appearance. They had been excited and ready to go down and visit him at once.

Then Rosamund discovered a description in one of the ancient texts about a metal box that matched the one on the table, and John decreed that freeing the feather took priority over Aleksandr. So Rosamund worked out the translation from Akkadian to English, Aaron and John had gone out to collect the necessary supplies for a potion, Jacqueline had read the spell—and Samuel had been knocked on his ass again.

"I could watch that over and over." Charisma helped him up again, and handed him his cane. "It never ceases to be entertaining."

"You should have been with us in Europe," Caleb said darkly. "You would have been entertained all the time."

Out of the corner of his mouth, Samuel said, "He's such an old lady."

Caleb huffed.

Charisma grinned at Samuel. "*Someone* has to act responsibly around here."

"What can I say?" Samuel spread his hands wide. "When Rosamund said she had the spell to open the box, I believed her."

"I said I *thought* I had it, Samuel." Rosamund glared. "Don't try to blame me because you're impetuous and can't wait to try out new things."

"Makes for a great sex life." Samuel hugged his wife. "Doesn't it, honey?"

Isabelle ignored him.

Of course she did. Isabelle was the most ladylike creature Charisma had ever met. She could drop a hammer on her own foot and never even say *shit*.

How they were such good friends, Charisma would never understand.

"Samuel, I wish you would let me fix your hip," Isabelle said.

"I let you fix my face. That's enough for today." Samuel touched the now-healed place on his forehead. "Really, honey, the hip is just uncomfortable."

"It's *cracked*." Isabelle looked worried and fretful. "Promise you'll let me help you before the big showdown."

"Hey, if this Guardian guy Charisma found is actually Aleksandr Wilder, we won't have to bother with a big showdown. Everything will get fixed, zip-zap, and all we have to do is pick the next seven Chosen Ones for the next seven years." Reflectively, Samuel said, "Poor bastards, whoever they are."

"Yes, Samuel." Aaron's voice dripped sarcasm. "Because everything we've done so far to stop Osgood has been so easy and so effective."

"Actually, darling, it doesn't seem that way to me," Rosamund said.

Jacqueline patted her on the head.

Rosamund looked around. "Oh. That was a jest. I get it."

"Actually, your reaction was right for how funny it was." Samuel glared at Aaron.

Aaron glared back.

John started to stand up.

"Time for dinner!" Martha called from the doorway.

"Thank heavens," Genny muttered to Charisma. "The frustration is getting to everybody."

Martha pushed a laden cart into the room, and smiled tightly at the Chosen Ones' exclamations of pleasure and anticipation.

So the tension wasn't merely getting to the Chosen Ones. Irving's housekeeper had been with him and the Chosen Ones' organization apparently forever—and heaven only knew how long that had been, because depending on her mood, Martha looked as if she was somewhere between sixty and ninety. When she was angry, her brown eyes snapped, her skin flushed a dusky rose, and she was the epitome of a malevolent queen of the Gypsies.

For more than one reason, the Chosen Ones stepped carefully around Martha. She had been part of their initiation, she had faithfully served them for almost seven years, she was privy to a lot of cool information—and at any time, she could poison them all.

"As always, Martha, everything smells fabulous, and you read my mind." Charisma took a plate. "The whole time I was gone, I kept thinking about your green chili enchiladas."

"Even I have my uses," Martha snapped.

Charisma lifted her eyebrows at Irving, who shrugged.

Martha did have her quirks. She was not gifted, which rubbed her wrong, because her younger sister was not only gifted—Dina was a talented mind-speaker—but had been a rebel and joined the Others. Yet when Charisma and the women in the group discussed Martha, they agreed her big issue was that no matter how wicked and undeserving Dina might be, Irving loved her. And Martha loved Irving. Probably in an underappreciated lifetime of service and dedication, that fried her more than anything.

Even so, she insisted that she personally fix Irving's plate, take it to him, and help him with the chicken tortilla soup, which he loved but, since he'd developed a tremor, found difficult to eat.

"Still can't get the box open?" Martha's tone made it clear she took their failure personally.

"We will," Charisma said. "If we have to sauté Samuel's ass to do it."

That brought a chortle from Irving and a lot of laughter from around the room. Which proved Genny was right—eating and the camaraderie that came with it restored their good tempers.

Afterward, Martha piled the dishes onto the cart and took them away.

"Great meal!" Charisma called again.

Martha royally ignored her.

Irving dozed in his chair until McKenna arrived to put him to bed. He went with a weary wave and the assurance they could stay and work on the box, because all he had to do was remove his hearing aids and he would never hear them.

So, since the good research material was in here, they stayed, concentrating on the still-closed metal box to the steady, comforting sound of Irving's snoring.

Rosamund still had enough energy to enthusiastically say, "Since we're not having luck with this spell, should we head down to meet Aleksandr?"

"I can't. I can't walk that far. I'm still recovering, and

this has been a long and difficult day." Admitting it almost made Charisma cry, for she wanted Guardian with a fierce and desperate ache.

"That's a task best left for tomorrow," John agreed. "We need to send Aleksandr word through Davidov, or he won't be there to meet us."

Charisma lifted her aching head off the back of her chair. "Should we send Martha tonight? Give her something to do, and him plenty of warning?"

"I don't send anyone out at night anymore," John said soberly. "Not onto the streets. Not into the tunnels."

Charisma dropped her head back again.

Samuel hadn't removed his gaze from the box. "What would happen if someone flipped the latch and just opened it? Would it be any worse than a blast that knocked him against the wall?"

"You're not flipping the latch and opening the box," Isabelle told him.

He tried to look innocent—an impossible task. "I didn't say *me*."

"Then who?" Isabelle looked around the room. "Who among the Chosen Ones can we afford to lose?"

Charisma closed her eyes and wondered whether they could afford to lose her. After all, they'd managed to retrieve the box without her. Her gift was past its expiration date. Her mark was fading. She had lost hope and strength. . . .

"Charisma." Isabelle's voice was right above her.

Charisma opened her eyes wide, trying to look alert.

"It's way too late for that." Samuel was grinning obnoxiously. "You were giving Irving a run for his money in the snoring department."

"I'm good." Charisma staggered to her feet. "I just need a good night's sleep. Everything's good."

"I'm the expert here. Let me check you out." Isabelle smiled at her, cajoling her, teasing her.

"Sure." Charisma collapsed back into her chair. "I've got this lingering fatigue. If you could swap that out for a little kick-ass energy, I'll be the old Charisma."

Isabelle stroked Charisma's hair off her forehead. "I like any Charisma at all, as long as she's here with us."

Charisma smiled sleepily and relaxed as Isabelle's hands skimmed her head, her throat, her chest, her legs. With each gentle touch, warmth and strength poured into her body, and support and optimism filled her. . . .

"I feel so much better," Charisma told her. "If you knew how sick I was, you'd understand. If not for Guardian and Dr. King, I would never have lived long enough for you to heal me."

"I wish I had been there for you." Isabelle's lips trembled. "I can feel it in your bones. You suffered so horribly."

"I'm good now. Just tired." Charisma smiled beneficently at the whole group. "I missed you guys. I'm glad to be back."

That was true . . . in its way.

At the same time, she longed for Guardian with a sharp, sweet nostalgia that made her wonder how so many life mates survived the separation of war and duty.

"Now I must go to bed and rest up for tomorrow." She stood. "Thanks, Isabelle, for sending my injuries off with a final good-bye. Tomorrow I'll fight at your sides. It's so good to be back."

With a weary wave, Charisma exited Irving's room.

Isabelle stood. Just stood. And stared after her friend.

No one spoke.

Finally Samuel moved to Isabelle's side. He put his arms around her. "What's wrong?"

She shook her head. She tried to speak. Once. Twice.

"Charisma looked . . . transparent, as if her spirit is in transition. That never happens unless . . . unless the body fails." Genny extended a hand to Isabelle. "Is that what's happening?"

Isabelle nodded. "The demon's venom has been driven back. But not defeated. I could still sense it, biding its time. It dines on her strength. It's a land mine that waits to explode and destroy her." She wept broken, helpless tears. "I can't save her. There's nothing more I can do. Charisma will die."

# Chapter 39

—◆◆—

Guardian opened his eyes.

He remembered where he was: in Davidov's brew pub.

He remembered what had happened: Davidov had spiked his ale.

While he was unconscious, his whole life had paraded across his brain, playing like a bad drama on the big screen.

He remembered growing up in Washington, surrounded by his boisterous, funny, devoted family.

He remembered coming to New York to go to school.

He remembered meeting Iskra, tutoring her . . . falling in love. That first, bright burst of ecstasy when every moment smelled like springtime and every touch of her hand was cherished.

Then . . . there was the uneasiness.

Why didn't she want to meet his friends? His family? Why did she urge him to abandon them?

But every time he returned to her arms, every time he looked into her sparkling brown eyes, he forgot his disquiet and basked in his luck at winning her.

In disgust, he flung off the blanket, staggered up off the wooden floor. He stood, swaying, trying to get his balance, and he forced himself to remember it all: going to the courthouse to get married, realizing the courtroom was a trap, screaming at her to run, hearing her laughter like a knife to his heart.

He remembered being in the back of a van for three days, bumping along back roads. He remembered arriving at the facility, being shot with a tranquilizer gun before they removed him from the vehicle, and waking up on the operating table with Smith Bernhard leaning over him. Bernhard had explained that he demanded perfect specimens for his experiments, and then they performed the first operation: his hand, to separate his fingers, without anesthesia.

He remembered . . . everything.

Most of all, he remembered giving up Charisma to the world above. It was what pained him the most.

He looked down at himself, still hairy, still misshapen, still a beast.

His past didn't matter. Nothing had changed. He had no freedom from the dark tunnels beneath the city, no chance to reunite with his family, no possibility of taking Charisma as his wife, of watching her swell with his children, of growing old and dying with her.

Davidov came out of the back room, and the handsome bastard had the guts to look concerned. "You okay?"

"I am the Guardian."

"Yes."

"I am also Aleksandr Wilder."

"Yes."

"I have no future."

"Not true!"

"Face facts, Davidov. This is the end of days. If I don't do my job, *no one's* going to have a future." He walked to the door. "Call me when the Chosen Ones arrive, and I'll go with them into battle. Until then, I feel the urge to indulge my wild side. I'm going to go battle some demons."

At the sound of a door closing, Charisma woke.

Where was she? What time was it?

Where was Guardian?

She was in Irving's mansion. It was the middle of the night. And someone had placed a tray beside her bed with a flute of champagne, a yellow rose in a black glass vase—and a pair of red patent-leather stiletto heels by Lanvin.

Picking them up, Charisma stroked them, held them, put them on . . . and cried herself back to sleep.

The next time Charisma woke, sunshine streamed through her bedroom windows, and she pressed her hands against her eyes and groaned.

She had that *I've been crying too hard* hangover, complete with headache and a dragged-down depression, and the earth's call hummed in her ears like a bad case of tinnitus. She needed distraction, something to improve her mood. . . .

Turning on her side, she gazed at her stiletto heels on her nightstand where she had posed them. Reaching out a worshipful hand, she stroked her shoes as if they were her pets.

Guardian had sent her shoes back to her.

What kind of guy recognized her obsession with glorious shoes? What kind of guy, in the middle of a war, after a heartbreaking separation, arranged to somehow present her with supershiny, fire engine red, absurdly high heels? And then, after they separated, what kind of a guy fixed it so she woke to the sight of those heels after they had separated?

She rubbed the tickle in her nose.

Guardian . . . It was something only he would do.

Someone knocked firmly on the door.

As she sat up, Charisma groaned again. She flung her feet over the edge of the mattress and mumbled, "Shit!"

Taking her precious shoes, she slid them out of sight under the bed.

Another knock.

"I'm coming!" she yelled, went to the door in her scruffy pajamas, and opened it a crack.

She expected to see one of the Chosen Ones telling her it was time to go down to Davidov's brew pub to meet Aleksandr.

Instead, there was Martha holding a breakfast tray and looking grim. "Miss Fangorn, Mother Catherine at St. Madeleine's Orphanage sent word."

Charisma wasn't firing on all cylinders. "Sent word?"

"Their phone and Internet appear to be out, and the convent is being attacked by creatures they don't . . . they don't recognize."

"Demons." The scarred remains of the bite on Charisma's shoulder gave a throb.

Martha nodded. "Sister Mary Louise said they looked like living gargoyles."

"Sister Mary Louise came here . . . ?"

"And asked for help. Yes."

Charisma didn't cherish a lot of fond thoughts about demons.

Unfortunately, she also didn't cherish a lot of fond thoughts about orphanages. She pretty much figured they were all lumpy oatmeal and cold baths. But Mother Superior Catherine Mary St. Ignacious had been running the orphanage at St. Maddie's since Charisma had come to the city, and, as old as she was, probably since the orphanage had been founded about a hundred and fifty years ago. Under Mother Catherine's guidance, the nuns really cared for their kids, and protected the ones who had gifts. Charisma had become a fan.

Charisma opened the door all the way. She didn't want to; Martha was a neat freak, and when she saw the plethora of books, stones, weapons, paintbrushes, and canvases Charisma had stacked around, she would do her patented icy-housekeeper routine. Martha always made Charisma feel like a chastised child. But Charisma wanted the breakfast, so she braved Martha's irritated glare to take the tray. "Thank you. Please, would you tell the other Chosen?"

"The Chosen Ones were called earlier to an attack on a subway station on Broadway. You were still sleeping. They're gone."

Charisma stared at Martha in dismay while chaotic thoughts tumbled through her brain. "They're gone? I'm alone?" Left to fight demons alone?

"I called Mr. John's cell phone," Martha continued. "No one answered, so the battle must be heated."

"I'll bet." Charisma had fought demons alone before. She'd done it successfully, too. It was just that last time, things hadn't gone so well.

She'd feel more confident if she were prepared. If only she'd had the stamina to work out a little more, train a little harder. If only . . . if only she could go back to bed and sleep for twenty-four more hours. "Okay. I'll get dressed and go down to the orphanage. I can do some damage. At least I can keep the demons away until the other Chosen Ones return."

"I told that to Sister Mary Louise." Martha nodded emphatically. "I told her you would save them."

At least, Charisma thought, she wouldn't have time to brood over her lost love.

And wow! That was looking on the bright side. With an eye to preserving her strength, Charisma said, "Ask McKenna if he'll drive me to St. Maddie's."

Martha slowly shook her head.

"Oh. I suppose he drove the Chosen Ones to their battle?"

"I'm afraid so," Martha said. "You can take one of the bicycles."

"That'll work." Much to Martha's disgust, the Chosen Ones kept a couple of sweet Cyfac racing bikes in the foyer. "St. Maddie's is only a few blocks."

Charisma snatched bites of oatmeal and fruit while she dressed in her jeans and leather jacket and gathered her weapons: two Glocks, fully loaded, knives and daggers stashed up her sleeve and down her boot, and her favorite weapon for fighting at close quarters—a medieval flail with a wooden handle attached to a chain and, at the end of the chain, a heavy iron ball with spikes.

She was good with the flail. The wildly swinging

iron morning star blew through the squishy-bodied demons with marvelous efficiency.

When she was ready, she headed for Irving's room.

Martha caught her before she got to his room. "What are you doing?"

"I'm going to report to Irving." Because the Chosen Ones always reported to Irving. John was their leader. Irving was their mentor—and their heart.

"He's asleep!" Martha said sharply.

"Oh. But he likes to know. . . . Is he having a bad day?"

"He's old," Martha snapped. "Of course he's having a bad day."

"Okay." Apparently *Martha* was having a bad day, too.

Turning the opposite direction, Charisma descended the stairs and moved toward the basement.

From the landing above, Martha asked, "Now where are you going?"

"We always gather in the kitchen after a battle. I want to leave them a note so they'll see it right away and come to help—"

"I left a message on John's cell."

"Sometimes after a successful battle, they don't remember to check their mes—"

"I'll text for you. And I'll tell them *as soon as* they get home."

"I don't want to take you away from your duties." Because Martha was known to be sharp and cranky when she couldn't keep to her schedule. Not like she wasn't anyway.

"I'll take care of the matter," Martha said.

"Okay. Okay. Thanks."

Charisma grabbed her bike and headed for the front door; she realized that seven years of work and worry—and hopelessness—were grinding at Martha, and probably at McKenna, too, and all too often the Chosen Ones took their services for granted.

On her way back, she would stop and grab Martha some flowers and a card. Then, when Charisma had time, she would clean her room.

Remembering the layer of dust on her nightstand, she planned for a *big* bouquet of flowers.

Flowers were like a promise of a better day.

# *Chapter 40*

---

Irving tapped his fingers on the library table. He looked around his beloved personal library, at the stacks of books and research material the Chosen Ones had flung hither and yon in their search for the key to open the still stubbornly closed metal box.

In their search for an answer, the Chosen Ones really believed that with enough investigation, they could find the answer to the question, *How do we break the spell that holds the box in thrall and free the feather?*

It never occurred to them there might not *be* an answer.

These Chosen Ones were young. So young. And earnest. In all his years as director of the Gypsy Travel Agency, he had never seen such dedication, such perception, such maturity gained in so short a time. They made him proud to be their mentor . . . although at the beginning, he had never intended to last the whole seven years.

He thought perhaps he had survived because the Chosen Ones had dragged him along in their energy wake.

Of course, in his business, it behooved him to consider that fate had been only waiting for the proper moment to take him.

For a moment in his mind he felt a brief flutter of protest.

He frowned. Interesting, that. He had considered himself to be resigned to the idea of dying. Although he would like to serve some higher purpose with his death . . .

Eyes narrowed, he scrutinized the box again.

When Martha moved into his line of vision, he jumped and gasped. "Martha!"

Inside his head, he clearly heard a woman's voice. *Oh, it's that bitch.*

He subdued an inner leap of excitement . . . and a smile.

At last. Dina had returned to him.

Martha waved and pointed at her ear.

He dug his hearing aids out of his pocket and put them on. "There," he said. "What do you want?"

"I wanted to ask if you or the Chosen made any advances on freeing the feather from the box."

"Here you see it." He indicated the box with his cupped hand. "Still locked tightly."

*You finally got the box out of the safety-deposit box?* It was Dina's voice in his head again, stronger this time.

He knew she felt his agreement, and kept his attention on Martha.

Sadly, Martha said, "It's a shame that the Chosen Ones are wasting so much valuable time on trying to open the box when the time left is now counted in minutes."

*She must be shaking in her boots that she threw her lot in with the losers. Martha always wants to come out on top.* Dina's sarcasm was awesome and biting.

Irving knew Dina was right: Martha despised the situation and the people who had failed to resolve it. He also recognized a vicious case of sibling rivalry when he saw it; after all, Dina and Martha were sisters.

*Yeah, it's true,* Dina admitted. *She was always pissed that I had a gift, and royally pissed when I joined the Others, and cosmically pissed when you and I hooked up. After all, she's so much purer than me.*

"Mr. Shea?" Martha waved her hand at him. "Are you okay? Or do you need new batteries for your hearing aids?"

"New batteries might be a good idea," he agreed. Better that than telling her Dina was back. "Top drawer of my bedside table."

Martha went into the other room.

He pushed his wheelchair over to the window and looked out.

There Dina was, standing on the street, smoking her cigarette and looking up at him.

She was the most powerful mind-speaker he'd ever met. With everyone else, she could project her thoughts into their brains and they heard her as clearly as a loudspeaker.

With him, all he had to do was think and she understood him. So he thought, *I've been waiting for you.*

*It wasn't safe before,* she answered.

*It's still not safe,* he warned.

*No, but Osgood is distracted, busy preparing the papers that give him ownership of the world.*

*You could come in here with me. I'd keep you safe.*

*I would only do that if I were dying. Or you were.*

Regret pierced him. *Sorry to disappoint you. I'm the healthiest almost century-old man you're ever going to meet.* And he turned away from the window.

*Don't be like that,* she coaxed. *It's not that I don't want to see you. It's that . . .*

*You don't trust me.*

A pause. *Yes, I do.*

Years ago, when they were young, he had used her, betrayed her, and abandoned her. Because of him, the Others had had her nose split from forehead to tip, a dreadful punishment that left her scarred and outcast.

He had earned her suspicion. He had no right now to wish he had been a better man.

"I can't find the batteries, Mr. Shea," Martha called.

"Forgive an old fool." Irving tapped his forehead ruefully. "I moved the batteries to the drawer in the headboard."

Dina's warm chuckle sounded in his head. *For an old guy, you're wily.*

*Old age has to be good for something. Pretending forgetfulness is it.*

*I know.*

*You're still young.*

*No. Not even compared to you, my darling.* She pulled out another cigarette. *So what's in the box?*

*A feather from Lucifer's descent from heaven to hell.*

The lighter paused halfway to her mouth. *Now, that's interesting. What does it do?*

*We're not sure, but we are almost sure it has something to do with one of Jacqueline's prophecies.*

Dina laughed so hard she went into a paroxysm of coughing. *Fucking prophecies.*

"Here you go, Mr. Shea." Martha offered him the two tiny batteries.

"I can't replace them, dear. My fingers aren't steady enough." He held out his hand to show her the palsy that shook him.

"Give them to me." Martha held out her hand impatiently.

Meekly, he handed over his hearing aids.

*When did she get so snappish?* Dina asked.

"We're all a little tense," he said out loud.

Martha looked up, startled and confused, and said something.

He tapped his ear again.

She shrugged and went back to work inserting the battery—which he was completely able to do himself.

*So how are you going to extract that feather from the box?* Dina asked.

*That's the question*, he replied, but this time he remembered to keep his mouth shut.

Martha offered him the hearing aids.

He put them in and smiled. "Thank you, dear. I don't know what we would do without you."

"I don't either," Martha said sharply. "I keep thinking about what Samuel asked last night."

He observed as she fidgeted, shifting from one foot to the other. "What's that?"

"He wondered what would happen if someone just flipped the latch and opened the box?" Nervous. Martha was nervous.

"I've wondered that, too."

"Which makes me worry. The dear boy is so impetuous."

Irving lifted his eyebrows—no small feat for a man with the weighty equivalent of Gandalf's eyebrows. "The dear boy?"

*The dear boy?* Dina echoed. *She hates kids.*

*They're hardly kids.*

*Compared to her, they are.*

*Crabby,* he thought appreciatively.

"Isabelle said he was not to open the box. But if we don't get it open soon, you know he'll try it." Martha spoke loudly and slowly, enunciating every word as if she knew she was competing for his attention.

She certainly had it, although probably not for the reasons she hoped. "What do you think is going to happen?"

"I don't know," Martha said. "But it could be dangerous."

"It could," Irving agreed.

*What's her angle?* Dina's voice echoed his own question.

Martha continued. "Isabelle said it best—which of the Chosen Ones can we afford to sacrifice?"

*That bitch.* In his mind's eye, Irving could see Dina tossing down her cigarette and, with a dramatic flourish, stomping on it. *She wants* you *to do it!*

*I intended to, anyway.*

*Bullshit, Irving.*

*Dina, I'm old. I've been atoning for my sins committed on this earth for a very long time—and my biggest sin was against you. It's time for me to meet my maker. Surely you can understand that? And approve?*

She didn't answer.

"Mr. Shea?" Martha stepped close to the table. "Are you all right? You look . . . distant."

He listened for another few minutes. Was Dina gone again? "I'm fine, Martha. Thank you."

Now Martha spoke too quickly, as if she had a schedule to meet. "Did you hear me when I asked which of the Chosen Ones could be sacrificed to open the box?"

"Yes. I heard you. Both times." In his mind, he continued. *The question for me is—why are you urging me on this course?*

"Because the bitch wants the feather for herself." Dina had run into the house and up the stairs. Now she stood in the doorway of Irving's bedroom suite. Her chest heaved; her eyes flamed.

Martha flung herself around to face the intruder. "You! What are you doing here?"

Irving had forgotten how much the sisters resembled each other.

Both were handsome rather than pretty, sturdily built rather than thin, with dark, gray-streaked hair, brown eyes, and tanned skin that betrayed their Romany heritage. Yet they were nothing alike.

Martha had elected to serve the Chosen Ones.

Dina had joined the Others.

Martha had served him long and well as his housekeeper, and he appreciated that.

More than fifty years ago, he and Dina had conducted a violent, passionate love affair, and it ended badly. His fault.

Yet he loved Dina. Loved her with an affection that only increased with age and distance.

Now the sisters faced each other like the adversaries they were.

Aggressive and angry, Dina slammed the door hard enough to make his collection of skulls rattle on the shelves. She paced around Martha. "What are you going to do with it, sister? Who are you going to give the feather to? Did you finally realize the Chosen Ones' ship was sinking? Did you feel the ice water lapping at your feet? Your thighs?"

"I don't know what you're talking about." Martha watched her as if she were a circling shark. "You shouldn't be bothering Mr. Shea. You shouldn't be here at all."

"But I am," Dina said. "And I heard everything you said. I was in Irving's head. You want him to open that box and take the chance that he'll be obliterated."

"The box needs to be opened. The feather needs to be rescued to fulfill the prophecy and save the world from being overtaken by the Others." Martha lowered her voice. "Having him try to open it is not such a stupid idea. He's close to one hundred years old, after all."

"New hearing aid batteries, Martha," he reminded her.

She whipped her head around to glare at him, then whipped back to face Dina.

"So you were encouraging Irving to open the box for the good of the Chosen Ones and to increase the likelihood that good will defeat evil." Dina smiled with cruel mockery. "Did you intend to remain in the room while he sacrificed himself?"

Martha leaped for the door.

Dina tackled her around the waist, slammed her against the table.

Martha gasped in pain, then twisted and pushed Dina to the ground.

Dina came up at once, gold candleholder in hand, and smacked Martha across the side of the head.

Martha staggered.

Dina caught her in her arms. She looked over her half-conscious sister at Irving. *Do it. We can never be together in this life. Too much divides us. Maybe we can be together in the next.*

"I love you," he said aloud. He ripped open the latch and threw back the lid of the box.

Magic roared out in an explosion that rocked the walls, blowing out and up in a blast of heat and light that disintegrated every life-form in the room.

Then, like a cool breeze, it slid across the shelves, ruffled the pages on the open books, whipped through the empty-eyed skulls, and dissipated as if it had never been, leaving only a three-foot-long gleaming white feather floating, suspended, above the box that had been its home.

# Chapter 41

———✦———

New York was never quiet. Even in the early morning, the city hummed with life and excitement: garbage trucks rumbling, early-morning commuters grumbling, shopkeepers opening their doors.

Yet *this* morning, as Charisma rode the three blocks to St. Maddie's, the streets were oddly empty and eerily silent.

Then from the south, she heard a hollow, rhythmic booming begin, as if someone were using a gigantic jackhammer to dismantle something big. Something like . . . the Statue of Liberty.

No. Osgood wouldn't dare. . . .

Yet the sound funneled through the streets, loud and ominous, and only a week remained until the Chosen Ones' chance was over and Osgood—and the devil—would reign for a thousand years.

*Better not think about that. Think about the job at hand.*

*Think about the orphanage under attack. Think about the nuns who would give up their lives for those children.*

Charisma rode faster.

St. Madeleine Brideau Orphanage had been built in the mid-nineteenth century near the then brand-new Central Park. The convent occupied a full quarter of a city block, big enough for the church, the sleeping quarters, the classrooms, and a small playground. Even during the best of times, a twelve-foot-high chain-link fence surrounded everything except the entrance to the church, which was protected at night by iron bars. Now Charisma saw that rolled barbed wire had been added to the top of the fence, and even in the daytime the bars secured the church.

Good thing, because demons, dozens of demons, clung to the fence across the playground from the ter-rified children who peered out the windows, facing off against the phalanx of nuns who protected the school doors.

Charisma skidded to a stop. She had never antici-pated this. She couldn't have packed enough weapons to deal with an attack of this magnitude.

In the past, demons had hidden from the sun, skulked in the dark, attacked on the sly.

Now here they were in bright light, bold and hungry.

She leaned her bike against the wall, crouched down, and studied the situation. She should have brought her Steyr machine pistol, difficult to control, but capable of shooting lots of bullets. Instead she was carrying two Glocks.

Not that it mattered; unless she could lure the de-mons away from the school, her pistols were of no use.

Positioned as the demons were, with the school behind them, she couldn't shoot at them. Her pistols were loaded with hollow-point silver bullets, filled with mercury and made especially for the Chosen Ones. Through trial and error, the Chosen Ones had discovered that these were the only bullets that, if aimed correctly, could send demons back to hell. The trouble was, bullets slid into those moist, amphibious bodies and fragments exploded out the other side, rocketing wildly onto the next target.

How Mother Catherine had managed to sneak one of her nuns out to send word to the Chosen Ones, Charisma did not know.

A diversion would have to work. If Charisma could draw the demons into the middle of the street, she had thirty-four rounds to use on the ugly, creepy, slimy little imps. Then the plan was to run like hell and hope they followed her.

With a shout, she sprinted forward and lobbed a smoke grenade at the fence.

Their grayish green heads turned in her direction. Their bug eyes widened in anticipation. Their tongues lolled and their teeth gleamed. Half of them leaped off the fence and cantered toward her. They grinned and chattered. Their rotten-fish stench filled her nose and lungs.

And suddenly, in her mind, she was back underground, surrounded and terrorized. Weak. Exhausted. Broken.

Bitten.

In a flash, she was no longer Charisma Fangorn, warrior and Chosen One.

She was a victim.

These demons had hurt her before. They would hurt her again.

They would kill her.

Charisma wanted to get out of here. She *had* to run away.

Then across the schoolyard, she heard it: The nuns shrieked their war cry. "Charisma! Charisma!" They raced toward the fence, rakes and shovels in their hands. They attacked the demons still clinging to the fence, knocking them off, scratching them, piercing them.

For shit's sake, they were nuns. Mostly *old* nuns. In sensible shoes. With sensible dark-rimmed glasses. They didn't know how to fight. They were going to get themselves killed.

Leaves from the dying trees skittered along the sidewalk. A wisp of smoke floated through like a lonely ghost. But no people, no dogs, no cats, not even a rat. Every living creature had abandoned the orphanage to its fate.

Charisma Fangorn would not do the same.

She ran backward, drawing the demons into the center of the street. Lifting her pistol in her trembling grip, she shot the ones in the clear. Five. Ten. Fifteen. She emptied the Glock and threw it, knocking out one demon more with the impact.

The bullets sent them flopping backward. Their heads exploded.

Some demons leaped on their remains, dining on their former comrades.

Some hissed and spit at her, their eyes gleaming with malice.

All drew back.

The nuns cheered.

One nun screamed, "Charisma!" and pointed up-ward.

A demon scaling the fence.

Flail in hand, Charisma ran forward, using the spiked ball to bludgeon demons out of her way. When she was underneath the slimy little cockroach, she shot and prayed the bullet didn't fall into the crowd of nuns.

The demon blew apart.

When she turned, she was surrounded, her back against the fence.

Just like before. Just like in the tunnels.

The bite on her shoulder burned at the memory.

She lashed out in all directions with her flail, driving them back. But no matter how many she took out, more and more pressed in on her, running sideways on the fence, attacking from the ground.

Panic built.

Behind her, the nuns screamed and battered the fence.

It didn't matter. She didn't stand a chance. *They* didn't stand a chance.

Her time had run out. There was no hope. Unless help arrived now, the evil tide would wash over her, take her to some new hell, and all the nuns and the children, too.

Sweat ran into her face.

Desperation seeped into her bones.

Where were the Chosen Ones? Where was her backup?

When would they come?

Then, with a roar that made the demons chatter and quake, Guardian burst from a manhole and leaped onto the street.

## *Chapter 42*

————❖————

With another roar, Guardian threw the hundred-pound manhole cover as if it were a Frisbee. It cut through the demons like a hot knife through butter, taking out two dozen as they scampered away.

The nuns screamed.

The demons wailed and fled in all directions.

But Charisma saw that hope had arrived.

Charisma attacked their enemies with renewed determination, using her blade in one hand, her flail in the other.

The demons ran as if pursued by . . . demons. They slithered. They jumped. They vanished into the storm sewers. And as suddenly as summer storm clouds appeared in the sky, they were gone.

Behind Charisma, she heard one of the nuns catch her breath and start to sob. She heard Mother Catherine comfort her.

But nothing mattered except Charisma and Guardian, alone in the street, staring at each other across a distance.

Two thoughts possessed her.

Seeing Guardian only intensified her love and heartache.

And . . . something was very wrong.

*Why had the demons run?*

"What's that noise?" one of the nuns asked.

Charisma heard it, too. At both ends of the street, she heard the growl of speeding cars.

She looked. Large, powerful, black Town Cars accelerated toward them.

A racket, a clatter . . . a chopping noise, close . . . and abruptly loud.

Right *there*.

Across the street, from over the top of the building, a helicopter swept over them, so low it cast a shadow on the pavement.

Tires screeched as the cars accelerated toward them.

*Trapped!* They were trapped!

"Charisma!" Guardian raced toward her.

The helicopter lowered a heavy rope net.

"No!" Charisma screamed. "Run!"

The net fell on him, knocking him to his knees, snaring him in its grip.

Cars shrieked to a halt. Doors flew open. Police officers piled out.

The New York police chief stepped from the car, looking smug and controlled in her crisp uniform.

Guardian struggled, lashing out wildly, a frantic animal in a trap.

Charisma ran toward him.

Officers caught her, held her as she struggled.

"God, what a monster!" she heard. "Look at the size of him." "Look at those teeth!"

Over and over, she screamed, "Guardian! No. Let him go!"

As Guardian fought the restraints, he stared at her, his blue eyes wide and desperate.

Then a man in a dark suit stepped out of one car, walked to the net, and waited.

Guardian glanced up. Saw him. Stilled. And shrank back.

The stranger was a tall man, middle-aged, sharply handsome, with brunette hair that curled in a wave on his forehead and pale blue eyes.

Charisma had never met him, never seen him before. But she knew he must be Smith Bernhard.

He was the real monster. He watched Guardian avidly, observing him with pleasure and greed. "What a delight to see you at last in your true form, Aleksandr. And what an interesting form it is. When I thought some trigger in your family's brain must be present for transformation to occur, I envisioned that an actual animal would be the result. This"—he waved his hand at Guardian—"this is very unusual."

Guardian snarled.

The police officers gasped and backed up.

Charisma struggled again. "No!"

"It's okay, miss," one of the officers who held her shouted. "We've got you. You're safe!"

As if she were afraid of Guardian!

Guardian's gaze shifted to the woman who uncoiled herself from the backseat of the car.

Charisma recognized her at once.

Iskra. The woman who had been at Aleksandr Wilder's side when he vanished.

The police officers who restrained Charisma moaned simultaneously, piteously, in the throes of desperate, needy desire.

Charisma glanced at them.

Both of them were riveted by the sight of Iskra's sinuous body, her flowing blond hair, her red lips and sensuously made-up eyes.

At that moment, Charisma recognized her as a *thing*. One of the Others. Like Ronnie, she had been given the gift of seduction. Like Ronnie, she had used it to destroy a member of the Chosen Ones.

No wonder Aleksandr had run off with her. He had known all was not right with her, but he hadn't been able to resist her.

Guardian *was* Aleksandr Wilder.

And Aleksandr Wilder had been fatally seduced.

"Guardian!" Charisma yelled. "Aleksandr! No! Don't look at her!"

He glanced at her. "Get away," he shouted. "Save yourself!"

Even with Iskra here, he recognized Charisma. He wanted to save Charisma.

As Iskra stepped forward, voluptuous and lovely, Charisma screamed again, "Aleksandr!"

This time, he didn't look back at her. He kept his gaze fixed . . . on Bernhard.

Bernhard, who gestured to the hovering helicopter to pull the net up.

Charisma screamed and cried until she was hoarse, straining against the men who restrained her. They wrestled with her, gently at first, then yelling in pain as she broke bones. The next bunch of officers subdued her with nightsticks to the head and arms.

She fell to her knees.

The police grabbed her by her arms.

"She's gone crazy with fear," one said.

"Or she's just crazy," said another.

The net began to lift off the street.

Guardian snarled and fought as he was lifted into the air.

From behind Charisma, someone plucked the remaining pistol from her belt. She heard the safety click off.

Also from behind her, the calm, imperious voice of Mother Catherine said, "Let her go."

The police turned.

Charisma turned.

Mother Catherine, withered, sweet faced, five-foot-nothing, pointed an imperious finger at the officers.

Sister Marie Clare, younger and with a cold, cool gaze, held the Glock steadily pointed at the police chief.

Sister Margaret, who had taught at the school for forty years, caught the ear of the policeman who held Charisma. "Young man, let her go!"

The police officers released Charisma.

Charisma seized the moment. She crawled to her feet, ran, and leaped to catch the net with both hands.

Guardian still struggled wildly.

"Guardian!" she yelled.

Still mad with terror, he didn't respond.

She crawled up the webbing, looked into his eyes, said intently, "Aleksandr."

He froze.

"Aleksandr, get my knife."

He came back to life, no longer a panicked animal caught in a trap, but a man. "Yes." Reaching into her vest, he pulled out her blade and instructed her, "Jump."

Fifteen feet off the ground, she dropped off the net and onto the street, crumpling in exhaustion.

The net rose closer to the helicopter. The helicopter headed over the building across the street.

And at the rooftop, Aleksandr slashed a hole through the net and jumped.

Bernhard yelled, "Get him! Catch him!"

Iskra stared, beautiful brown eyes narrowing.

Aleksandr ran along the rooftop.

The policemen raised their guns.

Bernhard hopped up and down. "Don't shoot. Don't shoot. He's mine!"

Aleksandr disappeared from sight.

Bernhard pointed at Charisma. "Take her. Keep her!"

The police turned.

In a firm tone, Mother Catherine said, "Thou . . . shalt . . . not."

The officers paused.

"You don't impress me," Bernhard said. "You have no authority here."

"No. Not I." Mother Catherine pointed to the spire of the church.

A disbeliever to the marrow of his bones, Bernhard turned red with fury. "Take the woman! We can use her to trap the beast."

One by one, the police officers looked at him, then at Mother Catherine, and shook their heads. "She works for somebody more important than you," one re-marked.

To her nuns, Mother Catherine said, "Pick Charisma up. Bring her inside."

Sister Marie Claire and Sister Margaret grabbed Charisma under the arms and dragged her into the schoolyard.

Mother Catherine adjusted her sleeves, adjusted her glasses, and followed.

# Chapter 43

As soon as the Chosen Ones arrived back at the mansion, Samuel said, "'Scuse me. Gotta go find Isabelle and tell her we're okay. She worries."

"Tell her we kicked some big gang booty!" Caleb lifted a fist.

"Tell her we're all healthy!" Genny rubbed her ribs. "Mostly."

Samuel watched everyone head for the stairs. "I'll tell her you're all sweaty and are going up for much-needed showers."

He got a unanimous thumbs-up on that one and headed to the library. No Isabelle. He checked the kitchen and found McKenna, who sent him then to the gym.

There he found Isabelle dripping sweat, working out with the weights, her face frozen in that fixed expression that said she was determined to do better this time than last time.

He loved that look. She got that look whenever she took over their lovemaking and made him cry for mercy.

Everyone thought she was such a lady.

She was.

Except in the gym.

And in bed.

"Hey, beautiful," he said. "We're back."

She leaped at him so fast he never saw her coming. She wrapped herself around him and kissed him deep and hard, then fiercely asked, "Are you all right?"

"We rescued those tourists from the stranded subway car, and exterminated an entire gang and half a dozen demons at the same time, and escaped relatively unscathed." He grinned at her. "And my hip is fine."

"Liar."

"It's good enough."

"Liar."

"I can get it on right here and now if you want me to prove it."

"No." She wrapped her fingers into his collar. "Listen. I've got a problem."

"You started your period." It was the only reason he could think of that she wouldn't want to get it on.

She sighed. "You are such a simpleton. Not every problem I ever experience is related to my reproductive cycle."

"I know, honey." But when she was holding his collar like she wanted to choke him, there was a pretty good chance. "Would you like me to tell McKenna to rustle you up a steak for dinner?"

"No! Listen to me." She thought. "That is, yes. A steak would be nice. Rare. Better have McKenna get out a steak for the other women, too."

"Women in prison cycle at the same time. Of course the female Chosen Ones will do the same."

"Would you listen to me?" Isabelle came as close to shouting as she ever did, and she backed him up against the wall.

He stood with his hands up. "I'm listening!"

"I think Charisma is pregnant."

He dropped his hands onto Isabelle's shoulders. *"What?"*

"I think Charisma is pregnant!"

"I heard you." He could scarcely collect his thoughts. "Why? Why do you think she's pregnant? Why didn't you say something earlier?"

"Last night, when I tried to give her strength . . . I thought I would cure her of any lingering malaise. Then I realized . . ." Tears filled Isabelle's eyes. She swallowed, but her voice wobbled as she continued. "I realized the venom in her system was still there waiting, and she couldn't be cured. I realized she was doomed. And she's my friend, you know."

"I know. She's my friend, too."

"I . . ." Isabelle released him, turned away. "I got distracted. I have feelings, too!"

"You're the most sensitive person I know. The most sensitive member of the Chosen Ones." Stepping up behind her, he placed his hands on her arms, rubbing up and down, trying to convey his concern for her.

"I can't fight a battle because when I inflict pain, it echoes back at me. So I have to stay home and wait to see whether you're killed in combat." She took a shaky breath. "It sucks. I hate it."

He knew it was tough on her. But it was unavoidable, and not worrying that she would be hurt sure made his battles easier to fight. "Honey . . ."

"The thing is, last night I got distracted by the impending death of my friend. But this morning I started thinking. . . . I'd noticed a faint pulse of life in her womb."

"But . . . how?"

Isabelle twisted out of his grasp and faced him.

"Okay, the usual way. Sorry. Dumb question. Who?" In a roaring burst of fury, Samuel shouted, "Was she raped?"

"No, I don't think so."

"Not raped?" He could see again. Breathe again. "That girl. She's like the sister I never had—and always wanted to slap down."

"I know, dear."

"She's such a smart-ass."

"So are you."

"She's always getting in trouble."

"She always gets out of it without any help."

"She's a bad influence."

"On who?"

He shouldn't have said that.

She wrapped his collar in her fists again. "On me? Really? On *me*?"

"She wears those clothes. And those shoes. And when you were mad at me, she encouraged you—"

"She told me you were the man for me."

"Really?" He perked up. "In so many words?"

Isabelle narrowed her eyes. "Can you focus on someone besides yourself for five minutes?"

"Right." *Charisma. Going to have a baby.* "You're sure she's pregnant?"

"Yes. The life was faint and new, but it was there."

"Who?"

"I guess . . . Guardian. Aleksandr Wilder, if that's who it is."

"Holy crap." Samuel groped his way to the weight bench and sat. "None of you women have ever conceived."

"We're all careful not to. Right now it's too dangerous, and we're needed on the front lines."

"Yes." Samuel was a realist. "But in the heat of the moment, things happen that maybe shouldn't, and us guys . . ."

"I can't speak for the other men, but I know you've done your duty."

"You make it easy." His half smile faded. "So, Charisma, who hasn't even looked at a man since that scuzzball Ronnie, went belowground, was chased by demons, bitten and almost killed, rescued by the beast that is probably Aleksandr Wilder . . . and had a grand time screwing her brains out with him?"

"Simplistic, I'm sure. But yes."

"And got pregnant." He tried to wrap his mind around the concept. "She's expecting. Got a bun in the oven. She's knocked up."

"She's with child," Isabelle said softly.

"Yeah." He smiled. "Yeah. This has to mean something significant. What?"

"I don't know, but we've got to tell Jacqueline and see if she's had a vision about this."

"Good idea. And get Rosamund working on the research books." He contemplated their next move. "How pregnant is she?"

Isabelle widened her eyes in pretend astonishment. "You can't be a little bit pregnant, Samuel."

"Smart-ass." He rephrased: "Does she know?"

"Absolutely not. She has an IUD with only a one percent chance of conception. One percent, Samuel! For her fertility to have coincided with this meeting with Aleksandr Wilder, for implantation to have taken place in her uterus . . ." Isabelle seemed to have trouble finding the words. "It's a miracle."

"Go, Aleksandr!" Samuel cackled with joy. "This kid's going to come out holding an IUD."

"She's not going to live long enough to have the baby!" Isabelle said angrily.

His brief burst of elation faded. "Right. I forgot. For a minute I felt hopeful, and I just . . . forgot."

Isabelle eased herself into his lap, wrapped her arms around his shoulders, put her head against his, and looked into his eyes. "I keep seeing this as a good omen; then I realize what we're facing, what will happen to Charisma, and . . ."

"Have you talked to her about it?"

"No. She's still asleep." Isabelle ran her fingers through the short hair at his forehead, stroking it back from his face. "And she was so exhausted I can't bear to wake her up."

"We have to talk to her."

"I know." Isabelle stood and straightened her shoulders like a soldier going into battle. "Come on."

He followed her out the door and tried very hard not to concentrate on the sway of her ass in the tight-fitting workout clothes.

As they climbed the stairs out of the basement, Isabelle moved more and more quickly. They ran up the stairs to the second floor and headed to the women's wing.

Seven years ago, when the Chosen Ones had first gathered together, all the women had slept over here. Now only Charisma kept a room there, and not that Samuel was sensitive or anything, but as he followed Isabelle along the corridor, he felt the loneliness of the empty rooms.

She stopped at one narrow door. She knocked.

No one answered.

She knocked again. She turned to Samuel. "I'm so worried about her. She's been asleep more than twelve hours. We're going to have to go in."

"You go," he said.

She nodded. She turned the knob, entered the room.

"Samuel!" Her voice was frantic enough to send him rushing in. "Samuel, she's gone!"

He looked around the wildly messy, feminine space Charisma had created for herself and shouted, "Where can the girl have disappeared to this time?"

"She couldn't have gone after Aleksandr by herself, could she?" Isabelle begged rather than asked.

"I don't know. If she's in love with him—"

"We've got to tell the Chosen." Isabelle caught his hand and pulled him out the door and down the corridor.

Then Jacqueline's scream sent them careening toward the men's wing. They met the other Chosen in the corridor, ran in a discombobulated mass into Irving's room, and halted at the sight of the open box, the floating white feather . . . and the empty wheelchair where Jacqueline knelt, sobbing.

# Chapter 44

———❖———

Slowly, stealthily, Aleksandr crept toward the Guardian cave, using his every human and animal perception to sense danger. Yet all was peaceful. Nothing was out of place. He could smell no new scent, see no nets or traps.

But he didn't trust even his senses.

Because he had been sabotaged. Suckered. Betrayed.

Taurean had come to him, warning him that Charisma was fighting demons against impossible odds. He'd rushed to her aid . . . and there he'd found his nightmare waiting to seize him once more.

A trap had been laid, and by someone who knew him, and Charisma, and what had passed between them in the safety of the Guardian cave.

Who?

He lingered in the shadows, waiting, his mind coldly checking off suspects.

Amber. She loved him. Could bitter jealousy have driven her to fury?

Moises. His childlike mind feared change. Had he helped stage the trap, not understanding it was Aleksandr who would be captured, not Charisma?

Taurean . . . He couldn't bear it if it was Taurean. She was the one person he trusted above all others.

Davidov. Aleksandr wanted it to be that handsome bastard Davidov. But he didn't believe it.

And one name stood out above all others. . . .

Aleksandr crept closer to the entrance. Closer.

He sniffed the air. Yes, his people were in there. His people, and . . .

He heard the rumble of a man's deep voice.

A grief-stricken wail rent the air. A burst of weeping and a groan of anguish.

The man spoke again.

Aleksandr knew that voice.

Dr. King. It was Dr. King.

Dr. King said, "I am so sorry. Guardian was betrayed. He was captured. He's not coming back."

Aleksandr crept inside and observed the scene at the table.

Dr. King stood on a chair looking kind and sorrowful.

Taurean was on the floor in the fetal position, rocking and weeping.

Moises scratched at his own face with his fingernails.

Amber stood shaking her head over and over, as if denial would change the facts.

No. Only the truth would change the facts that Dr. King presented.

In the shadowy places of the cave, the Belows stood weeping or staring in shock.

"I know how you all feel." Dr. King wore the usual: his black suit, his white shirt, a blue tie. He looked and sounded like the man in charge. "This is a shock and a tragedy. No one can replace him, so we need to think about closing the Guardian cave—"

"We can't give up on Guardian! He saved us. He cares for us." Amber swung around to face the Belows. "We have to rescue him!"

Dr. King intervened at once, projecting his authority and dominating these sad souls whom life had treated so badly. "We can't fight! These people have guns. They used a helicopter and a net to catch Guardian. They are all-powerful. We have to cooperate."

"No," Amber said. "I won't cooperate with the devil!"

Sternly, Dr. King said, "Then you won't survive."

Taurean muttered something.

"What?" he snapped.

Moises spoke up. "She said if you haven't met the devil face-to-face, maybe you are going the same way he is."

"That's ridiculous." Dr. King's tone softened. "But I understand your distress. I'm distressed, too, and I know that you are all upset—"

Aleksandr straightened to his full height. He stepped into the light. "*I'm* upset."

Dr. King spun to face him, and for one moment his eyes lit with joy.

Taurean rushed at Aleksandr, mewling like a cat. She embraced him, quickly, loosely, and jumped back.

Amber fell to her knees and raised her hands to heaven.

Moises walked toward him slowly, holding out his hand and weeping loudly.

Aleksandr took his hand and shook it, then gently moved him aside and advanced on Dr. King. "I'm very upset. Who told you I was captured? Who told you I wouldn't be coming back?"

Dr. King wet his lips. "Taurean . . ."

Taurean shook her head violently.

Moises said, "No, she didn't."

Amber caught on quickly, and leaned across the table. "Really, Dr. King, who told you?"

"I heard at my clinic." Aleksandr could almost see Dr. King's mind working. "A patient came in. . . ."

"You heard from a patient?" Aleksandr nodded as if he believed, then shook his head. "And you made it back to the Guardian cave before me? You're three-foot-nothing, and you beat a running beast back here?"

"Your mind isn't right," Dr. King said. "You probably lost your way. You probably blacked out."

"I know I didn't." Aleksandr stepped to the chair where Dr. King stood and, for the first time ever, deliberately towered over the tiny man. *"What have you done?"*

Defiantly, Dr. King tilted his chin up. Then he collapsed onto the chair. He sat with his legs straight out, his fists clutched tightly in his lap. "After you first appeared down here, and I found you, *they* came to the clinic. *They* came to *me*. I didn't go to them. I don't know how, but they knew that I'd found you. And they offered me money."

"You betrayed me for money?" Aleksandr hadn't expected that.

"Not money for me. For the clinic."

"Ah." That made more sense.

Dr. King continued. "You have to realize—no one

in the real world cares about the homeless. About the street people."

Aleksandr stared coldly.

"Except you and me," Dr. King added hastily. "Nobody official, I mean. Nobody with a checkbook. More important, no one believes it's possible for a black dwarf to care for them. I can't get government funding. I can't get charities to take me seriously. I had no funds, but I was treating people for disease, for hypothermia, for injury. I didn't have the most basic medical equipment. I was setting bones blindly, without an X-ray, using splints and rags. Treating disease with no medicines. Starving people came to me and I couldn't feed them. The homeless were sleeping on the floor of my clinic and I had no blankets to cover them."

"I got it. It was tough."

*"They* came to me and said that if I kept an eye on you, they'd support the clinic."

"They? Who are *they*?"

"I don't know. I don't know! I just know that for the past twenty months, I've had morphine and food and antibiotics whenever I needed them. I've done a lot of good. I stand by that." Dr. King was passionate. He was persuasive.

The Belows all shuffled forward a few steps.

He glanced around at them, then appealingly up at Aleksandr.

*Yeah, Dr. King. Who's going to protect you now?* "You told them about me, told them enough that they knew exactly how to bait the trap. You sent Taurean to me with the report that Charisma was under attack, knowing I trusted her implicitly, and knowing perfectly well that Smith Bernhard intended to take me captive."

"I was your friend!" Dr. King cried. "All this time, to the best of my ability, I have helped you!"

"Was the whole setup your plan? Did you tell them that the one foolproof lure to get me to the surface was knowing Charisma was under attack?" The beast in Aleksandr wanted to kill Dr. King. Or perhaps . . . Aleksandr himself wanted to kill him. "Did you ever think about Charisma? That she could have been killed?"

Dr. King began, "They promised—"

"And those people always keep their promises, do they?" Aleksandr saw before him a fool—and a future demon meal. "Did you really think that Charisma and I were such good *friends* of yours that we'd be willing to sacrifice ourselves so you'd have the cash to run your clinic?"

Dr. King hunched his shoulders.

"By the time you betrayed me, I knew what Bernhard had done to me, and you knew it, too. Operations without anesthesia. Torture and brainwashing." Aleksandr looked at his hands, warped, deformed, hairy. "He made me a monster."

Shaking with indignation, Dr. King got to his feet. "Get over it! I've always been a monster. I was born that way!"

"No. You made yourself a monster." Like a bully with a puppy, Aleksandr picked up Dr. King by the collar. He picked up the medical bag. He carried the choking, kicking doctor to the entrance to the cave. He wanted to throw him. Throw him as hard as he could.

Instead, he set Dr. King on his feet. He placed the bag next to him. "Get out," he said. "Go to your friends and tell them I'm back in the Guardian cave, and see what kind of support you get from them. And never, ever come underground again."

Dr. King straightened his tie, his jacket, his cuff links. "I didn't mean to hurt you."

Aleksandr snapped out a laugh. "You knew my story, you knew what had been done to me, and you double-crossed me anyway. Don't deceive yourself. No matter how many starving people you feed. No matter how many homeless you help. No matter how many of the sick you heal. You allied yourself with the devil, and you are going to hell." He turned and walked away.

"What difference does it make that you rescued Charisma?" Dr. King wasn't loud, but Aleksandr heard him clearly. "She's going to die anyway."

Aleksandr kept walking. "Not if I can help it."

"She's beyond help already. She beat back the demon's venom, but only temporarily. No one can escape the demon's venom, and sooner or later she will die, blind and in agony."

Aleksandr wheeled to face Dr. King.

With a small, spiteful smile, Dr. King concluded, "So even if you manage to escape Smith Bernhard, you'll be alone. Enjoy your years in wretched solitude, Guardian."

# Chapter 45

———◆❖◆———

Charisma remembered nothing from the time she saw Guardian escape the net until she woke to find herself standing in a dimly lit corridor full of doors, wearing pajamas, surrounded by nuns in nightgowns. She said aloud, "Either this is a weird dream, or I've been sleepwalking again."

Mother Catherine slowly reached out her hand and rested it on Charisma's shoulder. "You were sleepwalking."

"I was really hoping it was a dream." But Charisma knew better. She could still hear the earth beckoning, cajoling, demanding. "How long have I been . . . asleep?" she asked. *Unconscious,* she meant.

"Twelve hours. It's now eleven in the evening on the day of the demon attack." Mother Catherine tucked her arm around Charisma's. "Perhaps we should go to my office and talk."

The other nuns smiled kindly and drifted away, through the doors and into their stark bedrooms.

Mother Catherine led Charisma down the corridor and through a wide, ornate wooden door with a small plaque that read, PRINCIPAL'S OFFICE.

"I feel like I'm in trouble," Charisma joked. Except she meant it.

Mother Catherine gestured to a chair in front of a battered antique desk. "I think you *are* in trouble."

Charisma sat. "I guess I am. I just don't know which part of my trouble is the most important."

"This morning, after you passed out and we put you to bed, I stayed with you." Mother Catherine used her hands to lower herself into her seat. "I rapidly became concerned. You were talking aloud, begging me to tell you that Guardian had escaped—"

"Has he?"

"To the best of my knowledge, the poor thing has escaped."

"He's not a thing," Charisma snapped. "He's a man."

Mother Catherine lifted her eyebrows in surprise. "Of course. Forgive me."

Charisma subsided. She may have overreacted.

Mother Catherine continued. "After I reassured you of Guardian's safety, you then begged someone who was not visible to leave you alone, to let you live. Apparently whoever it was . . . is stalking you."

"Yes. That." Charisma wondered exactly how to tell a nun that the earth had given her a woo-woo gift. "It's more of a what than a who."

Mother Catherine showed her keen powers of observation when she said, "You do realize that in my days as the director of an orphanage and a convent, I've not only seen children with unusual skills, but I have also heard every story, and discovered some are even true. And now I've also been attacked by living demons from hell."

"I don't know if we can call them living."

Mother Catherine looked over her glasses at Charisma.

"Right. That's not important. Okay. Here we go." Taking a breath, Charisma told Mother Catherine everything, from the first moment she'd felt the earth bless her with a gift to her induction into the Chosen Ones, to the threat and the call that filled her head.

When she was finished, Mother Catherine leaned back and tapped her fingers together, her heavy-lidded eyes thoughtful. "You don't want to respond to the call?"

"If I stay here with the Chosen Ones, that's a good thing, too. They need me for all kinds of reasons." Charisma shifted, then caught herself. The chair was narrow and hard, and required that she sit straight-backed and very still. "They need a fighter, and I'm one of them, and maybe I can help figure out how to free that first feather from the box, and maybe I can help find the second feather."

Charisma might as well have saved her breath. Mother Catherine saw through her babbling to the heart of the problem. "When you follow the earth's call, what is it you fear?"

Charisma wanted to say more . . . but slowly she subsided, and answered the question. "I fear darkness. Forever."

"Death."

"Death with no chance of redemption. For eternity."

"If you want my advice—"

Charisma really didn't.

"—I'd say your choice is clear. You don't want to abandon the Chosen Ones when your vow was to stay with them for the seven years of your tenure. That's admirable. But your vows to the earth far precede your promise to the Chosen Ones—"

"I never took a vow to the earth!"

Mother Catherine said nothing.

But her eyes, made big by her heavy, dark-rimmed glasses, spoke volumes.

Charisma folded her hands in her lap and shut up.

Mother Catherine continued. "And if the earth is calling you now to redeem your promise, you must obey."

"I don't *want* to die alone and underground," Charisma said passionately.

"Do you *know* that the earth demands your life?"

"I've had so many dreams . . . about going into a tunnel in a mountain, a tunnel without light or hope. And I know there's another world on the other side, but I also know I might never find my way out. Not ever." Charisma swallowed. "Eternity in the dark."

"I have some experience with calls from the beyond, and women who fight that call for good reason. But I also know that you have to take the gamble. You have to hope that what good you've done on this earth will be a light on your way. Do you not?"

Charisma sighed. She nodded.

*Why* did she have to end up in a convent with a clear-sighted, honorable nun?

"Good." Mother Catherine opened her desk drawer

and dug deep. "You can't go to your meeting with the earth in pajamas. It's not respectful, like attending mass without your head covered." She pulled out a set of keys. "I've kept the clothes I wore to the convent in 1960, when I renounced the world and all its vanities. I think they'll fit you very well." She went to the tall cabinet in the corner, unlocked it, and smiled.

Charisma saw a plethora of papers, holy day decorations, and supplies. And graduation gowns in the school colors.

Mother Catherine flipped through the hangers and crowed with delight. "There it is. I've been saving it for a special occasion." With loving hands, she brought forth a cloth garment bag with buttons. She laid it across her desk, opened the buttons, and revealed a cream-colored Jackie O–styled jacket with matching trousers.

Awe brought Charisma to her feet.

"It's Chanel. Some might say I've been saving it out of vanity." Mother Catherine stroked the wool with her fragile, twisted fingers. "I say I've been saving it for you."

"It's . . . It's too much. It's a piece of history. You should keep this. It's yours!"

"Yes, and I wish to give it to one of my favored children, one who will appreciate the gift." Mother Catherine smiled at Charisma's reverence. "Now take it."

With reverent hands, Charisma accepted the suit.

"I wore it with a blue cotton blouse." Mother Catherine removed the hanger from the closet and frowned. "Oh, dear. It's a little faded around the shoulders."

"It's dark down there. I can wear the blouse"— Charisma took the hanger—"and as long as I keep the jacket on, the earth won't notice."

"No." But still Mother Catherine frowned. "I saved the undergarments." She pulled an old cardboard box covered with boldly colored flowered paper from the top of the closet and opened it. "Yes! And the shoes."

"Oh . . ." Charisma cooed as she lifted the cream-colored handmade Salvatore Ferragamo pumps out of the box. "These are fabulous."

"They work very well with the suit." Mother Catherine snapped the box shut and placed it on the desk.

"Thank you. But I can't . . ."

"Of course you can. I give it all to you."

"Thank you. Really. But I can't wear the heels to the cave. It's too far. And it'll be dirty."

Mother Catherine's eyes widened in horror.

They both contemplated the pristine shoes.

"I'll get your athletic shoes." Mother Catherine disappeared, and returned in only a minute carrying Charisma's black-and-fluorescent-pink training shoes. "There. You can wear these until you get there, and change before you step on sacred ground." Mother Catherine nodded decisively. "Now I'll leave you to dress."

"Right. Sounds good. Thank you," Charisma said again as the door closed behind Mother Catherine.

She kept on her own "undergarments"—not only did the idea of wearing Mother Catherine's freak her out, but the elastic in them had failed about thirty years ago. She didn't have hose, of course, de rigueur for 1960, but her workout bra and panties gave her a slim line under the suit, which was even more fabulous than Charisma had first imagined.

Donning her training shoes made her wince, but when Mother Catherine knocked and entered, Charisma spread her arms. "Well?"

Tears sprang to Mother Catherine's eyes. "My dear child. You do me—and Chanel—honor in your choice of garb."

Charisma closed her eyes in relief.

Mother Catherine slipped the pumps into their custom cloth bag and handed them to Charisma. "Now come."

"It's night. I'm going to need help getting out of the convent so I can go belowground."

"No, you won't." Mother Catherine shook her head and led her down the corridor, past the doors to the nuns' bedrooms, toward a small locked door at the end of the hall. She unlocked it and turned on the light.

Charisma peered down the narrow, steep stairway.

"When Sister Brigetta found you sleepwalking, this is where you were headed." At the bottom, Mother Catherine flipped on the next light.

The basement was storage for the school and convent, full of boxes and paintings and chipped holy statues. At the back, where the light was the dimmest, was another door, metal and secured with a series of locks.

Charisma's heart began to beat heavily.

Behind that door waited her destiny.

As Mother Catherine opened the locks, she said, "Remember, my child, you have to ascertain the right thing to do, and do it."

As the door swung open into the Stygian darkness, Charisma said, "You make it sound so easy."

"It is. You will do the right thing. I know it." Mother Catherine handed her a flashlight, lifted her hand and blessed Charisma, and left her standing, staring into the darkness and wishing she had Mother Catherine's faith . . . in herself.

# *Chapter 46*

———◆❋◆———

An hour later, Davidov found Charisma wandering slowly through the tunnels and led her to his empty brew pub. He set her on a bench at a long table. As he served her warm, rich beef stew, he said, "Mother Catherine tends to think of the broader picture, and miss the fact that you might need refreshment before you start out on such an arduous passage to the heart of the earth."

Charisma didn't ask how he knew about her journey or her destination.

Davidov knew everything.

But she did smile awkwardly. "Not that I don't appreciate this, Vidar. And I know you're right; I do need fuel to continue on. But the truth is . . . I think I waited too long to take the first steps on my quest."

He placed a restorative draft by her right hand. "What do you mean?"

She stirred her spoon around in the bowl of stew.

"I'm dying." She looked up fast, catching him frozen behind the bar, his expression rife with dismay and guilt. "You knew it, didn't you?"

"Yes. Last time I saw you . . . Yes." His eyes were sorrowful.

She had suspected, feared . . . but to have her apprehensions confirmed was a knife to the heart.

She wanted to scream denial, ask for a reprieve, go to Guardian and beg that he love her one more time. "I couldn't figure out what was wrong with me. Why I was so tired. And just an hour ago I was ready to make the trip into the depths to answer the earth's call, and now I can barely lift my spoon. It's the demon's venom, isn't it? Mother Catherine said I would know to do the right thing, but I've delayed too long. I'm too feeble and now I'm going to die." Putting her head down on the table, she closed her eyes and began to cry, weak tears that slid down her cheeks, mournful sobs that broke her body.

She heard a commotion by the door.

Davidov murmured something.

"Have you done everything you can to reach the heart of the earth?" Davidov asked from behind the bar.

"Yes. Yes," she said. "And now I'll die without serving the earth, and without finishing my term as a Chosen One. Now I can never rest. I'm doomed to wander the earth forever."

She felt the warmth of someone hovering over her. A hand tenderly brushed the hair off her forehead.

Her eyes fluttered as warmth seeped through her.

Guardian said, "But you *haven't* done everything to answer the earth's summons. You haven't asked for my help."

She caught her breath.

He leaned over her, awesomely beastly, beautifully hairy, fierce and frightening, dressed in his black superhero fighting suit, alive, free . . . and smiling tenderly. At her. "I'll go with you, Charisma Fangorn, to the ends of the earth, and if you're too weak to make it on your own two feet, I'll carry you."

Her heart leaped with joy, and she flung her arms around his neck. "You *did* escape!"

"Thanks to you, my brave and foolish darling." He kissed her.

Her blood heated. Her cheeks flushed. For the first time since she'd left the Guardian cave, she felt truly well.

Then he asked, "When do we leave?"

"I'm not going the ends of the earth. I'm going to the depths." She clutched her fingers in his hair. "You *will* have to carry me. And . . . I don't know the way."

"Then we'll have a good long trip together."

"Our first trip . . . and our last." She watched him as she made her pronouncement.

He trembled in her arms. "I don't believe that. I refuse to believe that."

"You knew, too!" Did everyone know she was dying . . . except her?

"Only a few hours ago, Dr. King told me." Guardian's eyes narrowed until he looked rather . . . beastly.

"Oh." Charisma put her head on his shoulder. "I shouldn't let you even try to come with me. It's dangerous, and it's selfish of me when I probably won't return, and you . . . I don't know how you'll find your way back on your own."

Determinedly, he said, "I don't know, Charisma, how you would stop me."

She smiled. "If you're determined to come, I am most grateful."

"Don't be grateful. Be well."

"I'll do my best. For you. For the Chosen Ones."

On the other side of the table, Davidov cleared his throat.

When they looked around, he put another bowl of stew on the table. "Better eat, both of you. You've got a long journey and it's later than you think."

While Guardian ate, Charisma changed into Mother Catherine's Ferragamo pumps. She stood and grimaced. "I was afraid of that. These really pinch."

"Someone else is giving you shoes?" Guardian asked with reserve.

"The mother superior at the convent," she told him.

His attitude changed to one of magnanimous approval. "How nice of her."

"It was, wasn't it?" She grinned at him. "Whenever you're ready, I'm ready."

Guardian rose. "Let's go then."

She climbed up on the bench.

He turned his back and bent.

She climbed on, wrapped her arms around his neck and her legs around his waist.

He straightened.

"Wait." Davidov folded a napkin and came to her. He tied it over her eyes. "You don't need your vision. Listen to your instincts. You were born to make this trip, Charisma Fangorn. You will get there if you rely on your instincts."

# *Chapter 47*

———✦———

"**W**e're almost there." Charisma's voice sounded in Aleksandr's ear.

"Stay with me," he said.

"I am trying, Aleksandr. You know if I could stay, I would never leave you, don't you?"

"Yes. I know," he said softly.

So this was the final challenge of their trip? He had to face the fact that just as he found Charisma, he would lose her? That a few gleaming golden moments together were all they would ever have?

Now that Aleksandr's amnesia was vanquished, he remembered every challenge he'd ever faced in his whole life.

Nothing compared to this trek into the bowels of the earth. He fought demons. He jumped a river of fire. He crossed an icy lake. Bats flooded toward him, tangled in his hair, flapped in his face. The farther they went, the more he was aware . . . that none of this was true.

Or rather, it was true, but it did not exist in the real world. The challenges were picked for him, playing to his fears, past and present.

But although he expected to see Iskra and Smith Bernhard, not even their phantoms would descend into the bowels of the earth to challenge his resolve.

No, it wasn't Iskra and the doctor that made him wonder if he could go on . . . it was Charisma's weight, growing ever lighter as they traveled. At first she had been a solid mass of muscle, a burden he was glad to carry, but a burden nonetheless.

Now, she was almost nonexistent, a feather on his back.

"How long have we been traveling?" she whispered. "Weeks? Months?" Time didn't seem to exist down here.

"I don't know." He only knew that the farther they went into the depths, the lighter she became, as if her spirit were lifting from her body, preparing itself to soar.

"Almost there," she promised again, her voice hoarse and drowsy. "I hate to ask . . . but can you carry me inside the cave?"

"I intend to."

"Thank you. I had hoped to spare you the final trial . . . but I don't have the strength to walk."

He stumbled.

"Aleksandr." She stroked his hair. "You have brought me so far. You can do this."

Lose her? No. No, he couldn't.

With Charisma on his back, he stepped through the arched entry.

The cave softly gleamed: the walls, the floor, the stalagmites and stalactites . . . the broad raised stone, smoothed into a shallow hollow.

"There," Charisma said. "Put me there on the altar."

When had she discarded her blindfold?

But when he placed her on the upraised stone, he saw she still wore it.

"It's beautiful. We are in the earth's living heart." Her voice was worshipful.

He looked around. They were in a cavern. Vast, colorful, with lofty stone formations. A spring bubbled forth from the wall, splashed down the stones, babbled across the cave. Yet the cave was barren and, except for the fire pit in the middle, stripped of all signs of humanity. In his opinion, the Guardian cave was larger and more impressive.

How did she know about the altar? What did she see without her eyes? What would this sacrifice demand of her?

He placed his hand on her forehead.

The heat of her fever burned like a fire. He glanced around. He needed to get her out of here, take her somewhere she could get medical attention.

"No." As if she heard him, she caught his wrist. "It's okay. I am dying, Aleksandr, but before you volunteered to bring me here, I thought I was going to die alone. You're here with me, and for that, I thank you."

"I don't want your thanks. I want you to live!"

"I want that, too." She shook her head. "I don't see it happening. Now . . . go sit by the fire, and keep warm in the chill of this winter day."

"It's not winter." Far above, in New York City, the sun shone for long hours of the day, and the heat penetrated even into the Guardian cave. He wanted her to remember that—to remember real life existed, that the two of them now lived in an alternate reality.

She seemed to hear his thoughts. "I know the city is there. But it's not more real than this. Let me rest. I promise to call you before I go."

Flames sprang to life in the pit.

He knew he had to leave her alone to do what she had to do.

He went and sat beside the pit.

Charisma lay prone on the flat, smooth stone and sighed with pleasure. The surface supported her. The rock gave her strength. Here, even with her eyes closed, even with Davidov's blindfold in place, she could see the energy of the earth, glowing, pulsing, alive and violent, soft and warm, sharp and frigid.

Was this cave a dream? An illusion? Did it exist only in her mind, or was it a location in the earth? She didn't know. She knew only one thing. . . . "It is a good place to die."

Then a whisper of a promise slid through her mind. She could hear the earth's song again.

*You don't have to die.*

The earth could work its magic for her. The earth could cure her.

She almost leaped at the chance. But some caution held her back.

*What's the price?*

*Not a price, but a choice.*

She could drink from the stream, and she would live a long life.

Or . . . she could have the second feather.

*The second feather . . .* The words skimmed her mind.

One of the two surviving feathers from Lucifer's wing . . .

Osgood had obtained one feather and placed it into the foundation of his building, weighing it down with tons of concrete, trapping it and putting it forever beyond the reach of the Chosen Ones . . . or so he had thought.

Foolish man. A feather that had survived the descent from heaven would not be contained. It worked down through the tons of concrete, down into the earth. It had moved, slid, glided through the ground.

Charisma had searched underground for that feather.

Now she turned her head and there it hung, pure and white, encased in a crystal-clear stalactite, waiting for the right person to free it.

Even with the blindfold on, she could see it, sense it . . .

A choice.

Charisma had a choice.

She could live.

Or she could take the feather to the Chosen Ones and save the world before her death.

*I can't take the feather to the surface. I'm too weak. I'm dying.*

The earth answered her.

One taste from the stream would restore her enough to retrieve the feather, use it, and finish her time with the Chosen Ones.

To drink from the stream would give her life—and strengthen the stalactite, encasing the feather forever.

A choice. One or the other.

A weight descended on her chest. She could hardly breathe.

She remembered her dream. The mountain. The dark. The hopeless search for a way out.

She wanted to pick life. So desperately.

Again she looked at the feather.

The crystal in the cave sparkled like diamonds and jewels, but nothing could compare to the beauty of that long, slender, perfectly formed wing feather. It hung suspended, waiting to be freed. And she was the only one who could free it.

She had to do her duty. She had to free it. *This* was why she had been summoned down into the depths of the earth.

She strengthened her resolve.

Then another temptation whispered through her mind.

*If Aleksandr drinks from the stream, he will be returned to his true form.*

She looked at Aleksandr, seated beside the fire pit, staring sadly into the flames.

*If you choose life, he'll take human form again. He can live in the sunlight, at your side. You'll be part of a family—his family, the Wilders, loving and supportive. You can have children, grandchildren.*

*If you die . . . he is condemned to life as a beast.*

*You said if he drank from the stream, he would return to his human form,* Charisma thought.

*Only if you drink, too. If you don't choose life, he will remain in his current form. They'll hunt and hurt him forever. He'll go mad with loneliness. You will have condemned him.*

The earth cajoled, *Choose life.*

She tried to remember what Mother Catherine had said to her about doing the right thing. She tried to remember what Davidov had said to her about listening to her instincts.

But weren't her instincts telling her to grab life at all costs? Wasn't life all that mattered?

Yes. Life was all that mattered.

She swallowed a sob.

Just not necessarily *her* life.

What mattered were the millions of lives she could save by retrieving the feather.

This wasn't a choice. Charisma had lived her life trying not to be her mother, selfish and shallow. If she did this now, took the temptation the earth offered, every effort she had ever made, every vow she had ever spoken, every belief she had ever held . . . would be betrayed.

And with that, Charisma had made her decision.

She sat up, took off her blindfold.

She could see perfectly well, and in this reality the cave looked like a cavern, large and colorful. But not the diamond-encrusted cavern she had seen before.

It was just a cave.

The fire in the fire pit died.

Guardian looked up. He was still long-armed, long-legged, barrel-chested, and hairy, and yet . . . for her, his blue eyes lit with concern and love, and if they had a long life to live together, and he remained more beast than man, she would be the happiest woman in the world.

If they had a long life together . . .

It was possible. . . .

She slid off the altar. "We're going to take the feather to the Chosen Ones."

He hurried to her side. "The feather? What feather?"

"It's here." Slowly, with his help, she walked to a long, slender stalactite, no longer clear and glittering, but dull and gray. "It's trapped in here."

He stared as if he didn't know whether she was quite sane.

"Trust me." She tapped on the rock, then tried to fracture it with her fist. "But I can't get it out alone."

"Let me try." Unwavering in his dedication to her, he tried his best to break the rock apart.

He could not.

She leaned wearily against the unyielding stone. The earth was not done testing her. "We have to take a taste from the stream."

Clearly he didn't understand her tragic tone. "All right. It's not a big deal. We'll get some water. We'll rest for a minute. Then we'll come and, um, free the feather." Which he obviously could not see, and possibly didn't believe was there.

"Yes. That's what we'll do."

They went to the stream and knelt. They cupped their hands and tasted just a few drops.

That sip was better than anything Charisma had ever tasted. Of course. Her fatigue vanished like a drop of water on a hot griddle. Energy filled her. In a life spent in study, in researching, in working too hard and fighting too often, she had never felt so good.

She knew if she drank a little more, she would live.

And if he drank a little more, he would be Aleksandr Wilder again.

It would take only a small amount. . . .

*Temptation.*

If they drank, yes, they would be healthy, but they would also live in a world corrupted by such wickedness, filth, death, and degradation, they would be miserable all their days.

She caught his hand. "One taste! No more."

Once again he wore that wary, concerned expression, as if the state of her sanity worried him. "What happens if we drink too much?"

"I'll be condemned to a lifetime of knowing I did the wrong thing." She shook her hands dry. "Let's get the feather."

They returned to the stalactite. They put their hands on it, ready to break the stone.

At their touch, the stalactite crumbled into dust.

The three-foot-long feather, pure white and faintly glittering, floated into Charisma's arms.

It weighed almost nothing, a piece of heaven displaced to earth.

In awe, Aleksandr whispered, "I didn't know whether I believed the feathers existed before. I didn't know whether I believed we could win this battle. Now . . . at least I have hope."

"Yes. This is hope given form." Taking off her cream-colored Chanel wool jacket, Charisma wrapped the feather as tenderly as a baby and carried it out of the cave.

As she crossed the threshold into the real world, she felt a jolt of approval, a pat on the head.

*You are a worthy servant, Charisma Fangorn.*

And the stones on her wrist sprang to life once more.

The earth song was as beautiful as she had remembered in her dreams.

## Chapter 48

The journey back from the center of the earth went all too quickly. It was as if the challenges that had assaulted them on the way down had disappeared into the mists of their minds. It probably also helped that Charisma's strength had returned, and, with the help of a change from her Ferragamo pumps to her athletic shoes, she was able to walk next to Aleksandr all the way back.

Now, at the end of the long, dark tunnel, the door of Davidov's brew pub glowed softly. Behind it, Aleksandr knew, was duty, civilization, the real world.

If he was going to speak, he had to speak now.

He stopped her with a hand on her arm. "Charisma." Her name was a treasure against his lips. "When we go through that door, if Davidov has done his job, the Chosen Ones will be there and we'll go to war."

"We'll do battle," she agreed, cradling the Chanel-wrapped feather in her arms. "Some of us won't return." *She* wouldn't return.

That was a knowledge that tore at him like a raven's claws. And that was the reason he said, "Before we go in there . . . I want to say . . . I have to tell you . . . I lost my mind for a while. For twenty months, I didn't remember my life before I was Guardian. And since, it's all been demon fighting, and blood and gore, sweat and pain, and, at the end, certain death. There's no escape in sleep, either; that's all terror while nightmares fight their way out of my brain." The recollection of Smith Bernhard and his abhorrent surgeries shattered him yet again, and for a moment he trembled.

She moved closer, her green eyes filling with tears.

But now was not the time for terror. Now was the time for Charisma, and him, and saying what needed to be said. He shook off the memories and continued. "Every minute with you has been golden, filled with laughter and sex and love."

"And you and me fighting," she reminded him.

"And you and me fighting. Good times." He turned her face up to his. "No one can ever take this time away from me. I have jewels to remember; the joy of realizing you were going to live and see, the way you attacked me the first time, when you were blindfolded—"

She cringed. "Yes, that was one of my better moments."

"It was, because you didn't recoil when you realized I was a monster."

Irritated, she said, "You're not a monster! Stop calling yourself that."

"The tone of your voice when you scold me." He smiled at her. "Your voice in every way, especially hearing you hum and realizing your singing *would* attract demons."

She shoved at him, and wavered between tears and laughter.

"How understanding you are of Taurean," he said.

"She's a nice lady."

"Not many think so. I love your two-tone hair." He ran his fingers over her head. "I loved seeing you in the waterfall the first time, naked and glorious. The sun shone in the cave—"

"It was night."

"The sun shone, because you were the most beautiful thing I'd ever seen." He cupped her cheek. "No matter what happens, you've given me memories. Good memories. On the day I die, today or tomorrow or fifty years from now, your name will be on my lips, and I'll remember . . . you."

Tears welled in her eyes. "I'll remember you, too. Wherever you are, that's where I want to be. Wherever you are, that's paradise."

There was nothing else to say. There was nothing else to do.

Charisma stood looking up at him, tiny, defiant, courageous, with tears in her green eyes, dirt on her face, her cream suit smudged, and her feet shod in her black-and-pink athletic shoes.

He had never seen anything more beautiful in his life.

Standing on tiptoe, she lifted her head.

He leaned down.

With the feather cradled in her arms between them, they kissed, a kiss of passion, love . . . and good-bye.

Stepping away from each other, they nodded. They clasped hands.

"All right, then," Charisma said. "Let's go."

Aleksandr opened the door to Davidov's brew pub.

She stepped over the threshold.

He followed.

She stopped.

He stopped.

Davidov had kept his promise. He'd assembled an army to fight Osgood and his evil. The place was full: the Chosen Ones and their spouses, Taurean, Moises, Amber, the Belows, people from the street, people from the mansions, police officers, former Chosen Ones. Davidov was putting out plates of food and drink.

And in front of them all, the Wilders. Aleksandr's family. His mother, Firebird, smiling with tears in her eyes. His father, Douglas, looking fierce and glad. His uncles and their wives. A *bunch* of the cousins. And his grandparents, Konstantine and Zorana, so much older than the last time he'd seen them.

What did Aleksandr feel?

A leap of joy.

A dollop of dismay.

He wasn't ready for them to see him like this. He was a beast. He was the Wilder who had betrayed his family's decision to turn away from any temptation to once again indulge in shape-shifting. Worse, he had done it to save his own life.

But it was too late. They were here, they had seen him, and he couldn't hurt them again.

Arms outstretched, he walked toward Firebird.

His mother ran to him, sobbing.

His grandmother, Zorana, hurried over and wrapped her arms around them both. His father joined them, holding them and saying, "Thank God. Thank God." His grandfather cried tears of joy.

As the rest of the family closed in, Aleksandr looked over the top of the smiling crowd to Charisma, who stood watching him with such tenderness, he knew he was the luckiest doomed man in the world.

While the Wilders embraced, shook hands, laughed, and scolded, the Chosen Ones surged to surround Charisma.

Jacqueline's eyes gleamed at the bundle Charisma held. "You found it!"

Charisma nodded and carefully unwrapped the shining feather. "We could have had it a lot sooner if I hadn't been such a coward."

Even Samuel laughed at that. "You put us all to shame with your courage."

Isabelle smiled at her. "For your reward . . . Show her, Sammy."

Samuel's eyes gleamed as he placed on the table a long object wrapped in blue cloth.

Charisma caught her breath. "Samuel! You figured out how to open the case without getting knocked on your rear?"

Her friends froze.

"What?" Charisma looked from one to another, at the guilt and grief etched on their faces. "What happened?"

"Irving freed the feather," Aaron said.

Charisma sank down on the bench and hugged her own feather close to her chest. "How?"

"We think he simply tore the latch open," Jacqueline said.

"He . . . Was he hurt?" But in her heart, Charisma already knew what they hesitated to tell her.

Genny hugged her. "He's gone."

"Gone," Charisma repeated.

"Everything in his study is untouched." For the merest wisp of a second, Rosamund looked relieved. Then her eyes filled with tears. "But there's nothing of *him* left. Jacqueline thinks . . . That is, she's pretty sure . . ."

"Martha's gone, too," Caleb informed her.

"Martha helped him?" Charisma asked. "I don't know. She always supported us and cared for us, but I thought it was to honor the idea of the Chosen Ones. Honestly, I didn't think she would ever have sacrificed herself for us."

"We talked about it, and we agreed," John said.

"In her case, I don't think it was a willing sacrifice. There're some pretty violent vibes in there," Jacqueline said. "And the dust of three souls who went on in a wave of magic."

"Three souls?" Charisma sprang to her feet. "Oh, no. Not McKenna!"

"No. Dina." Samuel attentively unwrapped his feather. "I'm pretty sure it was Dina. I tried to find her in my mind, and she's gone. So Irving and Dina died together, and Martha . . . I guess Martha came along for the ride."

"But Irving was just there, in his library, talking to us, guiding us. What will we do without him? He was our link to the former Chosen Ones, our mentor, our friend."

The exterior door to Davidov's bar opened. McKenna slipped in.

Charisma smiled shakily at him.

He nodded at her.

A movement on the table focused Charisma's attention.

In slow motion, Samuel's feather lifted off the table.

As people noticed, the noise from Aleksandr's reunion died.

The police, the wealthy from the mansions, people who had never witnessed anything magical stared with rapt attention as the feather rose as if on an invisible breeze. It swirled once in a full, graceful circle, as if celebrating its freedom from its long confinement. Then it floated toward Charisma and settled into her arms directly beside the other feather.

A moment of silence.

The room exploded in cheers.

John allowed the commotion for one moment; then he stepped up on a bench and flung out his arms.

The Chosen Ones quieted.

The civilians kept gasping, talking, marveling.

John shouted.

Still the babble went on.

Konstantine Wilder put his hand on John's shoulder. "Let me," he said in his accented English, and shouted, "It is time!"

Silence descended.

"No one exerts authority like the old wolf," Aleksandr said in Charisma's ear.

"So." Konstantine turned to John and rubbed his hands together. "What's the plan?"

"We're going to Osgood's building, and we're going to destroy him," John said simply.

"Easier said than done," one of the older Chosen Ones said. "Have you seen what's happening out there? It's the apocalypse. Thunder, lightning, black clouds rolling in from all directions, all headed right for SoHo and the Osgood building."

"That's what we have to do," John said.

The brew pub rattled as the earth shook.

"The building is miles away. We've got sixty-five people in here. How are we going to get there?" Davidov, Charisma saw, was packing up the pub.

The mysterious man was leaving them now.

McKenna cleared his throat and stepped forward. "I believe I have the answer to that."

# *Chapter 49*

The New York City bus McKenna had commandeered came with one pissed-off bus driver. Rosie sat in her seat, chomped on her cigar, and shouted for everyone to get in and sit down; she had a schedule to keep.

In a low voice, Aleksandr asked McKenna, "The streets are empty. The whole subway system is shut down. What schedule is that?"

"I told her we had two hours to get to the Osgood building and stop him from taking over the world." McKenna's voice was both fascinated and appalled. "She cursed me and asked why I didn't tell her sooner."

"Really, McKenna, why didn't you?" Samuel gave Isabelle a hand up the steps, then bounded after her.

The Belows shuffled to the back.

Taurean shuffled with them.

The people from the mansions looked bewildered, as if they didn't know what to do in a vehicle fragrant with the smell of pee and furnished with plastic seats, but they finally moved into the front seats close to the police.

Charisma was interested to note that Amber sat with them.

The former Chosen scattered themselves up and down the bus.

Moises sat next to one of them.

Rosie got up, looked down the aisle, and shouted, "Hurry and get your freaking seat! This isn't a freaking first-class flight, and I am not your freaking steward-ess!"

The pace picked up.

The Wilders filled in the middle left side.

The Chosen Ones filled in the middle right side.

Isabelle took the seat behind Aleksandr and Charisma—and the feathers, wrapped in the blue cloth and cradled in Charisma's arms.

Samuel sprawled next to Isabelle. In an aggrieved little boy's voice he said, "I don't never get to hold the feathers."

Charisma turned around and grinned at him. "The feathers like me best."

He fake-grinned back at her.

She was going to miss him so much.

"Charisma is the Chosen One of the Chosen Ones," Genny said as she seated herself with John in front of Charisma and Aleksandr.

"All right. I'm putting my ass in the driver's seat, and we're headed for the Osgood building. There's not much traffic today"—an understatement; there was no traffic—"and we've got to get there fast. So if you're on the wrong bus, get off!" Rosie pointed at the door. "Otherwise, hang on and I'll get you there on time."

"I love that woman," Rosamund said.

Rosie put her ass into the driver's seat, slammed the bus into gear, glanced in the rearview mirror, and they peeled out so fast they burned rubber.

Across the aisle, Konstantine shouted, "Powerful engine in this thing!"

Charisma looked around.

The passengers were divided between the people enjoying the ride, mostly Wilders; the people looking stern about the speed, mostly cops; and the terrified, mostly everybody else.

The bus screamed south on Fifth Avenue, past Central Park, past the stores, shuttered and dark. The city streets were empty, and the black clouds scudded across the sky, blocking the sun, turning day to night.

Konstantine leaned over to Aleksandr and spoke.

Aleksandr nodded, then leaned forward. "John, do you have any real plan at all?"

John shook his head. "Get there, hopefully in one piece. Get inside with the feathers. Confront Osgood and see whether we can figure out how Jacqueline's prophecy will work."

"Play it by ear. Got it." Aleksandr leaned back and spoke to Konstantine.

Konstantine nodded enthusiastically, hooked his elbow around Aleksandr's neck, and gave him a hug, then gave John a thumbs-up.

Charisma had to admire Konstantine, a man who faced the annihilation of his entire family, possibly during a bus ride before the battle, and yet who glowed with good cheer.

Aleksandr leaned over to her. "He figures this is his last battle, and it's a good one. Plus he's happy to see me."

"Aren't they *all* happy to see you?" Charisma asked.

Aleksandr wavered. "Well . . . within reason."

Charisma's temper started to rise. "They didn't criticize you for your forced decision to change forms?"

"They didn't mention the way I look. I didn't mention the reason I look this way." Aleksandr rubbed the hair on his cheeks as if to call her attention to the difference between him and the boring-looking humans. "I imagine we'll get to that when we finish off Osgood."

Charisma nodded. "Yes. When we finish him off."

Aleksandr continued. "But my father and uncles are a little tight-lipped about why I didn't make contact sooner."

"You had amnesia!" Charisma glared across the aisle.

"The women cried for me. The men grieved. My mother is still weeping. I put them through a lot."

"Oh." Charisma glanced across the aisle. She knew Konstantine from his earlier visits to New York, and the rest of the family in a peripheral way. The legend of Darkness Chosen had been well documented, and she'd studied the Wilder family's rare success in their battle with the devil. She respected them for their determination and admired them for their courage.

But somehow none of them were the people she'd pictured.

Firebird kept glancing over at them, and every time she did, she smiled tremulously.

Douglas spoke to her quietly, and the glances he sent their way were a great deal more stern.

At Davidov's, Zorana had embraced Aleksandr . . . and then taken him by the shoulders and shaken him.

If it hadn't been so heartfelt, it would have been funny, for Aleksandr towered fully two feet above her.

The people Aleksandr had introduced as his uncles and aunts were all holding hands. . . .

"I guess, since they're Wilders, they know what they're getting into better even than we do," Charisma said.

Aleksandr put his hand to his chest, over his heart. "I would not have brought this trouble on them if I could have avoided it."

"You didn't make this trouble."

"No. But they are here because of me. For me."

"You should sit with them," Charisma said in a low voice.

"No. I shouldn't. I should sit with you." He put his hand over her cold fingers and warmed them.

Charisma was glad. In a time of so many sacrifices, whether they sat together on this last ride shouldn't make any difference to her. It shouldn't—but it did.

The bus rumbled past Madison Square Park.

Here a few people were on the streets, standing and looking toward the roiling black clouds and the lightning striking the empty skyscrapers, or running in the opposite direction. But mostly there was that unnerving stillness, as if the world were waiting for a storm to break.

Charisma found herself listening too hard, holding herself too tensely, and she jumped when Jacqueline turned and made a speech to the Chosen Ones. "Aleksandr is back. This is the moment we've been waiting for. It's time for us to join hands and feel the energy between us."

The bus got very quiet. Everyone craned their necks,

including Rosie, who watched in the broad rearview mirror and never slackened speed.

Jacqueline offered one hand to Caleb and one to Aaron in the seat behind her. One by one, the Chosen Ones and their mates joined hands: Jacqueline and Caleb, Aaron and Rosamund, John and Genny, Samuel and Isabelle, and finally Charisma and Aleksandr. For a long, tension-filled moment, nothing happened.

Then the feathers in Charisma's lap lifted.

Lightning zapped through the Chosen Ones, clearing their minds and gladdening their souls. Before, that was all that had ever happened, and it was enough.

But this time, in each of their brains, a vision sprang to life, and each of the Chosen Ones saw himself or herself soaring on angel wings through the crystal-clear air, the world far below, the heavens above . . . while Osgood's building broke apart and vanished.

Then the vision melted, the feathers settled back into Charisma's lap, and each of the Chosen Ones was breathless with awe, reinforced in his or her determination, and exalted with a renewal of hope.

Then the bus hit a speed bump so hard they left their seats and landed with a thump, and they laughed as Rosie drove them through Little Italy, toward Osgood Headquarters now towering on the horizon.

Jacqueline turned. "Did everyone have the vision?"

Nods all around.

"What did you see?" she asked.

"I was flying with the wings on my back," Genny said.

"No, it was me," John said.

"Me!" Aaron said.

Rosamund straightened her glasses on her nose. "A

most unusual occurrence. What is commonly believed is that this means that any one of us can perform the task at hand."

Jacqueline nodded. "We have to get to the roof of the Osgood building. That's where Osgood is. He's calling in the storm, remaking the earth. The roof—that's where we'll take flight."

"Then the roof will be our goal," John said.

"Charisma carries the feathers." Jacqueline's low voice carried to every ear. "So whether or not she takes flight, she *has* to make it to the roof."

John stood up and shouted, "Charisma Fangorn has to make it to the roof!"

Around the bus, every head nodded.

Rosie turned a corner so hard John hit the window and remained plastered there until she straightened the wheel.

"Hope we live through the ride," Konstantine shouted cheerfully.

Isabelle put her hands on Charisma's shoulders.

Charisma felt the flow of warmth start, and sighed with pleasure.

"You're stronger." Isabelle's surprise told Charisma that Isabelle, too, knew of her fatal poisoning. "Oh! How marvelous! Your gift is back."

"Yes." Charisma touched the stones at her wrist. They sang to her of duty, of sacrifice, of a death nobly borne. "I can hear the earth again."

"What about— Oof!" Samuel gasped as if Isabelle had elbowed him hard.

Both Aleksandr and Charisma turned to see Samuel holding his ribs.

He fake-smiled again, that lawyerly smirk that made

Charisma glad she had never faced him across a courtroom. "I was going to say, what about me? You know how selfish I am. Isabelle should put her hands on me."

"Yes! And heal you!" Before he could say another word, Isabelle put both hands on his hip and grimaced.

"Woman, you try my patience." But the small, pinched frown between his eyes vanished.

"We need you, Samuel. We need every warrior." Isabelle took her hands away and leaned sideways, as if trying to alleviate the pain in her own hip. "And don't try to tell me it didn't hurt, because now I know better."

Samuel wrapped his arm around his wife and brought her close against his chest, closed his eyes, and rested his head on hers.

Aleksandr watched them, and his beastly yet beautiful face twisted in anguish. Then he looked at Charisma, and his blue eyes softened. For a moment, just the briefest of moments, she slid her arms around him and rested her head on his chest.

No one else could have made her happy. Except Aleksandr.

The moment of loving communion was all too brief.

The bus shrieked to a stop.

Rosie flung open the doors and yelled, "Osgood Headquarters. Everybody out!"

# Chapter 50

***

Aleksandr joined the others as they moved to one side of the bus and peered out the windows.

Osgood Headquarters rose straight up, bleak, stark, almost completely windowless, with a sickly-white sheen that reflected the black clouds swirling in a circle around the top floors. In an eerie silence, lightning snaked out of the clouds, striking like flaming cobras at the walls, the trees, the ground. The earth began to tremble, then to shake. Giant cracks opened in the street, then snapped shut again while waves of destruction emanated from the building's foundation.

Seemingly oblivious to the shaking, Rosie lit a new cigar. "No time like the present!" She stomped down the steps.

Clinging to the seats for balance, everyone stumbled their way down the aisle and onto the circular drive. A landscaped and lavish covered walk led to the cathedral-size bronze-cast double doors that opened to the lobby. They walked forward, exclaiming at the bronze arches, the stone benches, the perfectly arranged landscaping. The entrance resembled any entrance to a grossly wealthy conglomerate, except . . .

They all slowed.

They all looked around.

Rosamund said what they were all thinking. "Where are all the people?"

There were no employees. No visitors. No guards. No one watching them suspiciously.

"Something is very wrong here." Charisma cradled the feathers a little closer.

"Osgood declared this Worldwide Apocalypse Day and gave them a holiday?" Samuel suggested.

Nobody laughed. Not even Samuel.

Ten feet before they reached the doors, John waved everyone into a circle around him. "Gather 'round. Gather 'round. And listen. I'm the leader of the Chosen Ones, which means I'm your general." He bent a stern look on the older Chosen, on the Wilders and the street people, the wealthy, and the Belows. "I'm going to do everything in my power to make sure no one is hurt, but there's not much time left before Osgood gets all the trump in his hand and starts his thousand-year reign on earth."

The ground rattled beneath their feet.

Everyone looked up toward the top of the building, where the clouds circled faster and faster.

Aleksandr pulled Charisma close, and noted that there was no sign of life around them; not even birds twittered in the trees.

John continued. "We don't know what we're walking into. The Others are probably going to be in there, and heaven knows what other kind of creatures, and heavens knows what kinds of weapons. Stick together and stay behind me. I throw off energy, which means I can repel bullets and push people around. Remember—the elevators are at the back of the lobby. Our aim is to get as many of the Chosen Ones on them as we can and head for the roof."

"Osgood has control of the elevators," Aaron pointed out.

"We'll have to take our chances," John answered.

"What's your choice?" Rosie chomped on her cigar. "Running up one hundred and some flights of stairs?"

"Right." John nodded at her. "We haven't got a *good* choice, but for sure, Charisma and the feathers need to make it aboard that elevator. Innovate as you have to. And for just a moment, let's hold hands and—"

Behind them, Aleksandr heard a warning crackle. Heat flashed through him. He saw a blaze of fiery white light, felt the hair lift all over his body.

A bomb!

He flung himself around.

No, not a bomb. A lightning bolt had hit the bus, turning it into a pile of twisted, smoking metal.

"Why, you son of a bitch." Rosie threw her cigar on the ground and stared at the wreckage. "You killed my bus!" With a growl that started deep in her chest and issued from her mouth as a roar, she charged toward the bronze doors.

"Let's go!" John shouted, and ran after her.

The Chosen Ones encircled Charisma and Aleksandr.

The Wilders surrounded the Chosen Ones. The police, the wealthy, the Belows formed the outer perimeter.

The whole group followed Rosie and John, and barreled toward the heavy doors, into the lobby. . . .

They stopped. They stared.

They had found the people. All the people.

The gigantic room was a symphony of white marble, glittering gold, crystal, and cast bronze. And every inch was packed with employees, screaming, pushing, shouting, praying . . . begging. Begging the guards who held them at gunpoint to let them leave.

At the back, behind the security station, more employees emptied out of the elevators, packing the gigantic space tighter and tighter.

"Of course," Rosamund said. "To seal his deal with the devil, Osgood is going to sacrifice them all. He owns their souls. Now he'll take their lives. The bargain will be sealed in blood."

Aleksandr was tall, and could see all too well, looking over the heads of everyone else and deep into the lobby. He could smell the fear of a thousand bodies pressed together, feeding one another's dread. He could smell pain and terror. "Yes," he said, "and that's why he hasn't killed the Chosen Ones when at any moment, he so obviously could have. If we are part of the sacrifice, it is all the more decisive—and powerful."

Another earthquake rumbled the ground.

People screamed. They broke. They ran toward the entrance.

The guards opened fire, killing them and the employees behind them.

Blood spattered the white marble, splashed the bronze statues.

Shrieks of pain and fear echoed off the marble columns.

Rosie trembled with rage. She shouted, "You sons a bitches!" and charged again.

John charged after her, using his powers to block bullets, to knock guards aside.

More guards leaped to the front, firing at the people in the lobby.

John slammed the guards against the wall.

The police used their nightsticks with abandon, knocking out the guards, pointing out the way to the people rushing toward the door.

A wall of flame sprang up in the entrance.

As Aleksandr's fur burned and curled, he pushed Charisma farther into the lobby and away from the doors.

Fire caught one of the fleeing female employees. She screamed in agony.

Firebird Wilder ran into the flames. "Don't worry. We can walk through!" Putting her arm around the terrified woman, she led her to the door and outside.

"Good for your mother!" Charisma shouted above the din.

Yes, good for his mother. And what hell for his father, who abandoned the Wilders to run after her and ensure her safety.

The fire flared up higher, driving back the employees.

A female Other leaned against a marble column, a woman who smiled as she threw fire from her palms.

Samuel faced her. "You bitch. Don't even think you can get away with that." With a lift of his chin, he controlled her mind.

She staggered. Her eyes rolled back in her head. She fell to the ground.

The flames died.

Aleksandr saw his mother open the doors wide. She shouted and gestured the employees forward. The guards were still fighting, but the older Chosen blocked them.

The Belows sneaked up on them and, while pretending madness—or perhaps with real madness—smacked the weaponry out of their hands.

From the back, something unseen slammed Samuel. A blade rose and glimmered in the light.

Charisma shouted.

Isabelle reached out and grabbed an invisible arm.

The outline of a human being materialized over Samuel's prone body.

When Isabelle kneed him in the groin, he dropped the blade and doubled over.

She dropped his wrist and shoved him into the stampede of fleeing employees.

He disappeared from sight, then . . . disappeared in truth as crowds of people trampled him, tripped over him, cursed the invisible obstacle, and bludgeoned him with their tromping feet.

Charisma grabbed his wrist. "Aleksandr. Look!"

Taurean appeared, dragging two women toward the door.

A guard swung around and pointed his pistol at them. He cocked it.

Aleksandr howled and leaped through the crowd. He was too far. He wasn't going to make it. He roared again.

The guard looked over his shoulder. Saw Aleksandr. His eyes widened. He tried to bring his muzzle around.

Aleksandr grabbed him by the neck and the belt. He lifted the guard over his head and flung him toward the wall.

The guard screamed. He hit. He slid.

Aleksandr turned back to find Charisma.

She was gone.

# Chapter 51

The crowd closed in around Charisma. She could hear Aleksandr roar her name, but she couldn't see him. Her phalanx of Chosen Ones had disappeared as, one by one, they peeled off to take care of another crisis, to fight the Others. Violent eddies in the crowd caught her, shoving her toward the outer door.

But she needed to enter the inner lobby, where the elevators would take her to the top. To the roof. Where Osgood called in the forces of hell.

She clutched the heavenly feathers close to her body, afraid that the employees' panic would soon turn this into a riot and she would be trampled, the feathers lost.

She heard gunshots.

Saw more blood, dark red and horrible, spatter against the white marble.

The screams grew deafening.

She remembered John's directive: The Chosen Ones were to sacrifice anything to get her to the elevators.

She had to trust that Aleksandr could take care of himself.

Fiercely, she shoved and elbowed her way toward the back. She had to reach the elevators.

Like snapshots taken too fast, Charisma caught glimpses of her comrades.

Of Rosie and Konstantine throwing punches, and John at their side, using his power to flip the submachine gun–wielding guards through the air like playing cards in a strong wind.

She saw Genny and Zorana directing Osgood's employees out the door.

She heard Samuel shouting, knew he and Isabelle were fighting their way through the crowd, trying to catch up.

The press of employees toward the exit was a river, driven by desperation. Charisma fought, strained toward the elevators, gained feet and inches only to lose precious seconds. Air was in short supply. She was squeezed and shoved from all directions. She struggled to breathe, but irresistibly she was pressed backward. The gunfire grew sharper, closer.

The guards were taking people out at the doors.

*Oh, God. Genny.*

But no. Charisma had to trust in John's powers. He wouldn't let those bastards get Genny. He wouldn't let her die.

Charisma heard Aleksandr roar again.

He was alive.

And suddenly three of the older Wilder men materialized in front of her. His uncles. Something about them, their predatory stares and their attitudes, made people swerve away. Slowly, then with greater momentum, her guard pushed against the throng, creating a path for Charisma toward the back of the lobby.

At last she could draw breath.

Above the milling heads and off to the side, she saw Aleksandr cutting a swath through the crowd, his blue eyes focused on her. He seemed to have no trouble getting *his* way. Maybe it was because, when people saw him, they screamed and tried to run.

*Dumb shits.* Didn't they realize he was saving them?

Wilders in the lead, Charisma reached the guard station.

She gave a gasp of relief. They were almost there. The elevators were just beyond, nine sets of glossy doors that closed, then opened to discharge masses of sweaty, crying, cursing employees, then closed again.

The employees streamed out of the side corridors, too, coming down the stairwells, panting from exertion and fear.

The ground shook continuously now. Above the cacophony, Charisma heard the ominous thud of lightning striking the ground over and over. In her mind, she formed a picture of the fleeing employees facing the press of death inside the building, the fear of annihilation from hail, lightning, every biblical plague.

She caught a glimpse of Aaron, their gifted thief, sliding along the wall, Rosamund behind him. Maybe they would catch up with Charisma . . . but Rosamund was pointing not at the elevators, but around the corner into the narrow hallway, where . . . where a shock wave of sparkling black energy gathered strength. Like a foul wind, it blasted out, taking out everyone in its path. Charisma and the Wilders careened sideways, stumbling, scattering.

Charisma was alone again, isolated in the crowd. She clutched the feathers, but she didn't so much hold them as they clung to her, refusing to leave. Another powerful gust of energy sent her spinning in a circle, tripping over her own feet, falling beneath a hundred stamping feet.

Someone caught her. *Aleksandr* caught her. She clung to him as yet another gust of energy hit them. Aleksandr leaned into it, fought to remain on his feet.

John's power counterpart in the Others stood in the corridor, blasting them with so much power Charisma's heart squeezed in agony, then resumed its beat.

"We've got to stop him!" she shouted.

"Aaron's got it," Aleksandr shouted back.

Behind the Other, a smoky mist rose. Sensing something, the Other's head whipped around to see Aaron materializing behind him.

Too late. Aaron snapped his neck and dropped him to the floor.

Rosamund ran to Aaron and embraced him.

Aleksandr wrapped his arm around Charisma. "Come on!" Escorted by the Wilder men, they made it past the guard station into the elevator lobby.

Caleb appeared out of the melee, Jacqueline on his heels. "Jacqueline says it's these elevators." He pointed to the doors on the left. "They're the only ones that go all the way to the roof!"

"Come on." Jacqueline held the doors open. "Come on!"

"Have we lost the rest of the Chosen Ones?" Charisma shouted.

"Yes," Caleb said. "But we've got to go. Jacqueline says we can't wait any longer!"

At her wrist, Charisma's stones jangled a warning.

Something about this scenario was wrong. Very, very wrong.

She touched Caleb.

He was fine.

She put her hand on Jacqueline's shoulder, and the blast of enmity and evil glee made her spring backward. "That's *not* Jacqueline!"

"I don't know what you mean," the fake Jacqueline said.

"Of course it's Jacqueline!" Caleb viewed the shapeshifter with narrowed eyes. "Although somehow we got separated."

"Find your wife," Charisma told him. "This is not Jacqueline!"

Color drained from Caleb's face, and he turned and fought his way back into the crowd.

Aleksandr turned to his father and uncles and pointed at the impostor. "What is that?"

The Wilders surrounded the Jacqueline thing, focused on her. Her form wavered and changed into that of a middle-aged balding man who cowered at the sight of those grim, handsome Wilder faces. They backed him into the milling crowd.

Samuel and Isabelle arrived, panting and disheveled.

"I asked one of the employees. These elevators go to the roof." Isabelle hurried toward the smallest elevators at the back and punched the button.

Aleksandr suspiciously stared at her.

But Charisma's stones hummed happily. She nodded reassuringly at Aleksandr. "It's really them."

The four moved swiftly to the opening door of the elevator.

"Stop. Now!" One of Osgood's uniformed guards popped out of the crowd, pointing his submachine gun at them.

"You people are a real pain in the ass." Samuel sighed, then gestured to the Chosen Ones. "Go! I'll handle this."

Charisma and Aleksandr rushed into the elevator.

Isabelle stood beside her husband.

Samuel leaned toward the guard, read his name tag, and in his warm, convincing, lawyerly voice, he said, "Logan, you don't want to fire that gun."

The guard blinked. "I don't?"

Charisma held the elevator doors open. "Isabelle! Get in here."

Isabelle waved a *wait for us* hand.

"Logan, you don't want to fire that gun," Samuel repeated. "You want to help people exit the building in an orderly fashion."

The guard put the gun on the ground.

Isabelle walked forward and picked it up.

The guard walked into the crowd, shouting, "Follow me! I'll lead you outside."

Samuel and Isabelle ran toward the elevator—and staggered backward.

Aleksandr started out.

He stumbled backward. "Something's between us. A force field of some kind!"

Charisma heard the hum of the stones on her wrist. She looked down at the feathers she clutched tightly to her chest. She heard the message, accepted the truth. "Let the doors shut," she said to Aleksandr. "We're the only ones going to the roof."

"What?" Isabelle shouted.

Charisma looked out at Isabelle, at her friend, knowing she was abandoning them to a terrible fight, knowing she and Aleksandr faced this battle alone. "The feathers have chosen *us*. Let the doors shut."

Aleksandr stared at Charisma, and released the doors.

As they closed, Samuel tried again.

The last thing they saw was him falling backward into Isabelle's arms.

Aleksandr and Charisma were alone.

Aleksandr pushed the button for the roof.

The elevator started its ascent.

After the riot in the lobby, it was quiet. So quiet. Except . . . "I can't believe Osgood plays Muzak in his elevators," Charisma said.

"Proof he really is the devil," Aleksandr said softly.

They grinned at each other. They stood close without touching. All the words had been said. All the kisses had been exchanged. There was nothing left except to do this thing or die trying.

The panel showed one hundred and thirteen floors, and with each number that lit up, Charisma's stomach tightened. She swallowed. Her ears popped.

The earth trembled. The building rattled. The elevator swayed and clanked.

Charisma breathed deeply, gathering her strength to face the coming battle. "I can't believe Osgood's going to just *let* us come up to the roof to fight him."

"Don't worry," Aleksandr said. "We can do this. Think of how much you've already done. Fought demons. Loved a beast. Visited the heart of the earth, regained your gift, and come back with one of the two things we needed to make the prophecy come true.

You've been chosen by the feathers to carry them to confront Osgood."

Charisma shook her head. "I'm not *afraid*. It's more than that." The stones at her wrist started to burn her skin. "There's something very wrong," she murmured.

"Earthquakes? Lightning to fry a bus? Cloud vortices? I agree there's something wrong. And we know—" Aleksandr stopped talking. Stiffened in alarm. Turned his head slowly from side to side and sniffed the air.

He had caught a scent of trouble.

"What is it?" she asked.

The elevator began to slow.

He grabbed her shoulders and shoved her against the side wall. "Listen to me," he said. "It's an ambush. Smith Bernhard has come for me. Smith and Iskra."

"No!"

"They want to take you, too." Stepping away from her, he leaned down, loosened his boots, discarded them.

She observed without comprehension. "I won't leave you!"

"You can't help me. They want to use you against me. You *can't* get caught. You *have* to go to the roof."

The ninetieth floor dinged.

The doors opened. The room was dark, except for a spotlight on Iskra, blond, beautiful, slowly disrobing and smiling into the elevator. At Aleksandr.

"Charisma, everything depends on you." Aleksandr pushed the button for the roof. He leaped into the room.

As the door shut, the last thing Charisma saw was Aleksandr in midair. Then the spotlight clicked off.

The elevator resumed its ascent.

Would Aleksandr yield to Iskra's seduction?

Charisma didn't believe that for a minute.

Would Smith Bernhard trap him, torture him, kill him?

She had to believe that somehow Aleksandr would find a way back to her.

Charisma was alone with her duty and her destiny, and the cold, clear knowledge that Aleksandr was right.

She couldn't help him.

And at this moment, everything depended on her.

# *Chapter 52*

A leksandr had always known it wasn't over.
In his Wilder heart, he had always known what he could become.

As he leaped from the lighted elevator into the dark room, he did what he had sworn he would never do.

He denied his humanity, and wholly transformed himself into the beast.

His nose and mouth became a wolf's hairy snout with hungry, spiked fangs. His fingers grew long and misshapen, tipped by razor-sharp claws. His chest expanded, bursting the seams on his fighting uniform. His hips narrowed; the muscles of his thighs grew long, thick, powerful. His feet changed to paws capped with ten more lethal weapons.

With his new, even more acute senses, he breathed in the scent of the two eager game wardens waiting to take him. He smelled the dozen burly men who both feared him and wanted to catch him in their trap. He could smell Bernhard's evil anticipation, Iskra's sick excitement.

Even in this utter pitch dark, he could see the massive net the guards held, ready to confine the beast.

Dropping to the floor, he rolled to the left, under the net, slamming his weight against the guards' legs, slashing with feet and hands.

They screamed in surprise, those men who wanted the glory of snaring the beast. They dropped the heavy net. They fell.

As they hit the ground, Aleksandr ripped away their night-vision goggles, slashing their faces.

They screamed again and violently scrambled to get away from him.

The heavy nylon rope net with its six-inch holes had been created to capture a grizzly bear or to use underwater to trap a shark. That made it easy for Aleksandr to wrap his claws around the ropes at the edge, and use his weight and strength to yank it toward him.

The guards holding the other side stumbled forward, off balance, dropping their end, putting their hands out to stop their falls.

Net in hand, Aleksandr pounced, trapping them; the fly had turned the tables on the spiders.

One of the men threw the edge of the substantial net aside and rushed at Aleksandr. A knife flashed in his hand.

Aleksandr grabbed the wrist of the man who wielded it and heard a satisfying snap, then threw him across the room and into the other guards. The knife clattered across the floor.

He turned toward Bernhard, at the back of the room and to the left.

"Aleksandr. Stop." Bernhard's voice was accompanied by the click of a safety. He wore night-vision goggles, he held a Ruger pistol, and he steadily pointed it at Aleksandr.

As instructed, Aleksandr froze. And breathed, long and slow, absorbing, analyzing, and cataloging the scents around him.

In the whole room, there were only *two* weapons that used bullets. *Two* weapons that fired. That was all.

Of course. Bernhard would take no chance that one of the guards would see Aleksandr's horrible form and panic, and shoot his most precious creation. Bernhard always kept control of the violence in any situation. Bernhard dealt out the violence. No one else.

Iskra held a handgun. Yes, she wouldn't agree to bait the trap without the security of knowing that if the fight got out of hand, she could save herself.

But guards were not the brightest, and they lived for violence. They had arrived with other weapons, other knives. Aleksandr merely had to figure out who, what, and where.

Behind them, the man with the broken wrist sobbed and pounded on the elevator call button. It lit up, giving enough illumination for Aleksandr to see . . . everything.

If he was going to get out of here alive, and go to Charisma and help her destroy Osgood, Aleksandr had to use all his human intellect and all his animal cunning.

He knew Bernhard was an accomplished sadist; he was a highly intelligent man, not easily fooled. But also . . . Bernhard had a weakness. Bernhard always believed he was the smartest man in the room.

Not in this room, he wasn't.

"Aleksandr." Bernhard employed the firm, kind, logical voice he always used when preparing to torment and maim. "Listen to me. You think you're safe because you're loose. You think I won't shoot you because I made you what you are. But when this is over, when Osgood has won, he will give me hundreds, thousands of subjects to run experiments on." Bernhard's eyes glowed with greedy pleasure.

*No.* Aleksandr couldn't allow this to happen.

Bernhard continued. "I don't want to shoot you now, but I will if I have to. You have value for me in death, too. I can dissect you, see how your transformation worked, preserve your brain, slice it and put it under the microscope."

Iskra made an ardent noise.

"Yes, dear, you can watch."

She was too venal and stupid to realize how Bernhard patronized her. Or perhaps she didn't care, as long as she got to satisfy her need to view pain in all its forms.

She made Aleksandr's skin crawl, and yet . . . she had volunteered to be his bait, and as she had removed her bra, she'd smiled at him, imagining her gift still worked on him, that he was easily seduced.

She didn't realize the memories of Charisma's lovemaking had completely wiped Iskra, the seductress, from his mind. She didn't realize she was doomed.

And so was Smith Bernhard.

"Aleksandr, get on your knees and I'll let you live." With his gun pointed at Aleksandr's chest, Bernhard believed he held the upper hand.

As Aleksandr sank onto the floor, he groaned in deep, mournful despair.

The room fell silent. Everyone was watching: the

men in the net, the wounded guards and gamekeepers. All were eager to see Bernhard tame the beast.

From inside the big, heavy rope net, Aleksandr heard, "Bet you a hundred that in less than ten minutes, we've changed places with him."

"Fat chance. Two minutes, maybe. It's a *stupid* animal." A pause. "Damn thing ripped my cheek open. I'm bleeding."

Aleksandr recognized the second voice.

Troy, an intern from Bernhard's hospital, a bully who jammed in the needle when he gave shots, who applied the restraints too tightly, who starved Bernhard's patients and gloated.

Now Troy rested on his side, exalting in Aleksandr's humiliation, anticipating the moment when he would have him under his power . . . and as he grinned, he fingered his knife threateningly, lovingly.

Aleksandr had never thought Troy clever. Now at least he thought him useful.

"Aleksandr, tell me you're sorry," Bernhard said.

Aleksandr groaned.

"Tell me you're sorry," Bernhard snapped.

Aleksandr groaned again.

"My God!" Bernhard peered toward him, his night goggles giving the already vile scene an element of science fiction. "Is it possible? Can it be? Did this latest transformation move you so far from your human form that you cannot speak?"

Aleksandr hung his head as if in shame. He groaned pitifully and shuffled on his knees both toward Bernhard and to the side . . . toward Troy.

Bernhard held the pistol steady, but stepped closer.

Arrogant fool.

"Of course. You still *understand* speech, but you no longer have the tongue, the lips, the palate to speak."

For Aleksandr, that was the worst part. Bernhard was right: Aleksandr could no longer speak. But although he was a dumb beast, still he felt the press of time ticking away.

Charisma was alone on the roof with Osgood. She needed Aleksandr.

He had to finish this.

Hunching his shoulders, he whimpered pitifully, and once again slid on his knees toward the men in the net, toward Troy. Then, opening his mouth, he pointed and looked meaningfully at Bernhard.

"Yes! Your teeth, too, have changed." Bernhard took another step. And another.

Troy, bless him, crawled closer, too.

One thing Aleksandr could depend on: If Troy saw a chance to hurt someone, he grabbed it. Right now, he wanted a stab at Aleksandr.

One of the guys in the net with Troy punched him and told him to hold still or they'd be eaten.

Troy responded with a swift stab to the throat.

A spurt of blood. A death rattle.

Aleksandr groaned to keep Bernhard's attention away from the altercation, away from the knife coming within Aleksandr's reach.

Bernhard glanced toward the net full of men, but his pistol never wavered. He was in full mad-scientist tirade. "This is it. This is the proof I was looking for! No other subject has even started such a transformation, because no other subject had the genetics to make the change. The devil might make the bargain, but—"

Troy was one long arm reach away, wiping his knife on the dead man's sleeve, paying Aleksandr no heed.

Bernhard was a long arm reach to the other side, enthralled with his creation.

With bestial swiftness, Aleksandr grabbed Bernhard's wrist and yanked it forward and to the side, neutralizing the pistol.

With a roar, it discharged toward the side of the room. One of the gamekeepers collapsed.

Snatching the knife from Troy's careless fingers, Aleksandr used a bleak upward motion to plunge the blade into Bernhard's chest.

Bernhard had been so enthralled with his own genius, he never saw it coming.

His mouth dropped open in surprise. "You . . . I won't allow this. You—" He gurgled. Blood dribbled out of his mouth.

Aleksandr stared into Bernhard's eyes, speaking his contempt in the only way he could.

Then, with a twist of the knife, he pulled it free.

For three beats, blood pumped from Bernhard's heart. Then . . . it stopped. He crumpled to the ground.

Still holding Bernhard's arm in one hand, the knife in the other, Aleksandr rose off his knees. He looked around.

The room exploded in panic.

Guards squealed like stampeding pigs. They pounded on the elevator doors. They flung the stairwell door open and raced down the steps.

It was a long way down. Aleksandr wished he could chase them until they dropped.

Yet in the midst of the terror, Iskra's low, breathy,

grateful voice reached Aleksandr's ears. "My darling, you killed him. At last, you've freed me from my bonds!"

He couldn't believe it. He couldn't believe Iskra dared.

She rushed toward him, one arm outstretched, the other at her side.

Arrogant fool, indeed. *He* was the arrogant fool.

He had forgotten she had a gun.

He dropped the knife, grabbed Bernhard's shirt-front, and, in one smooth motion, lifted the body to use as a shield.

*Too late!* She raised the pistol and fired.

Heat, agony burst like fireworks in Aleksandr's chest.

She fired again, and again.

The bullets slammed Bernhard's body as Aleksandr hoisted the deadweight high and threw it at Iskra's head.

Bernhard's corpse knocked her off her feet.

Aleksandr heard the crack of her spine. And smelled the sweet, clean odor of her death.

He stood, chest heaving. Blood ran from his shattered rib cage. He had trouble getting his breath.

Punctured lung.

Too bad. He had a job to do. He had to help Charisma.

Out of the corner of his eye, he caught a movement.

Troy was crawling toward the pistol Bernhard had dropped.

With his new claws, Aleksandr could no longer grip a pistol. Could no longer fire a pistol.

So with Troy's own knife, Aleksandr killed him swiftly.

Then, with a snarl, he bounded into the stairwell, and in his mind he pictured Charisma in flight, with the angel's wings attached to her back.

# Chapter 53

The elevator dinged. Stopped. The doors opened onto the roof, concrete-clad and bare of seating or plants. A low, ornate Italianate balustrade surrounded the perimeter.

Charisma could hear the wind howling, but here, in the center of the storm, everything was preternaturally still. Blinding flashes of lightning snaked out of the clouds, slapping the earth, and the smell of sulfur filled the air. Black clouds swirled in violent circles around the building, while in a single patch in the middle of the roof, the sun shone.

There, in the only patch of light left in the world, Osgood, arms upraised, called on heaven to watch as he wreaked death and destruction.

*Good thing he's got his back to me. . . .* Charisma glanced longingly at the down button.

Then some asshole must have called the elevator, probably Samuel, because the down arrow lit.

And Charisma had to make her decision. Her *final* decision.

Heart pounding, she slipped between the closing doors and onto the roof. There was no going back now. She was stuck.

"Miss Fangorn!" Osgood's voice made her jump. "I'm so glad you decided to join my little party. It wouldn't have been complete without you."

His back was turned.

How did he know it was her?

Security camera in the elevator. Of course.

But she knew it wasn't that easy. She'd glimpsed Osgood only once, been surprised at how mild, short, and old he looked, like an employee in the Boring and Boring Accounting Firm. That had been three years ago; they had never officially met.

Yet they knew each other. They shared a war. For seven long years they had been opponents. She had watched and fought as his power grew. He had watched as she survived against all odds. They were enemies, forever opposed.

Now she had to do more than survive. She had to win.

Kneeling, she unwrapped the blue cloth from around the feathers. She picked them up, held them uncertainly.

If only they came with an instruction guide. How did she attach these things? Why hadn't she asked? She twisted, got first one, then the other to touch her shoulder blades.

Nothing happened.

Should she take off her blue blouse? Here in the sunlight? With Osgood on the roof and the apocalypse approaching?

That seemed so wrong.

Maybe if she just held one under each arm and jumped.

That seemed stupid.

But when did jumping off a tall building not seem stupid?

While she puzzled, one of the feathers took on a life of its own. It twisted out of her grip and skittered away.

She gasped, stood, groped for it.

As if dragged on a chain, the feather moved in jerks . . . toward Osgood.

He turned to face her.

He was still a mild-looking, stooped, and skinny old man with mottled skin. But his eyes were no longer a nondescript hazel. They glowed an eerie blue.

The devil looked out from Osgood's soul.

His voice was quiet, yet she clearly heard him above the shriek of the spinning wind. "Miss Fangorn, you were very foolish bringing that feather here. It's *mine*. It was part of *my* wings. I control it. It's mine to use." He spun his finger.

The feather whipped in a circle, faster and faster, a blur of white.

"Mine to destroy."

The feathers were indestructible.

Weren't they? Charisma stoutly said, "You already tried to destroy them once. You stuck that one in tons of concrete at the base of this building. It escaped. The feather won't be contained."

"That feather is still there." Then he caught a glimpse

of the second feather, the one she hid behind her back. With slowly rising fury, he asked, "What's that, Miss Fangorn? Is it possible? Did you somehow obtain *both* feathers?"

"*We* did. The Chosen Ones."

His voice surged. "What did the Chosen Ones intend to do with them, Miss Fangorn? Did the Chosen Ones plan to pay heed to the ancient prophecy?"

"The *ancient* prophecy?" No, it was Jacqueline's prophecy that Charisma had heard. "What *ancient* prophecy?"

Chagrin passed over Osgood's face.

Then the second feather jerked out of her grasp and slapped her hard across the face as it flipped into the air.

She cupped her stinging cheek.

"Don't play games with me, Miss Fangorn. If you wish to fly, I can help you off the edge right now."

He avoided the subject of the ancient prophecy.

She reached an inescapable conclusion—Osgood knew of an ancient prophecy, and he feared it.

So Jacqueline had nailed the truth. With those feathers, Charisma could fly, and when she did, Osgood's reign of terror would be over.

*Wow.* That was the best news Charisma had received for days. Months.

A gust of wind made her stagger toward the balustrade.

The feathers followed her.

*Osgood* followed her. "You shouldn't take these prophecies seriously."

"You believe the prophecy is false. Let me prove it. Let me have the feathers and jump. If you're right, I'll plunge to my death."

He lifted an admonishing finger.

Pain lanced into her brain.

"Do you know how many prophecies there are? How many crackpots and charlatans have made their living telling the ignorant and the desperate that they could read the future?" His voice pounded at her head.

She fell to her knees.

Relentlessly he continued. "Are you ignorant, Miss Fangorn? Or are you merely desperate?"

"I am hopeful," she whispered.

"The more fool you. Look around! Hope is dying. Soon, very soon, it will be dead. Dead for a thousand years. I will reign for a millennium. It will be a new ice age, a new dark age. But you'll die first." Osgood stood over her. "Did you realize the demon's venom is fatal, Miss Fangorn?"

The pain. She couldn't speak for the pain.

He pulled his hand back.

The pain eased. She sagged. She gasped. "Yes. I know."

"You know you're dying." He chortled. "No wonder you face the idea of jumping off the roof with such equanimity. When you already know you're facing the long dirt nap, it's not such a big sacrifice, is it?"

She had to keep trying. "If your ancient prophecy is false, give me the feathers and I'll jump."

He lifted his finger again.

Pain ripped into her heart. She gripped her chest, rolled, and moaned.

Still she could hear him speaking his words of misery, cruelty, and despair. "You Chosen Ones have done well. You survived the destruction of the Gypsy Travel Agency on this very site. You thrived without training, with few books, with little knowledge. . . . You should not have survived at all."

Through her agony, she noted his vexation.

He continued chatting as politely as if they dined in a tearoom. "Did you notice the measures I used to keep you and young Wilder apart?"

"Iskra." She gasped.

"From the first moment young Wilder arrived in New York, he never had a chance." Osgood dug his fingers into her cheeks and turned her face to his. "On your way up, did you by chance run into Bernhard? He has such plans for young Wilder."

"Aleksandr will win."

"Still hopeful. How touching. Young Wilder has no chance."

"Always a chance." Her gaze fixed on the feathers hovering just out of reach. "Give me the feathers and I'll prove it."

Her ribs squeezed her lungs. Squeezed . . . she couldn't breathe. *She couldn't breathe.*

"You never had a chance, either. When he escaped from Bernhard, I sent Ronnie to you. But you saw through him before you killed him. . . . Miss Fangorn, that's when I truly gained respect for you." Osgood was sarcastic. "For your endurance."

She started to slip from consciousness.

"Whoops. Can't have that." Osgood released her.

She gasped, sucked in air, took pleasure in breathing. In. Out. In.

Oxygen. Great stuff.

"But, Miss Fangorn, while you and Mr. Wilder have kept me greatly entertained for the last seven years, I am no longer amused." Osgood's glowing eyes blazed into hers. "To think that after all my efforts, after Iskra and Ronnie and so many obstacles, you could still find each other, still create a child."

A child.

The two words fell into Charisma's consciousness like a pair of dropped cymbals.

A child.

She was going to have a child.

# Chapter 54

———❦———

"**A**s I told you," Osgood said, "I don't believe in prophecies. But this child of yours . . . she cannot be born."

A child. Charisma's child. And Aleksandr's.

He pointed out, "So it's convenient that your death is minutes away."

*No.* She carried a baby!

Osgood's voice became a warm, pleasant croon. The blue glow of his eyes burned like coals. "Can you feel the demon's venom moving through your veins? The approaching chill of death?"

Charisma could. And did.

She turned her head away. But nothing could stop Osgood. He was activating the poison, encouraging it to take her.

"Do you remember the hours after you were bitten? The convulsions? The delirium? The fever?"

"No." Behind him, the stairway door was opening.

"You'll remember this time." Osgood glanced at his Timex. "Although I don't have hours."

A creature stepped through the door. A beast of unspeakable horror, not really man, not really wolf, its fur matted with gore.

Cheerfully, Osgood said, "Only a few minutes left until the apocalypse. So I'll hurry your death along."

"Don't do me any favors."

Blood dribbled from the beast's chest onto the ground.

It glanced at Charisma, dismissed her.

The poor thing looked about half-dead from the gunshot wound in its chest.

Then it fixed its gaze on Osgood . . . and the beast had Aleksandr's eyes.

She caught her breath and turned it into a long inhale.

Aleksandr. That thing was Aleksandr. And he was hurt.

Abruptly he bounded toward Osgood, his gaze fixed on his back. Closer and closer, lips peeled back, teeth exposed, claws . . .

Osgood flipped his hand.

With a yelp, the creature somersaulted into the air. Blood and fur flew. He landed on his back.

Osgood turned with a snarl that would have done the beast proud. "You! You survive. And *survive*. Why don't you take the hint and die?"

Aleksandr struggled to his feet. He crouched there, a wolf creature waiting to explode into action.

Osgood observed him, then threw back his head and crowed with laughter. "Look at you! Look at those fangs, those claws, that misshapen form. That appearance must be a humiliation for you, son of the Wilders. You're a throwback. A predator—but you've so thoroughly destroyed your own human form, you can never go back."

"No!" Charisma shouted.

"Don't worry, Miss Fangorn." Osgood's eyes gleamed with revolting pleasure. "When you are dead, I shall keep him like a pet."

"No!" she shouted again.

"Didn't you hear me? You'll be worm's meat. What do you care? But wait!" Osgood tapped his lips, and his eyes shone evilly. "Do you know what will be even more entertaining? Your beloved Aleksandr is half-mad with pain and rage anyway. *I'll have him finish you.*"

"No," she whispered. If Osgood succeeded in forcing Aleksandr to kill her . . . Aleksandr would never recover any semblance of himself. Never.

In a voice rich with magic and command, Osgood said, "Aleksandr, kill Charisma."

Aleksandr crouched, balanced on feet and claws. His head turned. His eyes fixed on her, and in their depths she saw rage and frustration.

"Kill the female," Osgood said. "Sink your teeth into her soft flesh. Disembowel her."

"Geez, you're a sick bastard!" Charisma protested.

Aleksandr stalked forward, gasping and dripping blood.

"Drink her fluids. Rend her limb from limb." To a mindless beast, every word must be an incitement.

Aleksandr bounded over to crouch over Charisma. His hot breath touched her neck. Red foam flecked his black lips. His mouth opened, showing formidable teeth. . . .

Osgood laughed, fearsome peals that controlled the lightning in the heavens. "Aleksandr Wilder reverts to a form so vile not even his ancestor Konstantine could match it. Not even the original Konstantine ever stooped so low as to eat his lover! And Miss Charisma Fangorn . . . what a fitting sacrifice!" In a low, vicious tone, he added, "Don't let her stones get caught in your throat."

His lightning spread wildly across the clouds, spreading outward from the closing hole.

The crackling made Osgood look up, and laugh again with sheer, vicious joy.

Delicately, Aleksandr licked her cheek.

His touch, his breath, was so counter to her expectations that she turned her head and looked into his eyes.

Aleksandr. She recognized him. Aleksandr. He wasn't a mindless beast. This was Aleksandr. Just . . . Aleksandr. Somewhere beneath the fur and the teeth, Aleksandr remained a sentient human.

She had to warn him. She had to tell him. . . . "Osgood is afraid of the prophecy," she whispered. "He wouldn't allow me to take the feathers and jump off the building."

Aleksandr looked above them.

Both long, snowy white, perfectly formed feathers hovered over their heads.

She reached out her hand, straining to grasp them, then collapsed. "I'm too weak. I'm dying. Aleksandr, it's all up to you."

He gasped, a long, nerve-racking sound that made her press her hands to his chest.

So much blood . . . it matted his fur, slid onto her hands and made them sticky.

He was dying, too. *Oh, God. Oh, no.* "Aleksandr, can you do this? Can you fulfill the prophecy?"

Valiantly, he nodded.

His agreement sealed a bargain; the feathers lowered slowly onto his bare back. . . .

Charisma struggled up on her elbows to watch . . .

. . . as the feathers attached themselves against his shoulder blades.

"Fly," she whispered. "Aleksandr . . . fly!"

Aleksandr tried to catch his breath.

Osgood turned back. He caught sight of them.

Seeing the look on that evil face, Charisma frantically pushed at Aleksandr. "Go!"

"Damn you!" Osgood said. Never had a curse sounded so sincere, so real. "You two never stop. And why? There are only two feathers left. I had wings! Whole wings! Still I fell from heaven. This building is one hundred and thirteen stories. With only two feathers, you won't stop until you've buried *yourself* six feet under."

The clouds paused in their circling. They started to close over the last bit of sunshine.

Osgood smiled, a slow, cruel smile. "Anyway, it's too late. The deal is done!"

"Go!" Charisma said. "Fly! Aleksandr, *now!*"

With a last, long breath, Aleksandr snatched her into his arms.

"No! Not me." She struggled. "Save your strength. You have to do it!"

He bounded forward, leaped onto the parapet.

She got a dizzying glance at the plunge to the ground.

"No!" Osgood shrieked.

Aleksandr leaped.

They plummeted.

The building flashed past. The wind tore at them. They spun like acrobats.

Charisma clung to Aleksandr, holding his fur, desperate and afraid.

Osgood was right. He was right.

The feathers were useless.

The ground rushed up at them.

# Chapter 55

Then . . . the feathers tasted the air. As if remembering their long-ago flight, they unfurled to become long, beautiful, white wings joined to Aleksandr's back.

Charisma pulled her head out of Aleksandr's chest.

Their descent slowed. The wind caught them. They began to glide in slow, wide circles away from the building.

They were flying like birds, like butterflies, like . . . angels.

She looked up at Aleksandr's face, and thought that angels came in all forms, for this man-beast was fearsome. She wrapped her arms tightly around his neck.

And she loved him.

He pulled her closer, one arm behind her back, another under her knees; he put his great head against hers, and together they experienced the miracle of flight. Together they soared like a giant eagle, fulfilling Osgood's ancient prophecy, Jacqueline's current prophecy, and the visions they themselves had experienced on the bus.

And no matter what happened now, no matter if they never saw another sunrise, they would always have this moment of oneness and wonder.

Behind them on the building, they heard a shriek of rage. "No. It's not possible. No!"

Aleksandr banked in a slow, long curve that brought them back to face the Osgood building.

Osgood stood looking up at the sky.

As the wind caught the black clouds, they showed ragged edges, and the lightning retreated. The sun shone more brightly.

Osgood lifted his arms. He projected his voice. "I command the earth to move!"

The earth remained stubbornly still.

Osgood's form wavered.

Charisma blinked.

He seemed to struggle with himself. He wavered again, stretched sideways; then, like cloth being torn in half, the devil tore himself free from the clinging tentacles of Osgood's soul and took his own form, as beautiful and cruel as the sea, with blue eyes that blazed with malice.

Even from this distance, the angry blue flame of Satan's eyes reached Aleksandr and Charisma . . . but nothing he could do would touch them now.

They were out of his reach.

They circled again, rising on an updraft of air.

When they came back around, they saw Osgood, feeble, skinny, old, and completely, totally human, clinging to the devil. He fell to his knees, begging, pleading.

Satan looked up at the sun, which was shining

brightly. He looked down at the earth, still and obedient to the laws of nature. He shook Osgood off as if he were nothing but a pesky flea, and, with his hands over his head, he leaped over the balustrade and dove toward the ground—and through it.

He left no trace of his passage, no proof he had for seven years been one with Osgood, working evil through a wicked man.

Osgood stood alone.

Lifting his fists to the heavens, he cried out a high, defiant curse.

A chill went through Charisma. "Defiance cannot be good. In fact, I think it's very bad. Let's get out of here. Fast."

She and Aleksandr wheeled away.

They swooped low and saw the people fleeing from the building.

"Look." Charisma pointed. "I see the Chosen Ones. There. And there." She pointed at several small groups. "They're looking up. I recognize John." She waved. "And Rosamund. There're Samuel and Isabelle."

The Chosen Ones waved back, then returned to their task—herding Osgood's employees farther and farther away from danger.

And none too soon.

The building gave a deep rumble.

The people looked back in terror, then fled.

"It looks like the Chosen Ones helped Osgood's sacrifices escape," Charisma shouted at Aleksandr. "No wonder the devil left Osgood. He failed!"

He nodded and flew north.

She looked behind them and saw Osgood's magnificent headquarters tremble, then shake, then break apart beneath him, collapsing in on itself, faster and faster, like cards folding back into a deck.

When the dust cleared, Osgood and the symbol of his evil were gone.

Aleksandr helped Charisma turn in his arms, to face out as they ascended and descended, and see firsthand the transformation of their world.

Overhead, the black clouds showed more and more holes, and sunbeams poked through to the earth like benedictions from heaven. The smog swept out to sea.

Here in the heart of the wind the air was calm, and far below, New York City was laid out like a living map. Sunshine outlined the island of Manhattan: to the east and north, the river, the glistening waters of Long Island Sound, the high-rise apartments and three-story walk-ups of Brooklyn. Charisma saw all the way to Fire Island and beyond, to the sparkling waters of the Atlantic. To the west and south, she saw the Hudson River, the cliffs of New Jersey, the Verrazano-Narrows Bridge. They soared so high, she felt as if she could see all the way to Ireland. The water glimmered deep and blue, glorious in its eternal promise.

Directly below, the SoHo streets were tangled and confused, but beyond they straightened into the familiar Midtown grid. There light reflected off the skyscrapers' windows, blessed the spires of St. Patrick's Cathedral—and brought the people out of hiding.

The city was coming to life again.

New Yorkers ventured out of hiding and onto the sidewalks, first in a trickle, then in a flood. Yellow cabs leaped out to catch fares.

Every horn around the city was honking: in ships at the docks from the West Side, from pleasure boats and yachts on the east, the ferries, and all over the island of Manhattan and its boroughs, the horns on every imaginable vehicle—taxis, cars, trucks, buses—created a cacophony of sounds. Even the railroad and the subways—horns bleating as they passed under the street-level grates—added their sound to the rush of rising air generated by their passing.

Then came the last entrants—church bells and chimes.

Not a recognizable melody, merely the sound of New York celebrating its victory over evil.

And from one horizon to the other, a rainbow arched over the earth.

Hope. Osgood had mocked Charisma for having hope.

Yet look at what hope and faith had done.

She breathed in thankfulness and exulted in the freedom, the glory, the promise of a new day.

"It's beautiful, isn't it?" Aleksandr's deep voice spoke in her ear.

Another miracle. She had feared he could never speak again.

She turned to look at him . . . and realized the breeze was blowing the beast away. Aleksandr's features had lost their ferocity and become human again. As she watched, a gust of air removed the hair on his face and dispersed it to the corners of the island.

His body was changing, too. His shoulders were straightening; his chest was sturdy, but man-sized. And . . . and where was the gunshot wound?

It had healed, leaving nothing but a scar to mark its passing.

Where she gripped his arms he had bare skin, and on his hands the claws retreated, his fingers straightened, and the last of his thick fur lifted off, whirled in the breeze, and scattered away.

She looked again at his face.

He was wholly human.

For the first time since he had disappeared three years ago, she could actually *see* Aleksandr Wilder.

He was visibly older, with lines etched into his cheeks and between his brows, lines cut by pain and anguish. His shaggy blond hair blew away from his face, and she thought she saw streaks of white beside the temples.

Yet he was only twenty-eight.

The last time she'd seen him, as he walked up the courthouse steps to Iskra, he had been thin, almost gaunt, as if the guilt of leaving the Chosen Ones chewed at him. Now his face had filled out, gained maturity, and as she stared into his calm blue eyes she saw the man inside. Through suffering and sacrifice, he had gained wisdom and proved his courage.

This was a man to cherish and respect. Forever.

They passed over Times Square. The giant billboards lit up. The Broadway show lights came on. On the ground, the rapidly increasing crowd craned their necks to watch Aleksandr and Charisma, and Aleksandr gave a few slow flaps of his wings.

The crowd cheered.

Charisma laughed with joy. "Show-off!"

Ahead of them, Seventh Avenue and the Avenue of the Americas stretched all the way to Central Park. As they glided along, descending slowly, lights came on in shops and restaurants, a tribute to the renewed life of the city, of the world, and to the resilience of the human spirit.

Charisma twisted in Aleksandr's grip until she could again slide her arm around his neck. Kissing his cheek, she said, "Aleksandr, you are a brave and noble man, and you deserve this reward."

"What about you? What reward will you receive for your bravery?" He smiled as if he already knew the answer.

"I have you," she said. "I need nothing else."

His arms tightened. "Really, Charisma? What about your life? Wouldn't you like that returned to you?"

Her face fell. In the exhilaration of their flight, she had forgotten about her weakness, her pain, her approaching demise.

But . . . she wasn't in pain anymore. Death no longer touched her with its cold fingers. With every breath she felt stronger, and her happiness at being with Aleksandr buoyed her and made her wonder . . . made her realize . . . "The demon's poison is gone!" She pinched her own cheeks. "It's gone! Can you tell? You could! How do I look?"

"You look healthy. You look rosy with happiness." Unashamed tears filled his eyes. "You look like Charisma, the girl I first met, and the woman who brought me back from the brink of madness and into love."

"I do love you. And I'm going to live? I'm going to live!" Putting her head against his shoulder, she laughed loud and long. "Aleksandr, you have no idea how important this is."

"I don't?" Now he laughed, too. "I have no idea how important it is that the love of my life will be with me all my days?"

As they circled Rockefeller Center, Charisma's heart soared. "I would like to marry you."

Aleksandr dipped close to the cathedral. "So you don't believe what Osgood said? That I'm a predator, a throwback, a humiliation to my family?"

"I believe that the first time you changed, you did it to survive. I know that the second time you changed, you did it to save me, and you did it believing you could never reclaim your humanity. You never have to prove yourself to me, Aleksandr Wilder." She put her cheek against his. "You already have."

As if he could express his happiness in no other way, he spread his wings wide. Aleksandr and Charisma rose high above the city, hovered, soared . . . while Charisma's stones sang with delight.

When they once more began their descent, he said, "We'll celebrate the wedding with our family and friends."

"I can't wait for your family to see you now!" The Wilders would be so happy!

"We'll travel; we'll find joy in every simple moment." Aleksandr took a breath, as if steadying his nerves. "Maybe, when we decide to settle down, we can start a family—"

Remembering, she chuckled. "It's a little late for that."

"What?" He shook his head, puzzled.

Now, as she tried to frame the words she had thought she would never have the chance to speak, her eyes filled with tears. "Osgood told me . . . he told me one thing I never suspected. But I know it's true. Because he was so furious about it. He said . . . he told me I was pregnant."

# Chapter 56

———❖———

"*What?*" Aleksandr sputtered. He actually sputtered. "B-but you said you were protected!"

"I know. One percent chance, Aleksandr. One percent!" And in a surfeit of bliss, anticipation, incredulity, and possibly hormones, Charisma started crying in earnest.

"You're going to have a baby? We're going to have . . ." He crushed her in his arms, rocked her as if she were the baby. "This is the happiest day of my life."

And suddenly they were both laughing. And crying.

"A baby girl," she said.

"A girl? But I'm a Wilder. We don't have girls."

"Are you calling Osgood a liar?" She laughed at his grimace. "Don't you think that maybe with all your changing and transformations, something might have changed in you?"

"Yes. Yes. Of course. It's possible." He laughed again. "I love girls."

"Me, too. All those cute little clothes. Ooh." She brightened even more. "And the little teensy shoes!"

"Most important," he said seriously, "baby girls don't squirt you when they pee."

Abruptly, she remembered Aleksandr came from a large family. "I don't know much about kids."

"I do." In a resigned tone, he said, "I have changed more diapers. . . ."

"Cool. You can change all of Shea's."

"Not even." He caught on and smiled. "You want to call our daughter Shea? Like Irving Shea?"

"Well, we can't call her Irving. I like the name, and I loved Irving Shea. He was valiant and bold, he never hesitated to help us, and he sacrificed his life to get us this feather so we could save the world and look like the heroes." Charisma wriggled as she made her case. "What do you think?"

"Shea." He tenderly spoke the name. "It's perfect."

They were headed for Central Park, flying north on Fifth Avenue against the still-sparse southbound traffic.

"We're going to have to set down soon," he said. "The wings won't last for much longer."

"What happened?" She hated to see these moments end. "Did you get a five-minute warning?"

"Something like that."

She settled down to enjoy the last moments of the coolest flight of her life, and at once her mind skipped forward to their life, to the hours and days and months and years of boring old normalcy.

She couldn't wait.

She declared, "I need to get some hair dye. Is there any color you prefer? Orange? Pink? Black?"

"All of the above." He sounded amused.

"Yes." She bounced in his arms. "Good call! A rainbow to commemorate this day."

"But if you're pregnant, should you use hair dye?" It wasn't so much a question as a statement.

Turning, she stared at him in consternation. "I never thought of that."

"When the women in my family are expecting, they go organic."

"Organic." Horrified, she asked, "You mean, like, for nine months I can't dye my hair?"

" 'Fraid not."

"But my natural color is so boring!" she wailed.

"It's blond, isn't it?"

"Yes," she said in disgust.

"So's mine." He cuddled her a little closer. "Do you think our little Shea will be blond, too?"

Immediately, the vision of their plump, long-limbed baby formed in her mind. "With big blue eyes."

"No, beautiful emerald green eyes like her mama."

"She's going to be so smart, and gorgeous."

Their flight dipped abruptly lower.

"Is our time over?" She glanced behind and saw the feathers vanishing in a shower of multicolored sparks from the tips first. "Uh-oh."

"I'm going to set us down by the pond. People are thronging toward Times Square. Hopefully not too many will be close by to see us—"

"It's New York." She pulled up her feet as they skimmed the treetops.

"I know. But even for New York, I have a problem with my clothing, or lack of it."

"Hm. Yeah." He *was* naked. "When you were covered with fur, it wasn't such a big deal." She giggled. "I don't mean *it*, exactly."

"I would hope *not*," he said sternly.

"I mean . . . you're right." She glanced down at him. He really was bare. It was time to get practical. "Land in as remote an area as possible. How long do you think it'll take the Chosen Ones to commandeer transportation to get here?"

"The Chosen Ones? Who needs the Chosen Ones?" He laughed. "Rosie will take care of that. I mean, would you give her any trouble?"

"Never. As long as she's . . ."

"She's fine." Aleksandr hugged Charisma tightly. "We have to believe everybody is fine."

Charisma nodded. "You're right. I hope Rosie does the driving."

"Why's that?" He aimed them for an open, grassy knoll.

Charisma grinned. "Because if McKenna drives, it will take them most of the day to rescue us."

"And if Rosie drives, they'll beat us to the park." He landed a little too soon, touching down within sight of Fifth Avenue. He ran about twenty steps. He slowed, and then he stopped.

As soon as he stood on sturdy ground, he kissed her, and in the kiss he promised a lifetime of love. Then, wearing only a knowing smile, he let her slide to the ground.

Predictably, the first man who rushed up shouted, "Cool stunt, man! What are you advertising for? A clothing store?" He burst into laughter.

"Funny," Charisma told him.

An elderly woman sat on a nearby park bench, looking bedazzled and bemused. "He's an angel!" she told the man.

With a dozen brilliant sparks, the last two feathers burned away.

"See?" she said.

One of the Central Park police officers stalked up. "If he's an angel, where're his wings, lady?"

"When they flew over, I saw his wings," she insisted.

"So did I," a businessman in a rumpled black suit concurred. "I've got video!"

"Look, angels." The officer spoke to Aleksandr and Charisma, his tone patiently sarcastic. "I know it's been a weird few days, but if you can't produce clothes, I'm going to have to arrest you both."

One of the kids came running across the lawn, dragged by a brown dachshund in a pink coat. "He hasn't got clothes because he's an angel!"

On Fifth Avenue, they heard the screech of a bus whipping around the corner, catching the flow of traffic heading downtown. It raced across all lanes of traffic, slid up against the curb, and slammed on the brakes.

"Rosie drove," Aleksandr and Charisma said together.

The doors whipped open.

John, Samuel, Rosamund, and Genny bounded out and headed toward Aleksandr and Charisma. John and Samuel stripped off their coats as they ran.

"If they can produce ID, will that be enough to satisfy you?" the businessman asked the officer.

"From where would you like him to produce this ID?" the officer snapped.

A jogger ran past. "Get a room, you two!"

"I love New York." Aleksandr was relaxed and at

ease, even when two middle-aged women stopped to ogle his behind.

Charisma imperiously ignored everyone. "You know what the best part of this whole thing is?" She traced her fingers over the tattoo that started on his left shoulder and descended across his chest. "We know what this represents now. The picture is filled in, and there we are, flying from Osgood's building over New York to our landing here. The colors are so vivid, and, Aleksandr, look!" She bared her own shoulder. "I have one that matches!"

He stared at her tattoo. He lifted his wrist.

Clearly marked on his skin was a brilliant etched tattoo that matched the stones of her bracelet.

They shared more than love. They shared their marks.

# Chapter 57

———❦———

McKenna stood at the kitchen door in the basement of Irving's mansion and watched the Chosen Ones traipse up the concrete stairs into the alley and then to the street.

"Fabulous meal!" they called. "McKenna, take care. Don't work too hard!" "Visit us in California as soon as you can!" "No, visit us in Seattle first!" "We've got a place in upstate New York. We're closest!"

He waved and smiled.

Their voices were fading, but he clearly heard Charisma Wilder shout, "Keep fighting the good fight!"

"I will," he said softly, and shut the door.

After seven years of struggle, fighting, heartbreak, and ultimately triumph, the dear children hated to leave Irving's mansion and, he flattered himself, they hated to leave him.

They seemed to realize how important their time here had been; they had walked through fire, sometimes literally, and now they moved out to face the world as civilians. But with such maturity and strength of character as they had developed, the world would be their oyster.

"They have done very well, indeed," Irving's ghostly voice agreed.

McKenna turned.

Irving sat at the head of the table, looking as he had in life, but once again robust, straight, and strong. He was smiling and nodding, and . . . he was a little misty around the edges.

"Mr. Shea, I thought I had seen you around the house." McKenna seated himself on the bench. "Yes, the retiring Chosen Ones are young women and men of whom we can be proud."

"I am. Very proud. But where's Jacqueline?"

McKenna hated to deliver bad news, but Mr. Shea deserved to know. "In the final fight in the Osgood building, she was hurt. Badly. She's still in the hospital."

"She'll be all right?" Irving asked anxiously.

"We believe so. She will live. She has turned a corner at last."

"I had hoped to see her one last time." Irving sounded wistful.

McKenna thought about that, then offered, "Sir, she has connections in the other world. Perhaps when she comes to see her mother . . ."

"Good point." Irving perked up. "I'll look into that."

"I'm so glad you're here, Mr. Shea, so I can thank you for leaving me the mansion. It has made the transition of power between this generation of Chosen Ones and the new generation of Chosen Ones so much easier." McKenna thought of the improvements he'd made to accommodate the seven, and he glowed with pride.

"So they'll stay here under your supervision?" Irving leaned back with a satisfied sigh. "I had hoped that would work out."

"I feel I cannot offer supervision, per se, but certainly guidance."

"You're too modest, McKenna. Those young men and women are not the only ones who have gained wisdom over this difficult time."

McKenna chuckled. "I suppose you're right, Mr. Irving. One simply doesn't think of gaining wisdom at my age."

"Pfft!" Irving waved that away. "You're fifty-six. A mere child!"

McKenna supposed Irving would think that.

Rising, he went to the pot on the stove and stirred it, tasted it, sprinkled a little fresh thyme into the sauce. "I've made the new Chosen Ones my Scottish lamb stew. Now that Martha is gone, I might as well get them ready to eat my cooking."

"Oh, I think you'll have some help. Look." Irving nodded at the high window that looked out on the street.

There was Taurean, her face pressed against the glass, staring fixedly into the kitchen.

"Good heavens. That girl!" McKenna hurried to the door and opened it, and, with great patience, called, "Taurean, I told you. You can come in anytime."

As usual, she crawled around the corner, then scooted down the stairs on her bottom. In the kitchen, she stood and dusted her rear. "I got the invitation."

McKenna noted she was wearing a flowered chintz apron. "What invitation is that?"

"To cook for the new Chosen Ones, of course."

McKenna glanced at Irving.

Irving shrugged.

Taurean continued. "I'm a good cook. I'll help out around the house, too." She looked around. "I like this place. I'm safe here. Is this the pantry?" She headed inside.

"Yes, it is," McKenna said.

She came out carrying the bread machine and his container of flour. "Later tonight I'll start some sourdough, but for today's meal I'll make butter rolls to go with the stew." As she brushed by Irving, she said, "Hello, Irving Shea; you're looking good for a man who's been dead more than a month."

"Thank you, Taurean," Irving said. "It's good to see you feeling better."

"I am," she said. "Do you know that, even though I was afraid, I helped rescue all those people before the building collapsed?"

"She did, sir. She was very brave." McKenna couldn't have been prouder if she were his own daughter. Indeed, he felt rather fatherly toward Taurean, which was perhaps odd, since she was at least ten years older than he was.

"Brava, Taurean!" Irving softly clapped his hands. But the sound was distant and far away.

Taurean used her apron to curtsy, then went to work assembling the ingredients for the rolls.

Funny girl, but perhaps she would work out.

Irving looked up suddenly. Then he stood. "McKenna, I have to leave now. Dina's calling me."

McKenna looked around, but saw no other apparitions. "What about Martha?"

Irving stopped and looked right at McKenna. "She's not with *us*. She cannot be with *us*."

"As I suspected." McKenna shook his head mournfully.

"She was a sad case," Irving said. "Martha wanted to be one of the Chosen Ones, not be a servant, and she wanted to be on the winning side. Eventually she came to believe she deserved what she did not have."

"If only she had held out, she would have won with us all. A sad case, indeed." McKenna stepped forward. "Mr. Shea, will I see you again?"

Irving smiled. "Not in this life."

"I had hoped for advice," McKenna said.

"The Chosen Ones who just walked out that door"— Irving pointed—"were mine to mentor. The new Chosen are yours, and after these, I see many more Chosen Ones waiting to take their turn. They are all yours, and, McKenna, I have every confidence in you."

The front doorbell rang.

"And there they are," Irving said. "What a good time you have ahead of you, McKenna. Enjoy every moment."

"Yes, sir." McKenna slipped on his jacket. "I will, sir."

Irving turned again. "I'm coming!" he called. He walked through the kitchen door and vanished.

Taurean waved. "Bye, Irving!" she called, and headed back into the pantry. She seemed to consider the appearance and disappearance of a ghost to be a normal, everyday occurrence.

Perhaps for her, it was.

But this particular ghost . . . McKenna swallowed his sentiment. It wouldn't do to have the new Chosen

Ones seeing him with tearstained cheeks. That would give them entirely the wrong impression.

Straightening his shoulders, and at his usual majestic pace, he walked up the stairs to the entry.

The doorbell rang again.

Such impatience, he thought. *You will learn.*

He adjusted his collar and cuffs; then, with the proper dignity of a well-trained butler—that was, after all, his first calling—he opened the door wide.

Seven new Chosen Ones stared at him, some resentful, some joyous, some awestruck, and all filled with trepidation, hidden or not.

"Welcome." He stepped and gestured them into the foyer. "Please come in and make yourselves at home."

# Chapter 58

*Four Years Later*

Aleksandr walked into the huge living room of his grandparents' guesthouse, holding his three-month-old daughter in a sling against his chest. "Where's Charisma? Emma's hungry."

Samuel looked up from his supervision of the nursery set up in the connected dining room. "How should I know where Charisma is?"

Taken aback by Samuel's savage tone, Aleksandr said, "Well . . . I thought you might have seen her."

"Are you kidding? Those women dumped these kids on me and disappeared, and they haven't come back."

Aleksandr surveyed the four three-year-olds. Two were playing school under Shea's supervision.

One sat in a little chair in the corner, kicking, screaming, and crying.

"They're not so bad," Aleksandr said.

"Not so bad?" Grabbing Aleksandr's collar, Samuel glared into his eyes. "I thought little girls were cute. They're awful."

"They have their moments." Aleksandr leaned down and gave Shea a kiss. "Having fun?"

"Yeah!" She turned her big green eyes on him, and smiled, then went back to her schoolroom.

"That girl is particularly irksome." Samuel pointed at the screamer.

Aleksandr looked the kids over carefully. The former Chosen Ones and their children had arrived yesterday evening, and what followed had been a hodgepodge of hugs, greetings, exclamations, and planning, as well as their small, deeply felt annual memorial service for Irving. But Aleksandr was pretty sure . . . "Isn't that girl yours?"

"Yes. Can you believe Isabelle produced a daughter with that temperament?"

Aleksandr stared at Samuel.

"All right! Fine! Z'ana takes after me! But don't you think she'd have a little of Isabelle in her?"

"Not if there's any justice." Aleksandr adjusted the baby on his chest. "What did she do?"

"She punched somebody." Samuel's forbidding tone made Aleksandr's heart sink.

"Oh, no." Aleksandr started toward Shea. "Are the other kids okay?"

"She didn't punch one of the other kids," Samuel said.

"Oh." Aleksandr pinched his mouth to keep from laughing. "Looks like you might have a shiner."

Samuel glared. "I caught her trying to sneak out to find Grandpa Konstantine."

Aleksandr got serious in a hurry. "We've always been terrified one of the little ones would disappear up here. Do you want me to talk to her?"

Samuel waved a consenting hand.

Aleksandr walked over and knelt beside Z'ana.

Z'ana stopped crying and looked at him, lip stuck out.

"Honey, your daddy is right." Samuel and Isabelle's daughter was a cutie, with dark eyes that sparkled with life and, right now, tears. "You can't go outside by yourself. There are woods out there, and wild animals, and acres of ground, and you could get lost."

"Grandpa Konstantine said he would teach me surviv-al." Her speech was precise, her tone fully as irked as her father's.

"He will. Grandpa Konstantine likes to teach little girls how to survive in the woods. When he's ready, he will come and get you." Sternly, Aleksandr asked, "And when did he say he would be ready?"

"After lunch."

"And . . . ?"

The lip went out farther. "After my nap."

"Yes. If you're lost and he has to come and find you, he will be very unhappy. We don't like to make Grandpa Konstantine unhappy. He yells." Aleksandr stood. "He can't teach you right now, because he's in the barn with Uncle John, watching him lift a tractor."

She sighed hugely. "That's boring. So I'll wait." She was obviously making a huge concession.

"Thank you." Aleksandr kissed her on the top of the head.

She jumped up and ran to Samuel. "Daddy, I love you!"

Samuel gathered her into his arms, kissed and hugged her. "I love you, too, pumpkin. Do you want to play school?"

"Yay!"

Samuel put his daughter down and watched her join the girls. "Isn't she the biggest drama queen?"

Aleksandr looked at him again.

"I am *not* a drama queen," Samuel said.

"No, you're a hotshot trial lawyer in Seattle. I suppose that's not *quite* the same."

"I may put it on occasionally to impress a jury," Samuel allowed. "Why is John lifting a tractor?"

Emma fussed.

Aleksandr patted her bottom. "Grandpa keeps challenging John with bigger and bigger objects. He loves to see John project his power."

"So it's like Yoda and Luke?"

"Yes, except if John had to lift his X-wing out of a swamp on Dagobah, he wouldn't first whine that he couldn't."

" 'Do or do not. There is no try,' " Samuel quoted *Star Wars*.

"Right." Aleksandr looked around. "Where's Caleb?"

"He's at the main house with his mom and grandma and the aunts. They're showing Grandma how to make that polenta-and-sauce thing for dinner, and she's teaching them to make paste chicken or something for the Fourth of July celebration."

"Patychky?"

"That's it." Samuel smiled. "Looking forward to dinner tonight and the food tomorrow is the only thing that got me through this last hour. That and Shea, who rules with an iron hand."

Aleksandr observed his daughter, who now pointed a ruler at the other girls and expounded on the letter G, which stood for *girl*, and was way more important than B, which stood for *boy*. "We named her right. She goes for the win."

"And she doesn't take any shit." Samuel lowered his voice on the last word.

But Shea heard, because she pointed her ruler at him.

"I'm surrounded by officious females." Samuel groaned.

"You love it."

Samuel chuckled. "I do."

Aleksandr walked to the window and looked out. "The women are coming back."

"Thank God. I hope they enjoyed their walk through the vines," Samuel said sarcastically. But he joined Aleksandr and watched with a faint air of anxiety.

Isabelle was hugely pregnant.

So was Genny.

So was Rosamund.

Jacqueline was the most hugely pregnant of all.

"Have you heard? How is Jacqueline?" Samuel asked.

"I asked Caleb last night. He said she's back one hundred percent."

"Thank God."

The shape-shifter who had taken Jacqueline's form in that final battle had also tried to take her life. Caleb had found her stabbed, broken, and unconscious in a stairwell in the Osgood building. He carried her out, and they were the last two out before the building collapsed.

The weeks that followed had been terrible as the Chosen Ones waited to see first whether she would live, then whether she would survive the surgeries, then whether rehab and hard work could help her speak again.

Now for the first time she was pregnant, and to catch up she was having twins. Girls, of course.

Emma fussed a little louder.

Aleksandr patted her and swayed back and forth, back and forth.

For a thousand years, Aleksandr's family had fathered only sons. Now he and Charisma had had two girls. He figured it was something Smith Bernhard had done to him, so apparently one good thing had come from the torture Aleksandr had suffered.

The other good thing was . . . if he'd stayed the whole seven years with the Chosen Ones, if he hadn't been captured, broken, and transformed, he and Charisma would never have found each other, loved each other. His character had needed to be hardened and shaped by adversity before he was worthy to be her match, and her mate.

He touched the steel plate that still formed part of his skull. The doctors had been able to remove the homing device Bernhard had placed in his brain, but they couldn't replace the bone he'd lost. The plate was there to stay, an annoyance when he went through airport security, and a reminder of what was important—his children, his family, and his friends.

# Chapter 59

———— ❖ ————

Outside, Charisma came running in from the vine-yard. Catching up with the women, she said something that made them all laugh.

Then they came inside, flushed from the summer sun and smiling.

The children ran to greet their mommies and get hugs and kisses, then ran back to Shea's classroom to play some more.

Charisma stared at Isabelle, then Genny, then gave Aleksandr a significant look, which he supposed he should have been able to interpret, but couldn't. He didn't know most of the time what she meant and what she thought, but the good thing about Charisma was she didn't expect him to guess. Sooner or later she would tell him what was on her mind.

Isabelle used her hands on the arms of one of the wooden dining room chairs to lower herself into the seat. "Looks like the kids were good."

Aleksandr got a significant look from Samuel, too. At least he knew what that one meant.

"They were angels." Samuel pushed an ottoman under Isabelle's feet. "How are you doing?"

"Good." But she winced and put her hand to her back.

He sat next to her and started rubbing her spine.

She smiled and relaxed into his touch.

"I always knew you women cycled together," he said. "But this getting pregnant at the same time is ridiculous."

"*I'm* not pregnant." Charisma took Emma from Aleksandr, gave her a kiss and him a more lingering kiss, and sat down.

Aleksandr seated himself on the arm of her easy chair and held the blanket while Charisma got ready to nurse the baby.

As Emma settled down to her meal, Jacqueline laughed. "Does she always grunt like that?"

"Like a little piggy." Charisma brushed the bald baby head and cooed, "Don't you, sweetheart?"

Aaron wandered in from the kitchen, got kisses and hugs from his daughter, Juliet, and said to Charisma, "The only reason Charisma's not pregnant is because you two got the jump on us with Shea. We've all been working to catch up ever since."

"Have you been in the kitchen the whole time?" Samuel demanded.

"No, no, no." Aleksandr thought Aaron's denial was a little too enthusiastic—and fishy, since he picked up the conversation so quickly. "I was up at the main house helping Adrik break into the family safe. Apparently one of the Wilder great-grandchildren somehow managed to reset the electronics on the lock. That kid has a future as a professional thief."

Caleb came in from the kitchen, received kisses and hugs from his daughter, Kara, and said, "I agree with Samuel. Your due dates are all within a week. Considering you don't live in the same house anymore, that's kind of spooky."

"Honey, we've got an e-mail loop." Jacqueline let him slide a stool under her feet. "We're in contact every day, and we talk all the time."

He leaned down and kissed her, and looked into her eyes. "Having twins to catch up is even spookier."

"I'll grant you that," she allowed. "It's not like I could have planned it, though!"

"Caleb, have *you* been here the whole time?" Samuel asked.

Caleb looked surprised. "No, I came in the back so I could put the polenta in the refrigerator. We made a ton, and, oh, Samuel—wait until you taste the sauce."

Samuel was up and headed for the kitchen. "I'm starving."

"Easily distracted," Caleb muttered.

The children all came to their feet. "We're starving, too!"

Aleksandr definitely knew what *that* Samuel-look meant.

Samuel and the kids disappeared into the kitchen.

Charisma turned to Isabelle. "He's like the Pied Piper!"

"I know. He and Z'ana are always butting heads, but they adore each other." Isabelle winced again.

Rosamund pushed her glasses up on her nose, observed Isabelle, and said, "You show all the signs of the first stage of labor."

Aleksandr, Caleb, and Aaron straightened in alarm.

"Maybe," Isabelle allowed. "But don't tell Samuel. He didn't want us to visit this close to my due date, and I insisted."

Charisma chuckled.

"Honey, if you're in labor, he's going to figure it out pretty fast." Genny displayed her logical turn of mind.

John came in from the kitchen, looking chagrined. "He caught me," he said to Aaron and Caleb. "I had to admit I sneaked into the house from the barn and hung out in there to avoid, um . . ." He saw that no one paid him any heed. "What's up?"

"Isabelle is in labor," Jacqueline informed him.

"I wondered whether that would happen with one of you. That's a washboard gravel road coming into the Wilder estate." Leaning down, he kissed Genny. "Promise me something."

She clung to the sleeve of his T-shirt. "What's that?"

"Promise me you'll wait until we get home to California before you have little Firebird's sister."

"I'll do what I can." But she looked worried.

Which made John look worried.

"Everyone's panicking prematurely." Isabelle sounded patient. "It's just a backache. If it turns into something more, you all will be the first to know. In the meantime, Charisma?"

Charisma raised her eyebrows.

"You promised us a *Downton Abbey* fest when we got here." Isabelle ignored the guys' groans.

"Which one?" Aaron asked. "Season eight . . . thousand?"

Charisma flipped on the TV.

"There aren't eight thousand seasons," Caleb said. "It only seems that way."

"It'll distract me," Isabelle said.

That stopped the groans.

The news flashed on the screen: *Riots in Hong Kong.*

Jacqueline held up her hand. "Wait a minute. I want to see this."

The broadcasters chronicled the rise of a mysterious new overlord who now controlled the drug and prostitution trades, and sought ever more power by dissention and murder. The overlord was named Sun Tai-shu, and the news show flashed on-screen the blurry picture of an elderly Chinese lady with a sweet face.

"Look at her eyes glowing," Jacqueline said dreamily. "Glowing blue with evil."

Samuel walked in from the kitchen in time to hear her. He looked at the TV. "I don't see any glowing blue eyes," he declared.

"Jacqueline's having a vision, Samuel," Isabelle said.

"I know." Walking over, he turned off the TV.

Jacqueline blinked and looked around.

Samuel faced them. "We've saved the world once, and now it's up to the current Chosen Ones. They have McKenna to direct them. We still have our gifts. If they need us, they know they can call us. But they haven't, and they wouldn't thank us for interfering. And according to tradition, there can be only seven. So let's let them do their jobs, and we'll love one another, raise our children, and live in peace."

For a long moment, it was very quiet.

Then Charisma said, "I say this so seldom, but . . . Samuel's right."

Everyone nodded.

"What?" Samuel cupped his ear. "I can't hear you!"

He got a chorus of "You're right." "You're right." "You're right." "You're right." "You're right."

And one, "We're having a baby."

"What?" Samuel shook his head and stared at Isabelle. "I know we're having a baby."

"No. I mean"—she pushed herself out of the chair—"we're having a baby *now*."

"You can't." Samuel clutched his forehead. "You promised that if we came to the Wilder Fourth of July picnic, you wouldn't have little Tasya until after we got home."

"I lied."

Samuel turned to Aleksandr. "Where's the nearest hospital?"

"No time for a hospital," Isabelle said more emphatically. "We're having this baby *now*."

"Oh, no," Genny whispered.

From her easy chair, Charisma immediately began to direct operations. "Samuel, help Isabelle to bed. Aleksandr, call your mother and your grandmother and have them come over."

Aleksandr pulled out his cell phone and stepped onto the porch.

From inside, he could hear Charisma ordering everyone around. "Aaron, Dr. Bloom's number is in the kitchen by the house phone. Give her a call and tell her what's going on. John, can you herd the kids over to the main house? Aleksandr has plenty of relatives to care for them. Genny and Jacqueline, there are towels in the linen closet by the bathroom. Get them all. Caleb, I know it's a cliché, but we're going to need boiling water."

When Aleksandr stepped back inside, the guests had scattered to do their duties, and Charisma sat in the living room, alone, burping the baby.

"Mom and Grandma are on their way." He grinned. "I could hear Grandpa shouting in the background. After what happened to Grandma when she had Firebird, he gets excited about a birth."

Charisma laughed, and lifted her head for his kiss.

"You're a superwoman," Aleksandr murmured. "You arranged that like a general, and all while nursing Emma."

"I had it planned out. I suspected this was coming."

He took the baby so Charisma could adjust her bra and shirt. "Are you our new seer?"

"Isabelle had that abstracted look, like she was looking inward." Charisma touched the stones at her wrist. "And she kept pausing when she walked."

"The stuff you women know," he marveled.

"Just using my powers of observation." Charisma waved an airy hand. "I gave you *the look* when I came in. Didn't you get it?"

"Oh. Is that what *the look* was for?" It was always good to have a woman explain woman stuff. "No, it never occurred to me we'd be delivering a baby today."

*"Babies,"* Charisma said. "Keep an eye on Genny. I think she's in the early stages of labor, too."

"I had no idea labor was contagious." Against his ear, Emma burped so loudly, Aleksandr shook his head to clear it.

"You guys so constantly exclaim about how we get pregnant at the same time. Surely it can't be a surprise when the babies arrive at the same time."

"You're right. Of course."

"Of course." She leaned her head against his chest and looked into their baby's face. "Someday, maybe all of us Chosen Ones will have sons together."

"I like girls." And he loved Charisma so much. Charisma, his wife: rebel, wild child, genius, lover. With her enthusiasm, courage, and determination, she had saved his life, his sanity, and his soul. Now Aleksandr knelt at her feet. "I've been thinking."

"Always dangerous."

"I love it up here in the mountains."

"Me, too."

"And with the success of my game, *Killing Demons for Fun*, our company has a lot of money."

Charisma was smug. "I know." Leaning close, she took his collar. "Admit it. Marketing it to the public was a great idea."

"It was a great idea," he repeated. "How often do I have to say it?"

"Once a day, at least." Before he could speak, she waggled her finger. "And no, you can't say it seven times on Monday and have that be for the whole week. I want you to remember it every day."

"I was thinking," he began again. "We love it up here in the mountains, and with the amount of cash we've got coming in, what if we bought the property next door?"

"Okay."

"I checked it out. It's seven acres of mostly forest, with a crummy little house and a great view. We could live there while we build a nicer home for us and the girls, and whatever little boys you want to bless me with."

"Okay."

"Work's not a problem. We can set up anywhere, and I know our little town of Blythe would be happy to get a business to stimulate the economy."

"Okay."

"Grandpa and Grandma are getting older. We could keep an eye on them. . . . Why are you smiling at me?"

"Okay." She kissed him. "Okay." She kissed him again. "Okay. I would love to buy the place next door. I would love to be close to your family. And as long as you're with me, I am happy to call anywhere home. Okay?"

He kissed her eagerly, lingeringly. "Okay."

Find out where Aleksandr came from!
Read the whole story about the Wilders
and their pact with the devil
in the book that launched
Christina Dodd's Darkness Chosen series,

## SCENT OF DARKNESS

Available now from Signet.
Continue reading for a special preview!

*The Beginning*

For centuries, the word *Cossack* struck terror in the hearts of the peoples of central Asia, and the family Varinski was the embodiment of merciless conquerors who murder, maim, and rape. Even today, the Varinskis reside on the steppes of Russia, known for their scouting abilities, proving themselves again and again able to discover their enemies' weaknesses. They leave a trail of blood, fire, and death wherever they go. Terrible rumors swirl around them, rumors that say Konstantine Varinski, the founder of the Varinski tribe, made a deal with the devil—and, in fact, that is exactly right.

A thousand years ago, Konstantine Varinski, a magnificent warrior of great cruelty, a man driven by his craving for power, roamed the steppes. In return for the ability to hunt down his enemies and kill them, he promised his soul to the devil. To seal the pact, he promised the devil the family icon, four images of the Madonna painted on a porcelain tile and fired to brilliance.

To obtain the holy piece, the heart of his home, he killed his own mother . . . and damned his soul.

Before she died, she pulled him close and spoke in his ear.

Konstantine paid no heed to her prophecy. She was, after all, only a woman. He didn't believe her dying words had the power to change the future—and more important, he would do nothing to jeopardize his pact with the Evil One.

But although Konstantine did not confess the prophecy his mother had made, Satan knew that Konstantine was a liar and a trickster. He suspected Konstantine's deception, and he comprehended the power of blood and kin and a mother's dying words. So to ensure that he forever would retain the Varinskis and their services, he secretly cut a small piece from the center of the icon and gave it to a poor tribe of wanderers, promising it would bring them luck.

Then, while Konstantine drank to celebrate the deal, the devil divided the Madonnas in a flash of fire and hurled them to the four ends of the earth.

To Varinski and to each Varinski since, the devil bequeathed the ability to change at will into a hunting animal. They could not be killed in battle except by another demon, and each man was unusually long-lived, remaining hale and hearty well into old age. Because of their battle prowess, their endurance, and their decisiveness, they became rich, respected, and feared in Russia.

Through czars, Bolsheviks, and even presidents, they retained their warrior compound, went where they were paid to go, and with flawless ferocity, crushed uprisings and demanded obedience.

They called themselves the Immortals.

They could breed only sons, a matter of much exultation to them. They took their women cruelly, and in their sprawling home they had a turnstile equipped with a bell. There the women who had been impregnated by the Varinskis' careless mating placed their newborn sons. They rang the bell and fled, leaving the child to be taken by the Varinski men into their home. There the men would hail the birth of a new demon and raise the child to be a ruthless warrior worthy of the name Varinski.

For no Varinski ever fell in love. . . .

Until one did.

No Varinski ever married. . . .

Until one did.

No Varinski ever fled the compound and their way of life. . . .

Until one did.

For the first time, cracks appeared in the solid foundation of the deal with the devil.

Heaven took note.

So did Hell.


*One Thousand Years Later, in Another Land*


The storm broke.

How appropriate.

Ann had broken into her boss's house on the wild

Washington coast. She'd showered, she'd donned her slinkiest gown, and now, at last, she was going to seduce Jasha Wilder—if he managed to make his way home through this unpredictable tempest that trapped her here.

She stared at herself in the mirror.

How could she look so good, yet feel so much like the Cowardly Lion?

Okay. She was going to go the great room, get a glass of wine, pose artfully in front of the fire, and wait for Jasha to show up. She could do it. All she had to do was walk downstairs—

Above the battering of the storm, she heard a blast of sound from outside.

A gunshot.

Running to the second-story window, she separated the curtains and peeked out.

Billows of storm clouds diffused the late-afternoon sunshine. Wind blew the rain sideways. Lightning flickered across the branches of the cedars and pines, casting them in bleak colors of black and white. She could see the shiny, wet roof of her car, but there was no sign of anyone on the driveway or in the yard, no glint of a gun or sign of movement in the forest that stretched for miles in every direction. Uneasily, she opened the bedroom door.

Someone was moving around below. Someone—or something.

Had she reset the alarm?

No. She hadn't. And someone in the forest had a gun.

Had someone who was not Jasha—someone crazy, someone like Ted Kaczynski—shot him and walked into his house?

She felt silly. Overly dramatic. She was plain Ann Smith, administrative assistant and nerd. Nothing harrowing ever happened to her. Yet she tasted fear. Taking off her stiletto heels, she held one in each hand as she walked quietly down the corridor. She paused on the balcony.

She heard growling. Panting. Those weren't human sounds.

Did Jasha have a dog?

She peeked over the rail.

Yes—a dog stood facing the fire. It was tall at the shoulders, long and gaunt, yet it easily weighed a hundred and fifty pounds, with a black and silver coat that gleamed with red and gold in the flames. It was growling, a constant low rumble of displeasure rising from deep in its chest.

Ann wasn't afraid of dogs, but she'd never heard such a menacing sound in her life.

Then the dog turned his head, and his pointed snout and white-fanged snarl sent her scurrying back against the wall.

*A wolf.* A wolf stood before the fire.

Her heart pounded so hard that it thundered in her ears.

How had a wolf broken into the house? Was the back door open? Had it crashed through a window?

*Where was Jasha?* If he walked in on this thing, he could get hurt.

She sidled forward and slid along the rail, examining the room from every angle.

No sign of her boss, but although the wolf's rumblings had subsided, Ann knew it was dangerous. A killer. A predator.

As she retreated, the clear-minded planning that made her such a valuable administrative assistant kicked in. *Return to my room. Lock the door. Call Jasha on his cell and warn him. Then call 911 so they can get Animal Services out here. . . .*

She stopped backing up, and stared.

The wolf looked different somehow.

She squeezed her eyes shut. She opened them again.

*I'm allergic to something. The new-car smell . . . Jasha's soap . . . I have to be. Because I'm hallucinating.*

*But no, really.*

He looked . . . longer. His muscular shoulders had lost hair, and his ears . . . his ears grew bare and rounded, and slid down the sides of his head.

The wolf had begun to . . . had begun to resemble a man. Had begun to resemble Jasha.

Oh, yes. She was definitely nuts.

Drawn by the same fascination that always plagued her in Jasha's presence, she walked toward the top of the stairs. Shock ripped away her ability to plan. Her mind was empty of anything but wonder, but she never took her gaze off the wolf, and she walked carefully, making no sound on the hardwood.

The wolf stood on its hind paws. Stood erect, like a man.

Her blood stirred. Her skin grew sensitive. The air in the house had grown thick and heated.

She recognized the signs. That *was* Jasha. That . . . that *thing* was really Jasha.

The pelt retreated to the top of his head and became hair.

He was naked. Nude. Absolutely without covering of any kind.

And apparently she was the weirdest perv ever to walk the earth, for even in the midst of her madness, she found the sight of his bare, toned butt riveting. She wanted to shut her eyes against the sight, to take a deep breath and give herself a stern warning about the dangers she faced.

But she didn't dare shut her eyes against the sight, to take a deep breath and give herself a stern warning about the dangers she faced.

But she didn't dare shut her eyes—as she inched down each step, she stared at the *thing* before the fire. And she certainly didn't dare take a deep breath. She couldn't risk any sound.

The transition was happening slowly, and once or twice, it—he groaned as if the growth and change of his bones pained him. The paws became hands, large hands with Jasha's long fingers, and he used those fingers to push back his hair in a gesture she recognized as exasperation and worry.

With each step down the stairs, her frozen disbelief became certainty . . . and fear. The man she adored was a wolf. A beast. Something unholy, unnatural. She'd finally worked up the nerve to chase her dream, only to find that he had become her worst nightmare, and she was stuck in the house with him. It.

Jasha.

Think.

Her keys were on the end table by the door. If she could get from the stairs to her keys, she could open the door and race to her car ahead of him. She could drive off, and for once she wouldn't care about the speed limit.

She would drive as if her life depended on escape—and it did.

Five steps from the bottom.

He hadn't noticed her yet.

She'd run as far away as possible. She would never look back. Never.

But first she had to get her keys. Open the door. Start her car . . .

She'd had this nightmare a million times, the nightmare of hiding from some supernatural creature who would hunt her, chase her, kill her.

And just like in the nightmare, the thing in the great room lifted its head and sniffed. Its head turned slowly in her direction. It looked at her.

Almost human. That thing was almost human. Except that deep in his dark blue eyes, a red glow burned. "Ann." Its deep voice sounded rough, as if it had a cold. It looked human again.

Like Jasha, the man she loved.

Her gaze fixed on the small dark-red smear at the corner of his mouth.

*Blood.*

He walked toward her. Naked. He was as glorious naked as she had always dreamed, and now she didn't dare take the time to check and see if the rumors were true.

Because he had blood on his face.

"You little fool," he said, "what are you doing here?"

She screamed and flung first one shoe, then the other, with all her might.

He dodged the first one. The second caught him squarely in the chest. The stiletto heel smacked his breastbone. She heard him grunt. Saw blood spurt.

She ran. Ran so hard she skidded into the door. She grabbed the keys. Her sweaty palms slid on the doorknob.

Any minute now and he'd have her.

She turned the knob. The heavy door swung toward her. The wind swept through the door, taking her breath. She ran onto the porch.

Behind her, she heard a growl. In terror, she glanced back—and saw it.

The transformation was reversing.

Inexorably, Jasha was becoming the wolf once more, and those red eyes were fixed on *her.*

# Christina Dodd

## THE NOVELS OF THE CHOSEN ONES

When the world was young, twins were born. One brought light to a dark world; the other, darkness and danger. They gathered others around them, men and women destined to use their powerful gifts for good or evil. Today, their descendants walk the earth as the Chosen, and the ultimate battle is about to begin.

**AVAILABLE NOW**

STORM OF VISIONS

STORM OF SHADOWS

CHAINS OF ICE

CHAINS OF FIRE

**"Devilishly clever, scintillatingly sexy."**
—*Chicago Tribune*

S0217

*SCENT OF DARKNESS*

Available online and in your
favorite bookstore.